OUR DEAL

OUR DEAL

NORMAN LEVY

AVON
PUBLISHERS OF BARD, CAMELOT, DISCUS AND FLARE BOOKS

For Tina Howe,
who led the way.

OUR DEAL

8/17/10

For Susan & Peter
New Friends, Old Friends,
Family

Love, Norman

Chapter One

◆◆◆

I COULDN'T BELIEVE our luck. It was like being in a movie. The three of us arrived for dinner at seven-thirty. A tuxedoed maître d' sat us on a raised banquette away from the dance floor. He knew our arrangement, mere diners. The slight elevation gave us a perfect view of the dance floor, bandstand and entire nightclub. The place was empty except for waiters fussing about the round tables, filling sugar bowls with rationed cubes, arranging centerpieces, salt-and-pepper shakers; fluttering side work. The music stands with CB monograms were still dark, but the lacquered dance floor was gleaming.

Suddenly Charlie Barnet's men appeared on the band shell, slid behind their music stands and began blowing their way into "Cherokee," their hit theme song. Barnet on tenor sax carried the melody. Trombones answered his call. Soon the stage lights brightened, and the entire band was alive, improvising a dialogue of syncopated brass, singing to one another, blowing their brains out, standing and sitting on certain choruses, waving metal hats over their horns to modulate the volume. It was starting!

My mother, Hannah, was aglow with happiness after a long day on her pins at the bookstore battling with salesmen, ringing the register, wrapping endless 49¢ remainders. This was a pleasure earned, and she eased back with it, the brunette waves of her hair shining, her intelligent eyes accepting it gratefully. Philly, my father, winced at the initial horn braying; strings would have put him more at ease. The female vocalist, Marjorie Hall, finally brought him relaxation with her ballad. She reached into her own hopelessness—"could have gone, but what for?"—bringing the lyric up from the middle of her stomach. "It's so different without you/ . . . Don't get around much anymore."

"Han, listen to her. She's really singing it." My father nudged my mother.

Hannah agreed. The voluptuous crooner had touched them both. As I was only eight, her melancholy tone did not arouse me as much as her skintight evening gown. We were in the Cocoanut Grove, a remodeled nightclub on the roof of the Park Central Hotel, twenty-nine stories above the war-dimmed city. The tan brick building with Moorish ornamentation was diagonally across the street from Carnegie Hall, occupying the entire block between 55th and 56th streets on 7th Avenue. To the north was an unobstructed view of Central Park; to the south, Times Square. The club had been refurbished for contemporary revelers during the spring of 1943 while North Africa was being liberated by the Allied Forces.

When Marjorie Hall finished her solo, the band broke out with "The Halls of Montezuma" and then settled into longing melodies which brought fifteen couples onto the dance floor. The club began filling up in anticipation of the first floor show.

"Here they come, Han, the two of them. What do you think?" my father stage-whispered.

"The big one certainly walks like a queen, but the smaller one could be hiding it better," my mother responded, deadpan, as two men in casual suits neared our banquette on their way to the backstage dressing room.

The Bensley Brothers were a riot. Their act was mayhem. They came on stage in standard nightclub tuxedoes and began singing the Andrew Sisters' hit "Don't Sit Under the Apple Tree With Anyone

Else But Me" exactly like the Andrew Sisters. Charlie Barnet's men were laughing, their instruments at rest. The brothers, Al, the smaller one, and Dick, the taller one, assumed all the Andrew Sisters' mannerisms and then some. I could never forget the first time I saw them.

"I told my mother, I told my father, and now I'm telling you./ Don't sit under the apple tree . . ."—which is exactly where Al sat. Dick importuned him not to go "march, march, marching home" as Al marched off with anyone else but him. Gales of laughter shot from the audience. I wet my pants. I had never seen anything so outrageous or been so happy. The Bensleys' mincing and tomfoolery were such a relief from the longing dance tunes. Suddenly as I clutched my wet thighs there was suddenly a scratching sound over the stage mikes that indicated a record defect. The Bensleys lip-synced the repeating record without missing a beat, thus revealing the source of their feminine voices. They finished their act doing Carmen Miranda in "Rum 'n' Coca Cola" and some Hope and Crosby duets. They were most adept at the women, however, which led to my parents' inevitable queries about their sexual preference.

"The little one isn't hiding it very well," my mother insisted with too much volume as the Bensleys passed our table on the way to their dressing room. My father hummed a bar from "Don't Sit Under the Apple Tree," and Hannah began laughing, quietly at first, then uncontrollably. Suddenly the Bensleys were at our table.

Dick spoke. "Wanna let me in on the joke, lady?"

"Nothing you'd be interested in," my father answered quickly, sensing his hostility.

The Bensleys turned and continued their walk down the aisle. My mother, however, was raucous with laughter. My father couldn't control her, and since his suggestive humming was the cause of her glee, he didn't try too hard.

Dick Bensley turned in his tracks and came right back to the table, very mad. "Still funny, lady?" His voice was threatening. "We're not part of your joke, are we?"

"You're hearing things. Back off!" my father said.

"I don't think so, shorty. Let's talk about it."

3

My father didn't move, which made Dick Bensley even more furious.

"Get up!"

My father remained where he was. I was scared, embarrassed. My mother had stopped laughing.

"Just make sure you're not talking about us, shrimp!"

Suddenly my father, who *was* only five feet tall, stood and stared down at Bensley. The banquette elevation made him appear six feet tall and very menacing. Dick Bensley was intimidated. They shouted, sparring with one another for a while. Then Dick Bensley walked back to Al. They both glared up at my tall father and continued on to their dressing room.

When the floor show was over, we took the elevator down to our suite, 2209. The large living room and bedroom faced Central Park, now dark except for taxicabs still making their way along its roadways. They formed eerie caravans. Their headlights, painted half black, a wartime precaution, cast a faint yellow light in front of each moving cab.

"Get ready for bed, Mitchell," my mother said, turning from the living room windows.

I scurried into the bedroom, pulled the slipcovers off my daybed sofa, found my flannel pajamas, undressed quickly, and put them on.

"Fold those slacks, Mitchell. Don't forget," my father reminded me.

He had come into the bedroom to use the telephone, call Mac, the night manager, at the bookstore. Saturday was always the busiest night of the week. Times Square was hopping.

"And your teeth," my mother urged from the other room. "Get all the sugar out."

I did my best with Dr. Lyon's tooth powder, brushing down, away from the gums. Then I moved my glass under the ice water spigot, pushing the stubby porcelain knob to fill it, and rinsed.

"I'm ready now," I announced when I was finished at the sink, back in the bedroom, finally under the covers, teeth chilled clean. My mother came into the room, sat on my bed, and ran her long fingers through my hair.

"Sleep tight, Mitchell." She kissed my eyebrows. "Philly, come on, it's enough with the store. Mitchell's got to sleep."

My mother went back into the living room. My father hung up, came over to me and kneeled beside my pillow.

"You can sleep late tomorrow."

"Sunday," I remembered. "We have breakfast together." The store was closed all day, it was special.

"How about pancakes?" my father asked casually.

"Pancakes!" I was ready to climb out of bed.

"In the morning, Mitchell." He pushed my head back into the pillow. "Your Grandma Lufkin did a nice job with your appetite." He laughed, walked to the overhead light switch, turned it off and quickly shut the bedroom door separating me from them.

"With maple syrup!" I gasped at the closed door. He didn't hear me. They were probably talking to each other. I couldn't hear anything. I stared out at the black sky.

Grandma Lufkin and I had been inseparable. She was my mother's mother and had shared a six room apartment with us on Walton Avenue in the Bronx until just ten months ago, when we moved into suite 2209 at the Park Central. She had taken care of me and the apartment while my parents were at their store. Lena Lufkin was one of the world's great cooks, and I developed into one of its premiere eaters, a wunderkind of the kitchen table, devouring her briskets, gefilte fish, chicken soup, matzo brei, chopped liver and home fries. Her food was all over me, inside and out.

She and her bounty had been replaced, however, by an entire hotel staff of chefs, maître d's, waiters and busboys when business picked up at the bookstore and my parents were able to afford a place of their own closer to Times Square. The hotel cuisine was bland, plentiful and definitely not kosher. For me it was like eating foreign food: Manhattan clam chowder, roast Long Island duckling, creamed kale, pureed corn, house salad, chocolate parfaits, a complete absence of chicken fat. By our second dinner, my taste buds adjusted and I gorged on it all.

Our deal at the Park Central—the American Plan—included dinner for three every night of the week. After Labor Day word came from the hotel management that American Plan residents would also be welcomed for dinner at the new Cocoanut Grove nightclub provided we finished immediately after the first floor show. My parents were thrilled. In October we began going up there a few nights a week. The food was just like the fare served in the dining room downstairs, except the portions were smaller.

"So pretty, Philly, those little headlights." Hannah was standing beside the living room window when Philly entered after saying good night to Mitchell and closing the door. She turned in the dark room. The foyer light helped him pick out her shape. Hannah was five feet nine without heels, a towering large-boned five feet nine. Philly adored her size. He reached for her hips with his strong hands. Hannah looked down into his eyes, smiling. He pulled her into his chest, his head crushed against her low bosom. He imagined the large pink nipples centered inside her rayon blouse.

Hannah could taste Philly's black hair, smell the cologne on his throat. Hannah loved the dapper little man and the midtown show biz world he had brought her into. She wanted more of him touching her.

"The night deposit, Jesus!" Philly suddenly loosened his grip. He shook his head free of Hannah's embrace. "I told Mac I'd come down."

"Forget it, Phil, please! For Christsakes, it's Saturday night!"

"That's why Mac gets flustered, can't make the drop himself."

"You make it for him, tomorrow. What the hell's the difference? The bank's closed till Monday."

"Suppose someone breaks in, steals the money in the deposit bag?"

"Come on, Phil, tell Mac to hide it. Stick it . . ."

"Where?"

"Guess!"

They both laughed.

"Call him, Phil. Go in the bedroom, tell him you're not coming . . . please." Hannah's arms were limp now, at her sides, her eyes beginning to water.

Philly saw them glisten. "I'll do it, Han." He turned on his heels and walked toward the bedroom. Then he stopped, twisted around. "What if I wake Mitchell?"

"He sleeps like a dead person."

"I'll only be a minute, Han . . . don't go away."

"Where would I go, Phil?" She tried to smile.

Hannah slumped down on the couch, wiped her eyes. She remembered their first meeting at the Monterey Hotel in Asbury Park. A summer weekend in '29 when the diminutive English Woolfs and the huge Polish Lufkins shared a large oval table in the sumptuous dining room. Philly was so different from Hannah's brothers—fat Sam, haughty Mordecai, the doctors; robust Morris, the building contractor. Philly had been a violinist, a real performer, starting with Gus Edwards's School Days Review at ten, going on to the RKO vaudeville circuit when he was a teenager, and finally playing with a series of popular orchestras, including Paul Whiteman's, when he matured. The fiddle had rendered him special. Philly moved through the meal with poise, approached and left his chair the way he had occupied the stage and taken curtain calls, oblivious of his size, aware only of his stature, an internal given.

On the Boardwalk and later, as they walked barefoot skirting the surf, it was Philly's show biz stories, his road adventures, not the Woolf mercantile saga of the Seven Seas from Liverpool around the Cape of Good Hope to San Francisco and finally Newark, that enthralled Hannah. Philly had left show business two years before they met for the steady income of the men's clothing business—the trade of his forebears—but it was Philly's artistry, his style that made their courtship so exciting.

Philly broke her revery when he came back into the room after his phone call. "Mac says we took in two hundred and fifty dollars tonight."

"Not bad," she whispered.

"I don't believe it, Han. But will it last for us after the war?"

"The war ended, Phil? When? I missed the headline."

"Come on, be straight. People are starting to talk about after the war."

"So that's good, isn't it?"

"But what will it do for business?"

"How can you worry about that too?"

"What if there's another depression when all the GI's come back?"

"You're kidding, Philly."

"Where are they going to find nine million jobs that weren't here when they shipped out? Even the *Times* writes editorials."

"Jesus!" Hannah shook her head in disbelief. "In the old days on 23rd Street we didn't have a pot to piss in." She meant the first store they had owned, Woolf's Haberdashery, from 1935 to 1937.

Philly smiled, recalling the paltry receipts, $19 a day, $28 on a good Saturday.

"Remember Murray Finer, the sales manager of Swank Accessories?" Hannah asked.

"With the black front tooth," Philly recalled.

"Chipped," Hannah added.

"And the cotton ball in his left ear with the yellow drops oozing," Philly said, completing the vignette.

"Well, he dubbed you the Weather Man. 'I call for money, you give me the weather report. What the hell are you? The goddamned Weather Man?' "

They completed the final epithet in unison and fell into each other's arms, heaving with laughter, weeping. Philly kissed Hannah's red mouth. She licked his tears playfully between kisses. They moved from the couch into the bedroom, undressing. Certain Mitchell was asleep, they made love, the naked little man moving quickly between her soft thighs. He rode her moist womb in a frenzy until he exploded.

"I love you Hannah . . . Hannah." He was surprised at his own avowal and joy. He rested his head on her nipples.

Hannah grabbed his buttocks and pulled him closer to her stiffened folds, trying to revive his lust.

"Stay, Philly . . . stay inside."

Old partners with differing rhythms. They tried to forget all the changes.

* * *

In the morning I was still facing the double bed when I woke up, only now my mother and father were sleeping in it, bundled in the middle. I slid out of my bed, went right to the bathroom, then eased into the living room and sat on the radiator cover in front of the windows. It was a bright November day. I could see all the way up to the Yankee Stadium, three blocks away from our old Bronx apartment. My stomach began to churn with morning hunger. I walked back to the tiny kitchenette off the foyer hoping to find a little something in the icebox. It was almost empty except for a can of tomato juice, one stick of butter, a lemon wedge, and a box of suppositories. I went back to the windows; I spent a lot of time in front of them waiting for my parents. I gazed at the continual flow of traffic making its way down the Central Park roadway from 110th Street to the grand opening at 59th. Each cluster of cars that emerged and disappeared from within the tree-lined swirls of the drive were like a finish-line group of Thoroughbreds as they roared past the New York Athletic Club into 7th Avenue. I could watch them race for hours. Each heat was a unique combination of black sedans, coupes, limousines and yellow taxicabs. It was impossible to pick the winner everytime. Anything could happen to them on their trip through the park.

I finally heard my parents moving in the bedroom. I remembered the pancakes, which usually meant Bick's on 53rd and 7th Avenue, a counter-top coffee place with four self-service tables beside the south window. On Sunday we always ate breakfast together somewhere outside 2209. Bookland was closed all day.

Fifteen minutes later I went into the bedroom to get dressed. My father assured me Bick's was the place when he came out of the bathroom, patting his neck with talcum powder. I couldn't respond vocally. My mother had gripped my chin in her left hand.

"Hold still, Mitchell!" She was recombing my hair, dissatisfied with the crooked part I had made.

"Do you ever brush your hair?" She looked down into my eyes.

"I just use a comb."

"This is the way to do it." She pushed my father's stiff-bristled walnut brush through my waves, "Now, let's see . . ." She reexamined my part, ran the tip of a black Ace comb down it, making one neat line. Her grip was tight but reassuring, our once-a-week grooming ritual. Next was my tie.

"How about Rumpelmayer's or the Russian Tea Room for a change?" Hannah suddenly asked Philly while pressing my Windsor knot into my buttoned dress shirt.

"Their prices are outrageous." Philly whipped around from his closet mirror. "Black market . . . Nice tie!" He had noticed Hannah's exquisite knot, her successful efforts with my hair.

"Couldn't he be in pictures, Phil? Such a handsome boy."

"He's certainly tall enough."

I blushed at myself in the closet mirror.

"But you have to be quick in school since you miss classes all the time with rehearsals and filming."

"I suppose." Hannah nodded. "You have to be quick in school for any line of work today, a good student, period."

Why did they have to bring up school? I wasn't doing well, but it was my day off too. I turned my eyes away from the mirror, confused by their praise mixed with criticism.

"Let's get going. I'm starving." Philly turned out all the lights and ushered us quickly into the carpeted hallway that led to the elevator bank, where the carpet's red floral backdrop gave way to a golden wreath with *PC* writ large in the center.

"Twenty-three skidoo," he yelped as the brass door swished open.

My mother and I started giggling as we entered the mahogany-paneled cab. My father cautioned restraint, pointing at the elevator operator.

"She'll think we're nuts," he whispered, which made us laugh even harder.

By the time we reached the main floor, Mary, the operator, was a party to our silliness. "Twenty-three skidoo," she echoed, opening the steel gate for us to exit.

The lobby was empty, so I pushed the revolving door around full circuit three times before I would allow my parents to join me inside.

"Come on, Mitchell, you'll lose your appetite," my father shouted into my wedge of the door on my last revolution.

"Maybe his part, never his appetite," my mother sassed as I regained my balance under the 7th Avenue hotel canopy and we assembled for our walk downtown to Bick's.

Hannah rallied on 53rd Street, "What about the Stage? It's right here. The best. Potato pancakes, blintzes . . ."

"Too greasy for breakfast. Maybe dinner," Philly added, relenting. "Besides, Mitchell loves Bick's pancakes. I promised him last night. Come on, Han, we're almost there."

He lead us across the street like the Pied Piper and pushed open the glass door, held it ajar for the two of us to file through.

The pancakes were sensational, thirty-five cents for a stack of three with plenty of butter and maple syrup to fill the yellow air pockets. Rich hot coffee was included, which I drank with my mother, a Sunday-only treat. My father had his usual cup of tea with lemon. A few silent men in gray hats sat at the counter, nursing bottomless mugs of coffee and smoking Lucky Strikes. My father took charge, brought our plates from the counterman to the table and made sure we all had enough butter and syrup. Hannah poked at her food. She gazed out the window, despondent, her long neck twisting away from our sticky faces. Her eyes were haunted, tracing the Sunday line of empty buses pushing downtown. Clean, hopeless Bick's. She wanted a more elegant place after working in the store all week, ten hours a day.

My mother opened Bookland by herself every morning at nine-thirty so my father could sleep late. He remained in the store longer in the evening, held down the fort while she went home, washed, and relaxed before we went out for dinner. Often he returned to the store while I was asleep to close up, count out the register and make a night deposit. My mother always waited up for him.

"Maybe we should stay open till twelve on the weekends," my father said after a long sip of hot tea.

"Why, Phil?" My mother turned her head back to the table.

"The business is there. Mac has to push the customers out of the store to close up at ten on Saturday night. Who knows? He probably starts shoving them out at nine-thirty. Let's take advantage—"

"Still worried about the next depression, Phil?" Hannah snapped.

"Come on, Han."

"The last one wasn't all bad. Look at the deal we have at the Park Central, $109 a month, dinner, maid service . . ."

"That was luck," Philly answered. "The American Plan was a legacy of bad times. The landlords didn't know things were getting better when we signed the lease in '42."

"We sure did. 'Books, the perfect wartime gift!' " My mother imitated a radio announcer, but there was a sarcastic edge to her mimicry.

"Thank God they are." He sighed, stung by her ridicule. "More coffee, Han?" My father broke the tension, pushed his chair back. "I'm going to get some more hot water." He picked up his teacup.

"Splurge, Phil, get a new tea bag while you're up there."

His face lost its color.

Philly did watch his money, their money. In restaurants he would nudge me under the table if I ordered a top-priced entrée. He double-checked the arithmetic on every bill. Hannah saw this. He complained about rising prices, excess profits taxes. It wasn't that he was cheap. He did spend money on his own custom-tailored suits and on Hannah's exquisitely made dresses. Though she didn't have a mink coat, the ultimate wartime extravagance, Philly bought her a durable muskrat. And we did live in a luxury at the Park Central that was unusual in wartime. Though $109 a month was a good rent with wages and prices practically frozen for the duration, it was still a big nut. Philly was careful, worried about money. Hannah no longer shared this anxiety. A wedge was opening between them.

After my father's tea and my second order of pancakes, which I shared with him, we left Bick's. Outside on 7th Avenue we huddled.

"I've got to go down to the store, make last night's deposit. Want to come with me, Mitchell?" My father started making plans for the rest of the day.

"You bet!" I was ecstatic—the two of us alone in Bookland with no customers, afterward the United Cigar Store full of penny candy, then the Broadway trolley ride back home.

"Just a second, Mitchell," my mother interrupted. "Don't you have homework for Monday? Remember, those tests are coming up soon." She was right. Monday, spelling, one hundred words; Tuesday, math—addition, subtraction, multiplication tables.

"I forgot all about that," my father agreed.

They were solid allies when it came to school. I had been startled by their united rage when I came home with my first third-grade report card at the end of October. I had failed three subjects. They were shocked, disbelieving. I'd never had any trouble before. My cousins were all very good students. Marshall, Uncle Sam's eldest, was first in his entire medical class at the age of nineteen. How could I fail? They were certain I wasn't dumb. It had to be my fault, lack of effort. They turned on me, furious.

"Don't you realize how important school is? What this means? College . . . everything! God damnit, you little punk!"

Slap! Slap! Stinging blows to each cheek from my mother. Tears streamed down my face. My father came at me with my commando machine gun.

"Come here, you little bum! What are you doing to us? What the hell is going on in that school? Get him, Hannah!"

They cornered me in the bathroom. My father slammed me over his knees and belted my behind with the machine gun until it broke in half. The weapon, a wartime toy made of thick cardboard, splintered black flakes over my pants, shocking and shaming him.

"Come on, Mitchell," my mother said, interrupting my recollection, "we'll have a good time at home." She clasped my palm in hers, pulled me to her side. "You do your homework like a good boy while I take a bath. I'm exhausted. Afterward we'll have lunch downstairs at the drugstore. Daddy will be home before you know it."

"Check the paper, Han. See what's playing at the Ziegfeld," he said, helping her out.

"Gaslight, I think." She was planning ahead also.

"I love Bergman," he replied. "Good actress."

"Nice and tall, huh, Phil?" My mother turned on her heels with me in tow and sauntered off like a big show girl laughing.

My father smiled, relieved at her mirth, and headed toward the downtown bus stop.

Upstairs in 2209 I collected my spelling lists and math tables, brought them into the living room and sat down at the neat hotel desk with Park Central stationery stuffed in its middle drawer.

My mother went into the bedroom, closed the door halfway and started running the tub water. After fifteen minutes at the desk I decided to look over some of my old tests. They were back inside the bedroom, where I kept my schoolwork. When I entered the room, my mother was standing in my path, beside her bureau, stark naked. I flushed. She reached for her robe, quickly placing it on her shoulders, clasping the sides together over her breasts.

"You should have knocked, Mitchell." Her hips were exposed as she walked quickly into the bathroom.

Their high plump curves were a surprise, like a bleached valentine with hair matted on the tip. Embarrassed, I grabbed my old tests and ran back into the living room. After thirty minutes of renewed study I was bored. I thought of asking my mother to quiz me but was too flustered by our last encounter to request it. Besides, my parents rarely helped me with schoolwork. Exhortation was their specialty.

When my mother finished her bath, she poked her shiny wet head into the living room.

"I'm going to lie down awhile, Mitchell. Let me rest."

So I was on my own until she woke up or my father got back from the store. I went up to the windows and sat down on the radiator cover, waiting, waiting.

There were only a few other kids at the hotel. Pearl Sobel, a hefty seven-year-old, lived on the eleventh floor. We were dining room pals, always trying to break away from our tables and sneak into the employees' dining area on the second floor, where a humming ice cream machine dispensed Dixie Cups, one for a nickel. Sometimes the machine malfunctioned and dropped three for a nickel, a jackpot. Unfortunately, Pearl's family had a country house where they all went every weekend, carting shopping bags full of delicacies.

There was another Mitchell Woolf with a different middle initial and straight blond hair on the fifth floor. I used to go down to his apartment for help with subtraction on my way to school. He was impatient with my requests but very quick with his own assignments, which he always put off until the last minute. He was so smart, he skipped right out of 3A into 4A, so I never saw him anymore.

Paul Rice lived across the street in the Hotel Wellington. His father was the manager. We often played together on weekdays after walking home from school: lobby games, helping the bellhops at his hotel or the elevator operators at mine, whichever group we could ingratiate ourselves with. Sundays were also special for him. His father was off duty and made certain the entire family spent the whole day away from the hotel.

Finally there was Fred Grosso, age nine, a large, sweet boy with delicate wire-rimmed glasses. He lived in the Essex House on Central Park South; his father owned the barbershop concessions in both the Park Central and the Essex House. Fred was always on the move, getting something for one of his father's shops. Unpredictable timing, surprise made our adventures exciting.

"Mitchell, wait up!" he'd screamed the last Friday in July, spotting me in the hotel lobby. I was pushing my way out the 56th Street revolving door on a retrieval mission, searching for paper clips and airplanes I had just thrown out of our twenty-second floor windows—my target, the cars in the gravel parking lot directly across the street.

"What's up?" Fred yelled, following me, his question muffled by the slice of door between us.

"I'm looking for clips," I said on the sidewalk.

"Clips?"

"Paper clips."

"Why? What do you need them for?"

"I dropped them out the window."

"What for?"

"To see where they land. How far I can throw them."

"I still don't get it," Fred said, following me into the gravel lot as I looked for my latest round of ammunition. By the time I found four clips, Fred was hooked, oblivious of his barbershop errands.

"Come up to the apartment, I'll show you how it works."

We took the express elevator up to the twenty-second floor and then ran down to our suite.

"Here's what you do, Fred." I approached the open living room window with a fistful of clips. "See the black car? Try to hit it in the lot . . . bang . . . bull's-eye!" I aimed and threw one. We watched its trajectory across the street.

"Where did it land, Mitchell? I didn't see it. Did you?"

"That's the fun. I try to remember and then go down and look for it."

"Let's go!"

"No, not for one. I throw at least ten."

"Go ahead, so we can find them."

"You try some." I offered him the clips. Fred began dropping them out the window, carefully at first. By his fifth one he was confident, hitting the lot with each toss.

"Terrific, Mitchell. Can we go downstairs now and find them?"

"Sure!" We left the suite. None of the elevators would come. We waited at least ten minutes.

"What's wrong?" I asked Fred.

"A breakdown maybe. Let's take the stairs."

"Twenty-two flights?"

"It's fun all the way down. Come on!" We entered the green metal stairwell and jumped, two steps at a time, down the twenty-two flights of stairs, gasping, laughing, exhausted but never stopping until we ran out through the wide service exit onto the sidewalk.

Fred found two of his clips, I found eight and we rushed for the elevators, but Fred stopped me.

"Let's use the stairs again, Mitchell."

"Up?"

"Yeah."

"Walk up twenty-two flights?"

"Why not?"

"We'll get tired."

"It's more fun than down."

"Okay, *vamos, amigo.*"

It was hard, and we did stop every five floors, winded. After reaching the fifteenth we both got a charge of adrenaline and were still running when we passed the twenty-second, breathless with laughter and agony.

"I can't stop my feet!" Fred gasped.

"Neither can I." We fell on top of each other, a heap of exhausted glee when we reached the twenty-ninth floor, at the top of the building. We peeked out the stairway exit and saw a lot of workmen hammering, making what looked like a new floor in the middle of the largest empty space I had ever seen. We edged into the noisy activity, but were spotted by a man in a gray suit.

"Looking for something, boys?"

"Paper clips," Fred squealed.

"None up here, buster."

"Can't we watch?"

"You kids might get hurt."

"Please?" I asked.

"Beat it, fellas. Out of here, will you?"

Down the stairwell we flew. Down was easier, and we ran repeating the man's orders in a mock-authoritative tone: "Kids . . . fellas . . . buster . . ."

At the twenty-second floor we returned to my apartment, moaning with little explosions of laughter, recalling the stairs up and down and the foreman's hostility. Fred used our house phone to check in with the barbershop. They needed him for a coffee-and-Danish run. He was gone. Silence again. I walked back to the windows, closed them and looked outward, way far out for a long, long time.

I was sitting beside those same windows now, waiting. Absolutely no chance of running into Fred on Sunday; the barbershops were closed. At two-thirty, just as my mother and I were finally on our way down to the drugstore, my father came home. We all went to the Stage Deli instead and then to the movies, where *Gaslight* had been replaced by *Since You Went Away,* a home-front love story.

The next morning I slid out of bed, dressed quickly, used the bathroom and went into the kitchenette to make breakfast: a glass of ice-cold tomato juice and a piece of buttered white bread. My parents slept until eight-fifteen on weekdays, so I left 2209 before they woke up.

I made my way across 7th Avenue and down to 54th Street, where I turned left. PS 69 was between 6th and 7th avenues. When we first came to midtown and I was only seven and a half, my parents insisted I use the BMT subway entrance on the 55th Street side of the Park Central to cross underneath 7th Avenue, coming up on the Hotel Wellington side of the street. Now a veteran of early morning two-way traffic, I was allowed to cross aboveground.

PS 69 was a grim preindustrial public school. The signs marking the boys' and girls' entrances and the *FUCK YOU'S* splashed all around the high fenced school yard were the only adornments on its limestone facade. My classroom housed three different grades, 3A, 3B and 4A. This format was not created to encourage a seamless learning process; rather the childhood population of our midtown area was too small for the normal one-grade-to-a-room pattern. Our class was composed of the few kids who lived in hotels and nearby luxury apartments and those who came from the walk-up tenements of 9th and 10th avenues. Concentration was a problem with three distinct grades in one room, all chattering different lessons. I never adjusted, caught on to my proper grade level, which was somewhere between 3A and 3B. I was always writing endless lists of misspelled words. Our teacher, Mrs. Hanley, believed in teaching by penalizing.

Monday's spelling test was hard, though there were only seventy-five words on it. Mrs. Hanley threw all the tough ones at us: *there, their* and *they're, swimming, difficult, grieve, deceive* . . . I was prepared for most of them, I thought. On Tuesday she went way beyond the triple-digit addition and subtraction she had promised to concentrate on, to the hardest multiplication tables, 7, 9 and 12. I would certainly fail and get another disastrous report card. On Wednesday, Mrs.

Hanley returned our spelling tests. I got twenty wrong, a 65 even with the class curve.

"Write each misspelled word ten times" was scribbled on my paper. After twenty minutes of communal spelling penance, Mrs. Hanley began going over the 3A math test—common mistakes with the 12 table and subtraction carry-over rules. She held our corrected papers in her right hand, waved them above her head, walked to the rear of the room, stood in front of our wooden lockers and then came back to the front of the class, dropping a graded math test on each pupil's desk except mine.

"Finish those word lists and you'll get your math back." She stared me down.

I twisted around to see how the other kids had done, what the right answer was to 12 × 12. When I turned my head back toward the desk, Mrs. Hanley's palm met my nose, which spurted blood all over my face, shirt and goddamned spelling words. Giving an eight-year-old boy a bloody nose, even accidentally, was serious. Mrs. Hanley had merely intended to tap the back of my head in order to return my gaze to the front blackboard, she explained by way of apology as my mother suddenly entered the classroom with the school principal, Mrs. Brice. Salvation! Just in the nick of time, like in the movie *How Green Was My Valley.*

I was taken out of the room to Mrs. Brice's office, sobbing, explaining the bloody nose to my mother, babbling about my math test. Mrs. Brice came back to her office after conferring with Mrs. Hanley. She and my mother talked heatedly while I waited outside. When my mother finally emerged, she was flashing mad.

"I'm taking Mitchell home right now!" she shouted toward Mrs. Brice.

"Have it your way, Mrs. Woolf, if you insist!"

"Let's get out of this awful school," my mother proclaimed as she led me down the wide stairwell onto 54th Street. "That goddamned woman is crazy, *meshugge!*"

I agreed.

It was chance my mother was in school at that moment. My parents had decided to send me to a private boarding school and needed the principal's permission and my official transcript. The incident she witnessed confirmed their decision despite Mrs. Brice's plea that I be allowed to complete the semester. My dramatic evacuation from PS 69 obscured the actual reason for this sudden shift in schools. There was an aura of salvation about a boarding school: I'd be going away to the country, better teachers, smaller classes. My parents promised: "You'll come home every third weekend, we'll come out and visit in between." There were also disturbing innuendos: Business was so strong the store would have to remain open until midnight every evening of the week and possibly Sunday afternoons during the Christmas rush, forcing my parents to work longer hours—which meant fewer evenings together at the Cocoanut Grove. And though our Sunday breakfasts at Bick's could still occur, Hannah's growing fatigue would render them less and less pleasurable.

The Lake Ronkonkoma School in the heart of Long Island was unique even in the slightly absurd universe of nonsectarian private schools. How my father found it was a mystery, as no one in the Woolf or Lufkin family had ever been sent away to school. I understood the obvious reasons for his choosing it once I saw photographs of the 150-acre campus. The Lower School children, grades one through eight, lived in real stone dormitories with slate roofs. At age seven, while we still lived in the Bronx, I had been sent away to Camp Lake Surprise in the Adirondacks and developed a series of ear infections and horrible colds. These forced me to come home two weeks early, tears in my eyes, different colored socks on my feet. The reason for my chronic illness, the family decided, was the open-air sleeping cabins we were housed in; no basement, no heat, just woods and air. The dorms at Lake Ronkonkoma had all the amenities Camp Lake Surprise lacked, a definite plus along with its moderate tuition.

Academically the school was mediocre, hardly a prep school of quality, though it did run through high school with most graduates going on to college. The headmaster's oldest son was even accepted at Columbia, and the youngest at Harvard, but they were both ill prepared and almost flunked out.

Physically the school was more impressive. The buildings and campus were developed by a group of visionary Christian Scientists in the late 1920s. It was called the Windward School, and from old yearbooks we came upon in various attics, it seemed to have been a thriving coeducational school, rich in activities, happy faces and upper-class affinities. The school attracted a benefactor of enormous wealth with enough capital intact after 1929 to underwrite an ambitious building program. His money and the enrollment fizzled by 1935. The construction debts were enormous. When the school filed for bankruptcy in 1938, the pine woods near the Lower School dorm were packed with slate roof tiles intended for five more dormitories. Fortunately, before going broke on stone quadrangles, the Windward School had erected other buildings of traditional wood, cement and birch shingle, including a four-story schoolhouse, dining complex, dormitories, and the largest indoor gymnasium on Long Island. Numerous athletic fields had been carved out and the entire campus agreeably landscaped with urban sidewalks installed as pathways, another plus with my father. All this was our legacy from that moment in 1942 when Roland Kennedy convinced the East River Savings Bank to let him refinance a reduced mortgage on the Windward School. He promised to bring the property back to life as the Lake Ronkonkoma School.

Mr. Kennedy was a charismatic, balding redhead with the obligatory Columbia Teacher's College degree. His educational philosophy was ideal post-Depression wartime rhetoric stated in the school's motto: Study, Work and Play. He had recruited a hundred male students, sixty in the Upper School, forty in the Lower by the time I arrived in early December of 1943.

"What's he like?" they all asked Roger Oaks, the fat black-haired boy who was my first roommate on the top floor of the North Dorm. Oaks cross-examined me after lights-out, aware of my first-night-away-from-home vulnerability, knowing I was close to tears yet wanting to confide and make new friends.

"Do you like the Germans, Woolf?"

"Are you kidding?" I was offended.

"Yes or no?"

"No, of course!"

"Well, then you like the Japs?"

"I don't like them either."

"Well that means you love the Italians. One or the other or both."

Aware that Oaks was testing me, I brushed his loyalty game aside and tried to elicit more pleasant information.

"Roger, do you ever go to the movies here?"

"Oaks, call me Oaks. Okay, Woolf?"

"Sure, Oaks."

I accepted their tradition. We were all known by our last names, as if our families had attended the school for generations.

"Do they ever take you to the movies?" I repeated.

"On Saturday we go to Smithtown. Sometimes we go to St. James on Sunday."

"Two movies a weekend! That's great!"

"Depends on what kind of movies you like. They show a lot of cartoons and love stories," Oaks announced with disgust.

"Oh, like what?"

"*Bambi, Gone With the Wind*, crap like that."

"Do they ever show *Dumbo*?"

"Not yet. Why? Is that your favorite?"

"I liked it."

"What about movies with real people?" Oaks pursued. "What's your favorite, Woolf?"

"I liked *Since You Went Away*. Saw it twice. Once with my parents and the next time by myself."

I missed them so much I couldn't say anymore. Would I ever see my mother and father again? Go home to 2209? Would they really come out to see me? Would they have the time now? Or care ever again?

Oaks was silent until the morning when he broadcast that I liked love stories more than war stories and that if the proper sequence of questions were asked, I preferred the Germans, Japs, and Mussolini to the Allied Forces. Oaks cast me as a sissified collaborator—a perfect target.

He and his cadre were effective. I could never ignore them for long.

"How's Dumbo today? Did you evah see an elephant fly?" They mimicked the black crows who befriended Dumbo flapping their arms.

I always broke down and chased the faster ones, Fritz, Zachery, and Daniels into the woods.

One morning, when I had assumed I was in the clear after two weeks of harassment, Oaks and his contingent surprised me on the steep sidewalk leading to the dining hall. I whirled on the fat bastard and tracked him into a cluster of blue spruce. His cohorts, sensing my rage, scattered, leaving him exposed to my fists and feet. Oaks was soon crying more than I was. He appealed to our teacher, Miss Green, who saw it all.

"What do you expect, Oaks? You keep on teasing him. You can dish it out, but you can't take it."

Miss Green had articulated the unofficial school motto, a turning point in my socialization and the key to proper conduct on the pathways, in the dorms and on the playing fields of the Lake Ronkonkoma School: If you dish it out, you'd better be able to take it!

Her own classroom was more civilized, even gentle, though I was confused by the difficult curriculum and disappointed to find the same jumble of three different grade levels (3A, 3B and 4A) in one classroom. What was the big deal about boarding school?

After a month of patient instruction and observation with little improvement on my part, Miss Green made a bold move. She parted the accordian-hinged oak doors that divided her room from Miss Wells's and quietly placed me in the 2B section of that room for prearranged remediation. It was a wonderful sleight of hand. I wasn't demoted, just visiting. The work was not as hopelessly complicated with Miss Wells, who taught all the first- and second-grade children. I was able to perform without despair because I could actually do the work.

Miss Wells and Miss Green were both fifteen years younger than Mrs. Hanley. They were friends, recent primary education graduates from the University of Massachussets. Miss Wells was pert, wore high heels, a lot of rouge and an upsweep hairdo with little ringlets for bangs. Miss Green was a tall, fragile Yankee who wore rimless eye-glasses, brown or black saddle shoes and a button-up-the-front sweater over her blouse. Her long blond hair was parted, swept down and up into waves which hid her ears but highlighted her white neck.

After three weeks I was returned to Miss Green's class a more competent student, able to keep up with my 3B section in math and reading. Success emboldened me. I wrote home for special books to read and began the Honey Bunch series, *Heidi, Heidi's Children,* and *Hans Brinker.* I still had relapses, when I lost the thread of a lesson and gave up, but Miss Green understood this mechanism of despair and would patiently snap me back to work. She also knew us outside of class as the faculty presence on our dormitory floor, where she lived in a two room apartment facing the central hall. Her governance was light and trusting, mostly timetable and housekeeping supervision.

"All up, everyone! Out of bed!" she shouted down each corridor at seven A.M., and "Lights out now!" with a quick walk down the same corridors at eight-thirty P.M. On laundry day she made certain we placed a clean sheet with neat hospital corners on the bottom of our beds, switched our old bottom sheet to the top just under our blankets and sent the soiled top sheet to the Blue Port Laundry with the rest of our dirty things. On bath night, the other end of laundry day, she dressed in pants and a U. Mass. sweat shirt, put her hair up, and was prepared to assist when necessary.

It was Miss Green who moved me and Oaks apart after our side-walk battle, realizing no amount of time could cool such animosity. She put me in with another relative newcomer, Jack Ronson, who was also having learning problems.

"Duh, Jack" was Ronson's daily greeting from the North Dormers like Oaks, Fritz, Zachery and company, though not for long, as he handled these demeaning assaults with dignity and casual disregard, never losing his temper or chasing anybody. He was two years older than most of us, had been left back twice in city public schools. Harassment merely disappointed him. Jack was stronger than his tormentors, lean, wiry, sure of himself despite his painful frustrations with reading and subtraction.

We became friends in Miss Wells's class. Ronson was a permanent member of 2B. He never made it back to Miss Green's classroom. His academic concentration and effort were so intense and his subsequent confusion so disheartening, I could never imagine teasing him. He sat at his 2B desk, yellow hair shading into silver around his ears, always trying, friendly.

He was a terrific roommate, neat, considerate, worthy of trust. After lights-out in the darkness, lying on our backs, we would release our family secrets and fantasies into the night, play them back and forth in whispers until Miss Green had finished the bed check, then allow our normal vibrato full range till, in mid-anecdote, one of us passed out and sleep closed up the room.

Morning broke with Ronson's Zenith radio blaring forth the seven o'clock news despite my anguished pleas for silence and more sleep. Ronson never lowered the volume, which kept me moving toward breakfast. In the late afternoon, while we changed into our jackets and ties for dinner, Ronson's radio, tuned into *Jack Armstrong, the All-American Boy*, became an asset. Sunday nights we got Lamont Cranston in *The Shadow*, Wednesday evenings after study hall, the *Lux Radio Theater*.

Every other Sunday Ronson's parents would drive out to see him in a '39 steel-gray Chevrolet. Mrs. Ronson had a large round head with a hair bun resting on the back of it. She wore the softest sealskin fur coat I ever touched. Mr. Ronson looked and dressed exactly like Jack, Rogers Peet tweed jackets and button-down shirts.

Sometimes they invited me on their afternoon excursions to Smithtown and Stony Brook. We crept along at thirty-five miles an hour, the wartime speed limit, trees and villages passing in slow motion. Our favorite place was Stony Brook, a reconstructed harbor village with a delicious sweetshop and, fifty yards off the green, Melville Pond, where Jack and I tossed stale bread to the ducks and swans. We drove back to school on a narrow dirt road that ran through tall locust trees and naked maples, up steep hills and down, past sudden glimpses of the Sound.

The first Sunday my mother and father came up for a visit, the Ronsons invited all of us along for the Smithtown–Stony Brook excursion. We were in the back seat, the Ronsons up front. Mrs. chattered, making friends. Mr. concentrated on the road and his machine, turning the pearl steering wheel gently with his soft leather gloves.

"Warren loves to drive," Mrs. Ronson purred. "He's so good with his hands, does all the engine work himself."

"Lovely car," my mother said, looking over the gray upholstery. Neither she nor my father knew how to drive.

"If we had more gas coupons, we'd come out every Sunday," Mrs. Ronson said.

Mr. Ronson finally spoke, turning his head slightly in our direction: "Take longer trips."

"Oh, this is fine for us, a treat!" my father assured him.

"Guess we have to win the war," Mr. Ronson exclaimed, steering us onto 25A outside of Smithtown.

"Eisenhower and Patton seem to be doing that," my father said.

"I still can't get any typewriter parts," Mr. Ronson exploded at the windshield. "Do they fire them at the goddamned German tanks?"

"Easy, Warren." Mrs. Ronson explained their dilemma. They owned a typewriter repair business which was thriving down on Nassau Street. Royal, Smith, Underwood, Corona no longer made machines for the domestic market. The only way to get a new typewriter was to fix your old one or buy a reconditioned model. But now it was almost impossible to get spare parts. Mr. Ronson had to fabricate countless delicate springs and spokes. A trying task when deadlines were involved. My father and mother were sympathetic, related their own difficulty in stocking men's clothing when the war began and their subsequent switch to books. The ice broken, they confided, opened up with one another like Jack and me after lights-out.

"Pretty town," my father commented as we drove up the Stony Brook green.

"Melville built it," Mr. Ronson explained.

"Melville? Shoes, isn't it? Thom McAn?"

"Right, Thom McAn."

"Why would he spend so much money and not open a store?"

"Melville lives here. He bought serenity, not another outlet."

"Is that like security?" my father mused.

"No, serenity costs more, Philly."

They all drove back to the city together and decided to make the trip both ways in Mr. Ronson's Chevy the next time they visited the school on the same Sunday. This would be convenient for my parents, but it certainly reduced our chances of being alone as a family. Nuzzling in the back seat of the Ronson's gray Chevy wasn't enough intimacy to last for three weeks.

When my mother first brought me out to Lake Ronkonkoma with my trunk and one valise a few days after her scene with Mrs. Brice, the two of us were alone. She walked the steep sidewalk paths with me, introducing the promised fresh air and trees.

"I wasn't lying about the trees and the air, was I?" she asked up in my new room shortly before her taxi was supposed to pick her up.

"No," I agreed, pouting.

"Come on, Mitchell, you'll like it here once you get used to it."

"When will I come home?"

"In three weeks."

"*Three?*"

"Daddy and I will meet you at Penn Station. We'll eat dinner at the Cocoanut Grove. See a double feature at the Ziegfeld. You'll see Grandma on Saturday afternoon."

I remained silent. My mother stroked my ears. I began crying into her dress.

"It'll be all right, I'm certain. Don't cry now. I love you."

She held me against her thighs. She began wiping tears from under my chin, straightening my tie, touching my hair into place.

We both heard the taxi.

"I have to go now, Mitchell."

I followed her down to the black DeSoto for a final embrace, and she was gone.

The trees remained. Oaks, maples and towering elms stood over fields of second-growth pine, a perfect setting for nighttime ring-a-levio and daytime fort building. I, however, was oblivious to nature per se. Instead the outdoors meant sports to all of us in the Lower

School. Football, soccer, rugby, softball, running, throwing, batting, hitting the ground with our bodies, it was exhilarating; all the shouting, competing, straining for mastery. For three hours every afternoon we abandoned ourselves to the season's sport. Played out, we returned to the dorms tired yet refreshed.

A problem arose on Fridays after dinner, when sports meant the Chief and boxing or other forms of combat. The Chief, descended from Sitting Bull, was a mythic campus figure with a huge beer belly shoved into tight black pants. He selected and conditioned the Upper School football, track and baseball teams from a scant sixty students and drove them to distinction and occasional victory. His reputation forced us to accept his orders at Friday night boxing without any questions. Grades one through eight would all be present in Windward Hall Lounge, seated against the walls, making the room a large boxing arena. We were the ropes. The Chief paired us with opponents. We laced up the heavy gloves. Some of the first and second graders began crying as soon as they hit each other. The Chief let them cry and bang around until their short rounds ended. There were no TKO's. I usually fought O'Conner from 4B, a tall baby face who I could take easily. The Chief liked that. Sometimes I fought Fritz, a more even match. We slugged out our mutual hatred. He was quicker, I was stronger, a tentative mutual respect took hold. I wanted to fight Oaks, but he was too small. The Chief paired the black-haired Roger against his older fair-haired brother, Fred. They pommeled each other senseless. As the Chief moved up the grade levels and the strengths and fears of the paired boxers became more divergent, he would place a blindfold on the stronger boxer and let the weaker one hit him at will. Sometimes the Chief would beckon a third boxer up to help slug the floundering blindfolded victim. Some of the kids squealed their approval, others just clouded over with fear, watching quietly. The Chief was unpredictable. Certain evenings he would switch blindfolds if a little kid didn't attack his blindfolded adversary with sufficient fury, couldn't dish it out.

One never knew. Was it caprice, or was there a moral order, some distant foothill lore operating inside the Chief's large brown head? I particularly wondered about his moods when I ate at his table in the dining room. The faculty members rotated every month to the head of a new table. They served the food, which was so low-grade, it was another new eating experience. Cereal and toast with margarine for breakfast. Grilled cheese on bread with mustard for lunch. The outstanding meal was Sunday lunch, roast chicken with moist bread stuffing.

I finally took to the food and learned to finish quickly in order to qualify for whatever seconds were offered. There was, however, a problem with this. We had to eat all or, depending on the table head, most of each portion put on our plates. There were two strange vegetables I had never encountered before, cabbage chopped into coleslaw, and beets, plain or minced into a salad. The very odor of beets made me retch. If only borscht had been one of Grandma Lufkin's dishes, I might have been invulnerable except for the coleslaw.

When I couldn't finish these vegetables, Mrs. Kennedy put them in the refrigerator and served them to me instead of the next meal. The only salvation was a subtle understanding with the faculty member serving the food that he or she would go easy on my portion of beets or look the other way when the student waiter cleared the dishes. The Chief was again unpredictable, as with boxing and the blindfolds. Once he had Mrs. Kennedy bring back my uneaten beets for three consecutive meals until I finally threw up. After that episode he usually rattled the beet serving spoon over my plate so the red juices trickled onto it with a few slivers of the vegetable, but I was never sure whether his beneficence would continue. It was so *dangerous*, eating on certain days.

Not at all like the Cocoanut Grove or Grandma Lufkin's kitchen, which made my visits home so comforting. They did occur once every three weeks as promised. My mother and father picked me up at the Long Island section of Penn Station and returned me in time for the Sunday 4:07 to Smithtown. But they never took me to the Cocoanut Grove for dinner or a double feature at the Ziegfeld. Instead I was whisked up to Grandma Lufkin's new three room apartment in Washington Heights on the IND for most of the weekend. The store was now jumping, so busy seven days and nights a week that no hands could be spared. Bookland was on SOS alert.

As a result it was Uncle Sam and Aunt Blanche, Uncle Morris and Aunt Renee, their children and Grandma Lufkin's Shabbas evening group who knew the selected details of my life away from home. They had never heard such goings on. An Indian chief with boxing gloves on Friday night! Shabbas! Whoever heard . . . They were captivated. I was Marco Polo telling the Venetians about Peking. I enjoyed their response but was surprised by their laughter when I paused in the middle of what I thought was a serious adventure.

My parents only heard abbreviated versions of these tales, going back and forth on the subway or eating late Sunday brunch at the Savarin in Penn Station. In our letters, however, there was more time, our voices were unimpeded, full of news and questions. My father's script was distinctive, sweeping high and low with elegant loops on the *W*'s and *M*'s. He covered both sides of Bookland's new blue-lettered stationery with graceful sentences and perfect spelling. My mother wrote less often on the hotel stationery.

One day, after three months at Lake Ronkonkoma, I received a letter from her in a strange envelope. *HOTEL DIXIE* was printed in the left-hand corner, as it was on the letterhead within. Why was she writing from a different hotel? It was on 42nd Street, one block west of the store, opposite the Laffmovie, but she lived in the Park Central with my father, with us.

Dear Mitchell,

I've been very sick this month. The doctor, Uncle Mordecai, says it's from standing on my feet such long hours at the store. I must keep off them, rest, exercise in the open air to get well. I'm going out West. Remember, I told you once how much I liked to horseback ride when I was young? Well, I plan to do some out West. I'll send you a real cowboy hat when I get there. I'm very proud of your progress at school.

Love and kisses,
Mommy

Where was my father? Why was my mother staying at the Hotel Dixie? Was it closer to the station? Would my father put her on the train? Which hotel was he living at? What the hell was happening between them? It was all so arbitrary, like Mrs. Hanley's classroom or boxing night with the Chief, eating or not eating beets at his dining room table. I had no answers, only the questions festering inside my stomach.

Violent rain swept through the spruce trees on the front lawn while I waited for a Sunday visit from my father, two weeks after the Hotel Dixie letter. I was desperate for details. Would they come straight out like in the Honey Bunch series, or would they be concealed, like in the Nancy Drew mysteries?

My father arrived in a taxi, late as usual, but with an excellent excuse this time. The Ronsons' car was washed out by the rain—the engine wouldn't turn over—so he had to take the Long Island Railroad, which was unreliable in any weather. He was very wet despite a large black umbrella, a fedora, and silly quarter rubbers. Rain pellets spotted his large nose. He gave me a Dentyne-scented hug, and then we went up to my room. The dormitory was empty on Sunday afternoons. My father took off his wet clothes and hung them meticulously on wooden hangers over the tub. I sat on my bed. He settled into Ronson's desk chair and lit a Garcia y Vega panatela. We could hear the rain outside, still going crazy against the trees. We were safe now, dry, alone.

"Where's Jack? The other kids?" my father asked.

"In the gym. Where's Mommy?" I asked. "Did you get her on the train?"

"Out West." He was matter of fact, looking at the rain.

"Where, out West?"

"Doesn't she write to you?"

"Not anymore. Not since the Hotel Dixie."

"Oh, she's in Nevada."

"Do they have horses there?"

"Sure, mountains, horses . . ."

"Will she get better and come back?"

Silence. He drew in on the cigar deeply, letting out the smoke gently, examining the panatela shape, looking through the smoke, hurt, quiet. No answer.

"Come back?" I tried again.

"Sure, sure."

He was back in the room now, just barely. My stomach twisted.

"Don't worry, Mitchell, she'll be back soon. I'll let you know."

"How are the Yankees?" I asked, changing the subject.

"Terrible, terrible. With DiMaggio, Keller, Rizzuto and Chandler in the Army it's not even baseball, for Christsakes! Snuffy Stirnweiss at second base, remember him? He's the Yankee slugger now, leads the whole American League in batting with .302. It's just not the same."

I agreed.

The rain outside stopped. My father decided to take me out for a soda and candy at the canteen, a white frame cottage near the dining hall run by Chef Swanson's wife. He put his damp rainwear back on, and we walked downstairs, passed the wet pines sweet with sap and rainbows. On the way I pointed out the swings, playing fields, and crosswalks that were now my landscape. My father's clothes were too expensive and elegant for this terrain. He talked about the store, the hotel, the number 7 bus, business, always business. I held my own, connecting his world to mine.

"Donny Faber's father works at the Stork Club. That's in midtown, isn't it?"

"West 40's somewhere," my father agreed. "Big crowded place, lots of celebrities."

"His father's the bartender. They leave him dollar tips."

"Hah, the mooches are really throwing money around now."

"Faber's got Stork Club ashtrays and matches tucked between his sheets in his bottom drawer."

"Does he smoke?"

"No. He looks at them sometimes before lights-out. They're shiny black with white storks."

"He's all right in the noggin?" My father smiled, tapping his fine black hair.

"He's all right." I laughed. "Has teeth like Bugs Bunny. No one ever teases him. He's very fast."

"Faster than Zachery and Fritz?"

"Much!"

"What's his mother do?"

"I don't know. I think she lives in Queens." I couldn't stop. "Fritz's mother died when he was born."

"Same day?" my father asked.

"Same minute."

"How did his old man manage?"

"He's a cop, captain of a precinct."

"Oh." My father exclaimed. He assumed Fritz was somehow nurtured in a Hillside station house.

"Paul Zachery," I continued, cataloguing mothers, "has a mad, raving one. She hurls him onto the platform of the 4:07 by the hood of his mackinaw as the train is moving out. She hates him for making them late."

"What does she do for a living?"

"Sells pots and pans, hardware. She's a businesswoman. Only you and Mommy and the Ronsons work together at the same jobs," I said, suddenly realizing how special their working together was.

My father let this discovery pass in silence.

"When am I coming home?"

"Mitchell"—ignoring my question—"did you know they have a camp here in the summer with swimming at the lake, girls, horses?"

"I've heard kids talk about it."

"Would you like to stay on for camp this summer?"

"What about the hotel? Mommy? Grandma Lufkin? Can't I see them after school?"

"Mommy's out West, Grandma Lufkin's having her apartment painted, and I'm busy at the store, day and night," he snapped.

"Grandma Lufkin can take me."

He nodded sideways, negative.

"Why not?" I shrieked. Tears took over my eyes, splashed down my face.

My father was resolute. "Why are you crying? There'll be other kids here between school and camp. Some of your friends."

Between school and camp, did he say? Jesus, the real lifers, Fritz, O'Conner. I cried defiantly. My father relented, surprised by my rage; he shook me quiet, brushed my hair back.

"Okay, okay, easy, Mitchell. I'll work something out at the Park Central, the store. You come home to me when school ends. Maybe we can even go to the stadium for a game. But you *will* come back for camp, okay?"

"Sure, if there aren't any earaches."

My father laughed, remembering Camp Lake Surprise, pleased with my wit under duress. I wiped the tears away with my palms, trying to calm down as we reached the canteen porch.

"Use this, not your hands." My father offered me his hand-rolled handkerchief. "I thought you liked it here, Mitchell."

"Sure, sure," I muttered, calming myself, thinking, *How much can you like a place for twelve months?* I told him about the Chief and beets, slipped it in. My best offense was still my stomach.

We were inside the canteen, and Chef Swanson was asleep in his caned rocker. Mrs. Swanson puttered around refilling an ancient icebox with soda pop. Startled, she turned around to greet us, a frail woman in her late sixties. My father nodded and invited me to order whatever I wanted, but there wasn't much to choose from. Wartime candy was a disaster, no chocolate at all—Milky Ways, Hersheys, Clark Bars, Almond Joys, all gone for the duration, fighting in the trenches. Wrigley's gum was also gone. Fleer Dubble Bubble gum was a hot black market item, fifty cents a piece if one could find it. On Long Island we made do with Topps gum, jelly fruits, marshmallow sticks and our mainstay, Islip Soda Pop.

I ordered a bottle of orange soda. We sat on the porch while I drank it. In the distance we could hear the Lower School kids coming toward the canteen from the gym. The Sunday night menu was so paltry, cold cuts and potato salad, that Mrs. Kennedy allowed the canteen to be opened before Sunday dinner as well as afterward.

I got edgy, not wanting to share my father with anyone. But he had to tell Ronson why his parents couldn't make it. Jack was saddened by the news, though relieved to know what actually prevented their visit. My father bought him a Fudgsicle and they talked about school. Other kids stared at us, envious, curious—"Woolf's father." Jealous, I moved him away from the canteen toward the gymnasium, the wonder of the campus.

It looked like all the other two-story brown shingled structures at the Lake Ronkonkoma School until we were fifty yards away. Then its enormous dimensions suddenly struck my father. Inside, the lacquered basketball floor was a clear shimmer. Two Upper School students perpetually swept sawdust across it to maintain that glow. I grabbed a loose basketball and started showing off at one of the side backboards. My father had never seen me play. After a few shots and some dribbling the Upper School sweepers began closing down the gymnasium, collecting the loose balls, turning off lights, hanging up the wrestling mats.

My father and I walked back toward the dining hall. It was almost six P.M. The Upper and Lower School kids stood around in clusters of four and five, mumbling about their day. I quietly pointed out Faber's teeth, my father and I smiled together in the dusk. No one was wearing a jacket and tie, which my father saw immediately. We did that for Sunday lunch, I assured him. While we waited for someone to hit the rusty gong with an iron pipe my father saw the Chief's silhouette against some hedges.

"Is that him, the Chief?" he asked me softly.

"Yes," I said.

"I want to talk to him."

"But you can't just talk to him. . . . About what?"

"Beets," my father replied.

Before I could stop him, he was at the Chief's side. I was too embarrassed to introduce or join them. I just hovered in their vicinity, eyes out of their sockets. The Chief's potbelly came to the middle of my father's lapels, but my father's hat and umbrella gave him equal leverage. They eased into a circular dance, facing off, turning— moccasins, cordovan loafers, the cigar smoke—talking quietly. Then my father was back at my side.

"Interesting guy, the Chief."

A car horn blew, parting the dinner crowd, and the car stopped just beyond the dining hall entrance. A frantic driver hopped out, spotted my father and exclaimed, "Mr. Woolf, your cab for the 6:35 back to New York! We'd better hurry if you want to make it!"

How could I say good-bye in front of the other kids? When the driver opened the rear door, we had enough privacy for a kiss, but no time for more questions about my mother. Only my father's assurance that I'd come home when the semester ended. The black cab drove off. I watched it as the dinner gong rang. I could see my father's hat through the rear window. It turned. He was looking back and waving. I returned the wave, then he did, then I did until the trees hid the taxi.

Spending June in the city gave me an opportunity to find out more about my mother. It was also a treat to be home with my father. Though I was almost nine, I was only a few inches shorter than he and had begun to assimilate his gait, if not his speech or physiognomy. In those respects I was still a Lufkin; with my mother's face, my grandmother's inflection.

We began each morning with a late breakfast at the fountain of the Park Central Drugstore. Its black marble counter top wound along the entire twenty-five-yard left side of the shop. Our feet barely touched the brass foot rests under our stools. Perfumes, bath powder, drugs and costume jewelry filled the other half of the store. The countermen and -women prepared and served eggs, pancakes, waffles, bacon and sausages with exquisite precision regardless of the dazzling variety of combinations ordered during the breakfast rush. They knew my father liked tea with lemon, a little dish on the side for the tea bag. My sunny-side eggs made with butter, served with rye toast and coffee, set me chattering. My father, still drowsy, listened with disbelief to my early morning energy. After his first cup of tea he bantered with me about the store and the Yankees. The weather report inside his folded copy of *The New York Times* broke the spell of our relaxed tête-à-tête. Instead of my mother, Harry, the day manager, was waiting for my father at the store, holding off salespeople, delaying his own chores. We headed for the number 11 bus. Fed, coffee-warmed, caffeine high, I dashed through the streets with my father.

Harry had worked alongside my mother, been there when she unlocked the door at nine-thirty. He was the first employee hired when my father switched from clothes to books in time for Christmas of 1942. In three hectic days Philly's Haberdashery had become Bookland, and Harry had cut open the cartons of initial shipments. He was the same height and age, forty-three, as my father, but shaped differently, with a larger chest and shorter legs. A kind, bald man from Buffalo, he was always in motion with his pocketknife and Scripto pencil striving for order.

My father was always late. Every day he arrived outside Bookland with me in tow at eleven. He checked the awning position, looked for faded book jackets in both windows and crushed cigarettes and debris in the lobby and then moved quickly into the store, examining the remainder tables for dust. When he saw Harry's anxious eyes, he deflected them with a smile and familiar promise, "Just let me set up, I'll come right back." He dashed past Harry into a crowd of salesmen standing outside his office, each one with a broken appointment.

"Mr. W., Mr. W." They reached out. Impervious, he barely acknowledged their greetings, ducked immediately into his office behind the Children's Section. He put his newspaper down, hung up his street paraphernalia, spent five minutes adjusting his tie, five more on his hair and jacket. Satisfied, he reemerged from his cubby, smiling, ready to orchestrate the day. First he had to placate Harry and go over the Bookazine list with him before the eleven-thirty deadline for same-day delivery. The deadline usually expired before Harry got my father's full attention. They argued about ordering books that were well reviewed in the *Times*.

"Let's be current, ahead of requests. Why lose sales?" Harry would plead, trying to slip in a few new titles.

"We're not a goddamned public library. If a customer wants a new book, get a deposit, and we'll have it the same day from Bookazine or Diamondstein. Why should we carry the publishers' complete list before we know what sells?" my father would respond, ending their daily argument. Despite these delays the Bookazine order always came through the lobby door at five-fifteen.

With proven best sellers like *The Robe* or *The Fountainhead* and standard reference works, my father would always replenish sold stock up to five copies, confident the jobbers would deliver additional copies the following day if necessary. They were an integral part of his inventory system. With hot sellers like *Forever Amber,* which could not be kept on the shelves, my father ordered direct from the publishers. He received 1,000 copies right after it came out and was the only store in the city with it for two months. Even Bookazine was sold out.

With remainders, Bookland's bread and butter, accounting for 60 percent of sales, my father also took risks. He would grasp a fat 79¢ romance, calculate its heft, hold it out at arm's length, take in the color, feel the paper, read the dust jacket copy, smile at the salesman's extravagant spiel, and suddenly order a hundred copies. He was a connoisseur of bulk merchandise. It had taken him only one month after converting to acquire this knack. All the salesmen had told him sotto voce that each book they showed him was "well written." After a week of this my father questioned the genteel Doubleday salesman, Mr. Ormsby.

"How do you know? Have you read it?"

"No, Mr. Woolf." He blushed. "Only this part here." He fingered the dust jacket copy. With this insider's technique revealed, my father became as well read as 98 percent of the salesmen who crowded into the Children's Section with briefcase samples.

I was awed by this ritual. How did he know when to say yes and when to say no? When to listen to a drummer's off-color road stories, when to cut him off? I was proud of my father's judgment.

Harry's incessant activity, unpacking cartons, checking inventory, preparing books for overseas mail, eventually drew me to the cash register–wrapping counter area in mid-store. Unfortunately I was considered too young to ring the register and make change, not because of faulty math abilities but rather because of the unprofessional appearance it would create. Harry taught me patiently how to wrap books, one, two, three at a time, hiding the taped bottom and showing off the clean yellow and gray Bookland logo when I presented the package to a customer.

He and Mel, his deadpan assistant, also taught me the essentials of inventory control. Whenever they sold a book, I located the table pile or wall slot it came from and "filled it in" with a fresh copy from stock. The challenge was to find the correct inventory pile for each purchased title. These were often hidden underneath the massive remainder tables or placed high up on wall shelves that had no relation to the book's display space. I scurried about, trying to fill up the tables and wall pockets evenly. I mastered the six-foot ladder, scaling high up to replenish hot sellers.

At twelve-forty-five my father would relieve Harry at the register for his overdue lunch break. Harry retrieved his *New York Times*, gave some parting instructions to my father and Mel.

"It's okay, Harry, enjoy your lunch," my father reassured him.

Pacified, Harry relaxed, cleaned his glasses and went to lunch. My father examined the clipboard holding a penciled list of each book sold. He slammed it down, then totaled the register receipts twice in five minutes.

"Jesus, it's slow! Nothing yet! Nothing!" he muttered toward the front of the store.

Mel just stared straight over his side of the counter into the Poconos, plotting yet another two-month escape as entertainment director of Lockover Manor. How to break it to my father so he could still get his job back in the fall was his tactical problem.

"It's still too early," Mel mumbled, returning to the store.

There was seldom a lunchtime rush per se. Times Square, with large movie palaces like the Roxy and Paramount and legitimate theaters east and west of Broadway, was not exactly an office worker's scramble. Only on matinee days was the twelve to two pace hectic. On light days my father would send Mel out for lunch with Harry, and he and I would man the register counter. Just the two of us alone. My father wrote up the sales in his looping script and made change quickly, courteously. I wrapped the books and filled in the stock, showing off my newly acquired skills. I imagined my mother and father doing the same things together. How did they divide the chores?

She was certainly able to ring the register herself and wrap books as well.

"Did Mommy use the ladder?" I once asked as I moved it against the middle wall to retrieve *Dinner at Antoine's* for the 79¢ table. My father was preoccupied with a group of browsers at the 49¢ table, so I repeated from the fourth rung, "Did Mommy use the ladder too?"

"What the hell are you talking about?" He was startled.

"The ladder," I repeated, hurt. "Did Mommy know how to use it?"

"No, her high heels got . . . Besides, her legs . . . Just a second, Mitchell. . . . For Christsakes . . ." and my father darted toward a chronic browser who had been absorbed in the same book for the last half hour. He stood behind him, took *The Complete Works of William Shakespeare* from a nearby wall slot, opened the fat volume and slammed it shut. Nothing. The browser continued reading unaffected. Next my father dropped the heavy volume on the stack of books in front of the browser and cleared his throat. Still no response. Finally he just grabbed the book clean out of his hands, saying, "Can I help you with this? Would you like to buy it?"

"Oh, I'm just looking at it," the startled browser gasped.

"For twenty minutes?" my father shot back.

"Oh, I didn't realize . . ." And out the door he went.

"Son of a bitch," my father muttered to no one, slowly walking back toward the cash register.

I placed the step ladder back in its corner and decided not to ask him about the past during working hours with fifteen customers in the store.

A Come In and Browse window sign did beckon them. During rush hours forty-five or more would mill around. These numbers precluded the genteel salesmanship found in Scribner's and Brentano's, the "May I help you?" greeting to everyone passing the threshold. Instead an intuitive screening process was perfected. It determined when someone was approached and who did the selling. My father was very good at picking or responding to "live" ones. He could work such a customer for twenty-five minutes, quick to open up the entire store to a special interest, often resulting in a spectacular $75 sale; he could also brush off deadwood with a pointed "No, we don't stock anything like that."

When Harry returned from lunch refreshed, ready to open twenty-four cartons and take on the world, we would still have to wait for Mel before we could go out for our lunch. This might not happen until three o'clock. I would be ravenous, unaccustomed to the retail waiting game, my father oblivious, preoccupied with his telephone calls.

When Mel finally returned and took his place behind the register, we would head toward the door for our luncheon date, but predictably my father would interrupt our progress, waving Harry toward us.

"See that mooch over there in the Woodford section?" Harry's ears would redden. "He's a shoplifter. Watch the son of a bitch! He clipped three *Ideal Marriages* last week from behind the register!"

Harry remembered the big hole. Stealing was an anxiety they agreed on. The fact that it went on in Bookland confused and embarrassed me. I never wanted to believe it, especially when I was starving.

At the Lake Ronkonkoma School, the food might be undistinguished, but it slid onto the oilcloth tables promptly at twelve-thirty. On 42nd Street I sacrificed punctuality for variety. There was so much to choose from, depending on my father's mood and schedule.

Chock Full O'Nuts, which had just opened a place between 5th and 6th across from Bryant Park, was for rushed lunches on busy days. My father was charmed by the interior design: tan marble floors, deep-blue counters, red stools, mirrored walls, stainless steel trim. The quality of their cream cheese on nutted raisin bread, the texture of their whole wheat doughnuts served by fast, polite hands for mere nickels and dimes made him a devotee of the chain. The first time we went, he let me taste his cream cheese sandwich, which I found strange on brown raisin bread instead of fat white bagels. I stuck with the predictable two hot dogs and a large orange drink.

"Mitchell, try their peach cream pie for dessert," my father urged.

I resisted. The puff white top made me squeamish.

"I don't know about . . ."

"Have a taste of mine. Another fork, please," he said to the waitress. "Try some, go ahead, Mitchell."

I plunged my fork into his pie.

"Real peaches, like Grandma Lufkin served with sour cream!"

I was surprised.

"Fresh, huh, Mitchell?"

The crust and cream sweetened the tart Alberta peaches without making them cloying like candy. My father was proud, as if he were responsible for the delicate balance of ingredients in the 15¢ piece of pie.

"One more peach pie," he ordered. "Be my guest, Mitchell."

By five o'clock, however, the pie and hot dogs had worked their way through my bloodstream. I was hungry again.

For more substantial fare we hit the cafeterias—Stewart's on the south side of 42nd Street next to the Wurlitzer Building, or the Governor, across the street from the Metropolitan Opera House in the center of the garment district.

"Isn't it remarkable, the variety?" my father once said as he lead me past the Governor's endless glass display case of food, which ran the gamut from fish salad and sliced meat sandwiches to hot potato pancakes and pot roast dinners. We skimmed our plastic trays over the chromium bars.

"Try a Danish, Mitchell," my father said in front of the drink counter, where pastries were displayed. "Baked on the premises," he boasted.

I chose a prune Danish to go with my tuna fish salad on rye. This combination pacified my stomach until six-thirty.

Stewart's and the Governor were popular, crowded, loud, even at three-ten. Since my father didn't relish waiting in line for anything, including food, cafeterias were for twice a week at most.

Rosoff's was his favorite restaurant, the place we went to eat and relax on West 43rd Street. It had a wooden bar with oak nooks beneath the windows, where we usually sat. On our way toward them we passed through the formal main dining room where many other

Times Square merchants were finishing their late lunches, dawdling over coffee and cigars. They sat in pairs or trios, never alone.

"Philly!" they saluted. "How's business?" *The* question.

"Fair, not bad, hot summer," my father responded, trying to rush toward his cool nook.

"So, Philly, how's it going? Some June, huh?" someone at another table exclaimed.

"Okay, okay."

"Ahead of last year?" they came back.

After bobbing and weaving past four tables my father counterpunched, "How's with you? You doing much business?"

A rush of anguish and despair burst from each table.

"Stinks!"

"Awful!"

"Worse!"

"Never seen anything like it!"

"I don't know how Moe and I are going to make it till Christmas, let alone Florida this year!"

"Boy, is it lousy!"

The crying towels were out, passing from one table to another, damp with self-pity, tears splashing onto wide silk collars as we dashed into the barroom for what was left on the luncheon menu.

"Nice and quiet in here," my father would say with a sigh as we eased into our dim oak nook. "What's still on?" he asked the busy waiter dressed in an apron skirt, black jacket and bow tie. The apron was an informal touch reserved for the barroom.

"We're out of the scrod, duckling and goulash. No fresh corn either."

"Do you still have the short ribs special? Mitchell, remember the ribs? How much you liked them last time?"

"Yes." I remembered.

"Two specials, and bring us some fresh rolls. Put a few salt sticks and raisin buns in the basket, will you?"

"I'll see what I can do." The waiter shot toward the paneled kitchen door. A busboy appeared immediately from the darkness with chilled water goblets and the requested roll assortment. The rolls were seductive. Some were just ordinary dinner rolls, hard, dusty shells with bleached, tasteless cores. But the salt sticks had rye centers wrapped in a crisp cone dotted with caraway seeds and diamonds of coarse salt. There were squat pumpernickel rolls and frosted sweet buns with juicy raisins tucked within each cinnamon swirl. Eating two of these after a couple of salt sticks and a goblet of ice water didn't leave too much space when the main course arrived. The ribs, however, were an exotic treat, barbecued with sugared tomato paste. My stomach expanded for the hot fatty beef. Dessert was problematic. Chocolate ice cream could possibly melt in . . . and usually did. Our 99¢ special completed, we returned to Bookland, my father relaxed, well fed, I bloated and uncomfortable, longing to sit off my businessman's lunch at the Laffmovie or a New Amsterdam double feature.

Only a unique event such as my father's trimming the window could dissuade me, command my full attention. He was supposed to change it at least four times a year, but the ordeal made him procrastinate. I remembered my mother cajoling him, commiserating with him, employing any strategy she could come up with to get him through the time when he did the windows. Some years he only changed them twice, before Christmas and in June. It could take him an entire week. The whole staff participated, lining up clean piles of new remainders near the windows with rubber bands holding each book jacket in place. Calm, silent Mel, not Harry, handed the piles and individual specials in to my father, who sat on an old haberdashery fixture wearing tan cashmere shoe mittens like Dr. Dentons over his wing-tipped dress shoes. He built colored pyramids just above the street, worked his way slowly toward three elevated glass trays of best sellers at the rear of each window. He could spend three hours or three minutes on a section of the window, depending on his mood. Sometimes, returning from lunch, he would see the half-dressed window from a new angle, change promptly into his outfit and work with inspiration and zest only to slump into cursing despair when that particular section of the window was realized and there was still so much more to do.

Usually my afternoons were a boring time stretch. I had the entire month of June to fill up with activity, thirty days, no PS 69 or Fred Grosso, who was still in school. Grandma Lufkin's apartment was being painted, so 42nd Street was it: home base. Sometimes I went to the penny arcades, where I attacked the Japanese and German navies, sinking their aircraft carriers and submarines with my own torpedoes. I drove automobiles through picturesque rolling farmland and walloped steel balls over a tin baseball stadium. After two weeks even these activities paled. I had seen all the movies, some twice, played all the games, and was always waiting, standing around the store rootless by late afternoon.

My father and I rarely left before eight P.M. A homeward-bound rush always swept the store into a frenzy of activity between five and seven-thirty, just as Harry's orders came tumbling into the store. The night crew, Mac and Albert, came in at five, but my father was essential after six, when Harry and Mel left and Mac, a retired Western Union night clerk, and Albert, an eccentric musician, were left alone at the dike. He relished the frontline activity—spitfire repartee with customers, the cash register explosions. I was exhausted, unable to play bookstore anymore. But my father could never abandon Mac and Albert until the rush gradually eased around seven-thirty or eight. By that time I was tired, hurt, and beginning to get my appetite back. Why couldn't he just leave them? Get the hell out? Take me home? Talk to me? Play with me? Anything! A burst of activity would come through the door at any moment introducing yet more customers, questions, sales. There was always some unpredictable force outside or within the store that determined when I ate or spent precious time alone with my father.

At first I was so overwhelmed with broken promises and fatigue when we finally left Bookland and ate dinner, I didn't pay much attention to the place or the meal, though I knew we weren't at the Cocoanut Grove. But on our third evening together, I realized we were in the Carnegie Delicatessen, right next to the hotel. Its aromas evoked Grandma Lufkin.

"How is she?" I asked. We were seated near the take-out counter.

"Fine, Mitchell."

"When can I see her?"

Hesitation. "After her apartment is painted. It takes time to dry. The oil smell lasts for weeks."

"Where is *she* staying if it smells so bad?"

"With Uncle Sam and Aunt Blanche."

"Does Grandma hear from Mommy out West?"

"Sure, sure. You'll see her when her apartment dries."

"Before I go back to camp?"

"We'll see, we'll see. If I can get away from the store to take you up there."

The meal blended into pajamas, corduroy daybed, my father sitting on the edge until I fell asleep. What he did until returning to the store at eleven I never knew because I slept so soundly until breakfast.

One night, ten days into my vacation, after I'd been asleep for several hours, a wild telephone ring woke me.

"Hello? Hello? Phil? It's Mordecai."

I was stunned. I had never heard Uncle Mordecai's booming rich voice on the telephone before. I replied shyly, "It's me, Mitchell, Uncle Mordecai. How are you?"

"Oh, Mitchell! Can I talk to your father?"

"Daddy, Daddy!" I yelled, looking around the suite before I realized he must have gone back to the store.

"He's not here now, Uncle Mordecai. He's closing the store."

"Tell him to call me when he comes home. It's important, Mitchell." The doctor's commanding tone now.

"How's Grandma?"

"Fine," he boomed.

"Are the painters finished with her apartment yet?"

No answer. Pause.

"How do you like your new school?"

"It's getting better," I replied with confidence.

"Don't forget to give your father my message, Mitchell."

Click.

I forgot to ask, wanted to ask immediately but understood by now I wasn't supposed to ask: *Have you heard from my mother?*

I had never been up alone so late in 2209. I was whirring with the strangeness of the hour, the darkness, the unfamiliar hallway sounds. I identified the elevators opening, closing, hoping it would be my father, but the footsteps always went down the wrong hallway or into the maid's pantry, accompanied by the sound of room service carts. I turned on the night table lamp, which eased the darkness out but illuminated the clock. One A.M. Where the hell was my father? He closed the store at twelve. Anger made sleep a hopeless, sweaty tangle. The hotel sounds were fearful. What did they mean? Two A.M. Where was he now? What did Uncle Mordecai want to tell him? Mordecai, the oldest, my mother the youngest. Where was she?

Tears fell onto my pillow. I buried my face in it to muffle my sobbing, dry heaving when I came up for air. Still no father. I pushed my head back into the pillow with fewer tears, but there was more sound when I resurfaced for oxygen. On and on I went, distraught, moaning into the night.

"Mitchell, Mitchell, are you all right? Please stop crying." I heard my name spoken outside the hall door.

"Mitchell!" Another voice. Both female. Soft.

I dried my eyes. The clock said three A.M. The doorbell rang.

"Mitchell," one of the voices entreated. "We have movie star pictures for you!"

The bell rang again.

"Who is it?" I asked.

"The Kesslers, Janine and Shelby." The maiden sisters who lived next door with their ancient mother. I didn't know them at all. They rang again.

"Please! Let us come in!"

I opened the door and they rushed in. Janine Kessler, the older, had an armload of eight by ten glossies. Shelby carried four recent issues of *Screen Gems*. They calmed me down, got me a glass of water and spread out their entire world of Hollywood stars on the carpet. They seemed to know most of them by special nicknames. They wrote for different film magazines. Janine was the editor of hers. She promised to have Roy Rogers autograph his photo for me if I calmed down and went back to sleep. Shelby agreed to sit in the living room until I did. Janine mumbled to her in the other room before leaving, "He shouldn't leave him alone so long at night. Talk to him."

The front door closed quietly. I was undone by their rescue mission. Exhausted, I fell asleep with Roy Rogers and Trigger glossies at my side.

The next morning my father was up before me, in his closet, by his bureau, selecting the appropriate shirt, tie, suit and shoes for the day. In the bathroom, hot and cold taps opened, his puffy face lathered, he focused on the medicine cabinet mirror. I slipped onto the commode, still weak from my nocturnal ordeal but eager to observe his entire shaving ritual. My father patted my head. *"Keppelah."* I lost all resentment and anger.

"So, what went on here last night, Mitchell?" he asked with a twist of guilt. "I read Shelby Kessler's note when I got in."

"When did you get home? What happened?"

"The door lock at the store was jammed, broken. It wouldn't catch. I had to wait for the locksmith to come."

"When did he come?"

"About one-fifteen in the morning, but then he had to go back to his shop on 14th Street for stuff. We'd just put in a special time lock."

"Were you alone?"

"Mac stayed with me, trembling, smoking twenty cigarettes. I sent him home when a cop came. It was all right. I put the store lights on. Some bastard must have tampered with the door the night before and screwed the whole lock up. How were you?" my father asked again. "What woke you up?"

"Uncle Mordecai called."

My father stopped. He and Mordecai rarely spoke to each other, never on the telephone.

"What for? What did he want?"

"He wants you to call him back. It's important."

His lips tightened.

"I'll call him from the store. If we ever get there this morning."

The shave over, I took my cue, scurried around picking up my wardrobe for yet another long day at Bookland.

That evening we returned a shade early, around eight-thirty. My father went next door to thank the Kesslers and explain the details of the emergency. He returned at nine, as charmed by the sisters as I had been. He brought Roy Rogers's autograph and Trigger's hoofprint, proof that the sisters' were as good as their word.

I drifted into easy sleep. There were horses at the Lake Ronkonkoma camp. I recalled Fritz and O'Conner bragging about them. The stable was near the lake, right across the road where the bus turned. In twenty days I'd be riding one of them. Like my mother out West.

Horseback riding on wooded trails near Lake Ronkonkoma was a thrilling once-a-week treat. An extra charge, my father let me know. I was actually scared of the large animals, though Blackie, the beginner's horse they put me on, was a docile creature. Riding him on the trails calmed my fears until the instructor turned us back toward the barn. Blackie followed the lead horses into a trot, which I couldn't control, and then into a rolling breath-stopping canter—exhilarating yet scary.

How could my mother do such things? Perhaps she just walked her horse on mountain trails. On my birthday, July 27, I did receive a special package from her, full of silver dollars, ten of them, one for each year plus one to grow on, like the extra candle on a birthday cake. There was also a note:

Happy birthday to my nine-year-old boy. I am coming home soon on a very long train ride. The horseback riding wasn't good for my legs. I miss you a lot.

Love,
Mommy

I was right about the riding, but still uncertain about her return. I pressed my father for details when he came out for a visit one Sunday in August. I was a slim brown stalk, standing on the edge of Lake Ronkonkoma in front of Raynor's Beach Pavilion. He was white, hairy in his silver-buckled swimsuit.

"What train will she take?"

"I don't know, Mitchell."

"How long a ride is it?"

"A week maybe. I'm not sure."

"Did she send you silver dollars too?"

"No, no." He looked into the calm lake.

I ran and dove in head first, showing off like a seal. We agreed that I would come home after camp before returning to the Lake Ronkonkoma School in the fall. Grandma Lufkin's apartment had finally dried. The Yankees played some doubleheaders in early September. It sounded inviting as long as I avoided asking questions.

I was tan and happy, a seasoned camper when I took the IRT from Pennsylvania Station straight to the bookstore, lugging my suitcase through the lobby. Harry and Mel greeted me with surprising warmth from their cash register island. I asked Harry where my father was, and he pointed to the rear office, gazing down at the rolls of wrapping paper under the counter. He seemed tense, upset. I dropped my suitcase in the Children's Section and poked my head through the office door.

"Hello, Dad. I'm back."

"Mitchell, Mitchell! Look at him, Philly! He grew a foot!" My mother roared with delight as I rushed into her blue dress, kissed her face and exploded, *"Mommy, Mommy, you're back!"*

"Yes, yes," she murmured into my hair, returning my kisses.

My father remained seated at his desk—there wasn't enough room for all of us to stand.

"Hi, Dad." I hugged him clumsily, kissed his cheek. He was preoccupied, with the store, Bookazine. He squeezed my hand. The telephone rang, and he picked it up.

"Yeah, sure. . . . Okay. I'll tell Harry you have it in stock. . . . Fine, four-thirty. . . . Good-bye."

"Phil, you didn't tell me how tall he was. And so handsome! Just like an actor! He could be a movie actor!"

The phone rang again.

"Allen, for Christsakes, when is that shipment coming in? I've seen those titles at two other stores. Where are they? You can't trace them? Jesus!"

My father's anger was building into a fury that would feed on itself. My mother sensed the coming torrent and tapped his shoulder at the next pause to suggest she take me next door to Schrafft's for an ice cream soda. He grimaced his approval.

I told her about all the things I had done at the Lake Ronkonkoma School, about camp and horseback riding. I wooed her with my adventures, so caught up in the telling, the foam on my ice cream soda evaporated before I noticed it had been served. She listened, enthralled, amused, proud, sipping a cup of coffee. Then I began losing her and noticed her pale face. I asked about the West, thanked her for the silver dollars. She said the horseback riding had hurt her right leg in a strange way no one could understand. Uncle Mordecai was looking after her now, trying to diagnose the problem.

We walked back to the store, fingers interlocked. As we entered the lobby my mother faltered. She reached up to the window with both hands for balance and slumped against the metal flashing. She was lame.

"I'll be all right, Mitchell. I just have to rest a moment. Don't worry. Stand with me." She inhaled deep breaths, held my hand and revived after three tense minutes. She had been so adept in her use of the window for support, no one else was aware of her ordeal. Eyes suddenly open, she looked in toward the rear of the store, resolute.

"Let's go see your father now and ask him to take us back."

"But we are back, Mommy," I answered. "You're back, I'm back, we'll eat supper together, won't we?"

She was silent; her eyes were not affirmative.

"Will you take us back, Daddy?" I burst out, seeing him at his desk. "Will you take us back?" I had internalized her desire, instinctively making her cause mine. My mother was behind me now, confused and embarrassed. She had planned to do the talking at the appropriate time, to make her own presentation. She came forward hesitantly and as she spoke, I ran past her back into the store, heaving myself against the Modern Library alcove. They talked. I understood their sharp words, not the events they signified. I felt their misery, the strange hatred binding them together.

Harry came to my rescue, whisking me off to Hector's Cafeteria for his coffee break. He wanted company, and so did I. But he wanted news about my camp, and I was through bragging for the day. I wanted silence, comfort, some news about my mother and father. Harry ordered an almond Danish ring with black coffee. I had a glass of milk. He knew my parents, had observed what had happened between them while I was away at Lake Ronkonkoma. But how could Harry describe what he had not seen or try to explain events I would not believe or comprehend? He rambled gingerly. We tried piecing together a past only my mother and father could know.

Hannah's melancholy had deepened. With Mitchell gone off to the Lake Ronkonkoma School she no longer hid her despair. She was getting very tired standing on her feet from nine-thirty A.M., when she opened Bookland with Harry, until six-thirty P.M., when she went back to the hotel with Philly for dinner. Afterward he returned to Bookland alone, counted out the receipts for the night deposit and locked up the store at twelve. The routine was leaden, and Hannah was losing her energy.

During the Christmas season of 1943, shortly after Mitchell was sent away to the Lake Ronkonkoma School, Philly hired a new man to help with the rush. Hannah found his temperament and jaunty pace pleasing, even delightful. They began noticing each other through the shared details of work—wrapping books, ringing the register, bantering about the customers. He was a deft, chipper spirit from Utica, new to the city, lively, smart and 4F. He charmed Hannah during their random coffee breaks in the midst of the feverish holiday countdown.

She particularly welcomed his easy laughter on Friday morning, December 22, when large snowflakes crowded the sky and Philly had awakened her with a weather report.

"Jesus Christ, will you look at that! It's really coming down!" he had yelled as he paced, looking at the curtain of snow falling past the 2209 bedroom windows.

"Shit! There goes Friday, Saturday, Sunday! The whole fucking Christmas! Hannah," he yelled, rousing her, needing her consciousness to augment his own rage, "will you look at this weather? Bang . . . just like that . . . the whole fucking year wiped out!"

"Please, Phil, take it easy," she moaned, eyes still closed.

"Look at it! Will you just look at it!"

She opened her eyes.

"Right on Philly Schmuck! Agh! The weekend before Christmas it has to snow! On me . . . *plotz* . . . right on me. Can you believe it?"

He scrutinized the flakes yet another time, hoping they were a mirage, part of a nightmare. Hannah pulled the pillows over her head to shut out the braying. She realized her only recourse was to get up, dress and open "the fucking store" as quickly as possible to avoid any more of his performance, which exploded in new expressions of mercantile madness just as she left for work, barely noticed.

"Why? Every goddamned son of a bitch fucking year! Why? Just look at the goddamned shit!"

It turned into a classic thick blizzard. The help was forced to remain in midtown manning the store, cleaning the sidewalk, waiting for traffic to move. They ate in shifts. Hannah and the new man were in the same shift. She was exhilarated by the snow, her cheeks throbbing red, 42nd Street miraculously white-clean. Over soup at Stewart's Cafeteria they held hands, and returning to the store, they tumbled into each other on the snowdrifts. Hannah and the new man became lovers during the storm, hidden by the emergency circumstances of close quarters. They sought and found wild release in warm thighs and full-mouthed kisses for two hours at the Hotel Dixie on dry sheets and a soft bed.

In the evenings, after the storm had cleared away and Christmas was over, Hannah went to the new man's room on Amsterdam Avenue when Philly returned to the store each evening. One night Hannah wasn't home when Philly got back. She returned at twelve-thirty, working the double lock expertly, quickly, hoping Philly was still en route. She saw the pantry light on and the bedspread pulled down.

"I went to see *A Weekend at the Waldorf,* the remake of *Grand Hotel.* Van Johnson sings with Cougat's band," she said as she breezed in. "He plays a war hero who writes lyrics and finally gets a chance to sing them in the Empire Room. Imagine, Philly, Van Johnson singing with Xavier Cougat's band!"

"You went by yourself?"

Philly was hurt. They always went to the movies together on Saturday night or Sunday afternoon.

Hannah undressed and turned over to her side of the bed. She could not dissemble. And her hostility grew as her evenings with the new man became more joyous and extended.

The next week Philly telephoned his older brother, Alfie, in Newark. He asked Alfie, who was in advertising and more experienced with women and the business world, to drive into the city for a late supper. Phil described Hannah's peculiar behavior and tone. Spoke about business, the store, the help. Alfie fingered the new man immediately. Philly was so overwhelmed with disbelief and pain that Alfie was even more certain of his hunch.

"It can't be. Just can't," Philly whispered.

"Let's find out. Maybe I'm wrong. Where does the guy live?" Alfie took charge.

"I don't know."

"Look it up on his Social Security form."

"What for?"

"We'll go up there and find out."

"That's not my style, Alfie."

"What is? Suffering?"

They took a cab up to 74th Street and Amsterdam. Hidden in a bar and grill doorway, they watched Hannah and the new man undress and fall into bed before the shades went down.

"Jesus . . . you were right, Alfie, you son of a bitch." Philly's eyes watered as he walked down Broadway, mourning for his life, their life—fifteen years. He didn't think about the store at all, only of Hannah and what she had done to him. And the guy, the new man, a nothing, a goyish drifter with starched collars and clip-on ties, a second stringer.

The next morning in the 2209 bedroom Philly confronted Hannah. She was sorry for his pain but proud of her new joy, her pleasure.

"I can't give him up. I'm too tired. I need his energy, his fun. I'll move out, Phil."

She went to the Hotel Dixie. After Philly fired the new man, he moved into the Dixie with her. She left Bookland the next day.

"Keep the goddamned store! You'll croak at the register!" she shouted.

"Hannah, stay! Please! You're killing me," Philly pleaded at last, surprising them both with his open heartbreak.

"What about my life, Philly? Where has it gone? Into a fucking book store! Under the register, that's where my blood is!"

She left the city after a few passionate weeks at the Dixie. They wanted their love made legal and went cross-country to Reno in a Pullman compartment, hoping to arrange a quickie divorce. Instead Hannah was broken by the arduous five-day trek.

The long brown train changed silver engines in Chicago, then laid over for eight hours, steaming, waiting for a connecting train. Next it stopped in frozen Omaha for coal and water. Then up the glazed Rockies to Nevada. Hannah's blood drained from her flushed cheeks as the altitude rose. Her legs got ice cold, difficult to maneuver. She was unable to enjoy the food in the lavish dining car after weaving her way through sleeping service men settled in the aisles. In Reno she was happy, but oddly weaker. Horseback riding was an effort, not the joy she remembered from high school. When she was finally unable to move her left leg one morning, her lover was alarmed. Though he nursed her, sought out medical care, even helped pay for it with his new earnings as a front desk man, he was not up to the responsibility of a thirty-five-year-old invalid. When her mobility returned, he left her alone one morning with a sweet note of farewell and courage.

She had enough money set aside for two months. Her brother Mordecai helped with checks and medical advice, though he was shocked by his sister's "emotional fling." A Lufkin in Reno . . . stranded by a goy lover! Finally Philly was asked to help. He contributed grudgingly, angry at her predicament—bitter. He sent the money via Mordecai, not wanting any contact with her; she was his wife in name only.

Her blood clot became acute in June, flared up. Mordecai implored Hannah to come back home, ordered her. Where was home? she asked. Home, he pondered. I'll call Philly. No, don't, please, she begged.

Mordecai asked Philly to take her back. He refused vehemently. Mordecai, a proud man himself, understood but persisted out of necessity. Alfie, informed of the request, also tried to soften Philly up. After two weeks of cajoling and bargaining he agreed to meet her at Grand Central Station and put her up. Where was left open.

It was a touchy reception. Hannah and Philly alone with two steamer trunks. She was wobbly, emaciated. He was drawn tight, his brown eyes liquid. They nuzzled. She cried on his topcoat collar. He took over, orchestrated their movements back to the Park Central, where she collapsed for three days of deep sleep on a special daybed brought into the living room.

When Harry and I returned from his coffee break at Hector's Cafeteria, my mother was settled on a high stool, my father's hand placed gently on her shoulder. They were talking quietly, smiling a little, not laughing.

"Mitchell, take Mommy home now. I'll get a taxi for you. Get your valise."

As he closed the cab door he assured us, "I'll be home by seven-thirty at the latest. We'll have a nice dinner."

At the Park Central, Maggie, the elevator operator, let me work the control lever up to the twenty-second floor. I started down our hallway with my bag, proud the bellhops had also acknowledged my abilities and not insisted on helping me. My mother trailed behind. I looked back for her when I reached our suite. She seemed unsure of her footing, paused, touched the wall momentarily. I heard the Kesslers' door, 2211, jar open, the safety chain snap taut, and saw over my left shoulder a slice of Mrs. Kessler's whiskered jaw through the crevice. She was observing my mother's progress, the vagabond woman of late hours and cross-country travel, not interested in rendering assistance as her daughters had with me. Her intent was to spy. She shut her door slowly as we opened ours.

My mother settled on the living room couch, legs covered with a blue quilt. I was on the floor beside her, arranging toy soldiers, artillery and books for an amphibious landing, not certain where to unpack my own baggage in the rearranged apartment.

My father actually rang the doorbell at seven-thirty. He swept out of his overcoat, placed his cigar in a mantel ashtray and presented himself in the center of the living room with a flourish.

"Where should we eat dinner? Upstairs at the Cocoanut Grove the Bensley Brothers are back in town."

We all laughed.

"Phil, I'm exhausted tonight," Hannah pleaded.

"Room service." My father snapped his fingers.

"Terrific idea," my mother responded, relieved she could stay put.

Thirty minutes later the room service waiter rolled in an enormous flap table dressed with nickel-plate food warmers and starched napkins. He pushed this all in front of my mother's couch, pulled up the flaps and left. I devoured my lamb chops. My mother picked at her roast Long Island duckling. After the main course, Philly lit a dark cigar. The smoke curled around our improvised nest. Safe, I began to doze.

"Get ready for bed, Mitchell." My mother's voice jarred me awake. Which bed, I wondered, my old corduroy couch in the bedroom or the new daybed in the living room? Did they sleep together now? Or in separate rooms?

"Your regular bed is fine," my father said, as though he had sensed my confusion. I kissed them both. I listened as they murmured long into the night.

The following days were a blur of happiness and mild anxiety. I was never certain how our familial dilemma would be resolved. On the Broadway trolley the next morning my mother burst into uncontrollable laughter over a remark my father had made the night before, after I was asleep and the waiter had returned for the room service table. Her outburst seemed disproportionate. She was preoccupied with Philly and what she had done to him. Was he a victim of her fatigue or the cause? He was back in the store, shedding his pride; still fond of Hannah, yet frightened by her confusion, her unpredictable mood swings, which shut him out. When I returned to Lake Ronkonkoma after my preschool holiday, I was hopeful my mother and father might work things out.

Back at school, there was an important development to balance the uncertainties left behind in 2209. Richard Stevens, our new Lower School activities director, moved into the faculty apartment on our floor of the North Dorm. He had been a successful member of the first graduating class (1942), yearbook editor and founder of the school newspaper. Rejected by the Armed Forces because of a congenital heart disorder, he went off to the University of Indiana to get a degree in journalism and returned to Lake Ronkonkoma after two disappointing years there to retool for a different kind of college. He was actually a postgraduate student as well as our mentor when the '44–'45 school year began. Within two months, however, Stevens gave up on prelaw study and devoted himself to us full time.

He coached our teams with skill and enthusiasm, drove us into Smithtown and St. James for weekend movies in the Kennedys' Pontiac station wagon. He was most comfortable, however, dressed in moccasins and a heavy plaid jacket, exploring wooded terrain with us at his side or single file at his heels. Stevens taught us how to use tools, build fences and forts and make roaring fires for warmth after sleigh riding or smaller hot ones for cooking bacon and eggs when we slept out. On those fall evenings, before we crawled under our blankets, he read us Poe's "The Pit and the Pendulum" with such dramatic tension most of us were exhausted into sleep, unaware of the cold night air. So unlike the times my father read to me and, lulled by his own boring monotone, fell asleep himself. I remained wide awake, wondering how the story would end.

We rarely spent Friday evenings with the Chief. Stevens insulated us with his special projects. One Friday evening, after we had all trudged through his room for our weekly allowance, Stevens whispered some of us back after lights-out for a treat. Ronson, O'Conner, Fritz and I sat around his hot plate watching him prepare a pot of hot chocolate.

"What about the other kids?" O'Conner asked.

"They're asleep. They don't have to know. It's my treat. You're my guests."

We were awed by his graciousness and our new status. We watched him open a can of tuna fish and mix it with globs of mayonnaise in a dining room cereal bowl. He spread generous amounts of mayonnaise on ordinary Wonder Bread, forked thin, even helpings of the fish on the five slices, sprinkled them with salt and pepper, mayonnaised the top piece of bread, sliced each sandwich in neat halves and gave us each one on a plate. Ronson dropped marshmallows in our cups while Stevens poured the hot cocoa.

We were speechless with delight, truly blessed. No teacher had ever invited us to his room for a party.

I carried these tales of good fortune home for Christmas, past Hicksville, Mineola, Jamaica, into Penn Station for the vacation—not realizing how eager I was to spread them out before my parents until my father told me in the store such an audience would be impossible to arrange. My mother had new complications in her left leg and was now recuperating at Grandma Lufkin's on Fort Washington Avenue. She had to rest in bed all day so the blood could circulate more easily and thus relieve the pressure in her leg. My father could no longer take care of her at the hotel.

He took me up there on the IND the following day. When he returned to the store, I fought back tears on the edge of my mother's bed. I held her long bony fingers, one at a time, stroked them and told her my Stevens stories. She listened quietly, dozed, held my fingers, looked at me peacefully. We did this for hours, days. Each finger a different story.

I spent most of the vacation in my grandmother's cozy three-room apartment. Where she slept was a mystery. I was on the living room couch. My mother was set up in the bedroom. That left the maroon overstuffed easy chair in the living room for Lena, though she was always up puttering in the kitchen by the time I opened my eyes. Breakfast served, Lena digested the *Daily News*. Fingers moistened, she turned the ingredients of each page toward her moving lips. Never satiated, she listened to the hourly war reports on her stand-up Emerson.

My father came up periodically to visit. Whenever he was in the room with my mother, I cleared out so they could be alone. The three of us were never together in her room. Everyone, even the important relatives who lived in the neighborhood—Uncle Morris and Aunt Renee, Uncle Sam and Aunt Blanche—fluttered aside when my father came. Only Mordecai would go into the room with them for consultation. After a few days I ventured out to my cousins' houses for afternoon comraderie. Blanche and Sam had two sons, Marshall, just finished with medical school, and Robert, eleven, my favorite. Renee and Morris had a boy, Douglas, twelve, who was preoccupied with his Lionel railroad set. They were all welcoming though our previous encounters had been limited to family feasts with Grandma Lufkin presiding. Still, their gestures of friendship could not hold me for long. I was always drawn back to my mother's bedside, where I held one wet hand while caressing the long fingers of the other one.

"Will you ever come back home with us to the hotel?" I asked during the last week of my vacation.

"When I get better, Mitchell. Of course I'll come back."

"And we'll be together then?" I added quickly for assurance.

She nodded affirmatively on her pillow, eyes sealed shut.

"When will you get better?" I asked as her eyes reopened.

"Uncle Mordecai isn't sure yet. I need more rest. All the doctors agree."

"Will she ever get well, come back?" I implored my father during the last two days of my Christmas vacation, which I spent with him at the Park Central.

"I don't know, Mitchell. Uncle Mordecai and the other doctors aren't sure. But I think she will improve."

"And come home?" I asked instantly.

"When she's able to."

* * *

The music swelled out of the loudspeakers on Raynor's Beach Pavilion. Stevens had discovered it was opened in February and brought us down to the frozen lake on a windy Sunday afternoon. We were ice-skating there, or trying to on weak ankles. The melody from Tchaikovsky's Piano Concerto No. 1, rearranged for Freddy Martin's Orchestra as "Tonight We Love," accompanied us as we swept across the ice clinging to the bows of three ruddered iceboats. They had tall, wide masts, like sailing ships, to gather the wind. We pushed when the owners requested it, falling, laughing until the mainsail caught the northeast wind and took us for an ice ride. Straight out, out, out, ankles taut now, stomachs on our sleeves, faces below zero, out to the middle of the four-mile lake. Raynor's Pavilion was tiny from this vantage point, but the wind still carried the distant music into our heads as we pushed the boats back toward shore, waiting for a new gust to give us wings once more.

"Here it comes. Hold on, you guys . . . tight! Woolf, Ronson, Fritz, tighter. Push! Let's go!" Stevens ordered.

Chill wind once more swept behind our mackinaws, pushing our backs forward, whizzing us toward land. My wings became my mother's legs.

Two weeks later I banged on Stevens's door. "I want to call my father tonight."

He opened it. "How come?"

"I haven't heard from him in six weeks."

"Maybe the mail got lost. No letters? Postcards?"

"None." Tears inside.

"Let me talk to Mrs. Kennedy about it, Mitchell."

He went downstairs to her apartment. The Kennedys had the only telephone on our section of the campus, thus making or receiving a call was serious, reserved for special communications. Stevens bounded back up the stairs in minutes, out of breath.

"It's okay, Woolf. You can go down there now. The door's open. Remember to reverse the charges."

Entering the Kennedys' dark overfurnished apartment was intimidating. The phone sat on Mr. Kennedy's leather-tooled desk. He wasn't in. Mrs. Kennedy greeted me along with her spaniel, Zing, a smelly old dog. She withdrew discreetly to her bedroom. Zing paddled into the connecting bathroom, where he lapped from the toilet bowl. I could hear him when the operator paused.

"Collect for . . . Mr. Phillip Woolf?"

"W-O-O-L-F," I spelled.

"Okay, will you speak to anyone else?"

"Sure, my mother, Hannah."

"Is that Woolf too?"

"Of course."

"Just checking, kid."

Riiiinggg.

"Hello?" It was my father.

"Long distance. I have a collect call for Phillip Woolf or Hannah Woolf."

"This is Phillip Woolf."

"Mitchell Woolf is calling long distance. Will you accept the charges?"

"Sure, yes, yes. . . . Hello? Hello, Mitchell? Is something wrong? Are you all right?"

"I'm okay . . . fine . . . I mean, worried."

"Why?"

"No letter for six weeks. . . . Is Mommy better?"

"I've been so busy . . . the store and Mommy . . . too busy to write."

"Is she back at the hotel?"

"Not yet."

"Still with Grandma?"

Long pause.

"Is she at Grandma's?" I repeated.

"No, Mommy's at the hospital."

"Why?" I stumbled.

"Tests, Mitchell, tests."

"Can I see her in the hospital?"

"We'll try, we'll try. When you come home for Easter in three weeks. Five-forty-five at the store, right?"

He remembered Easter. What did he mean, "We'll try, we'll try"? I wondered and tossed for hours, unable to subdue my panic after lights-out.

"They have a hospital rule. No children visitors allowed unless they are thirteen or over," my father explained when I was finally standing inside his office three weeks later at exactly five-forty-five.

"I'm almost ten."

"A large almost," my father countered with pride.

Indeed I was nearly his size.

"We'll try to pass you through as a thirteen-year-old."

"What if they find out my real age?"

"They won't let you in. You'll stay downstairs in the waiting room."

"With the new fathers, like in the movies?"

He laughed.

"Does Mommy know about this?" I asked, remembering how she always insisted on complete honesty. Except for the bad report card incident she had only slapped me one other time I could remember; when I had lied about sneaking some Louis Sherry miniatures from her handkerchief drawer.

"If you tell the truth, I'll never hit you," she had promised.

"Mitchell." My father's voice brought me back to the present. "She really wants you to come."

That settled the moral dilemma. My costume choice was trickier.

All my dress clothes were either suits with short pants for spring and summer or knickers for fall and winter. My mother and father ridiculed young boys in long pants dress suits as little midgets, miniature adults, not well-dressed children. So I didn't have a pair of long dress pants, which was the style for thirteen-year-olds.

My visit to Presbyterian Hospital not only forced me to lie about my age but also compromised my father's taste, for I was dressed in a long pants dress suit when I walked past the hospital information desk, expecting to be arrested on the spot. I got away with it downstairs. What about upstairs on the nineteenth floor? In the corridors? Her room? This fear of detection helped insulate me from the pain in my mother's private room.

Her legs were elevated, her bed seemed part chair. She was weak, there was little play in her fingers when I held them. She was glad to see me, but we couldn't talk for long except to celebrate my successful deception with nods and squeezes. There were so many doctors and relatives clattering about in the tiny room—whispering, shouting, coming to her bedside—that I was shunted toward a corner chair facing a yellow wall.

I never went back to that massive hospital. My mother was released three months later, the testing inconclusive. She returned to Grandma Lufkin's while I was at camp. During the next school year, my fifth grade, I spent most of the vacations with her until she was unexpectedly sent back to the hospital in the spring of '46 for new tests and physical therapy. I saw her in June in the break between school and camp in Grandma Lufkin's bedroom. Her hospital ordeal was over.

She was optimistic.

"The tests showed I can get better if I use my legs properly when I have pains in them."

"Will the pain ever go away?"

"Sometimes it does. Even now."

"Can you walk when it goes away?"

"Soon, Mitchell, soon."

That was a change. She was peaceful, damp-browed as I told her about our softball season at Lake Ronkonkoma. How we won our grammar school division championship.

"I made the Honor Roll in May and June. First time," I boasted, knowing it would please her.

"Wonderful, Mitchell!" She was tired but happy.

"Your ears? You don't get earaches anymore?"

"No," I assured her. "Or colds. Remember Camp Lake Surprise?"

"No colds either!" She was proud of my health.

"Daddy's taking me to see the Yankees play the Indians this Saturday as a present for making the Honor Roll twice. He bought reserved seats."

"That's nice for him too," she added with an edge.

My father had regained his interest in baseball now that DiMaggio, Keller, Chandler and Rizzuto were out of the Armed Forces and back in their elegant Yankee pinstripes. 1946 was the first full season all the teams had their veterans back, and the Yankees were once again the team to beat. They were playing Cleveland on Saturday. The Indians, strong pennant contenders, had a flashy, unorthodox owner, Bill Veeck, who experimented with night baseball and let his young shortstop, Lou Boudreau, manage the team. They also had Bob Feller, the fast-ball strike-out king of baseball: a legend before the war with his high kick windup and awesome overhand delivery. He was even more devastating now, having already pitched two no-hitters. He was scheduled to pitch against the Yankee prewar ace, Spud Chandler, a consistent twenty-game winner with a fast ball and some tricks of his own. My father and I were very excited. Central Park softball games were no longer a valid substitute.

When the day arrived, my father couldn't go to the stadium with me. A real heartbreaker which he felt as keenly as I did.

"It's the goddamned store. Harry's sick for the first time in three years. Mel just went off to summer stock again. I can't leave the place with the part-time weekend crew. They'll steal the whole fucking store on me. Cousin Marshall will take you instead. He wants to. He'll meet you downstairs in the hotel lobby at twelve. I'll leave the tickets with you."

I nodded grudging acceptance, and we went to the drugstore for breakfast.

Cousin Marshall was a paragon. At induction his Army test scores were so high, first in the Northeast, he was sent to a special three-year medical school which allowed him to bypass the traditional liberal arts curriculum and become a frontline doctor at twenty. The prospect of doing anything with him was so exciting, the letdown over my father's broken promise was partially assuaged during breakfast and almost erased when, out of uniform, dressed like a doctor, Marshall walked through the revolving doors to pick me up.

He drove us to the stadium in his doctor's car, a Mercury coupe. I wanted to be a doctor just like him—with his resonant deep voice, his confidence and his black hair he was more impressive than a movie star.

It was a bright, glorious day at the stadium. A capacity crowd, seventy-three thousand people. Though Snuffy was still on the team, the Stirnweiss era had ended. DiMaggio was actually loping after high fly balls in deep center field. The game itself became a standoff pitcher's duel between Feller and Chandler until Chandler, tired in the sixth inning, lost his control and allowed the Indians to score three runs. Feller protected this game-winning lead with his frightening speed. My father would have been mesmerized by the nuances of the contest, the strategy. Marshall was a dutiful cousin, but his mind was elsewhere. He was not a baseball fan.

After the game he drove me to his parents' apartment, where his mother, Aunt Blanche, and his kid brother, Robert, greeted us with open arms and rather somber faces. Marshall left immediately for hospital duties at Beth Israel. Robert hustled me to his room for a game of mechanical baseball, a recent birthday present. I shot marble-sized steel balls toward the batter's box, where Robert stroked at them with a miniature Louisville Slugger screwed to home plate. One could strike out or hit the ball into single, double or triple slots or loft it over the fence of the tin playing field. We each had three outs, like in a regular game. Robert was two years older and stronger than me. He had always been protective when introducing me to his neighborhood friends and their local variations of stick, punch, and curb ball. But he played to win after all these amenities. I was therefore surprised at the lopsided 8–2 score in my favor after we had played just three innings on his bedroom floor. He was pitching to me with such predictable ease that I had already hit three over the left field fence. My frequent visits to Times Square penny arcades gave me a certain advantage with this type of game, but I grew alarmed when my lead increased to twelve and Robert no longer dissembled. He stopped trying. He was letting me win, unable to concentrate when he batted.

Soon the giant Lufkin brothers, Sam, Morris and Mordecai, arrived with their wives, Grandma Lufkin and surprisingly my tiny father. I told him about the game at the stadium and my own victory against Robert. He was pleased. Everyone was solicitous, interested in my progress at the Lake Ronkonkoma School. I told them my Chief and Stevens stories. They were enthralled. Their joyous response no longer surprised me. Indeed, after certain bits of dialogue I paused for their laughter before continuing my bizarre narrative, cheeks flushed, roaring along with them. Wonderful prune Danishes and chocolate petits fours were served with tea and milk as I spoke. A long taxi ride back to the hotel with my father concluded the epic day.

The next morning, Sunday, my father and I walked through Central Park to the softball fields. Instead of going toward the stands, where a game was in progress, he steered me to the bleacher section of an unoccupied field.

"There's no game here, Dad."

"Let's just sit here a moment. Look at all the other fields. Pick out an exciting game."

We sat down on a green splintered board facing a game near the merry-go-round.

"Remember, Mitchell, the time you asked if Mommy would ever come back home?"

"Sure." I remembered vividly.

"Well, she can't come back now," he said softly, looking at the empty outfield in front of us.

"Why not?"

"She died yesterday afternoon."

I began crying, choking, holding my father's arm, quieting down, then sobbing with more abandon. I was ashamed of my tears in a public place. My father gave me his handkerchief.

"Blow, blow," he said gently. "It's all right. Use it."

I blew my nose, coughed, wiped my eyes, but each time I cleaned myself up, the merry-go-round, a leaf, a bird brought her voice back again.

"Cry. Cry all you want. Don't worry. No one is here."

He put his hand through my hair, squeezed it down to the soft part of my neck. His tenderness made me weep again. For both of us.

"Where was she?" I asked.

"At Grandma Lufkin's. It was a sudden attack. The blood clot moved from her leg to her brain."

"No warning? Couldn't the clot move out of her head?"

"Her heart stopped."

We lingered in the park without seeing a softball game. I couldn't stop crying long enough. My father held his arm around my shoulder as we walked back to the Park Central.

Philly was thinking about their last exchange. Hannah was wild. The clot had moved inside her head, exploding her bitterness.

"You'll marry again, Philly. You'll give your next wife everything! A mink . . . not a muskrat like me. You'll spoil her."

"Please, Hannah. Please . . . stop!"

"Cheap bastard."

"Don't!"

"Spoil her. . . . Your third wife . . . she'll get two coats!"

That evening my father took his old fiddle down from the closet shelf to cheer me up with show tunes. I resisted his efforts, wrapped in my grief. After a loud pluck in the middle of "For Me and My Gal" he did a soft-shoe twirl, and I gave in to laughter. Like my mother's it built and built until I was laughing clear as a bell. My father squeezed me tight and kissed my cheeks.

Chapter
Two

AFTER OUR TALK on the empty Central Park softball bleachers, my father and I pulled together. We were inseparable that June before I went to camp. For some reason I didn't see Grandma Lufkin or my cousins until camp ended, although my father did make one unexpected lightning trip up to Washington Heights in the middle of a hot June workday. He shot out the door into a cab after an angry telephone conversation with Uncle Mordecai, instructing Harry, "Take care of Mitchell, get him some lunch, I'll be back before Bookazine comes in." He wasn't, but Harry held the fort with me at his side, allowed to ring the register now that I wore long pants. At six-forty-five my father finally returned.

"How's Grandma?" I asked that night at dinner. "Sad?"

"Holding up, holding up."

"Did she cry?"

My father shook his grizzled, uneven jowls. He didn't know. The left side of his face underneath his chin hung lower than the right side, a legacy of clamping his fiddle there for twenty-five years.

"Who will live with her now?"

"No one, Mitchell. She'll be all alone, like before Mommy was sick."

"Then she'll get her room back. Will she sleep in the same bed?"

"I don't know," he snapped, losing patience. "She'll make do."

"Who will help her move the bed?" I couldn't seem to stop asking macabre questions.

"Her *big* sons will!" My father dropped his silverware, free fall, onto his dinner plate, and I concluded that line of inquiry. He wasn't mad at me. In fact he seemed somehow liberated once he had barked out "Her *big* sons" like an epithet, a dirty word.

"When can you take me up to see Grandma Lufkin?" I asked my father during my first full day back in the bookstore after I had returned from camp in late August.

"Soon, Mitchell, soon."

"When is soon?" I challenged.

"On the weekend, when business slows down."

That Saturday at one P.M. we took the A train up to 175th Street, walked down the short hill to Grandma Lufkin's building, pushed her apartment buzzer, rode up to her floor in the self-service elevator and rang her doorbell. I flew into her moist flowered apron, hugging her solid body in my arms, inhaling all her kitchen odors.

"Mitchellah, Mitchellah." She held on to me. "Goot boy, goot." Her eyes watered. "A giant, just like Hannah!"

We both turned and noticed my father still standing at the open door.

"So, Philly, come in, make yourself at home, take a rest."

"No, thanks, you two visit. I'll come back at four." And he was gone.

Lena didn't resist his departure. She moved me directly to a seat at her kitchen table and began ladling out the first course, fish stew with large pieces of carp and golden onions floating in the milky broth. A temperature change followed. Chilled gefilte fish with sliced baby carrots suspended in jelly. Then back to a warm sweet-and-sour fresh fruit compote for dessert.

"Nehm, Mitchellah, ess, ess, gesundheit," she cooed at me as I worked my way through the courses.

Lena finished her own cup of soup, buttered a heel of fresh hallah and listened to my camp news, shaking her head.

"Such goings on . . . a statue you won for good athlete? You did all these things, Mitchell?"

"Yes, Grandma."

I was afraid to look toward my mother's room, or was it Grandma's bedroom now? Its present use seemed irrelevant. I couldn't gaze down that hallway. I helped clear the white dairy plates, and Lena turned on the faucets. The afternoon sun flooded through the kitchen windows, spotlighting her wrinkled neck and yellowed white hair. As she moved her hands into the glare the gold watch on her left wrist refracted the sun's rays. I had never seen it or any watch on her before. She had always relied on the Westclox over the kitchen sink or the radio.

"Grandma, the watch," I blurted out because it was so bright, unexpected, alien on her rugged arm.

"It's fourteen karat, it's Vittnauer. Look, Mitchell. Even the hands are gold . . . the strep too."

She pushed it into my face. It was very golden but too large for her wrist, almost a man's watch in size and design. She displayed it like a strange trophy.

"Uncle Mordecai and Uncle Sam gave it to me."

"For your birthday?"

"No, no, a keepsake, a memento."

She flushed, moving the watch behind her apron.

"It's nothing, Mitchell, just a little keepsake."

"For *what?*" I had to know.

"So nosy, *boychik* . . ."

My eyes welled up at her unexpected reprimand. Lena sensed my hurt and embraced me. I tried to hide my tears on her shoulder towel as she concealed her watch inside her apron pocket.

The telephone rang us apart. Lena picked it up.

"Hullo?" She motioned me toward her, handing me the receiver.

"It's your father," she whispered.

"I'm at Aunt Blanche's," he said.

"Can I come over to play with Robert?"

"Not today, Mitchell. It's late. Almost five. I've got to get back to the store before Harry leaves."

"Can't I sleep over at Grandma's?"

"But who would bring you home? I'd have to make a special trip to come up and get you. Mitchell, I'll ring Grandma's buzzer in ten minutes. Just run downstairs. Get ready now, okay?"

What about me? I almost said, wanted to say when we were reunited in the lobby after my painful farewell upstairs with Grandma Lufkin.

My father was prepared for this attitude.

"Mitchell, notice the buzzer. Pay attention to the street as we walk to the subway. Notice the sign pointing to the downtown A train."

"Why?" I asked after dutifully taking in each object.

"So you can come up here without me. See Grandma and visit your cousins by yourself. You are eleven."

"Sure!" That was a good deal. The A train roared the stretch from 42nd Street to 175th in eighteen minutes. I reached for my father's hand as we went down the subway stairs and got on the express train that swept us back to midtown.

During the next three weeks of September before I began the sixth grade, I did take the subway up to Washington Heights two times. My cousin Robert and I had a fine time playing curb ball, shooting marbles and going to the RKO with his friends. They were all older than me, but my height and Robert's sponsorship made this age difference insignificant. His mother's example made him considerate beyond his years.

Aunt Blanche was a compassionate woman whom my father found especially appealing. Fortunately, during my last visit that September for a Shabbas eve at Grandma Lufkin's, she was present. I was sleeping over for the entire weekend. A real treat.

Aunt Renee was holding forth on the troubles of her brother Manny, who drove a number 5 double-decker bus along Riverside Drive and down 5th Avenue. Manny had two hazardous turns to execute on 72nd and 57th streets, but he was paid the same as regular single-decker drivers. Since wages and prices remained frozen immediately after the war, Manny had to live with this inequity. My father, however, could increase his profits by selling more price-fixed books and new titles, like best sellers which retailed at unfixed prices. Uncle Sam and Uncle Mordecai could see more patients, and Renee's husband, Uncle Morris, could build more stores. But it was my father's growing prosperity that particularly rankled Aunt Renee.

"The owners always get around controls. The OPA lets them. Philly . . . look at his business, he's rolling in dough. Up to here." She stabbed the top of her fat pink arm.

"Stuck up, vain little son of a—"

"Renee, control yourself. *Please!*" Blanche interrupted. "Not in front of Mitchell."

Renee stiffened. She sulked quietly in the large maroon easy chair. Grandma Lufkin refilled teacups and passed an assortment of coffee cake and petits fours around the living room again. My appetite withered. I had never heard anyone impugn my father before. A strange ache slithered through my intestines that evening, and on the train back to Times Square it flared up each time the doors whacked open.

Blanche had rescued me, saying, "Not in front of Mitchell." But what else did they say about my father when I wasn't there? I knew what *stuck up* meant. Something about girls. Was *vain* like that, but for men? I walked up the subway stairs, then west on 42nd Street toward the store, confused but eager to see my father and maybe ask him what was going on.

Philly had been drawn into a vortex of greed and recrimination after Hannah died. Propinquity had much to do with it, but resentment more. After Hannah returned from Reno, she spent one month resting at the Park Central; then her illness was managed by Uncle Mordecai, a board-certified internist, and her remaining time was spent at Grandma Lufkin's or in Presbyterian Hospital. Lena was in charge of her daily welfare as nurse, bed straightener, cook and sentinel. Philly was merely a visitor, a distraught observer, a rejected husband. Whether their twice weekly meetings helped him understand and forgive Reno and prepare for genuine reconciliation or merely reinforced his bent for self-pity, Philly was definitely not in charge. He carried all Hannah's personal effects up to the Heights when requested. Dutiful messenger, he brought her nightgowns, underwear, leather jewelry box, dresses for the hospital trip, anything she wanted, until most of Hannah's belongings were up at Lena's and out of 2209. The tiny jewelry box contained her slight collection: earrings, cameo brooches, engagement ring, some costume pieces from the hotel jeweler and a safe deposit key tucked away in a bottom drawer. She and Philly shared the same box at the Corn Exchange Bank on 41st and Broadway. Some war bonds and insurance policies were all they had in it. Philly's key was in the store, filed under *K* or *S*, he was never sure.

During Hannah and Philly's last visit, when her bitterness exploded into oaths and the prediction that Philly's future wives and their accoutrements would multiply, Lena, Mordecai and Sam overheard it all. The apartment was small, and they were poised radar screens, wired for sound, any shift in bodily rhythm, knowing Hannah's condition was terminal.

The three of them never had liked or approved of Philly. Hannah, the baby, the only daughter, deserved better. A professional at least, not a short merchant at the cash register. Hannah's outburst confirmed their old prejudices.

Cheap bastard. Who *would* he marry next? When? Their eyes flashed, wiping out the grudging deference Mordecai had shown Philly after he had helped bring Hannah home from Nevada.

How could they hurt him? Get back for the pain, the shitty life he had given Hannah? They dissembled when Philly came out of the bedroom, exhausted, eyes red. Lena gave him a glass of schnapps. Mordecai tried to console him with a walk in Tryon Park. Lena and Sam went straight into the bedroom. Hannah was still, glazed over, spent.

"*Nu*, Hannah? Finally you told the bastard."

Sam said nothing.

Hannah didn't hear. She looked past them for Philly. He was the object of her rage and love. She was sorry for him too now. What the hell did he have? A fucking bookstore, twelve hours a day, seven days a week. They didn't know how hard he worked. Her thoughts became audible.

"Poor bastard . . ."

"Bastard? Philly?" Lena asked.

Hannah went into a coma, her fine face up toward the ceiling. Lena embraced Hannah's chest, crying, until Sam gently removed her, took out his stethoscope to check her vital signs. Terrified, Lena slumped into the easy chair, fixated on Hannah's tiny leather jewelry case set on top of the cluttered night table.

Hannah stopped breathing forty minutes later. That evening after the undertakers had gone, Lena opened the brass-knobbed bottom drawer of the case and picked out a jagged key.

"Sam, Mordecai," she whispered to them in the empty room. "Put this in your pocket, Sam."

"What is it, Mom?"

"Hannah's safe deposit key."

Philly received a phone call from Mr. Garrity, manager of the 41st Street Corn Exchange Bank three days later. Garrity felt something was awry, though legal, and his customer should know.

"Mr. Woolf, some people were just in here with the key to your safe deposit box."

"Who, for Christsakes?"

"Lufkin, Dr. Mordecai and Lena. They had power of attorney as executors of Mrs. Woolf's estate."

"I'll be right over."

Garrity showed Philly a sheet of expensive rag paper with Hannah's tentative signature at the bottom, properly notarized by Morton Lufkin, attorney. It was the top section, dated May 20, 1946, that stunned him. Hannah designated Mordecai Lufkin and Lena as executors of her last will and testament to dispose of her property as they saw fit. Philly knew it was a fraudulent paste-up job over her tentative signature, drawn up by the family's lawyer, cousin Morty, at a special discount fee.

Hannah and Philly had never made wills, never had any property or assets to dispose of until the war years, when they began investing equal amounts in savings bonds for patriotic reasons as well as Mitchell's college education. His future needs also convinced them each to take out a five-thousand-dollar life insurance policy with Mitchell as the sole beneficiary.

Philly asked Mr. Garrity to get out the safe deposit box. He had remembered to bring his own key. Hannah's insurance policy was gone. Period. His remained. The few thousands in savings bonds were also gone, instantly liquid.

"Sons of bitches, they took the bonds too!"

"I wasn't in the coupon room, Mr. Woolf." Garrity shook his head.

"Crooks . . . thieving bastards!" Philly was livid.

He called Mordecai immediately and set up a family conference for the next day at their attorney's office near the George Washington Bridge.

"How could you do this shyster cops and robbers stuff?" Philly shouted at the tense, cramped meeting. "The bonds, the insurance policy?"

"Hannah didn't want *you* to have them," Lena came right back, though not as loud.

"What bonds?" Mordecai asked quietly.

"They were for Mitchell, not me, for college."

"How do we know he'll get them?" Lena's distrust was complete.

"The policy is in his name. The bonds I'll keep for him."

"What bonds?" Mordecai repeated.

"War bonds. War bonds." Philly realized they were gone for good.

"Mitchell's a minor. We'll make sure he gets his share of Hannah's insurance policy at eighteen," Mordecai announced, a model of fiduciary trust.

"*Share?* What the hell are you talking about?" Philly couldn't believe what they were doing. He should have brought Keppelstein, his own lawyer, with him.

"She didn't trust you anymore, with your new wife." Lena drove in her sharpest nail, but her wild accusation brought Philly clarity. He

realized that they had overheard Hannah's deathbed prediction and
become her surrogates, acting out her resentment to hurt him and
keep part of her for themselves.

"You can't do this, Mordecai. It's crazy. It's against the law, stealing." Philly attacked their moral heavy directly.

"Watch it," Mordecai bellowed. "That could be slander."

"Please, please, cousins," Morty fumphered. "Let's settle this
thing reasonably like family."

"Family? Hah! Family! *Mockie* bastards!" Philly screamed as he
slammed the office door and left them mortified.

He may have been cheap, but he was honest, loyal. So was Hannah. They shared everything until she took off with the new man.
And when she was stranded, ill, Philly paid for the train, doctor and
hospital. Philly knew it was the Lufkins who were responsible, not
Hannah. She wouldn't screw Mitchell.

After two weeks of tough negotiating the opposing lawyers drew
up a settlement. The bonds were gone, not traceable. The insurance
policy would go in three equal parts to Lena, the other Lufkin mi-
nors, and Mitchell.

"Outrageous!" Philly steamed at Keppelstein. "Sam and Mordecai are loaded. They can take care of Lena and their own kids. It
stinks!"

"They claim you got the store outright," Keppelstein answered.

"Thanks a lot, Keppy. They're really nutso."

"They could fight you on it if you don't settle. A lot of Hannah
went into it, Phil."

"But the lease, everything has my signature on it."

"Thank God, or they'd come after that too."

"*Mockie* bastards!"

"Easy Phil, easy."

"I won't let them see Mitchell again if they steal from him like
this."

So my father wasn't too shocked when I repeated Aunt Renee's
epithet, "stuck up, vain little guy," nor was he surprised at Aunt
Blanche's plea for discretion. She was the one who had negotiated my

recent visits with Grandma Lufkin. My father could break off with Lena and her family, but he knew and Blanche confirmed his feeling that it would hurt me more than the Lufkins if I couldn't visit my grandmother anymore. At least for the time being that's how Philly resolved matters. He never attacked them, and after Renee's outburst nothing was ever said against him in front of me. The Lufkins were the past for him—Hannah a bittersweet memory.

With Mitchell back at school Philly was utterly alone at night except at the store and a new cocktail lounge which had opened right after Labor Day in the 55th Street corner of the hotel. The Nite Lite was a discreet after-hours club where beige couches with a pair of leather bucket seats, tête-à-tête, ringed the mirrored walls. Onyx kidney-shaped tables floated in front of each seating arrangement. A relaxed instrumental trio, piano, bass and drums, slid through Gershwin, Berlin, and Rogers and Hart medleys. Business was slow, unheralded at first. Philly stumbled into the Nite Lite by chance after closing Bookland one stormy evening. Caught in an electric cloudburst, he ran for the 55th Street side entrance and dried off inhaling a scotch and soda. He was intrigued by the trio's clever arrangements of tunes he had once played on the fiddle. Few of the patrons, however, shared Philly's sophisticated ear. To enhance the trio and tasteful decor, the hotel had hired Charlotte Percy, a song stylist of warmth and magnificent proportions. She was a gorgeous choice, sheathed in a strapless gown of prewar taffeta which set off her straight black hair and blue eyes. Her vocal accompaniment fit nicely with the trio's standard sets. She augmented their sound with her own middle-range soprano, able to inflect an octave up or down the scale in "Manhattan" when her voice became the fourth instrument. With "Bewitched" she soared away in an octave beyond their rhythms.

On Tuesday evening, during her first week, Philly walked in and was seated just as she began her solo, "Bewitched." He was still drained by the bequest ordeal, raw. His battered condition made him particularly alive to the ironies within the rich new voice coming from the spot-lit bandstand.

"After one whole quart of brandy,
Like a daisy I awake,
With no Bromo Seltzer handy,
I don't even shake.

[pause]

Men are not a new sensation,
I do pretty well I think,
But this *half pint* imitation's
Put me on the blink."

"Who's that?" Philly asked his waiter after "half pint."
"Charlotte Percy, new singer."
"I'll have a scotch and soda, soda on the side."
"Sure thing, chief."
The trio welled up for the refrain.

"I'm wild again,
Beguiled again,
A simpering, whimpering child again.
Bewitched [pause, down an octave], bothered,
    and bewildered am I."

Now Philly recognized the tune from *Pal Joey*, but the lyrics he couldn't quite remember. He'd never heard them that way. Was she making them up for the club?

"I'll sing to him,
Each spring to him,
And worship the trousers that cling
    to him. . . ."

At the end of the song polite scattered applause came from the ten customers in the room. Philly was more demonstrative, riveted to with "Nothing Could Be Finer Than To Be in Carolina in the Morning" to more perfunctory applause. She moved quickly toward the powder room, passing Philly's table on the way. He was still applauding, more gently now. Charlotte noted his manicured fingers, brown eyes and handsome head. Philly registered her worried eyes and height. She was easily five nine—Hannah's size. They caught each other's stare. He waited for her to reemerge from the powder room, located just behind his couch. She came past his table again, was about to say thank you when Philly asked her to join him during her break. She did, surprised by Philly's invitation.

"That was really fine."

"Oh, thank you, Mistah . . ."

"Philly."

"Philly. But you're the only one who feels that way."

"It's a room full of stiffs. They were drinking, didn't hear a word, just the rhythm. It takes time in a new club."

"*You* heard."

"Some of it for the first time."

"Like what?" She was playing now, more certain, relaxed.

"The lead-in to 'Bewitched.' Did Hart write it that way?"

"Which stanza?" She could guess from the way he had to look up into her eyes.

"The daisy part." Philly almost blushed.

"Go on." Charlotte guffawed, grazing Philly's cupped hands, surprising them both.

She ordered a weak daiquiri. They talked about the music business; Philly about his vaudeville days, Charlotte about her genteel piano lessons while growing up in Richmond performing at the Newport News USO and her trip north after the war to stay with her maiden aunt and find work with a band like Dinah Shore had.

Philly was hypnotized by her cleavage, the moving white sides of her breasts, the delicate pores, the hint of pink aureole. He hadn't seen or looked for sixteen months.

When the trio reassembled on the darkened stage, Charlotte straightened up from the couch and placed her moist hand over his.

"Thank you. Please stay, will ya, Philly?"

He did, all night and the next and the next. He stayed with her arms, her breasts, her mouth, her whole body, he stayed and stayed, night after night in the lounge and in her tiny room at the Park Central, losing his grief in her succulence, finding his voice, his mouth, his own cry again.

I no longer grieved openly for my mother when I returned to the Lake Ronkonkoma School in September 1946 to begin the sixth grade. My public tears had been spent that June Sunday in Central Park. The mystery, the anxiety about my mother's travels and health were over. On long bus and train rides I wondered exactly where she was. Her face, what part of the universe did it occupy? Could I look into it? Could she see me now? Come back without my seeing her the way dead parents did at the Saturday movies in Smithtown?

Blessedly, new friends and their antics prevented my autumn morbidity from festering. Though Stevens remained in the North Dorm, an anchor, the Rafferty brothers, Jimmy, eleven, and Frankie, eight, shattered our comfortable menage when they arrived in October. They beat each other senseless out in the main hall, spilling over the couches, socking each other hard in the stomach, wrestling in the empty fireplace, ripping even bigger holes in their already tattered corduroy pants and plaid shirts. They were *real* brothers, yet they wanted to kill, or certainly maim each other. We were aghast as we watched them. Was this how my cousins treated each other when I wasn't around? How my uncles had acted when they were little kids?

Jimmy was dark and tall, and he had a high potbelly supported by slender legs. His soft Irish face with its mushy nose was vulnerable, like pictures of young Babe Ruth about to leave his Baltimore orphanage. Frank was fair, almost blond, with blue eyes, a cute turned-up nose, delicate wrists, his mother's image. Though tall for eight and rather agile, Frank was at least a foot shorter than his brother and thus no physical match for him when they went at each other. Frank had to rely on his wits, which often meant threats to phone his mother.

Elaine Rafferty was a nighttime long-distance operator for the Bell System. She had just transferred James and Francis from a dour

Catholic orphanage up the Hudson near West Point, where they had spent three years learning some Latin and their catechisms and committing venial sins. The change in schools was an emotional risk—leaving the nuns—as well as a financial drain. Elaine did have the discreet support of her new boyfriend, Tommy Powers, a prosperous mortician. Still, she was anxious and telephoned the boys direct from the switchboard whenever she was troubled. Her presence was real, giving validity to Frank's threats to reach her by phone.

"You call her, Frankie, and I'll really kick the shit out of you!"

"Try. Just try," Frank sassed, darting toward the stairwell, hoping to reach Mrs. Kennedy's desk telephone. When he could race down the stairs and plug into his mother's special number, Jimmy got his over the phone. But Frank got *his* immediately afterward.

"I'll kill you, Frank. I'll kill you, you fucking little bastard." And he almost did, throwing Frank down the entire stairwell.

Stevens finally put them in separate rooms at either end of the floor, which limited their blood enmity to one bout every month. Frank stayed with the younger kids, a slender loner, not a troublemaker, good in his studies, weak on the playing field. His fierce tongue protected him. Jimmy moved next door to Jack Ronson and myself. He was not verbally adept like Frank. His intentions were revealed in action. He was fearless in football, soccer and basketball. Though not a naturally gifted athlete, he had incredible stamina and was never intimidated by the stronger seventh and eighth graders.

One frozen afternoon I was cutting toward the goal line, football under my arm with only Freddy Daniels and Mark Gross in my path. They were cagey, tough seventh graders. Daniels, their quarterback, was out for blood, ready to knee me in the groin. Jimmy, the offensive blocker running with me, lobbed his stiffened body at Daniels's head, knocking him to the ground and breaking his glasses. I scored. Jimmy and I shared a smile before we had to fight Daniels and Gross, something I would have avoided without Jimmy in the trenches with me.

"I have a great new friend, Jimmy Rafferty," I announced to my father as I pushed my head through his office curtain at the start of my Thanksgiving vacation. "Rafferty and I can take the whole seventh grade in football, some of the eighth too. Just wait till basketball seasons starts. What a duo!"

"So, what about a new hat this year?" my father asked, unable to share my enthusiasm for basketball.

"Do you think they have my size yet?"

"With or without ear laps, sonny," my father said, mimicking the condescending salesman at Rappaport's on 84th and Broadway who always waited on us during our annual quest for a warm hat that would fit my large Lufkin head. The dilemma was similar to the short pants–long pants one. Size seven and a half was just too large for a child's hat, but I couldn't wear the grownup type sold at Dobbs or Knotts, where my father bought his demure size eight. I would have looked ridiculous in a man's fedora, and besides, it couldn't keep my ears warm and thus prevent the earaches that had plagued me in the Bronx.

We left Bookland at seven, fortified ourselves with a full course dinner at the Tip Toe Inn uptown and began the search, which again concluded at Rappaport's.

"Nothing! Nothing at all for *his* head, mister!"

Fortunately, my mackinaw hood kept my ears warm on frigid days, and I never got sick at Lake Ronkonkoma.

"How about shoes, Mitchell?" My father looked at my worn oxfords, remembering the one store that carried my size, eight and a half C, was only two blocks further uptown. Richmond's sold a special Boy Scout brand shoe designed and authorized by the Scouts. It had a full last, steel arch supports and sturdy leather construction throughout. Though my father shared my disdain for the Scout movement, he was a fan of their authorized shoe. Not only did it fit my long, wide foot, but it also corrected my tendency toward flat arches. When I was a toddler, Grandma Lufkin and my parents were so alarmed at the prospect of a flat-footed child, they shod my feet in ankle-high arch-supported shoes until I entered first grade. The Boy Scout oxfords were the next best thing.

"So, let's measure that foot, sonny. Lower it now. Stand up. Good. That's fine." Mr. Richmond adjusted the metal indicators.

"Well, he's not eight and a half C anymore. He's over nine now, nine D, to be precise.

"Jesus Christ," my father muttered to himself. "He can't stop growing."

"Let me see what I can find out back." Mr. Richmond returned with two shoe boxes.

"I'm sorry, they stop making the Boy Scouts after size eight and a half. Nothing much in his size unless we move to men's shoes."

"I don't believe it." My father sighed with a mixture of pride and disgust.

"Try this nine D just for size—try it."

It was a gleaming wing-tipped dress shoe.

"Just for size," Mr. Richmond repeated as he slipped the shoe-horn behind my heel. It was too snug.

"Stand, stand." Mr. Richmond shook his head. "There isn't enough room there. The Boy Scouts really fit him where he needs it."

My father felt the toe and arch and shook his head in agreement.

"Maybe he could wear the shoe boxes."

We all laughed.

"I just don't have much in men's shoes, Mr. Woolf."

"We'll try downtown tomorrow, Mitchell. 42nd Street is full of shoe stores."

It certainly was. Every major shoe chain was represented within three blocks of Bookland going east. Florsheim was practically next door, but their shoes were rather flashy and expensive. At least eight dollars. Thom McAn, also on our block, was cheaper, actually less than Richmond's. We went there during lunch. I tried on the right shoe of a heavy black oxford pair while my father examined the left one. Kneeding and smelling the leather, he tapped the raised hard toe.

"They're cardboard. Paper underneath!" my father exploded.

"We sell an awful lot of these, sir."

"To who?" my father snapped back. "Jerks?"

"Just a second, mister, you can't . . ."

"Let's go, Mitchell. Take them off."

Rafferty always got his shoes at Thom McAn. They did nick easily in the hard toe, revealing a white paperlike substance. But I knew he wasn't a *jerk*; maybe sloppy with his clothes and not exactly loaded like Daniels and the Venezuelans, but a jerk because of the shoes he wore?

Adler was next door to Thom McAn. Our next stop, I thought, looking in their window at all the glossy brown and black shoes. Not as boxy as Thom McAn's, a shade more expensive.

"Some shit!" my father said when he joined me at Adler's window. "Notice how thick the heels are."

He pointed at a display platform on which the difference between their heel and an ordinary one was highlighted. Theirs, the Adler Elevator Heel, was a good inch thicker.

"It screws up your foot, the way you walk."

"Why do they make them?"

"It makes short guys feel taller. Ridiculous . . . for schmucks!"

We ran for the crosstown bus heading east toward Coward, across the street from the Chrysler Building.

"Same people who own Thom McAn, only better quality shoes and they specialize in wide widths," he whispered as we entered a large double-level empty store. Two middle-aged salesmen stood like sentinels at the door. One, blond and balding, poured a fistful of pennies from one hand into the other as he rocked moronically back and forth on his heels. The other, a black-haired man who seemed like the manager, was adjusting his jockey shorts with his hands concealed deep within his pockets. He was desperately trying to rearrange his testicles, shift them back into the center of his shorts, certain no one could detect his covert activity. He withdrew his left hand in order to direct us to a younger salesman in the middle of the store.

They did have a large selection of shoes in my width, but the styles were not exactly youthful. One greenish-brown oxford was the best fit. My father questioned its durability.

"He's rough on them," he told the patient salesman as I walked around the store yet another time.

"You know Davega's, the sports store between 6th and 7th?" the salesman asked my father.

"Sure."

"They have a line of rugged shoes for hiking."

"I didn't know they carried shoes. We're going back that way.

How are they, Mitchell?'' My father felt and looked again as I sat down.

"Fine, they're okay."

"Well, let's think about them. We'll come back tomorrow or Saturday, okay?"

"Sure, mister. I'll put them aside."

"Thanks, chief."

"Still, try Davega's."

We did. Their hiking loafer was wide enough, but it had no arch support. It was constructed like a moccasin. I noticed a pair of black leather basketball shoes with high tops like the seventh and eighth graders on the Upper School JV wore. I showed them to my father, elaborated on who had them at Lake Ronkonkoma and how they'd replaced the sneaker in basketball.

"They must give good support in the ankles." My father held one up, impressed with the leather and built-in arch support. They were demiboot shoes with rubber suction soles.

"Do you think they have your size?"

"Ask, ask."

They did, and I got them, wrapped in a box. I hugged my father, too excited for speech.

That evening I wore them around 2209, finally placing them just under my bed near the pillow end when he tucked me in. I could smell the new leather. Freddy Daniels slept with his hand around a new leather basketball his parents bought him, hoping to stretch his grip so he could palm the ball like the varsity players. We were going to have tryouts for the Lower School varsity right after vacation. I was ready, sound asleep.

"The kid's in the next room." My father's voice woke me. The diction was strange. He had never used the word *kid* before. He was talking to someone, a woman, I finally made out. It was casual exploratory talk. They weren't old friends. They went into the foyer. My father showed her the kitchenette, turned the light on and off.

"Where does he sleep?" the woman asked.

"In there, the bedroom."

"Oh, we'd better lower our voices."

"He's a deep sleeper, like a rock," my father assured her. "Do you want to see the kid?"

"Sure."

Just as they began edging into the dark bedroom I realized I didn't want her to see me, so I turned toward the wall, pulled the covers as far over my head as breathing would allow and curled into a semicircle. They were both standing over me.

"What a big boy! You never said he was that large. How old is he?"

"Eleven going on twelve."

"How did he grow so big, Phil?"

"*She* was big."

"Oh." They were back in the foyer now.

"Kid," "she" . . . what the hell was going on with my father's vocabulary? The woman knew his name but not my size. Who was she? I decided to have a look as my father was helping her on with her coat, but the foyer was dim until the closet bulb illuminated her black Persian lamb coat. My father took it off the wooden hotel hanger and held it up so she could ease into it and walk toward the front door. I caught a glimpse of the bottom section of the coat: tight black lamb curls.

My father must have taken her to the elevator and downstairs to a taxi. I was alone. I reached for my new basketball shoes under the bed, touched the leather, making certain they had not been pushed out of position by my recent visitors, and turned toward the wall again to sleep.

The following day during our drugstore breakfast, later at the bookstore and during our return trip to Coward, where we purchased the greenish-brown oxfords, I was unable to ask my father who the woman in the Persian lamb coat was. I was afraid he might think I had been a sneak, spying on him at night, or he would feel I had been rude turning toward the wall and pulling the covers over my head. Maybe she wouldn't come back if I didn't pry.

On the last evening of the vacation my father opened the mirrored door of his large closet, turned on the overhead light and examined his exquisite collection of shoes. They were arranged in neat rows, wooden shoe trees blossoming from the opening of each pair, store labels embossed on them: Florsheim, Nettleton, Lloyd & Haig, Johnston & Murphy.

"Mitchell, do you still have your new shoes on?"

"Yes."

"Take them off but leave your socks on."

"Why?"

"Come over here and see."

I edged into his closet, looked over his compact shoulders. He was picking through his shoes—at least ten or twelve pairs, cordovan loafers, oxford walking shoes, black half-toes, wing tips with different swirling designs on each pair's toe and heel sections. He reached for a pair of black wing tips at the rear of the closet, pulled them into the light, blew the dust off, rubbed the shine back into them with a chamois cloth and handed them up to me.

"Try these on, Mitchell."

"But they're yours."

"Just see if they fit."

I took the Nettleton shoe trees out. The shoes slid on comfortably. My foot expanded into cracked expensive leather. I tied up the stiff leather laces.

"Walk, walk around in them."

I did, speechless, staring at the tiny circular pattern of holes punched out of each toe. They were grownup dress shoes.

"How do they feel? Enough room on the sides?"

"I guess," I replied, still dazed.

My father felt the width with his own thumb and finger.

"Plenty of room there, Mitchell. You like them?"

"Of course."

"They're yours, then. They were always too roomy for me. Never a good fit. Hardly been worn."

"But I already have a new pair from Coward."

"Now you'll have two. It's your ration stamp quota."

We both laughed, remembering the wartime shoe coupons we could never find when we went looking for new shoes.

"Thanks a lot, Dad." I kissed his cheek, gave him a long, tight hug. His whiskers made little indentations in my cheek.

"What about suits?" I asked. "Got any sharp ones that don't fit?"

He went right back to his closet and pulled out a wide-shouldered, double-breasted pinstripe which I hopped into. The pant legs were pinched, seemingly pegged. The jacket came down to my knees.

" 'I wanna zoot suit with a reat pleat./ With a drape shape and a stuff cuff. . . .' " I assumed the menacing stance of a zoot-suiter. My father smiled, acknowledging the skill and spirit of my impersonation. He immediately augmented it with an old key chain for the pants.

"Wait, wait," he shouted. "The hat, the hat! We need a hat, Mitchell." He found an old wide-brimmed black one on the second shelf of his closet, blew the dust off, boxed it into the appropriate flat shape and presented it to me. I did a reprise.

" 'I wanna zoot suit with a reat pleat./ With a drape shape and a stuff cuff. . . .' "

My father began snapping his fingers to my beat.

"I want a reave sleeve with a ripe stripe," he jived, still snapping his fingers.

"I want a zoot suit with a reat pleat." I scat-talked the intro exactly like Cab Calloway, digging my wing tips into the carpet for balance so I could lift my shoulders while twisting my midsection. "With a drape shape and a stuff cuff." I was gone, arms swaying to the beat.

My father continued snapping out, "I want a reave sleeve with a ripe stripe." He sent his stanza back, laughing so hard, tears came to his eyes.

Overcome by his performance, I couldn't stop my own. Back and forth we sang our stanzas, laughing, weeping, starting up again. Even when I was in my pajamas ready for bed and he turned out the bedroom light and went into the living room, we echoed each other's bursts of laughter. After ten minutes there was silence. I was glad I had suppressed my questions. Maybe that woman wouldn't come back if I didn't ask them.

I couldn't tell anyone about her at Lake Ronkonkoma, not even Ronson after lights-out, though I did hold him responsible for her first daylight appearance. The Sunday before our long Christmas break Jack's parents usually drove up to collect his dirty laundry in order to be all ready for their three week Key West vacation the moment Jack stepped off the 4:07 from Smithtown. It was their one chance for a family holiday, a slow season for broken typewriters.

This year they brought my father along with them, an unexpected surprise. Getting out of the Chevy right on his heels was a wide, curly-haired woman, introduced to me as Bea, my father's friend. I didn't hear the last name, Kagle, because I was staring at the tight black lamb curls at the bottom of her coat. It was her! The same coat!

We showed her the campus while Jack and his parents went up to our room to start packing. My father did most of the talking. I pointed out the buildings. He repeated all the details and anecdotes I had shared with him, which made me queasy.

"The gymnasium has the largest wooden playing surface on the Island. The varsity basketball team is excellent this year. Real contenders. They beat East Islip by two points, a real upset."

How could he tell her everything, divulge my secrets?

Mr. Ronson took us all on a drive to Stony Brook. I was in the backseat staring out the corner window at the trees, all naked now except for the pines. My father sat next to me, his crepe-soled oxfords straddling the drive shaft hump. Bea was at the other corner window, which she had opened a crack so the smoke from her Chesterfield could escape.

After hot chocolate and oatmeal cookies at the Stony Brook Sweet Shoppe, we walked over to the pond to see how the ducks were doing. My father was dawdling in the rear, talking to Mr. Ronson about business, this Christmas versus last. Jack ran ahead to the edge of the pond and began throwing stale bread at the ducks. Bea was at my side. We were alone on the brown grass.

"Your father talks about you all the time."

"Really?" I was pleased but wary.

"He's very proud of you. He told me you're very good at basketball. The only sixth grader on the Lower School varsity."

"That's true, except for Rafferty. He made the team also."

"Maybe during your Christmas vacation we could all go to see the Knickerbockers play at the Armory."

"Oh, that's not necessary."

"Don't you like the Knicks?"

"They're all right, I guess."

"Who's your favorite team?"

"Notre Dame and NYU." We listened to their intense, physical games on Ronson's radio, unaware of the symbolism—the subway Irish against the New York Jews—that actually made the Garden crowd so vibrant.

"Two teams?"

"Yeah."

"But they're colleges."

"Still, they play basketball."

"I didn't know they had any . . ."

I was off throwing bread with Jack.

Twenty minutes later on the narrow dirt road skirting the Sound, the potholes jarred the Chevy up and down, side to side. Jack and I loved the unpredictable motion. The grownups did not share our delight. After one spine-cracking upheaval I noticed my father was holding Bea's right hand, patting it with his palm. Perhaps the bumps had brought their hands together for the moment. I looked out the window through the naked locust trees into the icy Sound. Both my father's hands were resting on his tweed coat when we drove up the North Dorm gravel road. Bea was smoking yet another Chesterfield. Nothing to worry about. A lousy bump. That's all. A dirt bump.

"It's a tomato surprise," my father said.

"What's it doing in the icebox?"

"Staying fresh."

"Oh."

"It's for you."

We were both in our pajamas standing in front of the open icebox in the kitchenette. It was the second morning of my Christmas vacation. Seeing anything in our small icebox was surprising enough. In the old days when I went to PS 69, there were a few cans of tomato juice on the top shelf for my breakfast; milk, cream, butter, a loaf of Arnold's whole wheat bread for my parents' breakfast. Now the tarnished aluminum shelves rarely held more than a stale lemon slice, a pint of milk.

"Who made it?"

"It's a surprise." My father placed the chilled plate before me on the card table in the foyer.

I sat down holding my fork and eyed the wrinkled red sphere with skepticism.

"What's inside the thing?"

"You don't know until you taste it."

Some of the filling was coming through the opening in the tomato. It was whitish. I was starving. I drove my fork into the tomato and scooped out some of the filling. It was ice cold, so I couldn't really taste it until the second forkful began thawing in my throat. I could feel little bits of celery on my tongue and pulpy tomato without seeds. It was chicken mixed with an odd dressing taste, not Hellmann's. Grandma Lufkin's chicken salad was made with larger pieces of meat, patches of yellow skin still attached to the joint sections. There was no garnish celery subterfuge in her salad. It was plain. I gulped down a few more forkfuls.

"How do you like it?"

"It's supposed to be chicken, isn't it?"

"Do you like it?"

"It's different."

"That's all? Just *different?*"

"Who made it?"

"Someone who wanted to surprise you."

"Come on, Dad, who made it?"

"I'll let her tell you."

So Bea What's-her-name made it, I concluded.

"Are we still going to have breakfast in the drugstore, or do you get one of these too?"

"Not so fresh, kiddo. She was only trying to be nice. Get your clothes on."

So it was her.

We were ready to leave in ten minutes. Closing the suite door, we both noticed the half-eaten tomato surprise still in the center of the card table. Neither one of us could clear the remnant away.

"The maid will do it when she cleans up. Let's get down to the drugstore before the rush."

"I'm right behind you."

I did see Bea Kagle one time during the Christmas vacation. The three of us had a light dinner at Schrafft's and, as promised, went to a Knickerbocker–Syracuse Royal's game at the Armory. There was something incongruous and slapdash about watching a basketbal game in an amphitheater built for cavalry exercises. It was much smaller than Madison Square Garden, where the best college teams played.

I did, however, see the actual Carl Braun, Knick playmaker, dribble over the ten-second line and bounce-pass down to Bud Palmer at the high post, get the ball back, dribble to the top of the key, lift his left leg high like the arm of a water pump and push off a one-handed shot using his right leg for leverage. He scored two points on almost every shot. Braun's fluid motion was copied by Daniels on our Lower School team and by Mr. Kennedy's son on the varsity. It was much better in the original.

During the intermission organ recital, which featured the "Pennsylvania Polka" and "The Sidewalks of New York," Bea revealed her hand.

"Did you like what you found in the icebox Tuesday morning?"

"Oh." I was startled by her timing, not the question.

"Mitchell, something was wrong with it? Phil, you told me he *loved* it!"

"The mayonnaise was odd," I snapped in my effort to eradicate the verb *love*.

"How, *odd?*" She pushed her red forehead into my face.

"The taste was different."

"I bet it was the Miracle Whip I used instead of mayonnaise," she explained.

"I like Hellmann's."

"Well, I'm sorry. I just wanted to surprise you. If you hated it, just say so."

"I didn't *hate* it."

"Don't do me any favors."

Her cheeks were flushed. She stood up, walked over my father's feet into the aisle and up the ramp toward the smoking section of the arena. My father followed her. She lit a Chesterfield, pointing in my direction, and threw up both arms like a smoking windmill. My father tried to calm her down. He seemed embarrassed by her rage.

When they returned, the third quarter was almost over. She had been weeping, and broken capillaries webbed the whites of her eyes. Her nicotine-stained hands were trembling. My father was shaken, no color in his face, lips tight. I felt sorry for Bea, or anyone I made cry. She nudged my father. He didn't respond. Again her elbow in his ribs.

"Mitchell." He was mad. "Apologize."

"For what?" The words were a reflex, even though I was scared by his anger and disapproval.

"You know. Apologize," he insisted.

After one full minute I gave in. "I'm sorry," I said to Bea's black dress.

"We'll see, we'll see." She wiped her eyes. My father stared at the meaningless game.

The following evening we had dinner alone at Lindy's, the old smaller one on the east side of 51st and Broadway next to the Rivoli Theater.

"Jolson ate over there." My father pointed to a large round center table with eight chairs. "Berle and I were just kids then. We were against the wall near the men's room, but we could see his grand entrance, claque in tow, from the Winter Garden.

"Leo Lindy knew all the performers, Cantor, Fields, Jessel . . . where they wanted to sit, how they liked their meat—rare, well-done, lean, fat . . . constant attention to detail."

I didn't know what any of these performers, including Berle, my father's vaudeville partner, actually did on stage, but the timbre of his voice, the unusual cadence as he articulated each vowel made them mythic for me also. If alive and in town these luminaries went to the newer Lindy's, the big place across the street, three blocks north on Broadway. We never went there.

"A madhouse, overrun with moochers who got rich during the war," my father lamented. "Every *zhlub* from Brooklyn with twenty bucks in his pocket who didn't have a pair of shoes before the war has to run to Lindy's right away, wait in line outside to see the celebrities inside."

I listened, confused, unable to comprehend the cause of my father's bitterness, his unflattering evaluation of the postwar nouveau riche.

The original Lindy's was less hectic and served much better food at slightly cheaper prices. As we finished our last forkfuls of the cheesecake we were sharing for dessert my father took a postcard-sized piece of white cardboard out of his jacket pocket and placed it next to his teacup. Eight black domed buttons were clamped to it in neat rows. Specks of silver were sprinkled in snowflake patterns on the curved sides of each one.

"Look at these, Mitchell." He pushed the card toward me.

"They're beautiful. What are they for?"

"A dress."

"Whose?"

"A friend. She's a singer."

It wasn't Bea; my mind raced as my throat relaxed, allowing the last crusts of cheesecake to dissolve.

"Now, look at this one." My father took a solitary black button from his side pocket and placed it next to the card of buttons.

"What do you think? Is it a good match?"

The single button was older, duller, though its silver specks still sparkled as brightly as in the newer buttons. Its center had a round silver bubble at the very tip, like a nipple.

"That's different." I pointed to the silver bubble and blushed.

"I couldn't find an exact match, but it's close."

"It's certainly close."

My father held the old button, examined its design, felt its shape, as if it were a special talisman. Then he dropped it back into his jacket pocket.

"Check, check, please." He tried to get the waiter's attention, pretending his flat palm was a pad. He wrote on it with a make-believe pencil high over his head for all to see.

Outside Lindy's it was a clear, windless night. We walked uptown toward the hotel.

"Why are you crossing here?" I asked as we veered west toward Roseland on 52nd Street.

"I've got to take these buttons over . . ."

"To the singer," I said, trying to complete the sentence.

"To her aunt."

"But where's the singer?"

"Out of town, singing, natch."

We both laughed, walking toward the Hudson River.

"Where did she sing in town?" I asked.

"At the Nite Lite club in the Park Central. The new place next to the 55th Street entrance."

"Oh, sure." I remembered stepping inside it one late August afternoon while Fred Grosso and I were racing out the back elevators trying to evade the house detective. The carpenters were hammering black trim on the stage. Electricians hung tiny spotlights from the ceiling. It seemed a rather somber drinking and talking place, unlike the gay, expansive Cocoanut Grove. I recalled Charlie Barnet's female soloist and wondered if my father's "friend" was as beautiful in a low-cut dress. He probably went there after he closed the store.

"What's her name?" We raced across 9th Avenue to beat the light.

"Charlotte. Charlotte Percy." My father was winded after our dash.

In the middle of the next block we turned into the tile courtyard of a ten-story apartment building that was surrounded by shorter tenements. We were buzzed in as soon as my father rang. The aunt must have expected us. We rode up to the fifth floor in a small self-service elevator, pungent with disinfectant.

Miss Percy was a blue-eyed southern lady, her prominent white head set on wire-tight vocal chords.

"Pleased to meet you, Mitchell." She seated me at the dinette table facing the streetlight. After she started up her teakettle, my father gave her the card of buttons.

"Charlotte will love these, Philly," she assured him, holding them close to the light against the old button. "I'll send them along first thing. She's still in Cincinnati with Sammy Kaye, playing the Belle Queen Plaza. Held over. Second time."

"Wonderful news," Philly responded, up on *wonderful*, down on *news*.

"She's a fine singer, fine girl, Charlotte."

Philly's liquid eyes agreed. But what could he do, what could he have done to keep her in New York? They fell in love, such opposites. She had never been intimate with a Jewish man, nor he with a tall gentile woman. They spent entire weekends together in October, up in 2209 or walking in the park before she went on stage.

Manhattan became their joy until Charlotte received an invitation from Sammy Kaye to be lead singer on his winter road tour. The prospect of three months without her cut deeply into Philly's new peace of mind. He was desperate to keep her in New York but knew she had come to the city and sung at the Park Central to land just such a job with a big band. Her leaving him this way meant she had succeeded professionally. Philly was bereft. He couldn't leave with her, go on the road for many months more than three probably, hang around the dance floors; it was out of the question. He couldn't leave Harry in charge of Bookland for more than eight hours or they'd both spend the rest of their lives in Bellevue. Could he marry Charlotte, keep her in the city as a singer, as his wife? Was that possible? Only in Rogers and Hammerstein, not Rogers and Hart.

Charlotte wrote Philly long letters, then postcards from the road. She asked him to find the new black buttons for her favorite dress, his favorite dress, knowing Philly's good taste in accessories would guide him. He haunted old tailor shops and wholesale notions houses. When he found a set of nearly identical buttons, he took them to Miss Percy, Charlotte's maiden aunt. She had always been kind, approving. She understood Philly's heartbreak as well as her niece's ambition. She prepared camomile tea, her specialty.

* * *

"Mitchell, have some, it's delicious, won't keep you up. It's made from flowers," she assured me.

"Thank you." I took the cup and looked around the spare, dark room, through the orange fire escape into the street, while the grown-ups talked about Charlotte.

When we finally said good-bye and went back to the hotel, it was very cold out. The camomile only lasted one block. I was frozen as we swept into the Park Central lobby. Upstairs, in my flannel pajamas, under two woolen blankets, I thawed out.

"Tomorrow Grandma Woolf is coming over to visit. Have a good night. Sleep fast." My father kissed my forehead.

"Will she make us liver?"

"In our kitchenette? We don't have proper utensils. He touseled my large head on the pillow. "Still hungry?"

"Remember how she used to come to Walton Avenue on Sunday and make calf's liver her special way?" I continued, undaunted.

"Without the veins . . . like butter." My father was remembering, savoring the taste.

"How could she get them out?"

"A razor-sharp knife and patience."

I remembered her, tiny and crisp in a neat apron.

"How does she get here from Newark?"

"The tubes."

"You mean in those cans . . . like at Stern's when they make change?" I was thinking of their pneumatic tube system that sucked cylinders of money along the entire store and through the floorboards into a main cash register room. Even Grandma Woolf was too big for such a capsule.

"Dope, it's just like the subway." He was laughing.

"Then why call it the tubes?"

"Because it runs under the Hudson in a tube."

"Oh." Why were grownups such schmucks about naming things?

"How does she get to the store, then? All by herself?"

"On a crosstown bus or by foot. She's a tough customer, your grandmother. Now, good night, Mitchell!"

I thought about her in the darkness. She was three inches shorter than my father, but slender, maybe eighty-four pounds in all. She had his large nose and deep mouth lines, the same impeccable grooming. Her woolen coat and black dresses never had a speck of lint on them. Her calfskin shoes always had a deep shine. The total effect was one of decorum; white hair, washed and set before each journey, rimless glasses pinched to the bridge of her nose, pale water-blue eyes. Her soft voice still carried Liverpool undertones, modified by Yiddish inflections. Leah Woolf would materialize punctually in Bookland for her monthly visit, a tidy apparition popped up from the maw of Times Square.

"Mummy!" My father was always surprised. "How was the journey? You're looking well."

"I could use a spot of tea, Philly." She would adjust the long pin in her black hat and wait to be escorted to Schrafft's.

Since my enrollment in the Lake Ronkonkoma School, Grandma Woolf and I had drawn closer. Her annual birthday card with a crisp five-dollar bill tucked inside started it. I always wrote a thank-you note back. She answered me in real letters. Once a month I received her large yellow envelopes with *Master Mitchell Woolf* elegantly scripted in blue ink. Thus our actual conversations when we met in the bookstore, in the hotel or at Uncle Alfie's grand parties on his East Orange estate were hardly perfunctory. We were becoming good friends, eager to exchange news. Unfortunately Grandma Woolf was shy on ceremonial occasions. The trick was to get her alone. She knew everything about the past.

So I was not disappointed when the following afternoon she rang our 2209 doorbell at five-thirty without my father beside her. He was tied up in the store as usual.

"He'll be along," she assured me.

I helped her out of her soft woolen coat, its collar fringed with a circle of black Persian lamb. I hung it up carefully in the foyer closet, overcome by the special aroma of the garment. I followed it into the living room. It was Grandma Woolf's own sweet, dry smell. She gave me a two-pound box of freshly made chocolates.

"From Gruenwald's, been in Newark forty years, your deddy's favorites."

I struggled with the taut red and white string until she undid it for me. I tore off the tissue paper, exposing a layer of dark chocolate candies: pecan clusters, hand-dipped orange peels, paper-thin mints. The pecans nestled in a soft caramel and had a familiar taste and texture, but the chocolate surrounding them was different, unlike the milk chocolate miniatures Grandma Lufkin bought for her Shabbas-eve parties. These were very sweet at first, but had a bitter, almost powdery aftertaste that made them more difficult to swallow than milk chocolate. Undaunted, I worked my way down the top layer.

"Don't spoil your appetite, Mitchell," Grandma Woolf scolded playfully as I reached for yet another fistful of chocolates, orange peels this time. I paused, alarmed at the hard sour rind in my mouth. I washed the flavor away with a final runny mint.

"Would you like some tea, Grandma?" I asked, remembering her habit.

"Just a spot. I'll help you. Where's the kettle?"

We went into the kitchenette together, found the pot, tea bags, cups and saucers and watched the pot come to a boil as if a miracle were occurring.

"Will you join me in a cup, Mitchell?"

"Yes, Grandma." Tea was not my normal beverage, but when she brewed it, put proper amounts of sugar and milk into the cup and stirred them, it was a treat.

Resettled in the living room on the couch facing Central Park, she relished her life-sustaining cup of tea, took deep sips, breathed in the milky hot fumes and looked around the room at ease.

"Did my father start violin lessons at my age?" I asked suddenly, wanting to learn about him before sharing my Lake Ronkonkoma news.

"Your deddy took his first lesson when he was five."

"Five," I repeated in wonderment. "He must have been cute." Tiny, I meant to say, but politeness prevented my drawing attention to his size.

"The women in the market wanted to take him home, he had

such lovely curls, but they were gone when he was five. I had them cut off. We bought him a quarter fiddle. All the boys started lessons at five. Alfie, the piano, Tootsie, the clarinet, but Philly, your deddy, had real talent. His teachers told us right away. He had to practice every day."

"Did he like playing every day?"

"Not always. It wasn't easy. He was a good boy, though. He practiced."

"Is that why he went on the stage?"

"It certainly helped, but I was against his leaving school to play."

"How did he do it, then?"

"Well, I had this friend, Mrs. Berlinger, she belonged to our temple, Beth Torah, very nice woman—clean, intelligent. Her son, Milton, was a singer, two years younger than your deddy. Milton had also won a few amateur night contests at the RKO and received an offer to join the Gus Edwards's School Days Review. I told Mrs. Berlinger I didn't want Philly leaving school to travel so he could play his fiddle; it worried me. She said, 'Mrs. Woolf, I'm going with Milton myself for just that reason, to make sure he does his schoolwork, eats well and stays clean. I'd be glad to watch your Philly also.' They were like brothers, shared a Pullman berth, ate and did schoolwork together. Philly even graduated with his own class from Barringer High School. For almost two years they were on the road. I never worried. Mrs. Berlinger and I were friends for years afterward, even when Milton became a big star and changed his name to Berle."

I was dizzy.

"Tell me about New Zealand, the earthquakes . . . San Francisco."

She could start at any point on their trip around Cape Horn on a British steamer. There were always new incidents, details I had never heard before.

"Your grandfather Nathan was selling clothing—he was a drummer, really—in the backwoods of New Zealand; the bush practically. There was nothing for him in Liverpool when we left England after the Boer War. The mills were quiet, times were very tough. With a family he had to take a chance, had to earn a living. So there I was in the house with three boys, your deddy was two, Alfie five, Tootsie, I was still nursing him . . . all alone for days. Nate was off with his samples, always away from home, traveling, working. At night our doors were wide open for any breeze. Lions walked through them into the hallway, past the boys' rooms and out into the back bush again."

My mouth went slack on *lions*. Grandma Woolf didn't miss a beat.

"Then one day the earth broke apart, shook the house to the ground it seemed. We left after the next quake. I told Nate the lions and tigers trotting through the hallways at night were one thing. We were half-asleep, they didn't bother us, we didn't bother them. But the earth breaking open under my feet . . . that was beyond the pale!"

"Then you went to San Francisco?" I wanted the rest of the saga.

"Yes, in 1906. Perfect haven from earthquakes. *A mosel oyb Columbus.*" She threw her little hands in the air and slipped into the kitchenette for more hot water.

Did she know the present as well? I wondered.

"Do you ever see Grandma Lufkin?" I asked.

"No, no more, only at the wedding, your *bris*, the funeral." She paused, realizing how recent that was. The two women really had had little in common over the years except for birth and death, no small talk.

"Nice family, the Lufkins. Very tall." She raised her hand, wiggled her fingers toward the ceiling. "Professionals, doctors, very big." Fingers twinkling again. "Do you see them?" she asked me.

"Not too often anymore." I recalled my recent visits to Washington Heights. I was uncomfortable with the present also.

Precisely why our next meeting was such a surprise. It took place in the same living room two months later. I could see the black branches of the trees in the park from my radiator perch. I couldn't take my eyes off their configurations because I didn't want to look at what was taking place in our living room. Bea was sitting on the couch alongside my father. Grandma Woolf was in a wing chair next to her. They knew each other, were intimate, Bea drinking black coffee, puffing her Chesterfield, Grandma stirring her tea. They exchanged news like old friends. I wouldn't turn around even when they spoke to me.

"Bea and your deddy are in love, Mitchell," Grandma Woolf gently announced on her third attempt to include me.

"So?" I pouted into the windowpane.

"They want to get married." The word *married* echoed in the room, yet no one moved their lips.

I froze, tight. My father wanted . . .

"Mitchell, they would like your approval," Grandma Woolf continued with even more delicacy.

I was stunned. Words held in abeyance. The trees, the cars, the pedestrians were all pointless figurines. Why did they continue making the effort I could no longer make? I watched their pathetic motions, mesmerized.

"Mitchell, can't you answer Grandma?" my father said to my back. "Come on, don't be like this." He was embarrassed, frustrated.

I had never felt so betrayed, disconsolate.

Bea seemed surprised. I guessed Philly and my grandmother had predicted an immediate and favorable response—wishful thinking. And Bea had done her part, written three chatty letters to soften me up, tried to smooth over the basketball imbroglio, made a more successful tomato surprise.

"Maybe you want to think about it for a few minutes, Mitchell," my father said.

Philly had definitely taken his own time, thought about it for at least six weeks, from December into January, in a rational, weighing-all-the-alternatives manner. Bea could make them, him, a good home in the hotel. He wouldn't have to go out for dinner every night, spend so much money on dreck. She could look after Mitchell on vacations, take better care of him. These were the obvious considerations as their relationship progressed after a chance introduction at a Harlem Books cocktail party. Bea, a friend of a saleman's girl friend, was just back from a wartime secretarial job with the OPA in Washington. Philly's thoughts about wedlock had developed during five weeks of keeping company, dutifully taking Bea home to Brooklyn after they finally slept together at 2209.

Philly was overwhelmed by Bea's need, her unsophisticated pleasure and gratitude. She was seven years younger than he, thirty-eight. Pretty, with an expressive face, wide hipped, a mere inch taller than he. She had had a violent, abortive marriage immediately after high school and little subsequent experience with men. Philly's gentleness, his quiet manliness released her body. She was appreciative, hungry beyond his or her imaginings. She devoured the little man in her circle: full lips, dappled breasts, soft belly, plump thighs. Her convulsive, tight orgasms reverberated through his spine. He couldn't forget her in the store. The soft flapping body, his penis stiffened yet again inside her moist folds. She adored him, Philly, all of him . . . imagine!

Though Charlotte enjoyed his company, she had relished other men as well. Yet Bea cleaved to him, her hunger a permanence. She was euphoric, proud of her new man, Philly. She had almost given up on the gender after years of sisterhood mixers and a random string of 4F lawyers and accountants in Washington. Bea was through with the blind-dating scene. To avoid it, she even moved back into her parents' three-story frame house in Flatbush when she returned to New York. They and her older sister had also given up on her as a future wife and homemaker. Poor Bea would probably remain the family spinster, give her nieces and nephew thoughtful birthday presents, take them to Saturday afternoon concerts; unobtrusively keep an eye on her aging parents and her kid brother just out of the Army, also living at home. She was no doubt a top stenographer, a whiz-bang typist, had the makings of an executive secretary, commuting on the BMT early every morning. But men . . . a husband? Not in the picture, was the family consensus.

It was thus a triumphant turning of the tables when Bea presented Philly to her family the second Friday in January. They all saw and approved of the dapper retail merchant from Times Square, a widower, a *mensch*.

"So books is a good business?" Pop Kagle asked him. "Not seasonal like woodwork?"

"People turn pages, read all year." Philly winked.

Mom Kagle, more literate and worldly than her master carpenter husband, was charmed by Philly's obvious good taste; he was so unlike her son-in-law, Bruce, the scrambling accountant. Bea's sister, Marion, was ambivalent, relieved yet envious. How did she do it, the scamp? And getting out yet!

Philly, thus certified, was Bea's passport out of Brooklyn, the ticket she had to have for survival. The kid, Mitchell, as she learned to call him easily enough, would not be a problem. She was fond of children, enjoyed an effortless rapport with her sisters' kids. Her strategy crystallized after their Friday evening en famille, and she began to pressure Philly urgently for a decision. After all, a nice Jewish girl from Brooklyn just couldn't sleep with a man every weekend in his midtown hotel suite. A matrimonial conclusion had to be somewhere in the cards. Philly resisted her haste. Charlotte had certainly opened him up for Bea's companionship, but not quite for marriage, and Mitchell wasn't prepared at all. Not for a new mother after seven months. He didn't seem particularly fond of Bea. Or would he treat any woman friend of Philly's as a threat?

These doubts were resolved at the end of the month when, as a quid pro quid, Philly took Bea over to Jersey to meet the remnant of his family: Mummy, brother Alfie, and Gracie, his wife. Alfie had alluded inadvertently to Philly's affair with Charlotte one evening when Leah was a guest in his home. It was nothing serious, he added offhandedly, just a dalliance with a tall beautiful singer. Not Jewish, Leah scanned instantly. She was troubled but didn't meddle. Meeting Bea was thus a relief. Leah sensed the life-sustaining possibilities of their relationship. A wife, a mother, an end to the kind of loneliness she herself had endured since Nate had died twelve years ago. She had been in her fifties then. Her sons, grown, married men. It would have been unseemly for her to marry, and no one could replace Nate, her teenage Liverpool beau, anyway. But Philly was still a young man with a son to bring up.

Alfie and Gracie were not as impressed. They perceived the emotional hunger just beneath Bea's secretarial couture. It made them squirm. Leah surprisingly labeled the same excess as animal vitality. It was the essential ingredient for happiness in all the romantic fiction she had read since Philly had opened Bookland.

A few weeks later, just before Mitchell came home for the weekend, Leah had lunch at Rosoff's with Philly and Bea, both now ready to set a date for their wedding day. The only problem was how to tell Mitchell.

"He doesn't know your plans?" Leah was surprised. "Any of this?"

"He may suspect. I don't know for sure," Philly admitted.

"You never discussed it with him, talked with him?"

"Not directly."

Leah, puzzled, shook her tiny head from side to side.

"I didn't know how to go about it, Mummy. He's away most of the time. . . . He was hostile whenever Bea was with me."

Leah still shook her head from side to side, thinking, thinking. "Maybe, maybe let me tell him," she volunteered. "I could try to explain. He's such a good boy, sensitive. *Nu*, Philly? When will he be home?" She was in charge now, the matriarch. "If the wedding is March 10, it had better be soon!"

Philly was surprised at her decisiveness; he had been too young to remember the steamer trip across the Pacific, the transcontinental train ride to Newark.

"This Friday afternoon he comes back from school for the weekend," he responded.

"Good, I'll take the tubes over. We'll have tea and sweets from Gruenwald's. I'll buy fresh Saturday afternoon."

"Don't forget to polish your shoes, Mummy."

Her eyes twinkled, head no longer shaking.

"Mitchell, what do you think now?" Grandma Woolf broke the quiet hiatus, my time-out in front of the living room windows. "Do they have your blessings?" She was determined to get my assent.

I was inside the playground cliffs, part of the landscape, buried alive.

"Have you lost your tongue, Mitchell?" my father snapped.

"Bea wants to make you a nice home, take care of you and your deddy. You can't live here alone all the time." Grandma Woolf persisted.

"Why not?" It seemed like a perfect deal to me. *Our* deal.

"It's not right without a woman. You'll understand when you're older."

"It's *me*," Bea exploded from her side of the couch. "He doesn't like *me!*" Her face was red, her brown irises engorged.

"Easy, Bea, easy." Philly tried to calm her as large tears splashed from her eyes.

That scared me, a grown woman crying, bawling in the living room.

"Mitchell, you've hurt her. She only means good for you," Grandma Woolf explained.

"*So?*" I sassed, a trifle defensive, guilt working for their side now.

"So, say yes, they can get married, they have your permission!"

"I'm not a rabbi."

"Mitchell, please. . . . You love me, don't you?" Leah continued, undaunted.

"Yes."

"Trust Grandma Woolf. I love Bea. She's good for your deddy and will be for you. I wouldn't make you do a bad thing."

I turned and looked into her little face. I was crying now. Leah came toward my perch. I met her halfway, still crying.

"It's okay," I blurted out. "I don't care anymore. They can do whatever they want."

She tried to hug me, but her arms couldn't reach around me. She grabbed at my shoulders instead, reached up to dry my eyes with her lace handkerchief.

"You're a sweet boy, Mitchell, a good boy." She kissed my mouth with her thin, soft lips.

I still couldn't look back at the couch. Bea had stopped sniffling. My father must have been at her side with his big cotton handkerchief.

I wasn't invited to the wedding. It took place in March. Bea probably didn't want me there, afraid of my hatred or competition, as if my father would have had two brides to choose from. I was back at Lake Ronkonkoma, unaware of the exact date but certain the event would occur.

Chapter
Three

◆◆◆

THEY WERE DEFINITELY married when I returned for spring vacation six weeks later. I went directly to the Park Central instead of going to Bookland. Bea welcomed me with a wet kiss, which I deflected toward the side of my face. Her nose snuggled against my earlobe.

"Welcome home, Mitchell."

"Hi." No sound formed a name for her.

"Such a big boy!" She was thrilled, charged. "Do they have a stretching machine at that school?"

"No, just lousy food and team sports."

She smiled.

"Sense of humor, just like your father. Go unpack, then tell me everything while I fix dinner. Your letters are so brief."

Dinner—the letters flashbulbed around the inside of my skull like a Times Square headline. How could she make it in the hotel suite?

In the bedroom the colors had been softened to accommodate Bea. A floral spread lay on the large double bed. A beige fitted cover replaced the dark corduroy one on my daybed sofa. Both mahogany dresser bureaus were draped with lace scarves.

I quickly placed my shirts and socks in my father's half-filled bottom drawer. The second closet was now full of Bea's clothing, so I hung my pants and good suit in my father's closet, smiling as I stepped among his gleaming shoes. The moment my clothes were settled in, I was drawn back to Bea's culinary preparations, like a lemming to the sea.

Our five by four kitchenette was intended as a service pantry for busy hotel guests, not a work place in which to prepare full course dinners. There was no gas stove, only counter space for a hot plate plugged into an electric outlet precariously near the sink. The icebox was half the size of Grandma Lufkin's, but it was a real one, standing on the floor reaching four feet up toward the wall cabinets, the one generous component of the kitchenette. These framed the sink-icebox side as well as the entire left wall of the tiny room.

Bea was working over a quartered chicken on the left counter top, preparing it for cooking. Where? I wondered. Even though our old single burner hot plate had been replaced by a shiny chrome two burner, there was no oven underneath it.

"Broiled chicken." Bea indicated the bird with a sharp knife. "Your father loves the way I make it."

Where? I still wondered. Both burners had simmering pots on them. One smelled like cream of mushroom soup, and the other was a teakettle.

"Ronson's not coming back to Lake Ronkonkoma next year." I relaxed into my news.

"Why not?" Bea continued scraping nodules of fat from inside the broiler's thighs.

"He's not learning enough, not catching up to his grade."

"Which one?"

She turned right, pulled a bag of fresh string beans from the icebox and began washing them off in the sink.

"Sixth, like me."

"I like Jack and his parents."

She drained the beans in a new colander.

"Mrs. Ronson says he could learn more and get special help in a different kind of school, live at home."

"She must have looked into it."

"I'll miss him a lot. We've been roommates for three years."

Bea darted out of the kitchenette toward the living room. When I peered in, she was hunched over a stained oak table placed just behind the long sofa facing the window. She was dusting the surface, placing silverware at three settings for dinner.

"No more card table?" I sighed unconsciously to myself.

"This is much better, Mitchell, sturdy, for real meals."

"Did you throw it out?"

"No, no, it's still in the back of the hall closet, for cards."

I edged toward the new table, hypnotized by the chaste silverware. It wasn't hotel nickelplate. Bea noticed my stare.

"It's Gorham sterling flatware from Mom and Pop Kagle, a wedding present. Philly and I . . . your father, I mean, picked the pattern."

"It's beautiful," I had to agree. But how could anyone eat a meal with silver jewelry?

"You'll meet them on Monday night. We're going to Brooklyn for the first night of Pesach."

"What about Grandma Lufkin's?" We usually went there before my mother got sick. All my cousins came, Robert, Douglas, Marshall.

Bea was back in the kitchenette. I heard the faucets turn, water washing through the drain.

"What about Grandma Lufkin?" I yelled into the kitchenette. But she had vanished into the bedroom with the chicken parts before I got there. A trail of fatty water spots indicated her path. I wasn't sure. After all, why would anyone carry raw chicken into our bedroom? I couldn't just scream out my question about Grandma Lufkin's seder until I knew where to aim it. The bedroom door was almost shut. I heard pot ware clattering out of the closet. She must be in there. *She* . . . Bea. What would I *call* her?

"Ahem, ahem." I rustled against the door, trying to get her attention, save myself the embarrassment of naming her.

"Ahem, ahem . . . Bea." I peeped, uncomfortable with that choice.

"I'm in here. You can come in" echoed from deep inside the bedroom.

I pushed open the door. Bea was kneeling beside the round coffee table on the window side of their bed. She had placed the quartered chicken on the table alongside an enormous aluminum appliance that rose in circular layers toward a flat top. The cover part had three metal prongs coming out the back end and a long wooden handle on the front. She looked up at me, directly into my eyes, as I walked toward her.

"Please call me Mommy, Mitchell. That would make sense."

"What about Grandma Lufkin's seder?"

"She's not having hers this year."

"Oh. Is she sick?"

"No."

"Can I go up to see her?"

"We'll ask your father when he comes home. Maybe I could meet her some—"

"I go myself on the A train, twenty minutes from Times Square."

Bea lifted the aluminum cover off the base of the appliance and set it belly up near the chicken. I peered inside the cover. Its head was just like the top of our hot plate, gray coils embedded in hard white clay.

"What does it do?"

"It's a broiler."

"How does it work?"

"I place the chicken pieces on the bottom trivet." She began doing it. "Garnish with seasoning." She sprinkled salt, pepper and a little garlic powder on both sides of each piece. "Then I place the cover on top, push this brown socket onto the prongs like this and plug the other end into the wall adapter outlet." Bea didn't push the plug into the adapter but left it dangling on the carpet.

"Why did you stop?" I asked. I wanted to see the coils redden upside down.

"I can't start it till I know the minute your father will be home. It broils in fifteen minutes, and Philly loves his food hot, not warm, when he walks through the door.''

"I know all about that." She had my sympathy. "Why do you cook it here?''

"There's only one outlet in the kitchenette, and with the icebox and the hot plate plugged into it already, there's no room. Besides, the broiler's AC and needs the special adapter we have in here for the radio. It draws a lot of juice. We can't overload the lines, blow a fuse. DC is tricky.''

The Park Central was still on a direct current electrical system. Most postwar appliances were AC, needing alternating current. In order to use them, we plugged special adapter switches into the wall outlets which transformed the direct current to alternating so an appliance could operate on its proper frequency.

"Let's get the string beans ready." She flipped into the kitchenette. I followed her. She drained the tap water off the beans.

"Where will you cook them? Both burners already have pots on them.''

"In this." She pulled a new pot from the top cupboard, presenting it like a magician, hands waving each section before my eyes.

"It's a pressure cooker. Only has to heat up two minutes, then steam cooks the beans in seconds.''

The entire pot was a heavy-gauge alloy. Its cover was rimmed with thick rubber, which made the inner chamber airtight when the bottom pot and top cover handles were screwed together. A quarter-inch rod with a center hole leading directly inside the pot rose from the middle of the cover.

"I put this indicator on top of the rod to measure the steam pressure. You can help me, Mitchell.''

"How?''

"Tell me when you see the second red line on the rising pole.''

"What pole?''

"You'll see. It comes out when I put the pot on the burner. It's fun.''

The telephone rang in the bedroom. Bea placed the stubby indicator on the counter top and dried her hands on her apron as she moved toward the phone.

"Philly, hi. . . . I'll put him on. . . . Sure, sure. . . . Fine, fine, we're having a good time. When are you leaving? Five minutes? Definite? Promise? Five? So I'll figure fifteen you'll be home. I don't want to wreck everything again. Okay, Phil. Mitchell, it's your father, come say hello."

"Hi, Dad."

"Mitchell, how are you?"

"Okay. Okay."

"Are you and Bea getting along?"

"Sure, sure, everything's fine."

"Terrific. I'll be home in fifteen minutes. I want to hear all your news."

"Ronson's not coming back next year."

"Oh?"

"I may ask Rafferty to be my roommate."

"The new Irish kid?"

"Yeah."

"Mitchell, the Broadway trolley's just outside the door. 'Bye."

I reentered the foyer. Bea was whirling, darting back and forth like a dervish. Into the kitchenette, back to the dining table, out to the broiler.

"Bring me the butter, Mitchell," she yelled from the bedroom.

"Where is it?"

"In the icebox, for Christsakes."

She grabbed the fresh stick from my hand, smeared slivers of it onto the chicken sections. She plugged the broiler in and placed the cover over the chicken before I could see the coils inside the top cover redden. I heard them crackle on.

"Gotta start the beans." She raced back to the kitchenette, and I followed, magnetized by her energy. She poured a mere cup of water into the pressure cooker, spilled all the raw string beans into it, screwed the cover on, dropped the stubby indicator onto its post, took the teakettle off the burner and placed the pot next to the soup.

"Now, Mitchell, call me the instant you see the second red line on the pole."

I was paralyzed, not knowing what to expect or look for. Electric hot plates were confusing enough without putting new contraptions on them. Bea went back into the bedroom. After two minutes which seemed like an hour and a half, I could hear the cup of water come alive inside the pot, but the indicator was dormant.

Hssssss, hssssss. Vicious spurts of steam erupted from the base of the indicator, yet no pole emerged from its center. I froze, wanting to call for Bea yet unable to say her name, like at the end of a bad war dream. Then the pole began to rise. I saw one red line, then the second.

"You . . . you . . . yoo-hoo." I struggled with her name. *"Bea!"* I screamed running into the next room. "The second red line shows."

She was turning the chicken, grease smoke in her face. She held the broiler cover aloft in her left hand, turning the charred bird raw side up. The coils inside the cover were incandescent. Bea's face was scarlet from the heat, dripping wet.

"Jesus Christ, don't let that pot blow up, Mitchell. Take it off the burner right away!"

I raced back to the kitchenette and tried to remove it with a towel, but the live steam scared me. Bea suddenly reached in and grabbed the pot over my shoulder just as the pole reached an ominous fourth line. She placed the pressure cooker gently on the counter top. The metal pole slowly descended.

"Phew . . . close." She was spent.

Briiiing, briiiing. We both realized it was my father. I tried to move past her to open the door.

"I'll get it. . . . Commmming," she answered, undoing her apron and touching up the sides of her hair with her fingertips. "Commmming." She wiped a mustache of sweat from her upper lip and opened the door. "Philly." She embraced him. "Dinner will be ready in three minutes, by the time you wash up."

"Where's Mitchell? he asked.

Next in line, I rushed into his arms. He was chewing Dentyne and needed a shave. He looked terrific in his topcoat and hat.

"How are you, Mitchell? Do my shoes still fit you?"

We laughed together.

"Phil, wash up before everything burns. Mitchell, get the stick of butter, put it on this plate and take it in to the table . . . *please?*"

While my father hung up his coat and headed toward the bathroom I went to the broiler, empty plate in hand, looking for the stick of butter. I found a sodden puddle; the broiler had melted it back to liquid yellow. I scooped the translucent paper wrapper onto the plate and brought the butter residue in to the kitchenette.

"It melted."

"Why did you leave it there? It's ruined! The whole meal! No butter for the beans!" She opened the icebox door. "Wait, wait, here's another stick. Take it directly to the table."

"Wasn't my fault it melted. You were using it."

"Don't talk back, just take it in, or must I do everything around here?"

"*Everything,* huh?" I muttered into the sofa as I dropped the butter dish in the center of the festive dinner table. I waited near the sofa, wronged, wounded, not knowing which seat was mine until my father bounded in, refreshed from washing up.

"Mitchell, you sit here." He tousled my hair and nudged me toward the chair against the wall. He was next to me before the wide middle section of the table facing the window.

"Bea likes to sit here." He pointed to the end of the table opposite me. "So she's close to the kitchen." (He no longer called it a kitchenette.)

"So, Mitchell, how's Lake Ronkonkoma? You look healthy enough." He was pleased.

"Ronson's not coming back next year."

"You said on the telephone. Too bad . . . nice boy."

"His mom's putting him in a special school for slow learners."

"Where?"

"In the city."

"No more rides."

"No more roommate!"

"You'll get a new one. It works out."

"I was thinking of Rafferty."

"And I—"

"Soup's on." Bea entered with two steaming bowls of creamed mushroom soup, then rushed back for her own portion.

"Hot enough, Philly?" she cooed as my father savored each steaming spoonful.

"Perfect. Delicious, babe. Isn't it, Mitchell?"

I could barely swallow mine it was so hot, but it was tasty. I nodded approval.

"Wait till you taste my mother's matzo ball soup Monday night." She left the room to get the main course ready as my father finished his soup.

"*She* told me Grandma Lufkin's not having a seder this year."

"Oh." My father seemed surprised by the news as well as by my use of the feminine pronoun.

"When can I go see her?"

"Next week sometime, or after the holiday."

"How is she?"

"Fine . . . I guess."

Bea reentered with a serving bowl of bright green string beans; like technicolor compared to the canned variety at Lake Ronkonkoma. Three dollops of butter melted through them. Next came the sizzling platter of broiled chicken.

"Mitchell likes dark meat, the drumstick, don't you?" my father asked.

I nodded yes.

Bea obliged with a large one still attached to the thigh section. It seemed like I had half a chicken on my plate. I wasn't used to that configuration or the burned condition of the skin. I assumed the inside would be well done, dry, unlike Grandma Lufkin's stewed chicken meat, which slipped off the bone.

Hot juices erupted when I sank my knife and fork into the thigh, cutting down toward the drumstick joint, where streaks of blood came out of the socket, melding with the yellow grease. *It's still raw,* I flashed, but I got the initial forkful into my mouth. The bird was moist, slightly undercooked, yet tender, gamy. I'd never experienced such a taste. I was not as squeamish with the next forkful, or the next or the next or the next. Couldn't stop eating, hacking, sopping up the chicken skin and juices.

"He must like it, Philly." They looked at me, pleased, yet alarmed. I had worked my way down to the bone. My cheeks were glistening as I looked up, sucking the naked drumstick.

"Wipe your cheeks, Mitchell," my father reminded me. "Use your napkin . . . the napkin, that's it!"

I smiled up at them.

"Want some more?" Bea offered. "There's still another drumstick inside."

She and my father liked white meat, so they'd each had part of the breast section on their plates.

"Sure, I'll have more. Seconds." I laughed.

"Seconds!" She left the table in triumph.

"Better than the tomato surprise." My father nudged my kneecap under the table.

I reddened, nodding my head. "Much."

"Here, see what you can do with this." Back in the living room, Bea cut the drumstick from the thigh with a brown kitchen knife. It was even better than the first piece. I longed for the remaining section. Bea caught my eyes and answered them.

"Go ahead, take it, Mitchell, that's what it's for . . . to eat."

I sliced into it, mixing the crisp skin with the green beans. Seconds unlimited . . . what a deal!

"Mitchell, don't make yourself sick. It'll still be here tomorrow," my father cautioned, alarmed at my greed.

Dangerously stuffed, unable to identify the new broiled taste any longer, I paused, examined the partially eaten thigh and replaced it on the serving platter, acknowledging my father's admonition. I rested while the grownups finished eating. I imagined the disconnected broiler in the bedroom, the empty pressure cooker in the kitchenette, the teakettle simmering on the hot plate in its place. Bea had transformed our two room suite into a working kitchen. I was sated, drowsy for sleep.

* * *

"Didn't I tell you, Philly?" Bea poked her elbow into the side of his dark pinstripe jacket as he swallowed one of Mom Kagle's porous matzo balls.

"The soup too. The soup is so rich," my father murmured, adding to the chorus of praise coming from the seder table. "Not like midtown dishwater."

"Thank you." Mrs. Kagle was gratified. "I use real chicken for the base, meat still on the carcasses. No bouillon cubes. I let it simmer all afternoon. Three chickens."

"And the matzo balls. How do you make them so light?" My father continued his praise.

"That's my secret." She smiled at Philly from her end of the table next to the kitchen door. "All the way from Galicia."

"Mom, you got it from *The Joy of Cooking*," Marion joshed. "What is this old country routine?"

"Shh, shh, not so loud."

Indeed, Mom Kagle seemed quite modern. Though her hair was white, she wore it parted on the side in an attractive brushed out style. She was full of information and questions about the world, vibrant. She listened to WQXR all day in her enormous yellow kitchen. Drove a car, paid bills with checks, managed the entire household.

Pop Kagle was more European with his thick working man's forearms, balding round head and broken immigrant English.

"Vait, vait, Philly, you'll taste the brisket," he promised from his serving end of the table, where he sliced generous portions for everyone.

"And the kugel," added Myron, the six-foot-four baby brother, veteran of both the European and Pacific wars.

"And the kasha," chimed in Bruce, Marion's accountant husband.

It was exceptional food. Not so heavy as Grandma Lufkin's, with nonkosher touches like green salad, rolls and butter. I ate at a special children's table with Marion and Bruce's two younger children: Josh, eight, a tiny monkey-faced live wire, and Dianne, a serious junior-high adolescent with thick brown hair and large blue eyes. Their older sister, Jessica, a senior at Midwood High School, was at the table between her Uncle Myron and Pop Kagle, drinking Manischewitz with them. She was full-breasted, dark with light gray eyes.

It was so unusual being part of a family celebrating Passover in a three-story wood-frame house surrounded by maple, oak and sycamore trees. So American; a screened-in front porch, a long, narrow driveway leading to a two-car garage with basketball net and backboard screwed over the doors, two-wheeler bicycles everywhere. It was difficult to imagine this holiday Brooklyn as Bea's home. Everyone was comfortable, almost small-town.

After the main course the women, Marion, Bea, Mom Kagle and Jessica, cleared away the dishes and set out the dessert plates. The men strolled into the large front parlor, we kids right after them. My father took one of his sweetest corona panatelas from his vest pocket, lit it with his customary affection, sucked the smoke in and released it gently into the couch area. He was seated next to Bruce. Pop Kagle was catty-corner to him in his large blue easy chair. Yellow lace doilies were pinned over the head and arm sections where the slipcovers were threadbare. The men sniffed the aroma of my father's cigar, eyeing its circle of smoke with such pleasure, he offered them his three remaining ones, an unusual gesture on his part. Bruce took one, chewed the tip while my father lit the front end. Pop Kagle wasn't a smoker, but he knew his son Myron, who was just slouching into the parlor, would appreciate a quality cigar.

"Mikey, try one of Philly's cigars."

My father offered him one, which he accepted.

"Thanks, Phil. Thank you." Myron, like his father, was dressed in a soft open-necked beige sports shirt. He sat on the window radiator cover smiling at the older men, grateful to be at home alive.

"Let's show Mitchell our rooms," Josh suggested, realizing things might get very boring and smoky in the front parlor.

"Yeah," Dianne agreed.

"Last one up is a rotten egg." Josh scurried out of the parlor toward the stairs, where Bea was modeling her trim B. Altman suit, using the stairway bannister as a balance point for her exaggerated prancing. Josh was agile enough to slip beneath her flapping arms. He also knew where he was going. I had no idea and thus focused on his scampering feet, unaware of Bea's swaying form at the bottom of the stairs. Her arm caught the top of my head. This didn't slow me down or hurt me I was so excited by the chase. Bea unfortunately was spun off balance and teetered back against the bannister, shattered by my intrusion. Dianne, next in line behind me (the probable rotten egg), went to Bea's aid.

"I'm sorry, Aunt Bea, we were just playing." She tried to smooth out her suit, move her away from the stairs.

Bea was scarlet with embarrassment, enraged by my casual disruption. She looked up the stairwell to the first landing, unable to spit out the two syllables of my name. Her fury was too profound for enunciation. Besides, it might reveal the strains of her new motherhood to her own sister and mother, who put the blame for her anger justifiably on our entire band.

"Children, apologize to your Aunt Bea," they both implored.

"I'm sorry, Aunt Bea," Josh yelled down from the second floor landing.

"I'm sorry." Dianne sighed, looking into Bea's wild brown eyes.

I said nothing, though I was sorry. Whatever problems I had with "Mommy," she certainly wasn't my Aunt Bea.

"Go play, Dianne, go play. I'm fine." Bea calmed herself, smoothing the suit skirt where it met the jacket around her stocky hips, and resumed the fashion show. "The blouse is all hand stitched. Philly picked it out with me at Bonwits," she said as we kids hit the third floor landing.

"I win, I win." Josh jumped up and down like a yo-yo. "Here's my room, Mitchell."

"And here's mine," Dianne echoed from a charming book-lined alcove with two dormer windows. "Your . . . I mean, Aunt Bea used to have this room before she married your dad and moved out."

"Does everyone have a separate bedroom?" I asked.

"Yeah, Jessica is on our floor next to the bathroom, where she spends all her time." Josh giggled. "All the grownups are on the second floor. They have larger rooms."

"They *are* bigger," Dianne agreed.

"Want to see, Mitchell? Come on." Josh's monkey eyes twinkled.

We tiptoed through Mom and Pop Kagle's large front bedroom into Josh and Dianne's parents' room. Josh insisted on demonstrating their new clock radio for me despite Dianne's nervous objections. It was a white plastic GE. Josh turned it on. The sound was tinny, unlike that of our wooden Emerson with the green tuning eye.

"Now, listen Mitchell." Josh turned it off and carefully adjusted three tiny knobs. "Pretend you're asleep. Go on, lie down, or it won't go off."

Dianne and I both followed Josh's orders, our faces turned up toward the yellow ceiling, uncertain of the propriety of Josh's demands. The chenille spread was illicit, cool. We looked into each other's eyes and began to smile, then giggle.

"Be quiet, you guys, or you won't hear the alarm!"

These orders made our giggling uncontrollable.

Bzzzz bzzzz bzzzz. "And now a word from our sponsor" blared out of the plastic box. "Rinso white, Rinso bright . . . happy little washday song. Rinso . . ."

Dianne and I rolled around the bed, guffawing out of control. The Rinso song got so much louder, the volume knob was obviously broken. Josh had to disconnect the wall plug.

"Are you three all right up there?" Aunt Marion shouted from downstairs.

"Sure, sure," we yelled back in unison, after which Dianne and I had to gag our mouths with pillows to stifle our shrieks.

"Cut it out you two, please!" Josh implored. "I've got to fix this volume knob, or I'll really get into trouble."

We laughed until we tumbled off the bed . . . *crash!*

"I'm coming up in one minute," Aunt Marion yelled.

"Please," Josh whispered.

The fall and Aunt Marion's threat shocked Dianne and me into responsibility.

"You go downstairs while I try to fix this."

"We'll help you, Josh," Dianne offered.

"No, it's better with you and Mitchell downstairs. They won't suspect anything."

"Okay," we agreed as we left Josh frantically twisting dials.

"No laughing," he admonished sotto voce again.

We walked downstairs poker-faced, trying to be invisible until we made it past the dining room into the front parlor. Fortunately Marion and Bea were stacking dishes and boiling water in the kitchen. Mom Kagle and Jessica were resting at the bare table, which gleamed with the dessert plates and silverware. When Dianne and I caught their eyes, wide grins creased both their faces. Mom Kagle even put her index finger to her lips, indicating caution and whose side she was on. They never commented on Josh's absence, nor did the men in the parlor, now so caught up in conversation they barely acknowledged our reappearance.

"Roosevelt knew how to talk with the Russians," Myron said directly to his brother-in-law, Bruce.

"You mean like at Yalta?" Bruce snapped, his chewed cigar lying dead in a ceramic ashtray. "He gave the whole thing away, just let them take it."

"Bruce, they were there, for Christsakes. The Red Army was all over Berlin, Poland, Prague."

"We let them in at Yalta and crossed the t's at Potsdam."

"The Red Army pushed the Fascisti back to Berlin from Moscow," Pop Kagle erupted. "Twenty million dead, three years alone, they fought Hitler."

"But what about free elections?" Bruce challenged. "Nothing. The Russians don't keep their word."

"It's because of Truman's threats there aren't elections," Myron countered.

"Varmonger, capitalistic bastard," Pop Kagle concluded about the President of the United States, his hammer fists pounding the yellow doilies on his blue easy chair.

"Henry Wallace, he knows how to talk to the Russians the way Roosevelt did. He was supposed to be vice-president, wasn't he?" Myron asked.

"Thank God it was Truman. At least he's not a pinko!" Bruce snapped.

His red-baiting provoked no anger or countercharges. Myron and Pop Kagle had such contempt for Bruce's politics their hostile silence shut him out, so he turned to my silent father, still smoking next to him.

"Philly, how do you feel about Truman?"

"I voted for Governor Dewey."

"But he's a Republican." Now it was Bruce's chance for moral outrage.

"He's a good governor, put in rent control, fair employment before Truman . . . and his voice, rich, baritone—wonderful speaker."

"But Dewey's really bad for the working man, the middle class."

"He's been good for the small businessman in New York City," Philly continued.

"Goot, goot." Pop Kagle looked toward my father's shiny black hair. "You at least vote your real interest. Not like 'the friend' of the working man next to you."

"A regular Lenin, my brother-in-law." Myron tapped Bruce on the shoulder.

"Watch it, kiddo." Bruce hopped up, wiping Myron's large paw off his gabardine jacket. "Pop"—Bruce pointed—"you're doing all right in this country. In Russia no shop, no house, no car."

"No delightful family conversations either," Myron roared. "Free love instead."

"How about dessert, everyone?" Marion popped her head into the parlor. "Hot tea, fresh coffee, homemade pie?"

Dianne and I ran back to our little table hoping Josh would make it downstairs unnoticed. Miraculously he did. Slid into his seat just as his father and the other men walked through the wide oak doorway.

"I fixed it finally," he whispered. "They'll never know."

"Pie, children? Apple or mincemeat?"

We took the lattice-crusted apple; only the grownups could appreciate the bittersweet mince. I noticed my father savoring both the apple and the mince. He had half-portions of each on his plate, and he ate them slowly, satisfied, delighted. He looked around the long table, grinning into Mom Kagle's eyes when they met his gaze, acknowledging his gratitude. She was the model, the source of Bea's culinary skills.

Marion added scoops of vanilla ice cream to our apple pie, which made our table special, a la mode, like a birthday party. Who to sing to was a problem.

"Rinso white, Rinso bright," I began slowly, "happy little washday song."

"Shh, shh," Josh admonished, connecting the jingle to the radio fiasco. "They'll find out."

"How?" I whispered. "It's fixed—only the Shadow knows. Rinso white, Rinso bright," I continued. "Now you start a round, Dianne."

She did, in a strong soprano. "Rinso white, Rinso bright, happy little washday . . ."

"Now you, Josh."

"Rinso, white, Rinso bright, happy little . . ."

The three of us were singing rounds of the jingle. We couldn't stop. Everyone at the big table was watching us enthralled. Tears came into Josh's eyes, then mine, finally Dianne's. We linked arms, swaying, laughing, crying our new friendship.

"Humiliated! In my parents' home! Philly, what are *they* supposed to think of *me* if *he* treats me like that?" Bea pointed her finger directly at me. I was slumped on a jump seat, head resting on the cool taxi window. As we were too late for the Brighton Beach BMT back to the city, my father had magnanimously ordered a taxi.

"He didn't have the decency to apologize! Marion's kids did!" She was foaming now, bubbles of saliva oozing over her lips. "He crashes right into me against the bannister. I could have broken ribs! Disgusting," she screamed at my dark coat. *"Disgusting!"*

The cab driver shut his glass divider.

"Easy, Bea, easy. Everyone had a good time. He didn't mean—"

"And *you.*" She turned straight into my father on the back seat. *"You* let him get away with it! Didn't say a word! Lift a finger!"

"I was in the other room."

"Where it all began, their roughhousing. You don't care."
The Belt Parkway rhythm stilled her momentarily.
"I want him to apologize . . . *now!* Say he's sorry."
I feigned sleep, then passed out against the window.

"Whoever *'gives'* first loses, Woolf."
"How do we know? There's no referee."
"Damn right. Just say 'I give,' if you can still talk."
Freddy Daniels laid down the rules for our battle in the field of second growth pine and hay, west of the softball diamond where our face-off had begun. He was about my height, but heavier, muscular heavy. The toughest seventh grader at Lake Ronkonkoma, in the entire Lower School, for that matter. He placed his wire-rimmed glasses under a fir tree and picked up a gray weather-beaten stick.

"See this, Woolf?" He placed the stick on the left shoulder of his flannel shirt. "When you knock it off, the fight begins. Anything goes."

I was paralyzed, staring at it and then at his unfamiliar naked eyes, blinking, nearsighted. They were ringed purple where the wire frames had touched his tan face, vulnerable yet scary, like a lizard in daylight.

"Just tip it off, touch it, and we can start."

I didn't want to start. I was frightened, unaccustomed to serious combat in private places. In this premeditated duel brought on by Daniels's challenge I was truly alone. He was unpredictable, menacing. He might gouge my eyes out, kick me in the groin, choke me unconscious. What the hell was I supposed to do?

"Listen, I don't want to do this. I didn't mean all those things."

"You called me a shithead, Woolf, you can't deny that. Let's go! Come on! Just touch it off. Breathe on it."

We had been having tryouts on the softball field for the Lower School varsity. I was on first base, where I had played for two seasons on the JV team. I had a long stretch off the bag and good control of my first baseman's mitt. Rafferty was in right field, just behind me. Stevens was tagging fungo fly balls to him. Rocko was in center field, Alexander in left. Daniels, who had mastered the same lightning-fast underarm delivery as the best pitchers in Central Park, was on the mound, zipping the ball across the plate to fat Nesbitt, the catcher. Stevens called time out and then announced two teams for a practice game. Our group out in the field against the second team on the bench plus Stevens, who would play and bat with them for balance. They were up first. Daniels mowed them down with his speed and accuracy until the second inning, when Stevens was up. He batted righty. He caught a piece of Daniel's third fireball, lofting it toward the opposite field. Rafferty got a bead on the ball, but it spun out of his flat little kid's glove, rolling into the woods. By the time he retrieved it, Stevens was coming around third. Jimmy relayed the ball to me, and I lined a one-bounce strike to Daniels covering home plate, but there was no play. Stevens had scored, 1–0. Daniels tore past me out to right field.

"What the hell is wrong with you, Rafferty? Can't you buy a real glove with a pocket?"

"You rich shithead, lay off!" I shot at his back.

He rushed me like a mad bulldog. We wrestled on the base path. Rafferty on top of Daniels now, me underneath. Stevens broke us up.

"We're all on the same team, you guys. We want to beat Kings Park and Center Moriches, not each other! Not on this field!"

After the practice game, which our side ultimately won, 3–1, Daniels approached me on the sideline. I was sitting down on a log bench with Rafferty, Fritz and Ronson. Daniels had a few seventh and eighth graders at his side.

"Let's settle this alone, Woolf. Just you and me. Fair fight. Up there." He pointed toward the west field, where we played ring-a-levio on Saturday nights. He wasn't yelling. It was a straightforward challenge.

"You can take the mother," Rafferty whispered. Fritz concurred with a nod.

"Beat the shit out of the loudmouth for once," Ronson said.

There was no choice, no out. We had marched down the maple-lined path to the west field in fierce silence, Daniels and me.

"Brush it off, just touch it, tip it," Daniels continued, eager for battle.

"You knock it off yourself."

"It's not a fight if I knock it off, you son of a bitch!" Daniels responded to my ridicule.

"That's *my* mother you're insulting, you fuck!" I flipped the gray stick into a tree. We rolled around in the fir needles, pommeling each other. When my filial pride subsided, I was overwhelmed with fears of mortal injury. Daniels maneuvered me into a neck lock, both of our heads together on the ground. I could smell his hair.

"Come on, Woolf, fight back. *Do* something!"

Why? I thought. For what? *She's dead.* I remained silent. A neck lock was pretty safe, a good way to rest in a fight, buy time. Daniels's arm was pressed against the side of my neck, not underneath the Adam's apple in a choke hold, which would have been perilous.

"Give, Woolf, say it. Give!"

I wouldn't respond; the pain was bearable.

"*Say* it!" Daniels squeezed harder. "God damn you!" He was frustrated, realizing he couldn't put more pressure on my neck since I was also squeezing him in a neck lock which he couldn't get out of. Daniels was stymied by our status quo. I was relentless, mute for three minutes, determined to avoid humiliation while Daniels struggled to tighten his grip without success.

"Say it, do *something!*"

Nothing. Silence.

"Okay, I win, Woolf. Don't forget it. I can't spend all day with this chicken-shit stuff." He released my neck. I released his. He sprang up, brushed the pine needles from his stomach, found his glasses, put them on carefully and strode off back to the softball field.

I sat on the ground watching him. It was over. I got up, wiped some tears from underneath my chin. I must have cried. I couldn't remember when. It wasn't near the end. I was calm then. Would he tell the other kids about me? What happened? I hardly knew myself what had happened as I began the long walk back to the softball field trying to forget yet remember the details of our fight.

The other kids had returned to the dorms to wash up and dress for supper. I could see Daniels's fat ass swaggering ahead of me, up the tar road leading to the dormitories. He was skipping rocks through the pine trees by the road, breaking stray sticks with his sneakers, prowling for something to smash.

Daniels didn't tell much about our fight. "He got what was coming to him," was all he offered when asked what happened by a group of seventh and eighth graders playing stoop ball on the North Dorm steps. Then he went directly to his room. He didn't say anything to Ronson, Fritz or Rafferty on my floor either. Perhaps because I didn't "give" and he was merely the self-anointed winner, or maybe during our long mutual neck locks he realized the difference between his bravado and my quiet resistance was a slender one.

I was always confused by my fights. What they revealed made me uncomfortable, nervous. I never looked for trouble; it was always brought to me from outside, like Roger Oaks's harassment when I arrived at Lake Ronkonkoma or slugging it out with Daniels and Gross after Rafferty and I had run over them at the goal line. I fought these battles in public when the issue of right and wrong was clear to me and most of the onlookers. There was safety in their presence, a rough justice guaranteed. But what happened to me when I was right yet all alone, as with Daniels on the field of second growth or Bea in 2209 or the taxicab? Where could I find the courage to fight back when no one else said I had to? When the only voice was my own?

That evening at dinner Daniels brought the entire hall to silence with one of his monthly laughing jags. Something said at his table caught his fancy, and he exploded. Katz asked for seconds in string beans when creamed corn was actually the vegetable. Freddy's wild open-throat response was infectious. We laughed at Daniels laughing which made him roar louder. He was out of control until the absurdity of it all turned in on him and his laughter grew hostile, metallic, a warning for the rest of us to back off.

"She's going with you because of the dentist." My father was annoyed. He knew I didn't believe him.

"Why can't I visit Grandma Lufkin alone? She can take me to the dentist's. She always has. Isn't Cousin Stanley related to her?"

"Bea wants to make sure he takes an X ray of that space between your bottom teeth, get it squared away before camp starts."

"Grandma Lufkin can tell him."

"Well . . ." His hands flew up to his ears. His uncertainty was justified. Grandma Lufkin was normally intimidated by the family professionals she took me to, especially as their services were rendered at a discount fee. But who cared about teeth? I hadn't seen her since April, two months ago. Besides, with Bea along how could I sneak off and play with my cousins? She would be unescorted, lost. Bea had never met the Lufkins, not even Lena. Although she'd certainly heard enough about her culinary magic. She naturally seized this opportunity to observe, confront and hopefully demystify the legendary matriarch I couldn't stop comparing her to when she prepared meals or I consumed them.

We took the IND up to 175th Street. I led Bea along Fort Washington Avenue to Grandma Lufkin's apartment. My dental appointment was set for one-thirty. I was looking forward to a nice dairy lunch.

When Grandma Lufkin opened the door, I ran into her clean floral apron.

"Mitchellah, Mitchellah, so big!" She held me away from her chest, examined my face carefully. "Just like your . . ." She sensed Bea's form on the doorsill. She had been expected, but thus far unseen. "Like . . . Hannah," she finished in my hair.

"Grandma, this is Bea." "My stepmother" would have offended Bea; "my mother" might have satisfied her, but it would have devastated Grandma Lufkin. Lena had come up with the appropriate title months before. "Philly's second wife." She shook Bea's damp hand.

"Velcome, velcome, sit, sit." And she stared down the hall toward the bedroom.

She moved toward the stove and turned on the gas under the kettle.

"You'll have a cup tea after the trip?"

"Thank you, don't go to any trouble. We can eat after the dentist." Bea seemed surprised. Grandma Lufkin was more European than her own father, Pop Kagle, and older, like a peasant woman in a Russian newsreel.

"What's trouble?" Lena waved her off. "A *bissel* water, a

cookie?" She served the tea in ordinary drinking glasses. Then untied a box of fresh bakery cookies, put them on a dairy plate and passed them to Bea.

"Thank you. How nice!"

But they weren't nice. They were plain flat sugar cookies, no filling in the middle, not even a piece of fruit, a glazed cherry. What about the rest of the meal? Where was the soup? The gefilte fish? The fruit compote?

When Bea asked to use the bathroom and walked across the living room and down the hall, smoothing out the waist of her new Bonwit tweeds, I leaned against Grandma Lufkin's stirring arm.

"What's for lunch, Grandma?" I cooed.

"Nothing."

"Why?" I was hurt.

"I didn't make any, that's why. You can't go with *schmutz* in your mouth to Cousin Stanley."

"But I'm hungry."

"Have a piece hallah, Mitchell." She offered me a rumpled bag. I took two slices. They were dried out. Friday night's loaf. Besides, there was no coffee to dunk them in, only tea.

When Bea returned to the room, she looked at her watch. "Well, Mitchell, it's after one. We better get ready."

"*I* could have taken him," Grandma Lufkin said at the door, staring directly into Bea's eyes.

"It's no trouble. Why should you bother? I can take care of things now."

"What's trouble? Mitchell's such a good boy." Lena pressed her hand into the top of my shoulder till it hurt. I wanted to cry I was so hungry.

I led Bea two blocks further south on Fort Washington Avenue. We turned left and walked up a tiny hill overlooking the river.

"It's the next building up," I told Bea, who was winded but game in her sensible walking shoes. She hadn't smoked a cigarette since we'd left midtown.

Coming out of Cousin Stanley's lobby like the little engine that could was Aunt Renee with Cousin Douglas behind her. He was in high school now, Bronx Science. I was very excited; maybe we could get together later, set something up.

"What are *you* doing here?" Aunt Renee said, addressing us both.

"Going to the dentist, checkup," I chirruped. "Aunt Renee, this is Bea. Bea, Aunt Renee and Cousin Douglas."

"Oh . . . Douglas just had his."

"How's high school? Your trains?" I was jumping up and down like a puppy.

"I'm all right, I guess." Douglas stared down the hill away from me.

"We have to go, Douglas." Aunt Renee pulled his thin arms, dragging him off down the hill.

"Rude, rude," Bea mumbled to herself.

After the checkup (I was missing a permanent second tooth in the front), on our way down the block to the IND, I assured Bea that Robert and Aunt Blanche were not like that, and Grandma Lufkin, I thought to myself, was still the best cook in the world.

"Mitchell," Bea said as we pushed into the wooden turnstile, "there are other dentists and doctors near the hotel." She reached down and held my hand as we ran for the incoming train. I pressed her palm, absorbing some of its moisture.

"Come on, Mitchell, give it a try. I'll hold on to you." Myron steadied the seat of a balloon-tired two-wheeler in front of his Brooklyn home. "If I can teach Josh, you'll be a cinch."

"Okay." I got on the seat gingerly.

"Now pedal. I've got the bike, don't worry. Forget it's a two-wheeler, just pedal and steer. That's it. The balancing will take care of itself."

Myron gripped under the seat bar with his large right paw. His other hand was on the left handlebar touching mine. I pedaled furiously, trying not to look at the gutter, to forget the iron manhole covers I could break my head on. Traffic was sparse, just cars parked in front of every house.

"That's it, Mitchell. That's the way, you're getting it."

Suddenly Myron released his grip on the handlebar. I was floating solo down a one-way street, stomach in my throat, eyes gleaming—traffic light!

"How do I turn? How do I curve?"

"Just like a tricycle. Move the wheel where you want it." Myron was at my side again. I made the circle without falling.

"Pedal now, keep pedaling . . . thaaaat's it."

And I sped to the other end of the block, turned slowly and sped back toward Myron blowing past cars, houses, trees.

There were no bicycles at Lake Ronkonkoma School, so hardly anyone there knew how to ride a two-wheeler. Nor were there bikes in midtown that I knew of, so my old Bronx tricycle was the last one I had mastered. Josh, who wasn't well coordinated even for eight, was just making the transition it had taken me almost twelve years to achieve.

The two of us rode and rode that June afternoon, back and forth on the one-way street. Dianne soon joined us on her maroon Schwinn. Then Jessica came out of the garage with an English racer. She lead us out of the neighborhood onto the Ocean Parkway grand promenade. I was so intrigued by her hand brakes, which allowed her to reverse pedal without stopping, that I forgot how to apply my own brakes at a crosswalk and had to stop with my feet. The bike twisted on top of me.

"Mitchell, Mitchell, are you all right?" They gathered around my pile of bike and legs.

"I'm okay."

Jessica helped me up. The worst had occurred, and I survived without a scrape. Relieved and carefully reinstructed on the proper reverse pedal stroke for braking, I continued with the others on our ride homeward.

Bea had been summoned to Brooklyn as soon as we returned from my visit to the dentist. Mom Kagle had a weak heart and that morning had complained of chest pains. She was rushed to Coney Island Hospital, where the doctors ran a series of inconclusive tests and released her in the afternoon. Complete rest at home was prescribed, ordered. Bea and Marion were ministering to her, calming Pop Kagle, and with Myron's help keeping all the children occupied outside the house. Dinner was unprepared, forgotten until we returned to the driveway with our bicycles.

We rested on the porch steps, our stomaches gastric calliopes.

"What about supper?" Josh stood erect. He had the smallest stomach, but it emitted the most poignant squeals.

"Shh, Grandma's sick," Dianne admonished. "Mommy and Aunt Bea are taking care of her."

"I'm still hungry," he persisted.

"Josh," Dianne said despairingly.

The porch door swung open.

"Are you kids hungry?" Myron asked.

"Hungry? We're *starving!*" we shrieked.

"Let's go to Nathan's," he offered.

"Nathan's!" they squealed, hopping off the porch stairs. "Nathan's!" They ran toward the curb.

"What is it?" I asked.

"The best hot dog stand in the world," Josh proclaimed.

"Hot dogs?"

"They have everything—hamburgers, chow mein sandwiches, shrimp, fried clams, roast beef," Jessica reeled off.

"And french fries," Dianne added.

"Come on, no one goes hungry. Get in!" Myron shooed us toward an ancient black sedan. "Girls in the back. Mitchell sit in front, next to me. I'll show you Coney Island."

"That's where they have roller coasters and stuff, isn't it?"

"The greatest amusement park in the world." Josh, the booster, again. "Rides, freaks, everything."

"But I thought we were going to Nathan's?"

"We are, we are," they sang. "Nathan's is *in* Coney Island!"

Myron slammed his door. "Everyone lock up."

Josh, at my right, next to the door, pushed the brown button down. Dianne and Jessica did the same with their door buttons. Myron turned the ignition key and reached for a metal stick, which he released downward, and then another one with a gray plastic ball on top, which he moved around as the car gained speed or slowed down.

"Model A Ford, best of the prewar cars." He turned to me. "Old man Ford had lousy politics, but he designed a beautiful automobile. Listen to the engine, four-cylinder baby, still turns right over."

"What's that?" I asked, pointing to the stick, which kept vibrating.

"The shift."

"What's it do?"

"Gears, meshes them to the drive shaft."

I kept shaking my head like Grandma Woolf in Times Square, taking in the new rods, smells, sounds; all incomprehensible, yet wonderful, mysterious.

"This hot dog tastes like pastrami," I said as grease from my first bite seared the roof of my mouth. We were standing behind Myron, who was at the head of our line, one of ten long ones strung out from Nathan's outdoor counter.

"How many is that?" Myron turned his enormous head toward us.

"Three, Uncle Myron," Josh chirruped.

"Three more dogs with mustard."

"The mustard's over there, buddy," the middle-aged counter man barked, indicating a round chest-high condiment bar with several napkin cannisters.

"Three fries," Myron continued.

"Make it four," I shouted.

"Four fries." Myron echoed. "One chow mein sandwich and one fried clams."

"That it, buddy?"

"Three Cokes, two root beers."

"Jesus." The counter man took off his white buck-private-style hat, passed his hand over his bald spot, replaced the cap and assembled the rest of our order in three cardboard boxes. We got mustard, ketchup and salt at the condiment bar. I started in on my cup of fries as we ambled toward the Boardwalk, away from Nathan's greased chaos. Myron was still pulling clams from a paper bag. Dianne had given up on her sloppy chow mein sandwich. Jessica was in the lead, eager to see the ocean and buy saltwater taffy. We found the ocean and the taffy, but the taffy wasn't in the salty waves, as I had imagined. Next it was candied apples. Then Josh insisted on electric cars, which we could drive ourselves.

"You promised, Uncle Myron!"

"Okay, Josh."

Each car had a long aerial soldered to its back side that reached up to the electrified ceiling. Inside, on the floorboard, a tiny pedal allowed one to regulate the current on or off like a real accelerator. The steering wheels were rubberized, like the thick bumper guards that ringed each car, permitting us to crash at will into one another.

First a bike. Now a car. I was delirious with motion. Josh was at my side, the copilot, still too young to drive his own electric car; ten was the magic age. We bumped Dianne, were spun around and around by Jessica, rammed from the blind side by a total stranger. Josh wet his pants laughing. I had steered us into the clear for a clean shot at Jessica when the current died down.

Myron was standing at the iron gate, grinning at our performances. We swamped him with hugs and laughter.

"Some drivers!" He beat off our mock blows. "We better get home, it's after nine. I promised Bea, you have to get back to the city."

We followed him down a corridor of sideshows, rides, games and custard stands toward the Model A.

"What's frozen custard?" I asked Dianne.

"You never had it?"

"No. I don't like regular dessert custard . . . ugh!"

"It's not like pudding, more like ice cream, but softer. Uncle Myron," she pleaded, "can we have some frozen custard? Mitchell's never tasted it. Just a small one? Please?"

"Okay, you guys. Holes in your stomachs."

"What'll it be?" the custard man demanded in front of five sweating silver machines. Each one spit out a different rippled column of custard which could be joined in one multiflavored cone for a nickel a flavor, up to six inches high—banana, blueberry, vanilla, chocolate, pistachio. We shouted our choices.

"How much?" Myron asked.

"For you a special price. Sixty-five cents."

Myron reached for his wallet, then grabbed his back pocket. Nothing there.

"Holy shit! Someone picked my pocket!" He was astonished and embarrassed. He reached into his front pockets: a dime, his car, house and shop keys, nothing else.

"You still owe me sixty-five cents, Mister."

"Yeah, yeah, take it easy, you'll get your money, take it easy. Don't sweat."

"I've got money," I volunteered, eager to help out. I pulled a five-dollar bill from my front pocket. "Here." I handed it to Myron.

"Give it to the custard man. I've got to find my wallet. My discharge papers, my driver's license, everything's in there." He ran back toward the electric car ride.

"Here's your change, kid." The custard man handed me four bills and silver. Bea had slipped me a five on the BMT in case I had to pay my way for anything. I shouldn't be a *schnorrer* with my *new* cousins.

We ran after Myron, our cones dripping. Shocked. How could anyone harm him? He was a giant, had been a sergeant in the Military Police in Rome, Berlin and, briefly, Tokyo, outside of General MacArthur's residence with a gun and club.

We found him staring at the ground outside the electric car ride. He had stood there by the iron fence during our rides, mesmerized by our squeals, a perfect setup, a soft touch. Myron asked the owner selling tickets if he had found anything outside the fence.

"Like what?"

"A wallet, billfold."

"What was inside?"

"Discharge papers, driver's license."

"What's the name?"

"You found something?"

"What's the name, mister?"

"Kagle. Myron Kagle."

"Just a second." He opened a tin box. Its contents were hidden by the ticket counter.

"I got something here. You spell that last name, mister?"

"K-A-G-L-E."

"You got it, Sarge." He handed a black passport-style billfold over to Myron. "Guy turned it in five minutes ago, said he found it in one of the cars."

"Where did he put the money that was inside?"

"I don't ask questions when people turn items in. Lucky to get anything back in this zoo."

"What did he look like?" Myron insisted.

"I don't remember. So many faces. Look, Sarge, whoever found it probably took the dough, right? Seen your papers and handed them to me, patriotic-like. You're fortunate. He could have thrown the whole thing into the ocean."

"You didn't find my wallet yourself, did you, Buddy? You seem to know so much about it!"

"Hey, watch it, Kagle." He had trouble pronouncing the surname. "This ain't Germany or Japan. It's Coney Island, 1947. We won the war. You're lucky, Sarge."

"Sarcastic bastard," Myron shouted.

"Get lost, will you, soldier boy, before I call the police." He slammed the chain link gate around his cockpit.

"I'll wait here all night for them."

"That's trespassing."

Myron shot his long fingers through the link mesh, shaking it like an accordian. The owner hid under the cash register counter, out of sight, terrified, until Myron had vented all his rage on the metal gate.

We walked back to the car. The owner's head was still submerged as we turned out of his alley. We drove most of the way back to the house in silence, awed by Myron's anger.

"It was only ten dollars." A wide grin suddenly opened his face. "Forget about it, kids. What's a ten spot in a lifetime? I got my papers back, so don't worry the grownups with this. How much I owe you, Mitchell? Keep track!"

"Nothing, Uncle Myron," I answered, calling him Uncle for the first time, just like Josh, Dianne and Jessica. That was easy enough.

When we returned to the house, Uncle Myron offered to drive us back to the Park Central. It was almost ten P.M., much too late for a subway ride. He insisted even though Bea wanted to call a cab.

"I feel like driving tonight. Take my big sister into Manhattan."

"You and cars!" Bea slapped his shoulder.

"Get in!" he ordered.

Bea sat next to him, pulled out her Chesterfields. I had the entire back seat to spread out on, a worn gray couch.

"Will you ever get a new car, Mikey?"

"Why?" The engine refused to turn over. "Maybe," he mused. "Studebaker has a new model coming out."

"The one with the odd rear end, looks like the front of the car coming or going," I added from my back seat.

"But under the hood they have a brand new small six, not cosmetic like the body, but it costs money. If I stick with Pop, I'll have enough for a down payment in January. But I may go to the Pratt School of Engineering on the GI Bill. Still help Pop out part time. I have to decide."

"College would be terrific with your knack for machines," Bea said encouragingly.

"It's not machines in college. It's theories about how to make them."

"Could you do that, Mikey? Not work with your hands?"

"Well, I'm not sure."

Back and forth till the Brooklyn Bridge. Then they switched to Bea's life in Manhattan. What she did every day, wanted to do, finally Philly and the bookstore. It was like Ronson and me after lights-out. Bea was a different person talking to her kid brother, no tension, no flashes of craziness. I'd never seen her relate to anyone like that before.

Myron drove up 7th Avenue. Bea pointed out her window to Bookland when we crossed 42nd Street. The lights were out.

"Philly must be home."

In front of the Park Central, Myron made a U-turn. He caught my eye.

"Still owe you 65¢, Mitchell."

"How come?" Bea asked.

Myron told her quickly how his pocket was picked and I paid for everyone's frozen custard at Coney Island. His anger was gone.

"It's not like before the war, Mikey. You've got to be careful outside."

"There were pickpockets before."

"Not as brazen. Everything's quicker. Come up, have a cup of coffee."

The doorman opened her side, and she got out.

"I want to look in on Mom, make sure Pop goes to bed." Myron opened his own door. "If Coney Island's faster, Manhattan must be a racetrack. I'm only driving a beat-up four cylinder."

"Smarty pants!" Bea laughed.

They embraced on the curb. She wet his grizzled cheeks with kisses.

"Good night, Uncle Myron."

He swept me off the sidewalk into a bear hug. The Lufkin uncles, Mordecai, Sam and Morris, never touched me.

Bea pushed into the revolving door. I was behind her in my own compartment. She had some of Myron in her, same mother and father. So different from the stepmother in 2209, the sister in the Model A Ford.

June, the month between school and camp, was always a slow one. I had usually spent most of it at Bookland, at the movies, or waiting for my father to take me to a Yankee doubleheader. With Bea, there was another source of adventure. Though I was initially hesitant about spending time with her because of the potential for flare-ups, Bea's primary activity, shopping for food, appealed to me. We were one in our pursuit of produce, meat, fish and canned goods for the dinner table.

The little grocery store directly across from the Park Central on 7th Avenue had a limited choice of staples for customers on the run:

breakfast foods, fruit, herring, fresh rolls, coffee, tea, butter, cream cheese, canned fruit cocktail, all at exorbitant prices. The "thieves," my father called them. "Run across the street to the thieves and get some fresh salt butter and light cream, Mitchell." They were convenient, open until ten every night including Sunday, and they had sold us butter "spread," the code word, and other staples without ration stamps during the war. But customer loyalty aside, their stock was limited.

Bea searched the neighborhood for reasonably priced food stores with variety. There wasn't much in our immediate midtown vicinity, mostly restaurants, expensive clothing stores, jewelers, hairdressers, all catering to transients, big spenders. So Bea worked her way over to 9th and 10th avenues, where women made dinner for their families every night. On 54th Street there was a huge A & P, the size of our Lake Ronkonkoma football field. The produce was bountiful. With the canned goods, the Ann Page bakery products, the fresh ground coffee, it was a festival of fairly priced foods with red banner decorations and spacious shopping carts to hold every selection.

Bea was a regular by the time I went along with her.

"How's Mrs. Woolf today?" the produce manager sang out.

"What's fresh, Adam?" she asked.

"Everything! You know that, sweetheart."

"For tonight, ripe?"

"Nice string beans, carrots, spinach?"

"My favorites," I gushed.

"Who's your boyfriend?"

"Oh, Mitchell, this is Adam."

"Hi, oh, hi." He dried his hand on a red A & P apron.

"He's home from school."

"Big boy, got to fill him up."

The store manager, Mr. Reilly, the coffee grinder, Al—they were all solicitous. Only Russel in meat was a problem. He was cheerful like the others, but harassed, badgered by the women in front of his empty cases.

"Sorry, that's all they sent me, ladies, chicken and ham!"

"Oh, God, again?"

"No red meat, Russel? Chopped meat even?" an old woman pleaded.

"Maybe for the weekend."

"Soup bones, that's what he'll have on Friday!"

The crowd cleared away.

"Any calf's liver, Russel?" Bea asked gently.

"Let me check." He disappeared into a wooden meat locker and came out with a slab of mottled purple and gray meat on a piece of yellow waxed paper.

"What do you think, Bea?"

"Looks dead."

"Some onions and peppers . . ."

"I don't know." She wasn't pleased.

"Try a ham. They're on special. Very nice."

"I don't have an oven, dearie, remember?"

"A nice broiler, Bea . . . fresh from the Island."

"Which one? Rikers?"

"Funny lady. I'll wrap up a tender one."

I pushed the cart while Bea scouted ahead scooping essentials from each shelf. The wagon was piled to my eyeballs when we reached the check-out counter.

"Will this be a delivery?"

"No, I can't . . . the hotel," Bea muttered, angry for the first time.

"Sorry, I always forget, Mrs. Woolf. So shopping bags? How many do we need today?"

"Four, I think, will do." Bea was unloading the cart.

"Four? How can you manage?"

"My son, Mitchell, will help me."

"Oh, I didn't notice. Glad to meet you, Mitchell. You got a terrific mom," he assured me. She had never called me her son before. Was it the shopping together that had changed things?

We each grabbed two full shopping bags and headed out the doors. On the sidewalk Bea rearranged the bottles and large cans in her bags to redistribute the weight. She had the heaviest load.

"They were really nice in there."

"Terrific fellas," Bea agreed.

"What was that stuff about delivery? I didn't follow."

"The hotel prohibits grocery deliveries. They don't want us cooking meals upstairs."

"Why not?"

"They want us to eat in their expensive restaurants."

"Can they force us?"

"No, Mitchell, but they can give us a hard time about cooking upstairs. It's in the lease. The kitchenette is only meant as a convenience, like for tea, coffee, drinks, not for making full course meals."

"Will they enforce the lease?" We crossed 9th Avenue on the green light.

"They're starting to make trouble. They let us know *they* know we're cooking and they disapprove. Like no more deliveries." She put her heavy load down to rest against a stoop.

"Well, it's fun helping. I like carrying things."

"Especially food." Bea winked.

"I'll be the delivery boy."

We continued our long trek back to 7th Avenue.

The squeeze was on. The Park Central wanted the American Planners out so they could rent our large suites at exorbitant daily rates. The demand was intense, the city alive with money saved during the war and earned in fistfuls since it ended. Everyone wanted things in short supply—rooms, nylons, cars and red meat.

"Wait here," Bea cautioned me as we approached the 55th Street entrance of the Park Central. "I want to check the elevators."

Her bushy head flew in and back out the revolving door. "The coast is clear." She beckoned me in. I took both shopping bags directly into a waiting elevator. Bea came charging after with her bags. The elevator operator was friendly enough. She didn't care. It was the front desk managers who made trouble.

On the twenty-second floor we still had to lug the groceries down a long corridor and make a sharp left. 2209 was located next to the front elevator bank, not the rear. I raced ahead with my lighter bags to the end of the corridor, waved Bea forward like a Marine scout at Iwo Jima.

"Coast is clear," I whispered as she leapfrogged past my position, dropped her bags in front of 2209, unlocked the door and gave me the all-clear whistle to bring my bags into the suite.

Two sets of front elevator doors slammed open just as I dropped my bags in the foyer.

"Phew, close, Mitchell, close call!"

"Who is it?" I asked. "The manager?"

"No, Fatty Arbuckle and the Ritz Brothers!"

I roared at the incongruity. Bea cuffed my head.

"Not so loud."

We collapsed on the living room couch, both rubbing our palms, still raw from the shopping bag cords, at home now in our own laughter.

One week before I returned to camp, Bea and I found a rich new supply of beef and lamb on Fulton Street. After spending the previous week tracing false leads on the Lower East Side, we were thrilled with our haul. A thick sirloin steak, lean round beef good enough to eat raw, and six beautiful rib lamb chops.

"Will Daddy be surprised! I didn't tell him about the lamb chops!" Bea gasped, starting the evening meal. "He'll be home in fifteen minutes. I'll get the fries going, you set the broiler up, Mitchell."

I was pleased with my new responsibility. Took the broiler out of its hiding place, assembled the clean parts on the bedroom coffee table, slid the brown plastic socket onto the cover prongs, expecting electrocution even though the other end of the chord was not plugged into the wall.

Suddenly Bea's potatoes and minced onions were in the bedroom. Smell, smoke, and crackle worked into my head, making me faint with hunger. I came into the kitchenette where she was stroking the sliced potatoes with a serving fork, tears on her cheeks from the raw onions.

"The pan was too hot when I put the Crisco in. Damn electric coils! Can't judge the heat from their color!"

Smoke rushed into the cool foyer. There was no exhaust in the kitchenette.

"Mitchell, just watch these, turn them when they smoke too much. I have to start the chops. Then wash up for Daddy."

The lights dimmed when Bea plugged the broiler into the wall. In seconds burning lamb fat mingled with the potato odors in the foyer. With the meal underway Bea started washing up, creaming her face for my father.

Briiiing, briiiing. It was the front doorbell.

"Don't move, Mitchell," Bea hissed. She was instantly at the bedroom door, eyes blazing.

"Maybe it's Daddy."

"Shh. He uses his own key now."

Briiiing, briiiing, briiiing.

"Who is it?" Bea called out.

"Walsh, house detective. Open the door!"

"You can't come in here."

"You're cooking in there, lady?"

"No!"

"I smell the food in the hall coming from your transom."

"Nothing in here." Bea shut the bedroom door. I closed the kitchenette off. Bea advanced to the front door, holding a bath towel around her slip, as if she had just come out of the tub.

"Go away. I'm naked, my husband isn't home."

"You're cooking, lady. It's against hotel rules."

"Go away, you"—her mouth opened wide—"rotten bum!"

Tears flooded her eyes, which were fixed in terror on the door, its brass chain and double lock rattled by Walsh's pounding fists.

"Go away, you bum! Go away, I'm naked."

Pound, pound.

She was weeping uncontrollably as he slammed his open palms against the metal door. For two more minutes he pounded. Then, frustrated, outwitted, he retreated toward the maid's supply room.

"No cooking, lady. Not in this hotel. I'll stop you!"

Bea was flushed. She dropped her towel on the rug, weeping in her slip against the bolted door. I ran to her side, touched her freckled arm. "He's gone, he's gone. I heard the elevator."

Her tears hit my hands.

"Mitchell, what am I going to do? What will happen to us?"

She was crying in my hair, holding on to my shoulders. I put my arms around her heaving slip to steady her. She held on tight and kissed my face. She was on fire, her heart throbbing against my shirt.

"I'm sorry, Mommy," I said and kissed her frightened mouth.

"Oh, Mitchell, it's not your fault. You're a good boy, a good—The chops! The potatoes! Jesus Christ, the whole place will go up!"

She tore into the bedroom, threw open the windows and turned the flaming lamb over expertly. I opened the kitchenette door and was overcome with onion smoke. Bea's hand appeared instantly behind me through the fumes, turned off the hot plate switch and tossed the scalded frypan onto the Formica counter top. The potatoes had a thick brown crust and looked promising. The kitchenette smoke billowed through the cool foyer again. Bea dashed into the living room and jarred the windows open. She raced into the bathroom, turned on the faucets and returned with wet towels. She hung one over the front door transom and stuffed another against the doorsill.

Ten minutes later, when my father tried to open the front door, he pushed into the wet towel on the sill.

"What the hell is going on?"

"Just a second, Philly." Bea removed the towel. "Welcome to the Maginot Line that held firm," she added quickly, now in her dinner blouse.

We were breathless with our victory story.

"Bastards, bastards," my father repeated louder and louder as the tale unwound. "They really want us out, the bastards. I'll have to take care of that fucking house dick!"

"Well, Philly, wash up. Mitchell and I did rescue the meal."

He was at the table in two minutes. I could smell the Yardley soap on his hands. His collar button undone, Windsor tie knot loosened, we began the meal.

"Lamb chops! Holy mackerel, babe, where did you get them?"

"Fulton Street, kosher butcher. Everyone thinks fish down there, but I found this old place."

The chops were pungent, charred, tasty, the fries crisp chips with soft potato centers. The meal was special for me. I had done more than set the table.

"So, Phil, what do you think?"

"Lamb's a trifle tough," he mumbled through a mouthful.

"What is that . . . English? 'A trifle,' " she mimicked. "You don't like them."

"They're fine, Bea, they're fine." My father sensed danger building.

"Overcooked, aren't they?" she persisted.

"Just a bit, but they're really fine." He slid a discarded mouthful underneath the bone.

"What the hell am I supposed to do around this place?" She pushed her plate away, left the table, came back with her cigarettes and lighter.

"The broiler, the kitchenette, the schmuck house dick—what the hell am I supposed to do at mealtimes? Be a goddamned Houdini?"

"I'll take care of the house dick, what's his name? Walsh."

"Philly! You don't even know what I'm talking about, do you? *Do you?*"

My father was ashen. I stopped eating.

"I can't go on like this." She inhaled so deeply the smoke never came out. She drew on her Chesterfield again, the glowing butt searing her yellow fingers. "I want us to live like a real family."

"What?" Philly was confused. The Park Central, the store, me at Lake Ronkonkoma, that was our understanding, the deal. "What do you mean, 'a real family'?"

"You know, Phil. . . . Think!"

"A kitchen. You want a gas stove. That's it, huh?" He was hurt, thought he had given her enough.

"A stove with an oven would be nice. Mitchell could have a room of his own maybe, a bar mitzvah when he's thirteen, like a real family."

"Where, Bea? Where do you find that?"

"Aha!" She raised her hands upward. "That's it, that's just the point. Look, look around. Queens maybe, Rego Park, Forest Hills."

"Queens? You trying to kill me, Bea? Let's move back to the

Bronx. Why not? Queens Boulevard, it's the same *megillah*, same goddamned subway ride!" Philly paused, sucked in his tension, held it there, his lips tight over his bridgework.

"I'm not a money tree." He narrowed his eyes at her. "Three months, you want everything!"

"I want to make dinner without fear."

"Do it here, damnit! I'll figure it out."

"Do you love me, Phil?"

He was mute with bitterness at her demands.

"Do you love me? Please . . . say something, Phil!"

He got up from the table, grabbed his jacket in the foyer. "I can't take this crap anymore." He slammed the front door hard as he left the suite.

I felt bad for her; a little affection after a lousy day was all she wanted. My father couldn't *say* it, like Fred MacMurray and Dana Andrews in real families.

I cleared away the dishes while Bea stared out the living room windows, smoking, furious. I decided it would be wise to disappear. I went into the bedroom, pulled the slipcover off my bed, puffed out the pillow, got into my pajamas, slid between the covers.

What would happen to us if he stayed away like my mother had? I started to doze. . . . Went to Reno on a long silver train smoking a cigar? If Bea never cooked another meal in 2209 and went away in a Model A Ford wearing a beige slip, smoking a cigarette? Grandma Woolf was holding both events inside two balloons in her hand, coming up to me from behind.

"Mitchell." She tapped my shoulder.

I didn't feel her fingertips, yet I turned into her pale lips.

"They're both dead. Gone off."

I screamed into the blackness around my bed. I saw the bathroom light on, the door ajar, heard water in the sink, the ice water spigot pushed down.

"Mommy!" I cried.

Bea swept out of the bathroom toward my bed. She was in a satin negligee. She sat on the edge, put her hand on my forehead.

"Mitchell, easy, take it easy. It's all right. You're not alone."

"Where's Daddy?"

"Out walking."

"Will he come back?"

"I hope. Doesn't he always?"

"Mommy." I repeated the word.

She reached down and held me against her chest, rocked me into her bosom.

"I love you, Mitchell."

"I love you."

We were both crying. I held on to her neck. We kissed each other's cheeks.

"Sleep, Mitchell, sleep. He'll be back soon. I'll take it easy. We can stay here," she whispered.

"I don't mind this bed," I said, lying my head back down on the pillow. I looked up at her freckled cleavage, the pink lace around her brown nipples.

"Good night, Mitchell."

"Night, Mommy."

She scooped me up again. We rocked until the phone rang.

"Sure, Phil, sure. He's going back to sleep now. Okay, hon. . . . I love you too, Phil."

He must have said it into the phone.

Chapter
Four

ALL MY NEW socks and underwear were missing when I unraveled the brown package they were supposed to be in on the second Monday of camp. The Blue Port Laundry had become careless. I included this information in the Tuesday postcard home we were required to hand in at the dining room door before breakfast. Ma Kennedy collected them, smiled as we trooped past. She was almost affectionate with the old-timers like me who attended the Lake Ronkonkoma School. So I was shaken when she approached me after breakfast.

"Woolf, I can't let you send this home." She shoved my postcard into my face:

Dear Mom and Dad,
Camp is fine, but the laundry lost all my new socks and underwear.

Love,
Mitchell

"But it's true, Ma," I protested.

"*All* your socks?" She pointed to my ankles. "What are those?"

"They're old socks."

"So they didn't lose *all* your socks, just some new ones!"

"All my new ones, five pair!"

"Maybe they'll come back next week. They have name tags on them, don't they?"

"Yes."

"Well, let's wait."

"Can I send the card then if they don't come back?"

"Sure, sure, Woolf." She tousled my hair. "What do you think I am, a censor? Go make up your room now." She chuckled to herself. I smiled.

When the socks didn't show up the following Monday and more undershirts were missing, Ma let the postcard through the lines.

Bea's response was immediate. She sent me a brown fiberboard laundry box especially designed for the mail. I stuffed a full week's dirty clothes, sheets and towels into the bottom half, closed the top snugly over it, tied two gray straps around both halves and pulled them taut through their chrome buckles. I then turned the address card over, replacing it inside its celluloid window so the "Mrs. Phillip Woolf, Park Central Hotel" side was showing. Ma Kennedy mailed it parcel post with everyone else's postcards, charging the stamps to my canteen account.

Within ten days the brown box reappeared at mail call with my name shining through the plastic window. Inside were my clean socks, undershirts, sheets and towels. Tucked beneath the linen was a cache of Milky Ways, Clark Bars, and an eleven-ounce package of Uneeda biscuits made into peanut-butter-and-strawberry-jam sandwiches.

A week before Bea and my father's first camp visit, a letter tumbled out of the brown laundry box when I lifted the top cover off.

Dear Mitchell,

Now that you're twelve, eleven months from your thirteenth birthday, Daddy and I have talked over the possibility of your having a bar mitzvah when you reach thirteen and become a man in the Jewish faith. Daddy was bar mitzvahed, Uncle Alfie, and their father before them. Cousin Josh goes to Hebrew school and will have a bar mitzvah when he is thirteen. It's an important, happy occasion, the whole family comes to celebrate in the temple, and afterward there's a wonderful party. You also get nice presents from everybody. We can discuss it next Sunday. Until then,

Love,
Mommy

I'd never thought about having a bar mitzvah before. Where could I prepare for it at Lake Ronkonkoma? No religious training for any faith was available. Only church on Sunday for the Catholic and Protestant kids during the regular school year. They were driven into Smithtown or Ronkonkoma by Stevens. The Raffertys always went to Mass. Jimmy knew what to do because the nuns at the orphanage had instructed him. He had a rosary and missal he took with him. So did Francis, although his missal had bigger print and more illustrations. Fritz thought his mother had been a Catholic but wasn't certain. His father was Protestant, so he chose the Lutheran church because their services were in English and he enjoyed the hymns. Ronson never went. His father was against the whole idea.

The dozen Lower School churchgoers usually returned with treats from town: crullers, Tootsie Pops, the Sunday papers, comic books. Rafferty always brought the fat Sunday *Mirror* and a bag of jelly doughnuts back to the dorm, which he shared with us heathen.

There was no synagogue at all for the Jewish kids like Gross, Zachery, and me to attend. The nearest one was in Patchogue, fifty miles away. How could Stevens have taken us on Friday evening, ring-a-levio night, or Saturday morning, before the movies? No one even considered it. Religion at Lake Ronkonkoma meant Sunday morning services, doughnuts, and newspapers. It was a brief escape.

Most kids had to call home to figure out which church, if any, they should attend.

Curious that Bea should bring it up in her letter. Somehow she connected it with being a family, like having a gas stove and a larger apartment. A bar mitzvah for Mitchell was one of her demands that night she argued with my father. The same evening Walsh, the house detective, had pounded on the door of 2209 and I had called her Mommy for the first time. I knew there was serious preparation involved, specific Hebrew prayers and songs to learn for a bar mitzvah. I had actually gone to Hebrew school for two months every Wednesday afternoon at two o'clock while I was at PS 69. I thought this Released Time Religious Program was part of the war effort, one of FDR's Four Freedoms, not necessarily a family prerogative.

My Hebrew instruction had taken place on the fourth floor of the Actors' Temple on West 47th Street, an aging neighborhood shul attended by show biz luminaries, clothing manufacturers and garment workers. Like my father, they usually came only during the High Holy Days, Rosh Hashanah, Yom Kippur, and Yortzeit observances. The class met in a large open room where fifteen antique desks were bolted to the floor. In age and ability we ranged from seven to just shy of thirteen, from know-nothings just beginning Hebrew, like me, to the eager bar mitzvah boys three weeks away from the ultimate Saturday morning service.

I was at the *aleph-baiz* level, still amazed that all the books started backward. The class was a madhouse, and we required individual attention, but the teacher, Mendel Rifkin, a talmudic scholar, had contempt for our primitive skills. We, in turn, mocked his old-fashioned shtetl attire and immigrant's English with spitballs and simulated anti-aircraft fire. Mendel Rifkin never had a chance. Each Wednesday afternoon we provoked the poor man to madness and bitter, abusive rage at our ungodliness.

I had barely learned the alphabet symbols when my slapdash Hebrew schooling ended as I set out for the nonsectarian Lake Ronkonkoma School. So where would I start now at age twelve? Who would teach me all I missed and had to learn in eleven months?

* * *

"Mrs. Kennedy will let you come home every other weekend in the fall for bar mitzvah lessons," Bea announced the following Sunday after a short conference in the Kennedy apartment.

"But I don't know any Hebrew."

"You don't need much. Most of the service is in English at Temple Bnai Sholem."

"English? Is it Jewish?"

"Sure, Mitchell, it's Jewish. A Reform temple is just modern, more American, you'll see."

Bea had entered the fold of Reformed Judaism just before the war when her mother insisted that the entire family join the Kings Highway Synagogue. Mom Kagle had been raised in a nonkosher yet religious Jewish household and thus wanted Myron, her only son, to have a proper bar mitzvah with Pop Kagle in attendance. Bea stayed on afterward and was drawn to the Young People's League, a social group without danger. The young men were neither threatening nor appealing, unlike her first husband. It was a safe place for her energies and idealism. She became a spokeswoman for the Popular Front, a premature antifascist with her father's hearty approval.

After the war and her stint in Washington she still found solace and friendship in the Reform temple, though she was no longer politically active. Thus it was not at all surprising that she insisted Philly attend a Reform service after he took her to the Actors' Temple one Friday evening, where she prayed from the upstairs women's balcony while he said kaddish with the swaying men on the floor below. She picked Bnai Sholem because of Rabbi Perlmutter's reputation. A Friday evening when his sermon, "The Best Seller List and God," was sure to captivate Philly. He was impressed, comforted by the choir with music, and still able to say kaddish in Hebrew.

In September I went to a Saturday morning service at Bnai Sholem, a Moorish limestone synagogue off Central Park West. I sat between my father and Bea. None of the men wore yarmulkes, though most of them did have a silk *tallis* draped over their pinstriped shoulders. The women sat with their husbands wearing tailored suits or muted dresses. The few children in attendance were also in their "best" clothes.

"Mitchell," my father whispered, "here's the prayer book. You can follow the service."

He opened it to page 3 and placed it in my hands. The chief rabbi and cantor rose from their upholstered mahogany thrones, stage left and right, and moved forward, placing their tassled prayer books on the onyx top of the altar. They were dressed in formal black robes and wore crownlike yarmulkes. They spoke English most of the time, leading us in responsive prayer. Some of the songs, however, were in Hebrew, as was my father's kaddish prayer, the same *"Yitgadal veyitkadash shemei raba"* he chanted in the Actors' Temple. I wondered if he still remembered my mother in it.

The small cantor was accompanied by a mixed choir hidden in the second story of the sanctuary. They made a magnificent sound against his guttural baritone. He spoke English with a slight accent, like the men at the Actors' Temple. The rabbi, however, looked like President Roosevelt, tall, white haired, pince-nez clipped on the bridge of his long nose. He was impassioned, visionary in his sermon, pleading for support of Israel's nationhood at the UN General Assembly.

"Isn't Rabbi Perlmutter wonderful?" My father nudged me during a pause. "Brilliant man, speaks like a stage actor."

After his sermon Rabbi Perlmutter made some general announcements, among them, the news that Tommy Henrich would play in the Sunday doubleheader against the Red Sox, which everyone found amusing. When he raised his hands over the congregation for the benediction, manicured fingertips reaching for the heavens—"The Lord bless thee and keep thee; the Lord make his face shine upon thee and be gracious unto thee; the Lord lift up his countenance upon thee and give thee peace"—it seemed to me he was in contact with forces beyond mortal comprehension that might bring one peace and understanding.

We filed out of our cushioned pew and up the carpeted aisle toward the exits. The rabbi and cantor were standing at the head of our red aisle shaking hands with everyone, saying "Good Shabbas!" Bea introduced me to Rabbi Perlmutter, his immense soft hand suddenly firm.

"Pleased to meet you, Mitchell," he boomed, reaching immediately for the hand behind mine. Next came the tiny cantor.

"This is my son, Mitchell." Bea nodded.

Cantor Gluck picked up his cue. "Yes, Mitchell, one of our new bar mitzvah boys."

I was flattered but still confused about the lessons and my responsibility.

"I'll see you soon, *boychik.*" His handshake was bones and leather, no excess.

We passed into the entrance lobby, Bea headed toward a glass case where a group of women were huddled selling religious books and temple artifacts.

"I'm going to help out for a while, Phil. See you later. About two, okay?"

"Sure, Bea, I'll bring Mitchell back here."

My father and I walked up to Central Park West and turned south. We were part of a procession of congregants going uptown or down, cutting sideways after a block or two into wide crosstown avenues. They were on parade in austere black finery. Some of the white-haired women wore hats with gossamer veils; a few of the men had on topcoats with gray velvet collars. Occasionally one group of walkers hailed another, but most family groups kept to themselves, savoring the fall sun rising in their faces over Central Park. Comfortable, sanctified, they promenaded toward their awninged apartment buildings where three-course luncheons awaited them.

My father clipped along, pleased to be among them.

"Invigorating, isn't it, Mitchell?" he proclaimed as we passed Theodore Roosevelt astride his gigantic bronze horse on the front steps of the Museum of Natural History.

"Yes." I nodded, not realizing how rare such a walk in the noon sunlight was for my father, who would probably return to Bookland after lunch to relieve Harry.

At the corner of 72nd Street I saw a group of taxis spin into Central Park down an entrance to the tree-lined roadway that circled the entire park and became my racetrack finish line at 59th St. I'd never seen it from this perspective before, been able to look up at my 2209 perch instead of down. I tried to pick out the twenty-second floor by counting from the top of the Park Central down to our windows. Then I noticed the Hampshire House with its green mansard rooftop, two elegant white chimney stacks thrust out of its copper seams. The tan Essex House next door had its neon sign turned off.

"Why don't they wear hats?" I asked my father as we headed toward the Oliver Cromwell Coffee Shop for lunch.

"Who?" My father was surprised.

"The people in the temple."

"Yarmulkes," he said, labeling them properly.

"The rabbi and the cantor wore them. Why doesn't the congregation?"

"They're Reformed."

"They're not Jewish?"

"Of course they're Jewish."

"What kind of Jewish?"

"Mostly German Jews. They brought Reformed Judaism to America."

"What were they in the Actors' Temple?"

We were seated in a comfortable leatherette alcove, given ice water, silverware and yellow menus.

"They were Orthodox Jews there," my father answered.

"Were they German?"

"Some, not many."

"We're English Jews, aren't we?"

My father nodded. He was ready to order. "Mitchell, they have terrific hamburgers here, juicy, thick."

"Okay, I'll have three medium-rare."

He smiled and ordered two medium-rare hamburgers, one with onions, when the waiter came to our table.

"How's the soup? Hot?" he asked.

"Very!" the waiter assured him.

"One," he ordered. I nodded.

"Make that two hot chicken vegetable soups!"

"What do we believe?" I continued.

"It's all the same, Orthodox, Reform, same God, different customs."

"You mean like the hats?"

"Exactly! It's a habit, a custom."

"Who started it?"

"I'm not sure . . . in Poland or Russia or Spain. I don't know. We have different ways now in America."

"So it's not a sin?"

"No, Mitchell, stop worrying, your soup will get cold!"

After our delicious hot lunch my father walked me back to the temple to meet with Cantor Gluck in his third-floor study. He was in charge of bar mitzvah instruction at Bnai Sholem. He received us at his door dressed in gray street clothes. He looked even smaller, more adorable than in the pulpit, his sixty-eight years visible in his smile lines and crow's-feet.

"Come in, Mitchell." He grabbed my hand again.

My father stayed at the door. It wasn't his lesson.

"I have to get back to the store now, Mitchell. It's almost two. Harry must be starving. Mommy will pick you up afterward in the lobby downstairs, okay?"

"Sure." He was gone.

Cantor Gluck lead me into his walnut-paneled office, across an Oriental rug.

"Sit here, Mitchell. Pull up a chair next to me."

I joined him at the front of his long desk.

"That's a good boy. I can tell we'll be friends. Well, have you had any religious training?"

"A little." I was too embarrassed to elaborate, so I confessed directly. "I can't read Hebrew."

"It's all right, don't worry. All my boys are bar mitzvahed if they follow the lessons in this book." And he handed me a thin, flexible black and white composition notebook with my name and *Bar Mitzvah Prayers* written on the dotted lines of the white label.

"So open it, Mitchell, open it."

I turned the cardboard cover over. On the lined paper in blue-black ink the cantor had scripted *The Order of the Bar Mitzvah Service*, with a number beside each prayer.

"They're not in Hebrew," I exclaimed.

"Not in the Hebrew alphabet," he replied. "But read the syllables."

The prayers were printed in clusters of accented capital letters. I tried sounding out a word: *"Bo-re-choo."*

"Choo, choo, the accent is on the '*boo*,' " he indicated gently.

Again I tried: *"Bo-re-choo!"*

"Good, that's better. Continue."

"Es A-do-noy." A familiar phrase, but the next word was difficult, even spelled out in English letters: *"Ha-me-vo-roch,"* I pronounced falteringly.

"Listen to me, Mitchell." Cantor Gluck read the entire eight-line prayer as if he were in the synagogue. It was beautiful, like one of Grandma Lufkin's prayers over the Shabbas hallah.

"Follow me now, Mitchell, we'll try together."

He traced under each syllable with his yellow fingernails as we read the first prayer together: *"E-lo-hay-noo*, good . . . *me-lech* . . . no, no," he shouted. "It's *me-lech*, accent on the *e!"*

It was going to be hard.

"You must try to learn one prayer for each lesson."

"How to pronounce it?"

"Yes, just like I do."

I tried to memorize his Hebrew pronunciation so I could mimic it for my next lesson. *"Bo-rooch a-to, A-do-noy, no-sayn ha-to-ro,"* I concluded, my thick tongue exhausted.

"What does it mean, Cantor Gluck?"

He turned the page. "Here it is in English."

Praised be the Lord, to whom all praise is due. . . .
Praised are you, O Lord, Giver of the law.

"But what does each word mean, like *bo-re-choo* and *A-do-noy?"*

"For that we need years, Mitchell, many years! We have less than a year, *boychik."* He pinched my cheek like Grandma Lufkin used to.

"This is the best way to do it, Mitchell. It will be difficult. Together we'll do it."

He got up from the table. The first lesson was over.

"Before you go back to school, we can meet every week. Afterward, once every two weeks. Just let me know two days ahead when you'll be in the city."

I wasn't sure how I could do that.

"Your mother can call me." He wrote his address and phone number inside the cardboard cover of the notebook with his gold-tipped Sheaffer pen. We shook hands again in his doorway. I took the elevator down to the marble lobby and waited for Bea. She was still in the basement cleaning up after a sisterhood-sponsored Oneg Shabbat where coffee and miniature Danishes were served by the ladies.

I paced the temple lobby waiting for her, gazed at the memorial tablets in the foyer. There was a large scroll with four columns of names commemorating the Bnai Sholem men killed in the Great War. On the opposite wall tablets memorialized the Second World War dead. Further inside the main hall were wall inscriptions listing both women and men. I thought about my mother; her name wasn't included among them, couldn't have been. Was it on the walls of the Actors' Temple? I sat down in a high-backed chair near the stairwell and heard laughter climbing toward me. It was Bea with another woman slightly older than she.

"Mitchell, this is Claire Benjamin, president of the Bnai Sholem Sisterhood. Claire, my son, Mitchell."

"Your mother has told me all about your bar mitzvah, commuting back and forth from boarding school. Impressive determination!" Her blue eyes twinkled, and thick blond waves of hair fell over her powdered cheeks. We all walked outside together and down the temple stairs.

"I'm delighted you can help out with Sunday school registration next week, Bea. Good Shabbas!"

Mrs. Benjamin grazed Bea's right cheek with her left one and kissed the afternoon air with her pink lips. Then she swept uptown as we walked toward the Park Central.

"Sunday school?" I tugged at Bea's Persian lamb sleeve.

"Yes, Sunday school!"

"I thought *we* had Hebrew school and the *others*, Sunday school!"

"We have both. You can go on the Sundays you're home."

Terrific, I thought.

"They have girls in the classes."

"Girls in Hebrew school?"

"No, it's *Sunday* school, remember?"

"Oh, *that's* really different!"

"How was your lesson with Cantor Gluck?"

"Okay."

"Is that all? Don't you like him? He's adored at Bnai Sholem!"

"Sure, he's a very nice man, but I'm not going to learn Hebrew from him, only the sounds written in English."

"So?" Bea countered.

"Isn't it better to know Hebrew?"

She stopped walking. "Most people think it's better to cook meals on a gas stove with a real oven, but look how I make dinner. An electric hodgepodge, and it comes out tasting pretty good, doesn't it?"

I smiled. She was getting funnier.

"It's the results, Mitchell, that count. How we achieve them doesn't matter."

We continued walking along the edge of the park.

"And dinner?" Her homily revived my appetite. "What are you making tonight?"

"It's a surprise, Mitchell." She tousled my hair. "Is that all you can think about?"

That evening while Bea was clearing the plates from the table for her washing bout in the kitchenette my father asked, "How did it go with Cantor Gluck?"

"Fine, except it's not in Hebrew letters."

"Let me see."

I ran into the bedroom and returned with the flexible black and white composition book opened to the first prayer.

"See!" I showed him.

He studied the page and began intoning the prayer with meaning and cadence.

"But the letters, the words," I interjected. "What do they mean?"

"Letters, schmetters, who understands the words?" He put the book down on the dinner table.

"Even in Hebrew you wouldn't understand the words?"

"It's the sounds, Mitchell, the sounds of the words I understand. I've heard them so many times before you were even born."

"Like the violin?" I suggested. "Like those chords?"

"I'd never thought of that. Just like the violin!" He squeezed my forearm with his manicured fingers.

I returned to Lake Ronkonkoma at the end of September for the seventh grade with Cantor Gluck's black and white lesson book packed in my suitcase, determined to memorize the assigned prayers for each bi-monthly meeting. The bar mitzvah itself remained something I did back *there*, apart from my life at school. It could not compete for attention with the social and academic changes our new principal, Mr. Ryson, brought to the Lake Ronkonkoma School, along with his wife, Dorothy, and their eight year old daughter, Clara. Ryson convinced Mr. Kennedy of coeducation's economic potential—increased enrollment achieved with a slightly larger teaching staff. Mr. Kennedy not only bought the argument in time for the fall semester, but he also placed the responsibility for daily operation of the school in Mr. Ryson's large hands. To take full advantage of this development, the seventh and eighth grades were departmentalized, allowing us to share some of the new high school staff for courses like Contemporary Problems, Math and Spanish.

Ryson pushed his economizing one step further when he eliminated our tiny seventh grade—Fritz, Rafferty and myself—by skipping us all into the larger eighth which included old timers like Gross, Daniels and Zachery and some exotic new kids, but no girls. Most of them were in the high school, except for two in the sixth grade and tow-haired Clara in the third.

This academic sleight of hand hardly mattered to me or my

friends. A lot was changing. Ronson wasn't back, Rafferty and I roomed together instead on the upper floor of the North Dorm. Fritz and Zachery were on our end of the hall. Daniels and Gross were on the other. There were also newcomers sprinkled in among us. A few were refugees from the war. Their accented English, courtly manners and odd play clothes were certainly foreign. Albert Weil was a Parisian, born in Belgium, where his family had been in the diamond business for generations. His English was more American than British, though French rhythms came bubbling through on occasion. He wore polka-dot bow ties to dinner with his tight-ass continental blazer. He was terrible in all sports, uncoordinated, hopeless, with his bandy legs, glass ankles, and thin wrists. But his detachment from the games he was screwing up and his complete lack of ability saved him from ridicule. He was outside the event, neither a contestant nor an obstacle. In the evenings during study hall he helped Rafferty, Fritz and me—and even Daniels—with difficult math problems. This generous assistance protected him from dormitory pranks. Once he had completed his own homework—usually in a mere twenty minutes—Albert spent the rest of his evening reading Dumas or Hugo or leafing through *Information, Please!* savoring trivia about the world.

Ferdinand Castille was his roommate. He had more difficulty with English but was too embarrassed and possibly proud to ask for help. He spent his study hall writing endless letters on thin blue airmail stationery to his father, who still lived in Spain, and his mother, now in Manhattan. Ferdinand was dignified, sedate, like a man in our midst. Even on the soccer field, where he excelled, his speed, concentration and strength were not that of a boy.

Max Austria was actually an American from Danbury, Connecticut. His father, a prosperous optometrist, wanted Max to attend a good Connecticut prep school and felt his chances would be enhanced by a year at Lake Ronkonkoma instead of the scrappy public school he attended in Danbury. Lake Ronkonkoma was like a prep school for a prep school in the doctor's confused eyes. Austria was rather gaunt, bony. He had a faint adolescent mustache and an enormous cock, the largest in the Lower School. Without an erection it was like a miniature baseball bat, which surprised us because he was so thin. He was one of the few kids who came from a normal family, lived in a real two-story house with brothers and sisters. The room directly across from Rafferty's and mine was empty, waiting for a new kid who never came. Why not? We were intrigued, puzzled.

One Saturday morning three weeks into the term Daniels and Fritz snuck through the empty room and then edged over my doorsill with a pail of water, ready to douse me. Their eyes were on the rim of the bucket, so they didn't notice mine had opened. I closed them instantly, feigning sleep until they were next to my bed.

"You bastards, get the hell out of here!" I erupted in my flannel pajamas.

Rafferty woke up too. Fritz and Daniels were stunned by my discovery. I chased them down the corridor, the water sloshing out of their pail and finally spilling completely in the main hallway, dousing the common room, seeping into the gray fireplace.

Stevens woke and burst out of his suite, tying his plaid bathrobe sash.

"What the hell is going on here?"

He saw the water, the overturned pail on the floor, Fritz and Daniels scarlet with shame, trying to sneak down the opposite corridor.

"Daniels, Fritz, get back here!"

Rafferty and I watched, secure in our hallway. Weil and Austria poked their heads out of their door for a look.

"Clean this up immediately! There's a new kid coming today. You want his mother to get the wrong impression? I want everyone's room spick and span after breakfast! Back in your rooms, and get dressed!"

He knew we were all listening at our doors.

"Can't even sleep late on Saturdays." He slammed his apartment door.

Breakfast was at eight-thirty on the weekends instead of seven-thirty, giving us an extra hour of sleep. Some of the kids still woke up at seven and had an hour on their hands to relax or make trouble, the obvious choice of Fritz and Daniels. At ten, after one of Stevens's public inspections, I decided to look in the empty room across the hall where the new kid would sleep. His bed was naked, like mine had been on my first day. I stared at the dull mattress buttons, remembering Roger Oaks, the early days of teasing and harassment. Fritz pushed the mirrored bathroom door ajar and entered the new kid's room from the side. His room and the empty room shared the same bath. He was also checking out the bed.

"Thanks a lot, Woolf, you prick!"

"What's eating you, Fritz?"

"No movies because of you!"

"What did I do? You guys were ready to drown *me!*"

"Thanks, I'll remember that this afternoon."

"Stevens caught you himself." I started to laugh in spite of my best efforts to keep a straight face. Fritz sat on the new kid's bed, put his sneakers on the headboard, sand spilled out of them onto the feathered pillow.

"Fritz, give him a break, will you?"

"What do you mean, Woolf?"

"Don't screw up his bed."

"Why not? No one's in it yet."

"Come on, Fritz, get off his bed."

"Make me, wiseass!"

I wasn't afraid of Fritz. He was a familiar adversary. We had been fighting each other regularly since third-grade boxing nights with the Chief. We were so equally matched, though physically different (I was heavier, he was quicker), that our combat had a predictable, comforting pattern to it, unlike my solitary fight with Freddy Daniels.

"Come on, off, Fritz, get off!"

I grabbed his arms, he pulled me on top of him, I pinned him down, he threw me against the headboard.

"Shit, that hurt!" I yelled, getting up, rubbing the back of my head.

"Good, shithead."

We were both standing over the bed. He grabbed me around the neck, forced me down on the mattress. I got him in a neck vise, and we rolled around the bed, grunting abuse into each other's ears.

"What's going on here, Woolf, Fritz?" Stevens shouted from in front of the bed. "Get out of here at once! Stay in your own rooms!"

Fritz and I were startled but slow to release each other. I looked over his arm into the mirrored bathroom door, which reflected the new kid and his mother on the threshold of the room. They were frightened by our wrestling.

"Fritz," I whispered, "get off, the new kid's here."

He sprang off me. We both stood up. I brushed the sand off the bed, and Fritz straightened the pillow.

"Out, you two," Stevens repeated.

Fritz darted out the side bathroom door he had come in by. I, however, had to exit through the front door where the new kid and his terrified mother were frozen. Stevens helped me out.

"Mrs. Mayer, Alex, this is Mitchell Woolf. He lives next door. He's really a good egg. Old-timer. Woolf, how many years you been here?"

"Three and a half." I was embarrassed. "We were just horsing around. Sorry. If I can help with anything, let me know." I made it into my room.

"What's he like?" Rafferty asked. Still ashamed, I told him what had happened. Rafferty rolled over and off his bed, stomach clutched, unable to stop laughing.

"Cut it out! Jesus! They'll think it's a regular nut house on this floor!"

Fifteen minutes later, after Stevens had returned to his room, Mrs. Mayer stuck her tense dark head into our doorway.

"Excuse me, Mitchell, could you show us how the windows open, please?"

"Sure." I bolted into Mayer's room, eager to erase their first impression.

"Like this." I grabbed the brass handle, twisted it down, and pushed the leaded window open.

"Good to get some air in here. So stuffy." She sighed, moving her long fingers across her cheekbones, through her black hair, encouraging the breeze to follow her delicate touch.

Alex was short like her, small even for a sixth grader, yet compactly built. He had her wonderful jet-black hair, traces of which covered his arms and upper lip. His other features were round, not angular or apprehensive like his mother's. A wide smile creased his oval face, took one in. Alex was smiling at me when I finished unlocking the entire row of windows.

"The bed's been empty a long time," I said, still trying to apologize. "Weren't you supposed to be here at the beginning of the semester?"

He winced, and the smile dissolved. It was obviously none of my business.

"I'm sorry, we just didn't know."

"It's okay, Woolf," he assured me, indicating he knew the ropes about last names already, just from Stevens's little exchange with me.

"We should have been here sooner, as you said, Mitchell, at the start of the term." Mrs. Mayer averted her eyes, stared out the open windows, inhaling more cool air. "But Alex was kidnapped."

"Kidnapped?" I was flabbergasted! That happened in newsreels.

"Kidnapped," she repeated.

"Mama, please!" Alex was stern, but a little teary.

I remained incredulous. "By whom?"

"His charming father, Dr. Mayer. Wonderful dentist. Uses laughing gas on his patients. He snuck into my apartment while I was giving a recital, took Alex away to the movies. Of course Alex went right off with him, always looking for a good time. Never thought of me, what I'd sacrificed. My career, to make a real home for him. . . ."

"Mama, we only went to the Loews 86th Street," Alex responded in what appeared to be a familiar ritual.

"He wouldn't bring him home. Wouldn't give him back until I got a court order reaffirming my custody rights! Judge Kaufman was shocked at his newest liaison with an alien. Imagine, how could that be a *real* home?"

"They're married now," Alex corrected her, tears falling from his elegant lashes.

"Thank God! You see, my former husband will do anything to retain his visiting rights, even marry an *alien* . . . German!"

"Please, Mama, it's all settled. He won't kidnap me again. He'll visit."

"Don't let him take you away again, Alex, *keep* you!" She was crying now, tears rolling through her mascara over her powder, exposing tiny strands of her fine mustache.

"I always want to live with you, Mama." Alex rushed into her arms. They hugged very tight.

"Always?" she whispered.

"Yes, yes!" He kissed her tears.

I left the room as soon as I could get around their swooning bodies.

"Look at this hand!" Dr. Mayer unclenched his thick fingers, revealing an empty left palm.

"Where did it go?" We were surprised.

"Where could it be?" he asked me, Alex, Rafferty and Fritz sotto voce.

"In the other fist!" we shouted.

"The right one!" Fritz challenged.

"Was it a dime or a penny?" Dr. Mayer asked.

"A dime!" we shouted.

"Let's see." He opened his right fist and revealed a dime.

"How did it get there?" I asked.

"It's magic," he replied.

"We thought you were a dentist."

"I am. A funny dentist."

We roared.

"Don't be silly, Dad," Alex pleaded through his own laughter.

"Use a bigger coin this time, Doc," Rafferty insisted. "So we can see it move from one fist to the other."

"I'll use two." He jingled a quarter and a nickel out of his jacket pocket, placed the quarter inside his left palm, the nickel inside the right one. "Look closely now. Which hand will they end up in once I close my fists? Abracadabra." He raised both fists, crisscrossed them three times, moaning, eyes closed, swung them in the air around his bald head. "Abracadabra." We were mesmerized.

Fritz, Rafferty and I had befriended Alex the moment his mother left for the city. He had no roommate yet. We filled the void, always in his room setting him straight about Lake Ronkonkoma, finding out about him. Alex didn't like war movies, preferred the second features without music that we saw on Saturday afternoon in Smithtown, liked talking about them before lights-out. He could handle Fritz's snide remarks by ignoring them, evade Daniels's efforts to get him on the football field with his quick feet, sing charming ethnic folk songs for us without the least embarrassment. So it was not surprising that we were all in his room sitting on the bed playing Monopoly when his father came for a visit three Sundays after his arrival.

What did surprise us was his father. His clothes seemed odd for a dentist, at least compared to my Cousin Stanley's. Dr. Mayer wore an olive corduroy sports jacket, charcoal pants, a checked open-neck sports shirt and moccasin-type shoes with crepe soles. He was a thickset, large, happy man, physically and temperamentally the exact opposite of his former wife. Yet his head was the original for Alex's, except for the bald spot on top. Father and son were look-alikes, animated, cheerful look-alikes.

"Concentrate now!" Dr. Mayer stopped his abracadabra chanting and placed both fists in front of our enlarged eyes. "Which one has the quarter and which has the nickel?"

"The right one . . . the left, the left . . . both, both the right and the left . . . the left alone!"

"One at a time." He tightened his fists, his forearms flexed. They were muscular like Alex's.

"The quarter here!" I tapped the left fist. "And the nickel in there." I touched the other one, playing it safe.

"The nickel here!" Fritz indicated the left fist. "The quarter there!" He would go against my choice. Typical!

"They're both in there, Doc." Rafferty pushed the right fist, hoping the coins would jingle and confirm his hunch.

"Well, Alex, last but not least," Dr. Mayer smiled Alex's smile.

"The nickel's in this one." He grazed his father's right fist with his own. "But I'm not quite sure where the quarter is."

"What do you mean?" we asked him.

"I can't feel it yet."

"Try!" we urged.

"I can't . . ."

"Time's running out," Dr. Mayer boomed.

"It's not in there."

"Okay, here we go." Dr. Mayer slowly opened the fingers of each hand to reveal nothing, no quarter or nickel, alone or together, in either palm.

"Where are they? Where did they go? Are they lost?"

"Did you see them move, Rafferty?" Dr. Mayer asked.

"Na, nothing. Didn't see a thing. You're really a good magician, Doc, quick hands from drilling teeth with laughing gas."

Dr. Mayer roared. "Wait a second, just hold everything, kids. I think I see something now. Just let me feel in . . ."

He rose, moved toward Alex, stuck his left index finger into his right ear. "Poouf, see the twinkle?"

The nickel tumbled out of Alex's ear.

"The quarter, the quarter!" we shouted, wanting both coins.

"Here it is, look." He pointed to the center of Alex's head, where the strands of his hair came together like the spokes of a wheel. The quarter rested there, a silver moon in the black night.

"Wow . . . Jesus . . . terrific!" Fritz, Rafferty and I clapped.

Alex reached for his father, grabbed his neck. "I love you, Daddy Magic!" he whispered, hanging on as his father moved toward the leaded windows. Then, remembering where he was, Alex released his grip and turned around to face Rafferty, Fritz and me. Dr. Mayer looked outside toward his car, a '47 Olds with a woman passenger in the front seat. He was trying to catch her attention. He narrowed his eyes, focused hard on her fair neck. Suddenly she turned her face up in his direction. He jerked his head toward the room, indicating he wanted her to come upstairs and join him. Alex, still facing us, back to back with his father, was startled by his abrupt motion.

"Well, what will you do for an encore?" Alex wanted more.

"Let me think," his father said, staring out the front door of Alex's room as though searching for inspiration. We all followed his hypnotic gaze. Footsteps came down the hallway toward the door as if drawn by Dr. Mayer's commanding eyes. It was the fair woman, bearing a gift across the threshold.

"Alex, I brought you a nice Linzer torte from Bauer's, a present. You will like it."

He was undone. The blood left his dark face, then gushed back.

"You promised in your letter . . . you wouldn't bring her. I don't want to see her!" He wouldn't even look at the woman. "Or you!" He was purple, spitting out the words. *"Screw your tricks!"* He ran out the side door into Fritz's room, slamming the mirrored doors on each side of the bathroom.

Dr. Mayer lurched after him. "Alex, come back! Gilda wants to be your friend." He struggled with Alex's bathroom door, sprung it open, but then had to undo Fritz's. When he finally opened it, he was spent, angry, startled by his own desperate image reflected in both doors; like a magician caught with his cape down, the actual mechanics of the rabbit trick revealed.

We were confused by this duality. Which was he? The charming dentist who loved his son or the magician who made a stepmother appear while beguiling him with tricks? That he might be both at the same time never occurred to us.

Donald Duck floated into the court separating the two squat towers of the General Motors building. Tiny strings pulled his yellow beak and sailor cap back toward Broadway, bumping his stomach against a limestone cornice supported by Doric columns, the sole adornment on the massive headquarters. Donald survived this scrape, moving safely back to hover over the middle of the street.

I couldn't see the ground-level curbside parade route, only the tops of floats sweeping through the steep corridor of office buildings and car showrooms south of Columbus Circle, past 57th Street, 56th, on their way to Macy's. It was their first postwar journey in a Thanksgiving Day parade, at least the first one I observed from my twenty-second floor radiator bench. Directly beneath me on the northeast corner of 56th Street was the Broadway Presbyterian Church, its twin spires reaching up toward the floats. I was watching the top half of the parade, startled at first by the unheralded appearance of the huge inflated Donald Duck and Mickey Mouse. I didn't notice the marching band until I traced Minnie Mouse's flight down past the church. They were following after her high-heeled shoes. The sun reflected off their brass horns and silver xylophone keys. I heard their affirmation that Santa Claus was indeed coming to town.

Where was Dumbo? I wondered. My heart went out to the baby elephant, not the fast-quacking incomprehensible duck or the squeaky mouse and his three-fingered girl friend.

"Dad!" I rushed into the dining room. "Where's Dumbo?"

Bea was sipping her bottomless cup of breakfast coffee, talking about their afternoon luncheon party at the Russian Tea Room.

"Isn't he in the parade?" I persisted. They weren't at all interested. My father had been so casual when he mentioned the parade the previous evening, his description so vague, I had no idea what to expect.

"I don't know, Mitchell. Maybe there is no Dumbo balloon." He shook his head, unable to alleviate my disappointment.

"Tell us if you spot him, Mitchell, okay?" Bea was more encouraging.

I raced back to my perch. The instant I was seated at the window, Dumbo's flapping ears sailed through the canyon of buildings, blue eyes twinkling, trunk turned up to the heavens. I relished his wide smile in silence, just the two of us, exchanging glances in midair. What the hell were they talking about anyway in the living room? Wiener schnitzel? I overheard their replay of how Bea's family, Mom and Pop Kagle, Marion, Bruce, their kids and Uncle Myron were invited over to our place for Thanksgiving lunch.

Bea had instigated the event three weeks before, saying, "Philly, we can't keep going to Brooklyn without reciprocating, having them over to our place at least once."

"Can you feed all of them up here? How many is that?"

"Let's see." Bea counted in her head.

Philly used his fingers. "Five!" Philly held up his hand.

"Eight with the children." Bea raised three of her fingers.

"The kids come too?"

"Sure, it's Thanksgiving, Philly! What should they do with themselves? Besides, Mitchell will be home."

"That makes eleven with us." Philly shook his head at the prospect. Even Bea could not feed that many people in 2209, so he would have to take them all out.

"How about the Russian Tea Room?"

"The Russian Tea Room?" She couldn't believe her ears. It was really expensive, and for eleven people . . . !

"It's special, your father will love the borscht, the blini, all authentic."

"Isn't it too expensive, Philly?"

"Well, it's the best. Besides, maybe we can get a deal for a party of eleven. Josh hardly eats, he could split an entrée. The cutlets are immense! I'll look into it tomorrow." They kept repeating their conversation over and over, still unable to believe they had done it and everything was all arranged two weeks before I came home for Thanksgiving vacation. The names of the dishes intrigued me until I found out that borscht was beet soup.

When the parade was over, I rejoined my father and Bea at the dining room table.

"I don't like beets. Do I have to eat the soup?"

"Don't worry, Mitchell, the Chief won't be there." My father winked.

"You'll love the Wiener schnitzel, the main course," Bea assured me.

"What is it? I never had it before, did I?"

"It's a breaded veal cutlet."

"I've had those at Grandma Lufkin's house."

"With an egg on top of it," Bea continued.

"Egg? Hard-boiled?"

"No, fried!"

"Sunny-side up? On top of a veal cutlet? What for?"

"It's delicious. You'll taste it this afternoon, Mitchell."

At twelve-forty-five the phone rang. It was Marion and her children downstairs in the lobby.

"Sure, bring them up," Bea said into the house phone, then

turned to us. "The table is reserved for one-thirty—we still have forty-five minutes. Josh and Dianne are coming up, Mitchell. Are you dressed?"

"Just about, shoes shined, Windsor knot in place, ready to fly like Dumbo."

"Well, don't take off yet. Aunt Marion wants Josh and Dianne to clean themselves up, use the toilet. They were very wild coming over in the car."

They appeared calm enough when they rang the doorbell and entered our foyer. Josh, bundled in his plaid mackinaw, was subdued, diminutive, awed by the express elevator ride and the swank lobby. Dianne was more assured in her fall coat and velvet party dress. She peered through the living room, out the windows into the vast blue sky. Marion caught her breath. None of the Kagles had been to 2209 before.

"How lovely, Bea!" she purred, helping Josh and Dianne off with their coats. "So much bigger than I imagined."

Josh used the toilet first and quickly. When Dianne was through, I brought them fresh towels and soap for their mandatory wash-up and gave them each a clean glass so they could taste some ice water. I pressed the stubby knob down.

"It's ice cold. Try some, Josh."

He was so enthralled, Dianne had to finish drying his face.

"Where's your room, Mitchell?" Josh asked as he left the bathroom.

"Well, this is it," I said.

"But there's a double bed in here. Isn't that your parents' bed?"

"Yes, mine is next to the window."

They both ran over to the beige daybed and sat down on it. They wanted to make sure it was really a bed and not just a couch.

"I can see all of Central Park from here," I said, standing in front of the double windows, inviting them to join me.

They stood on either side of me, not as close to the windows as Fred Grosso or I would, especially when heaving paper clips out of them.

"There's the Polo Grounds straight ahead, a few miles beyond the park. See it?"

"I think so." Josh strained. "Kind of dirty cement pillars?"

"That's it," I assured him.

"Boys and sports," Dianne mused. Her eyes followed the gleaming dark cars and yellow taxis as they raced through the park.

"Now look right across the East River. That's the stadium, see?"

"Wow!" Josh burst out. "You can see the Yankee Stadium from your bedroom!"

"When there are night games, I see the lights from up here."

"And the cars," Dianne asked, still taking in the park, "what are their lights like at night?"

"Streaking diamonds."

"Come on, children, get your coats on," Bea urged from the living room.

"Okay," I answered her, "we're coming," but the three of us remained at the windows another moment, Josh and Dianne still ten inches further back than I.

My father was already at the Russian Tea Room checking on the arrangements, each detail, when the five of us pushed through the brass-plated revolving door. Mom and Pop Kagle and Jessica were waiting in the red vestibule, unwilling to surrender their coats until Bea gave her Persian lamb to the hatcheck girl and got a numbered plastic chip in return. Myron and Bruce were still looking for parking spaces. On a holiday no one had to move their cars, so they'd probably have to put them in a garage or lot, like the one across the street from the hotel.

The maître d' lead our party through the restaurant to a private dining room in the rear. Three waiters dressed in tan native tunics were ready for us, ice water in each goblet, silver gleaming, cloth napkins under every fork. Pop Kagle sat at one end of the table with a glass of vodka nestled in a cannister of ice chips. My father peered from the other end, very pleased. The waiters seemed to have our orders in advance. There were no menus. They came out with a choice of appetizers, chopped liver or marinated herring. For the grownups sipping vodka there were also two dishes of tiny black eggs with onion garnish and slices of lemon which were passed around the long table as if they were caskets of jewels. I tensed when our appetizer plates were removed by the busboy and two of the waiters carried in trays of soup. Here they came, the deadly beets. I panicked. A bowl was placed in front of Jessica at my right. The borscht was that awful deep red, and there were slivers of the offensive vegetable floating around the entire bowl. In the middle of it was a mound of sour cream, the one redeeming ingredient. The waiter passed over me, and the busboy took my golden underliner dish away. I glanced at my father, who smiled. He had remembered. I broke open a seeded pumpernickel roll and knocked off Josh's untouched portion of herring so no one would notice my soupless state. Would the Wiener schnitzel require more subterfugue? Some deal! It was supposed to be a party! Fun!

The breaded cutlet was thicker, larger than anything Grandma Lufkin ever served, but the sunny-side-up egg on the top was familiar. How would they go together, though? Why did they have to? Eggs were for breakfast. I cut into the edge of the cutlet, avoiding the egg entirely. It was moist, pink in the middle, the breading spicy, crisp. I was enjoying the veal so much after three mouthfuls, I wasn't conscious of puncturing the yolk with my fork as I speared yet a fourth bite. The yolk flooded the tender middle of the cutlet, oozing onto the rim of the plate. I couldn't avoid the burst of yellow liquid and hope to eat more of the veal, so I put the soaked forkful into my mouth. The film of yolk made the veal taste even better, bringing out the contrasting flavors and textures of the pink meat and the breading. I relaxed with this discovery, my portion of Wiener schnitzel no longer dangerous like the borscht. I looked around the long table. Everyone except Josh, who merely picked at his tiny slice of cutlet taken from Dianne's portion, was savoring their main course as much as I.

We all wandered over to the Park Central after the meal. Bea served fresh coffee and tea with chocolate petits fours, just in case anyone still had room left for "a little something." Marion, Bruce, and Mom Kagle shared the couch looking out over the park. Pop Kagle sat across the room from them in my father's upholstered easy chair. Myron was on the radiator, taking in the view. Bea puttered in the kitchen, and my father actually helped serve the tea and coffee, an act I had never seen him perform. It was the first time company had been up to the apartment. The Kagles were impressed with Bea's home; the panorama, the furniture, the pictures, all the accoutrements were taken in, their *style moderne* noted. It was Philly's taste, they realized, but she was part of it now, serving second cups of coffee from her new Silex. Philly passed around his pigskin humidor with a dozen fresh Havana panatelas inside. He had bought them for the occasion.

"Wonderful leaf!" Myron sang from the radiator, lighting a stick match against his thumbnail. He repeated the trick for my father and Bruce so they could light up. My father told stories about the store, everyone listening, laughing at his subtle punch lines. I sat on the floor with Josh and Dianne, looking up at all their wide faces. So many in our suite 2209, a real family, I thought, as Bea offered the men individual ceramic ashtrays.

When the Kagles left, hugging and kissing us with compliments, we were so flushed with our triumph we could not contain ourselves in 2209. We went for a walk along Central Park South, the pale sun descending over our shoulders. We strolled past the Plaza, down 5th Avenue by the carriage trade bookstores, Doubleday, Scribner's and Brentano's, where they sold no remainders and let customers charge purchases. Brentano's was always on the verge of bankruptcy because of this loose credit policy, my father told us, and Doubleday never made any money because their 5th Avenue rents were so high. They were lucky to break even. We turned back toward Rockefeller Plaza to admire the towering New Hampshire Christmas tree, partially trimmed for the holiday season the Macy's Thanksgiving Day Parade had just inaugurated.

In front of Radio City Music Hall my appetite revived. "What's for dinner?" I asked.

"Are you kidding, Mitchell?" my father exclaimed. "We just had that huge lunch and the petits fours. How can you be hungry again?"

"Just am."

"Well, it is six o'clock, Philly," Bea said in my defense, "the time he normally eats at Lake Ronkonkoma."

I nodded my head in agreement.

"The kitchen's a mess. I'll have to clean it up before I get something on the table. Can you wait an hour or so, Mitchell?"

Reluctantly I nodded once again. Bea knew I would be picking over her shoulder in the kitchen while she washed the dishes and tried to pull an evening meal together, so she turned to my father.

"Let's grab a bite while we're out, Phil. We can each have exactly what we feel like."

"Twice in one day, eating out? Jesus, what is this?" Phil was annoyed.

"Thanksgiving, remember."

She was getting stronger. My father sulked for several blocks. We were on 53rd, nearing the corner of 7th avenue, walking past the wide open windows of Bick's. I remembered my mother's forlorn gaze tracing the empty Sunday buses down the avenue toward Times Square, our breakfast of thick pancakes nearly over.

"Well, where should we go, Philly? It's almost six-thirty. I could use a cup of coffee, a little something myself."

Bick's was out of the question for Bea. My father knew that. Couldn't even suggest it.

"How about the Stage? Something for everyone." Philly smiled, giving in to her demand.

We got home at eight-thirty. I was uncomfortably stuffed, barely able to move through the doorway. A hot tongue and swiss on rye, a side order of potato salad and a bottle of Dr. Brown's cream soda churned within my stomach cavity. A white envelope with *MR. PHILLIP WOOLF* typed in capital letters sat on the doorsill.

"What the hell is this?" My father picked it up swiftly from a graceful crouch and went into the living room to rip it open. He had only ordered tea and apple strudle at the Stage and could still maneuver with some dexterity.

Bea followed me into the bedroom and stripped the beige slipcover from my bed while I hopped into my pajamas and brushed my teeth.

"Jesus Christ, Bea, look at this, will you! Just look at it!"

"Night, Mitchell," Bea said, rushing back to the living room.

I figured my father was screaming about the message in the envelope. I stared at the ceiling from my pillow.

"Bastards!" my father exploded. "They want a hundred and fifty dollars a month . . . a thirty-eight dollar increase!"

"That's thirty-five percent. Can they do it?" Bea was startled too.

"Their lawyers say wartime rent control has been modified by the state legislature. They can charge what they want in a *hotel*. I'll have to check with Keppelstein tomorrow . . . I mean, Monday. Bastards! Why did they slip it under our door on Thanksgiving? Couldn't wait a minute once they could raise the rent a dime . . . had to ruin the whole fucking day!"

"Shh, shh, we'll work it out, Phil, calm down. Mitchell has a lesson with Cantor Gluck tomorrow morning at nine. Let him sleep."

Their voices lowered.

"For that much money we could live in a palace," my father protested.

"Maybe we should look around," Bea snuck in. "No more services here anymore. They cut out everything."

"Maybe we should look," my father agreed, not realizing it had slipped out.

The tongue and potato salad were entering my intestines, which suddenly took on the muscular life of a snake that had swallowed a small field animal.

Chapter
Five

◆◆◆

ONCE PHILLY CONCURRED with Bea's suggestion that they look around for something else, looking around became her obsession. Her quest began on the Upper West Side, home of most Bnai Sholem congregants. Unfortunately the few vacant apartments on Central Park West and Riverside Drive were enormous, containing twelve, fourteen rooms. Philly wanted four and a half rooms at the old 2209 rent, $109 a month, with a large eat-in kitchen and a gas stove for Bea.

"Can't you find anything smaller and cheaper, Bea?" Philly asked at Sunday breakfast when she presented him with her findings after two weeks of actual looking with realtors and a fresh scan of the *Times*.

"Six rooms are a hundred and fifty a month, seven, one seventy-five . . . on up, according to size and location. Smaller than six rooms is almost impossible to find unless you try residential hotels, and that's tiny rooms, dingy. Less than one fifty a month, I'm telling you, Phil, doesn't exist. I've seen everything."

"But we don't need six rooms, Bea. Mitchell's away at Lake Ronkonkoma nine months of the year."

"I'll look for five, but that means key money, schmearing the super with three months' rent up front."

"Jesus!" Philly smashed the table with his fist, rattling his empty teacup.

"The war is over." Bea steadied his fist. "Lots of people are making money and need places to live. There's a housing shortage. You read the newspapers, Philly, come on!"

Bea was relentless in her quest. Mrs. Benjamin helped with inside leads from sisterhood members. Through one of these Bea found a charming, light five-room apartment between West End and Riverside Drive for $180, just on the market. She whisked Philly uptown without telling him the price. He admired the master bedroom river view, the orange sun ball slipping behind Hoboken.

"How much a month?" he asked, staring at the river.

"One eighty, Phil."

"Son of a . . . And the key?"

"Only one month's rent."

"Terrific!" he paced off the living room, trying to imagine their furniture in it. The kitchen was large enough to eat in. They walked the second bedroom together.

"Wouldn't it be less than one fifty without this room?" Philly asked.

"No fours in this building."

"One eighty will kill us!"

"Why, Phil? Business is good, better than during the war."

"But costs are sky-high—wages, paper, electricity, everything is up, up!"

"Listen, Phil." She lit a Chesterfield, inhaled deeply. "If Mitchell lived at home, the money you saved on Lake Ronkonkoma would pay for the extra room, wouldn't it? More than pay."

"Where would he go to school? The public schools stink. Private school tuition is prohibitive."

"Stuyvesant is public and it's excellent. The director of Bnai Sholem's Sunday school is chairman of the History Department. I know everything about it—there's a special entrance test in December."

"Well, maybe if Mitchell . . ." Philly was off balance.

"I'll arrange for him to take it. He's a bright boy, always on the Honor Roll at Lake Ronkonkoma even after skipping a whole grade."

"Wait a second! Not so fast! Would he like living here with *us?*"

"With *me,* you mean." Bea flushed. "I know what's inside your head."

"I can't stand this tension." Philly regained the offensive.

"Phil, be fair to me." She doused her cigarette in a container of coffee left by the painters and reached into her alligator pocketbook for her handkerchief. "The bar mitzvah is working out."

"So far." Philly knew there were still nine months to go plus the catered affair at the Bolivar to arrange. Since Bnai Sholem didn't hold bar mitzvah services during the summer when Mitchell actually turned thirteen, they would have to wait until early September for the event.

"He calls me Mommy, Phil," she moved the embroidered hanky towards her wet eyeballs.

"Easy, Bea, easy. We'll see what Mitchell wants, and try to work something out."

Bea rested her curly head against his glen plaid jacket.

The next day she found out everything she could about the test for Stuyvesant—except its contents. She also intensified her search for a less expensive five-room apartment in the 70's, 80's, or low 90's between the river and Central Park. She was dogged, even though Philly wouldn't commit the super's key money until the location of a future school was settled. Bea understood. It was a fragile equation: the apartment, the school, Philly's nerves, the money, Mitchell. Any one of these factors could upset the familial balance. If she succeeded, however, got Mitchell out of Lake Ronkonkoma and into Stuyvesant, all three of them out of 2209 into a larger apartment, the payoff would be breathtaking! Instant domesticity, an end to household improvisation. Bea could take care of apartment hunting easily; prying Mitchell loose from Lake Ronkonkoma before the September 1948 semester began would require more finesse. Without his tuition money a new apartment was "unaffordable"; and without Mitchell as a fulltime resident Bea would remain an idle stepmother.

Despite my pending bar mitzvah and the new intimacy Bea and I shared, my attachment to the Lake Ronkonkoma School was deep and loyal. I was center of our basketball team, probable shortstop for spring softball, and most important, a substitute player on the Upper School JV basketball squad, able to go on road trips even on week-nights. So far, I had adjusted to the rigors of the eighth grade, my leap over the seventh successful. The new high-school faculty Mr. Ryson hired to share in teaching our group were demanding yet inspiring.

Mr. Rosenthal, our favorite, the Upper School history teacher, exploded into our homeroom every day before lunch, 5th period, with books, pamphlets and questions about the real world.

"Okay, Woolf, say you're a cabbie in New York, own the cab yourself," Rosenthal began the week after Thanksgiving break.

"I can't drive."

Rafferty, Fritz, Austria and even Weil guffawed. Rosenthal paused, waiting out our laughter.

"Listen, Woolf, this is important. You drive your own cab, you're that guy. It's real. You have a flat tire on 47th Street and Broadway, open the trunk for the spare, find out it's almost thread-bare but strong enough to carry you into the Texaco gas station on 10th Avenue, where you get the flat patched."

All of us were mesmerized, staring into his weak black eyes, which were magnified by thick lenses.

"Now, what's your problem, Woolf?"

"Two lousy tires."

"Worse! At the gasoline station, when they hoist the cab up on the hydraulic lift to see which tire should be rotated to the spare posi-tion in the trunk, the mechanic shows you the three 'good' tires are ready to pop, next month, next week, tomorrow maybe. No telling. How come? Does anyone know how this happened?" Rosenthal sud-denly demanded.

"Woolf's a stop-and-go driver," Fritz says, recalling his father's police car antics.

"Let's say he's careful, even rotates his tires every six months at the Texaco station."

Austria waved his bony wrist in the air for recognition. "How old is the cab, Woolf?" he asked me when recognized.

"A forty-four DeSoto," I replied.

"Wait! Think, Woolf, about the year," Rosenthal said, interrupting my fantasy ownership. He had been a Seabee, had come ashore with the supplies at Normandy. "Who made new models during the War?"

The entire classroom helped me out: "No one!"

Austria jumped, alive with social insight. "The tires are really old, prewar, which is why they're all worn out!"

"What does Woolf do now if he needs four new tires at seven ninety-five each, but he only makes twenty bucks a week?" Rosenthal was presenting the postwar dilemma. "What do you do?" He walked over to my desk and sat on top of an empty one beside mine, as if we were in the Texaco station.

"And I only make twenty bucks a week? Plus tips?" I pleaded for a few extra bucks.

"No, the twenty includes tips—everything."

"But I need thirty-two for the new tires. What am I supposed to do, Mr. Rosenthal?"

"Borrow the money for the tires."

"Borrow money?" I repeated the alien words in disbelief. My father never did that. He saved for all improvements, paid cash.

"No time to save. Besides, twenty a week doesn't leave much for a savings account. If the other tires go, you're out of business altogether."

"So who's going to loan me the money?" I asked.

"The Texaco guy will give you credit to buy four new tires because you're a regular customer. He knows what you earn and that you own the cab."

"He'll give me the thirty-two bucks?"

"No, he'll sell you four new tires on credit if you sign an installment purchase contract, agreeing to pay him back, a few bucks at a time plus some interest."

"So I'm still in business, but I owe Texaco thirty-two dollars?"

"Make that thirty-three, thirty-four with the interest added."

"I pay them a few bucks each week out of my twenty?"

"Each month."

"Each month! That's not a bad deal!"

Briiiing, briiiing, briiiing. The electric bell went off outside in the hall, indicating the period was over, it was time to change classes.

"To be continued"—Rosenthal cuffed the side of my neck—"at the garage tomorrow." The spell was broken, and he grabbed his books for Ancient History, already searching his mind for examples of barter economy and slavery. We scraped our desks and chairs apart, collected our books and moved into the hallway toward Miss Brazell's math class, through the Upper School bodies also changing rooms and floors. She was a statuesque woman. Unfortunately her heavy bosom was always well hidden beneath a white blouse and pastel jacket. Only her wide calves were exposed in sheer nylons, a pencil seam splitting them into firm sections beneath the hemline of her skirt. We could learn anything her contralto voice sent our way. Miss Brazell exploited this attention, introducing us to algebra and hints of geometry before snowflakes took over the landscape in December.

Bea's suggestion that I take the entrance examination for Stuyvesant High School while I was home for Christmas vacation was thus a challenge, an opportunity to show off and measure my recent promotion and problem-solving skills at the best high school in the city. According to Bea *everyone* had gone there: Bernard Baruch, Felix Frankfurter, Louis Mumford, doctors, lawyers, scientists, all brains, all successful. We never discussed the consequences of my passing the two-hour examination, though implicit in my taking it was an understanding that if I did pass, I might consider going to Stuyvesant. The possibility of failure was never imagined.

Bea took me down to Stuyvesant on the 7th Avenue IRT one Saturday morning in late December. The closer we got to 14th Street, the more thirteen- and fourteen-year-old boys appeared holding fistfuls of sharpened yellow pencils. They were crowding into each car, some with anxious parents, others in neighborhood groups. At the 14th Street stop the wide platform was swarming with bodies climbing stairs, heading into yet another set of turnstiles leading down a steep corridor toward the Canarsie Line. The scene was like the IND at 163rd Street when the Yankees played a Sunday double-header. Only this mob was mainly kids, yelling, dashing, walking, a few of them faking jump shots with woolen caps. We all tumbled out of our subway cars at the narrow 1st Avenue stop, eager for daylight.

Bea was disoriented. We followed the moving bodies into the venerable high school on 15th Street between 1st and 2nd avenues. Bea pointed to a coffee shop across the street from the school.

"Meet me there, Mitchell, after the test. Good luck. I'll be waiting." She reached into her purse, desperate for her cigarettes, backtracking across the street.

All of us trooped inside the school auditorium and sat down on hard wooden theater seats with flap-hinged writing surfaces tucked beneath each right arm. The moment these were discovered, everyone snapped his into place. Some didn't work, the lock joint was broken, or the writing arm torn off. Murmurs of abuse and disappointment surrounded each defective writing arm until a teacher appeared on the dim stage.

"Okay, hold it down! And spread out! There must be at least one empty space on either side of you before we can begin."

I was suddenly standing in the aisle with no seat.

"The monitors will hand out sample questions and work sheets the moment they have your admission tickets. The first test will be distributed in ten minutes. Look at the clock over the balcony. Make sure your name is clearly printed on each section of the test. Everyone standing in the aisle without a seat follow Mr. Schimmerhorn upstairs to the biology room."

About twenty of us trailed a small man in a purple sweater and blue pants out of the vast auditorium and up a stairwell.

"Quickly, boys, we musn't be late!" he purred back at the stragglers. There were yellow cotton balls stuffed in his ears, as if he had just taken drops. He was gentle with us, but harassed by endless responsibilities. A chain link fence ran up the center of each flight of green stairs we climbed. After two floors I realized this metal cage divided the entire stairwell from the basement floor to the top of the building. A precautionary device, I supposed, to keep the students moving in one direction from molesting the students going the opposite way. What could they possibly do to one another on a stairwell?

The biology room contained fifteen rows of desks arranged in semicircular tiers, like a movie house balcony, except we stared down at a long slate laboratory table with a sink depressed in the middle and gas jets sticking up at either side for experiments.

"All right, boys, please find seats so we can begin." A different teacher with white chalk marks on his gray lab coat welcomed us. "Leave an empty seat between you and the next student."

I was in the middle of the seventh tier, leaning forward, both number two Ticonderoga pencils stickpin sharp. The room was lighter than the main floor auditorium. Altogether there were only forty-five students taking the test with me. The tests were handed out by student monitors, four-page booklets.

"Okay, boys, listen. Twenty minutes on each section, multiple choice. Black in the correct answer, A, B, C, D or E, and move on to the next question. Answer as many correctly as you can. Don't dawdle. Watch the clock."

I was ready, clearheaded. I moved through the initial computation questions confidently, then some stuff I was unfamiliar with but could figure out probable answers to. But number 5 took my breath away:

It costs n cents to manufacture 1 dozen neckties. At the same rate how many cents will it cost to manufacture neckties?

A) $50n$ B) $\dfrac{50}{n}$ C) $\dfrac{5}{2n}$ D) $\dfrac{2}{5n}$ E) $\dfrac{5n}{2}$

I reread it: It cost n cents for a dozen neckties . . . how many cents for 30? n wasn't cents—how could a letter be money? Twelve didn't go into 30 three times evenly. The suggested answers were no help. Guessing was impossible. $\frac{5n}{2}$ . . . what the hell was that? Nothing in Bookland cost $\frac{5n}{2}$. Rosenthal's situations were no help, and Miss Bazell never gave us word problems, just straight equations, no fucking tricks. I reread the problem six times, stunned. Number 5 came with an illustration, letters and numbers . . . hopeless! I was dizzy with grief, unable to continue. An electric buzzer went off.

"Your twenty minutes are up, boys."

The next booklet was vocabulary and reading comprehension. *Fling* and *routine* were easy enough, my confidence was partially restored. *Manipulate* and *adroit* were more problematic. I had seen *adroit* before, but I wasn't really sure what it meant. I took a guess. At least I had one chance out of five of being right. I was still in the game.

The next section began:

Plants that are structurally adapted to withstand severe desert conditions are called xerophytes. Some desert plants such as ocotillos and Jatrophas go into a state of dormancy that plant physiologists call drought endurance. With the rains the plants leaf out rapidly; then, with the onset of the dry season, they shed their leaves and return to dormancy.

The second paragraph became even more complex, scientific and unpronounceable. After three more long, detailed paragraphs the comprehension questions began. I read the second paragraph over and over and wanted to choose E on the first question, but I knew that was a direct contradiction of the first sentence of that paragraph. Hopeless and stymied, my eagerness ebbed away, despair overwhelmed me. I couldn't read through the rest of the questions, though I tried feebly. How could the other kids in the room keep going? Understand such horseshit? I was out of the game on the sidelines, staring at the black hands of the large Telechron clock on the front wall of the amphitheater. Diamond shapes had been cut out of the sharp hour and minute hand. The bronze second hand had a dagger point. Twelve noon was the magic hour of release when all these hands came together in a slick line. What a ludicrous ordeal!

Bea sensed my despondency when I found her in the coffee shop as soon as the test was over.

"How was it, Mitchell?" she asked from her mound of cigarette butts.

"Lousy!" I snapped.

"How did you do?"

"I don't know! What difference does it make anyway? Who gives a sh—"

"I do, Mitchell, I do!" She grabbed my hand and lead me out to the sidewalk. "Let's have a nice lunch."

"I'm not hungry."

"There's a famous restaurant on 14th Street near Klein's. Let's go there as a treat, Mitchell."

"For what?"

'Come on, you probably did really well."

I knew I hadn't, but lunch was lunch.

Luchow's was immense, charming, old-world. Red and green Christmas decorations were hung from dark wooden nooks and crannies. A large spruce tree with gold and silver ornaments occupied the center of the vast restaurant. Tuxedoed waiters rushed about with serving plates stacked up their arms. Bea ordered for both of us, sauerbraten with dumplings.

"You'll love it, Mitchell, just wait!"

The sweet sauce with hot raisins could not revive the dry beef it was poured over. The dumplings were tasteless mush, like Cream of Wheat cereal without salt and butter added. I could only eat half of the meat and a forkful of dumpling, indicating to Bea that my despair over the test was not fake modesty but rather a clear sign of failure.

Within three weeks Bea discovered Forest Hills High School, across the river in Queens. It was just as good as Stuyvesant. Some argued it was better. It had a newer building and excellent teachers, including a few with PhD's. Of equal importance there was no entrance exam. Residency was the sole requirement. So Bea had to find an apartment somewhere off Queens Boulevard within the boundary lines of the school.

Philly had to be lured back underground aboard the IND subway. It was a twenty-five minute express ride on the new Queensborough line from Bookland to 71st Street and Continental Avenue, the Forest Hills stop. Bea showed him lavish half-page advertisements in the Sunday *Times* real estate section: modern luxury buildings just completed on the west side of Queens Boulevard with five-and-a-half-room apartments priced close to the old Park Central rent.

They took the F train from 42nd Street and 6th Avenue one mild Saturday after Harry had returned from lunch. Bea lead Philly directly to the newest red brick apartment building, the Mahan House. The model apartment on the eighth floor had an efficiency kitchen leading into a dining alcove which opened onto the largest living room either of them had ever been in. The master bedroom was almost as big as the entire living room at 2209. Each room had high casement windows, the most dramatic running fifteen feet, wall to wall, across the living room. Philly stared out of the center pane, surprised at the haphazard vista. The Empire State Building and Chrysler spire were still visible, yet vacant lots, barren fields, frame houses and brick garden apartments were right underfoot.

"Phil, what do you think?" Bea came up behind him, snuggled her hand under his cashmere lapel.

"Fields," he murmured, focusing 500 yards out. "So many fields. Who owns them?"

"Isn't it lovely, Phil? And there's a landscaped park—you can't see it from this side—for exclusive use of the building's residents."

"What's the nut again?" he asked.

"A hundred and ten a month, including utilities."

"Not bad." He shook his head from side to side. "What about security? Didn't you say—"

"Three months," Bea answered.

"That's three hundred and thirty dollars Minskoff and Son hold interest-free until we move out! Crafty!"

"All the developers require security deposits, Philly. It's a seller's market, even in Queens."

"Where does everyone get the money?" He shook his head again, this time at the new prosperity.

"See the high school off to the right?" Bea pointed half a mile out.

"That's Forest Hills High?"

"That's it. Some spread, huh?"

It was much bigger than Barringer High, which Philly had attended in Newark, and the style . . . so American—red brick, a Greek Revival facade. Like the United States Congress or a state capitol, it was crowned with a pillared cupola.

"When was it built?" he asked.

"During the World's Fair, they told me. Thirty-nine, forty."

They took the self-service elevator back to the fluorescent lobby, picked up a promotional flier, spoke with the rental agent and strolled outside to the private park.

"It's landscaped, Phil, see?"

"Huh! Some job. What the hell are these?" He pointed to a row of thin seedlings in front of the Mahan House, one planted every twenty feet, wired to supporting two by fours.

"Trees!" Bea answered.

"What kind?"

"I don't know *kind*, Phil."

"I do!" Philly hopped onto the protective sod around a seedling to better inspect the green bark, sniff it for bouquet.

"It's a . . . Minskoff tree!"

Bea cracked up. "Philly." She hugged him in a rush. "Character! What a character!" she whispered in his ear.

They marched off, arm in arm, to the IND, repeating the name of the new species every half-block until Philly had tears in his eyes from laughing so hard.

Getting Mitchell to Forest Hills and into the high school was more complicated. He had taken the Stuyvesant test as a lark, not connecting his performance with leaving the Lake Ronkonkoma School so they could afford a larger apartment. He knew he'd done very poorly. Bea didn't have to tell him the official results, though she used them as evidence of Lake Ronkonkoma's deficiencies in arguing her case for bringing him home to a public high school. Philly was not convinced.

"It's just a test, Bea. One lousy test. Mitchell's not used to them, that's all. He has to want the change before we take him out of Lake Ronkonkoma."

When I accompanied Bea and my father out to Forest Hills one Saturday afternoon during my spring vacation, I assumed they were "looking for something else" because of the outrageous rent hike at the Park Central. Our first stop was Burleson's paint and wallpaper store on Queens Boulevard, where Bea and my father leafed through four cumbersome books of wallpaper in the "decorator corner." All the subdued patterns my father wanted for the dining alcove were not included in the group Minskoff and Sons would pay for as part of the decoration allowance. Neither were the quality paints. My father was infuriated.

"Cheap *mockie* bastards!"

"For just a little extra we can have what you like, Phil."

"It's the principle, Bea, the principle of the thing!"

They argued about the aesthetic merits and the additional cost of each swatch of wallpaper, each paint chip they carried with them to the model apartment of the Mahan House.

When we arrived, the sky was overcast. I couldn't see the Empire State Building or the Chrysler Building, as promised, and the radiators were recessed within the walls, leaving me no perch, though I would have my own long room with a single casement window to peer out of.

"Let's show Mitchell the high school," Bea suggested casually.

"Why?" I asked.

"It's so close by," she said, covering her tracks.

"Impressive set up." My father was helping her out, bending his neutrality. "Let's take a look!"

We left the Mahan House and strolled toward the high school down a tree-lined avenue with two-story brick houses on either side. The buds were ready to crack open on the trees. Yellow crocuses were already out along slate walks leading to each front door. This street emptied into a semicircular one with larger homes of stucco, wood and brick.

Forest Hills High School was set back fifty yards on the other side of this curved street on its own thirty-acre campus. I walked up to the Greek Revival entrance of the school past a towering white flagpole. I was awed by the gold letters below the stone cornice spelling out *FOREST HILLS HIGH SCHOOL.* Trumpet salvos would have been in order as part of the decor. At ground level the granite cornerstone had *1940* chiseled into it.

"See, Phil, it was during the World's Fair," I heard Bea mutter.

"How many kids go here?" I asked her.

"Twenty-five hundred."

"That's as many as Stuyvesant!"

"They all fit into one session here, Mitchell."

The facade of the three-story high school had enormous double-hung windows, six panes wide, which let sunlight into every classroom. The parallel sides of the H-shaped structure, however, were grim and endless, with fewer windows. Metal gates protected every pane of gymnasium glass on the right wing of the high school.

I grew nervous, recalling the inside of Stuyvesant, the amphitheater, the test. Bea sensed my apprehension. To pull me out of it, she suddenly turned me and my father around on our heels so we were facing the opposite side of the street, looking at a row of new one-family houses that were open for inspection, just on the market.

"Let's take a look, Phil."

"At a house? I thought we were interested in a five-room apartment."

"Just a look, Phil, it's free, to get an idea of comparative costs. Besides, it's even closer to the high school." She winked.

He threw up his hands. Bea reached for mine. "Come on, Mitchell, what do you say? Pick a house, any one!"

I was as eager to get to the other side of the street, away from the high school, as Bea was to look at a model house. We chose a gabled Tudor one with a garage attached to the front. There was a fenced terrace above the garage. Another couple was on the second floor, methodically inspecting the bedrooms with a saleswoman, so we had the entire downstairs to ourselves. My father joined us reluctantly, skeptically. Bea and I rushed hand in hand into the living room which was as long as the one we had just seen at the Mahan

House, though not as wide. It lead into a full-size separate dining room. The kitchen was just beyond the swinging door. It had wall to wall built-in cabinets, Formica counter tops connecting the base cabinets, a stainless steel sink and General Electric appliances.

"Is there room for a table?" Philly entered the kitchen.

"A small one maybe, near the back door."

"I mean, for the whole family to eat in the kitchen at the same time?"

"We'll have to measure it, Phil."

We moved out of the kitchen and discovered a convenient half-bath tucked under the staircase. A few feet farther and we reentered the living room. Philly stared into the flagstone fireplace.

"I wonder if it works."

"Of course it does!"

"Sometimes they're fake now."

"We'll ask the saleswoman when she comes downstairs."

I placed my hand on the bannister, my left foot on the first oak step, and pushed off. It seemed as though the pressure of the hard wood against my leather soles was propelling me up the stairs. At the second floor landing I heard the saleswoman out on the terrace with the other couple. I peeked into the master bedroom and two smaller ones, saw the full bath. I jump-stepped halfway down the stairs, favoring my left foot, hopping softly on my right.

"Psst, psst, come on up! It's terrific!"

"We'll wait till the others are done."

I sat down on the fourth step from the bottom, intoxicated. Imagine having your own stairs! And living on two separate floors! I waited for my parents and the other couple to switch levels. Bea caught my enthusiasm when she turned away from the fireplace.

"Phil, look at Mitchell! He's about to burst!"

"I'm not, but we're here, so let's—"

"Thank you, Mrs. Forbes, we'll be in touch." The other couple came down the stairs. I scurried out of their way and stood waiting with my parents for Mrs. Forbes, a middle-aged realtor, to show us up the stairs. Bea was enthralled with the master bedroom and its adjoining terrace; she would be able to take her morning coffee on it in her negligee if she wanted.

After the upstairs tour we returned to the living room, where Philly let loose.

"These walls." He ran his strong little hands over the one separating the living room from the foyer. "They feel like cardboard. Are they plaster?" He didn't wait for an answer. "And these moldings"—he pointed to the base of the wall where it met the floor—"are so skimpy. And *this!*" He twirled around, pirouetting until his hand struck the fireplace rock. "Is it real?"

"Of course it's real." Mrs. Forbes was stunned by Philly's rapid-fire attack.

"Does it work?" he continued.

"Certainly, Mr. Woolf! This is a customized home, made of the finest materials available. No one uses plaster anymore. Sheetrock is fire resistant and uniform."

"Is it strong though?"

"Very! Like a rock!" She twinkled.

"And quiet? Doesn't sound travel right through paper?"

"Practically soundproof, Mr. Woolf. This is not Levittown, mass-produced." She fluffed her blouse, realigned her jacket. "Each one of these homes is unique, different exterior trim, different layout, which is why they cost twenty-two thousand five hundred dollars."

The price tag ended their Ping-Pong exchange about details. My father brooded over the numbers, digested them, one digit at a time.

"How . . . how . . . how can anyone afford that? Who, who . . . who has that kind of money?" Philly had a nest egg from the war years, but nothing that large. "I mean that does seem like a . . . like a . . ."

"Mr. Woolf, you're not expected to put it all down in cash. No one ever does. We help you secure a three-percent thirty-year mortgage at the Ridgeway Savings Bank. You only have to come up with twenty-five percent in cash—that's fifty-six hundred and twenty-five dollars. If you're a veteran, FHA can arrange even better terms with a smaller down payment."

My father seemed upset, confused. He had always been a transient in hotel suites, apartments and leased stores; a renter looking for the best location, the best deal. He never settled in one place. Borrowing almost seventeen thousand dollars for thirty years meant a shift to permanence, an end to wandering. My father didn't understand owning a home.

The realtor sensed his anxiety. "Mr. Woolf, everyone, even the wealthiest homeowners have a mortgage. It's actually good business sense. Let me show you." And she sat down with Philly and Bea at the French provincial dining table and pulled out an interest table and her clipboard with white paper already set in place. She drafted a monthly payment schedule.

"Now, your debt service on the mortgage—"

"Debt?" Philly cringed. He only borrowed money to finance Christmas inventory.

"Your carrying charges would be seventy dollars a month, that includes interest and amortization. Gas and electric would be seventeen dollars, heating fuel averaged over twelve months, fifteen dollars, taxes—sewer, water, sidewalk, real estate—about forty dollars."

"A hundred forty-two a month!" Philly added it up quickly. "That's more than we pay now!"

"But, Mr. Woolf, you get a tax break on the monthly interest charge and real estate taxes."

"How?"

"Deduct them from your own taxes according to your bracket. Say it's forty percent . . ."

Philly was mute, refusing to acknowledge her guess.

"Just for the arithmetic. So you *actually* pay thirty-two dollars for heat and utilities, twenty-seven for amortization, and ten for non-deductible taxes. Now let me figure the break on your interest and real estate taxes. Let's see . . . altogether you save about twenty-nine dollars on the remaining seventy-three dollar payment, so your *actual* monthly debt is just under a hundred and thirteen dollars."

"How do I get the twenty-nine bucks back?"

"At the end of the year your accountant takes it off your tax bill, what you owe Uncle Sam. He'll figure it out."

"But I still pay the hundred and forty-two each month out of pocket?"

"True, but your equity is building up every day as you pay off the mortgage, and the value of real estate in Forest Hills keeps shooting up, has each year since the war ended."

"Which way did it shoot in 1935?"

"Those days are gone forever, Mr. Woolf. It's 1948!"

Philly wasn't certain about the future, especially if his money was going to be used in new ways. Bea, however, was not afraid of home-financing credit arrangements. From her parents' experience with their Brooklyn home she at least knew the words and tried explaining them on the subway ride back to Manhattan.

"It's still one forty-two a month, Bea," Philly continued, his voice louder, shriller as we left the express train at the 50th Street–Rockefeller Center stop to catch the uptown local for Columbus Circle. We were going home, not back to the store, so we had to change trains.

"Philly, you didn't listen to me. The tax and interest deductions—"

"All bullshit. It's still a hundred and forty-two bucks a month out of my pocket."

Bea sat down on a long wooden bench. Unable to smoke, she was restless, irritated by Philly's public swearing. My father was being unreasonable. I could accept the mortgage rigamarole because of Rosenthal's classes on installment buying. Why couldn't he? It was temperament, not business acumen. If one was optimistic about the future, it made sense.

"Where the fuck's the train?" Philly brayed at the white tiles, the empty uptown tracks. "Jesus Christ, twelve, fifteen minutes already. . . . It'll take us a goddamn hour to get home!"

Bea knew it was hopeless to argue when Philly was enraged. If they moved to Forest Hills, they wouldn't have to switch trains at Rockefeller Center to get to the Park Central. They could stay on the express train all the way to 42nd Street and be at Bookland in twenty-five minutes flat. For Mitchell's bar mitzvah lessons with Cantor Gluck, however, a switch to the uptown local would be necessary, but an hour's ride once in a while wasn't such an awful sacrifice for a larger apartment with a kitchen, or maybe a Tudor house. Bea's colon began twitching, from nerves, excitement about the future. The pain of her spasms increased as Philly's tirade intensified. When they finally made it back to 2209, Bea rushed into the bathroom, safe at last. But Philly pursued her, stood outside the bathroom door ranting.

"Prewar they built houses with real fireplaces."

"This one's real, it works," Bea answered from her toilet bowl sanctuary.

"They built real walls, not cardboard shit then. The whole fucking house will fall down in ten years, before it's even paid for!"

"Phil, please, take it easy. I got these cramps . . . awful cramps."

My father stopped in mid-bleat. His face reddened beneath his Saturday bristles. He moved away from the bathroom door, embarrassed. "We'll talk about it later, Bea, later." He withdrew to the living room window. Bea flushed the toilet again and again, then opened the bathtub faucets, let them run for fifteen minutes. She was creamed and relaxed when she emerged from the bathroom in her satin dressing gown. I was sitting on the daybed reviewing my bar mitzvah notebook for a lesson with Cantor Gluck on Sunday. Bea walked over to me, put her throbbing hand on my head. "You liked it, Mitchell, didn't you?"

"The house?" I looked into her stomach, wanting to be sure of the subject.

"Yes, the house."

"Sure, it was terrific."

"What did you like most about it?"

"The stairs."

"I thought so." She wiggled my head, still holding on to my hair. "What didn't you like about it?"

"That it was across the street from *that* high school!"

"Why?"

"It was so big."

"The house or the school?"

"The school, silly. You know."

"I know what you mean, Mitchell." She held my head against her red satin robe and peered out the windows into the park. "Maybe we can find a smaller one." She smiled. "Philly, you're right—they built better houses before the war," she called into the living room.

He was reading the Saturday *Times*, finally quiet. "You all right, Bea?"

"I'm fine now." She walked into the kitchenette. "When does the Sunday *Times* arrive at the newsstand?"

"Nine, nine-thirty."

"Can we get it tonight?"

"Sure, Mitchell can pick it up."

"Along with a Clark Bar," I bargained.

At nine-fifteen I left for the elevator, a fifty-cent piece in my palm. Bea stuck her head out the door.

"Mitchell, make sure it has section eight."

"Okay, I'll look."

"It's the Real Estate section." She blew me a kiss and closed the door.

"Woolf, hold it right here with both hands. Rafferty, get it down there, steady. Fritz, take the end, that's it." Stevens got us into position, supporting an eight-foot two by four against the studs of an old chicken coop we were restoring in the field of young pines east of the softball diamond. He drove a six-inch nail clear through the two by four into the gray foundation beam. Our hands vibrated with each blow of the hammer. Stevens never missed, four blows to a nail head. When the entire frame was rebuilt, we hoisted pine clapboards into place against it. Stevens used two-inch nails on these warped slats. There were curved ridges on the top of each board which fit snugly into the hollow groove of the next one. We moved quickly up toward the pitched roof.

"Take five. Let's see how cold our Cokes are." Stevens paused.

We climbed off our ladders. Stevens mopped his brow with a bandanna handkerchief and walked over to a cast-iron tub in the shade of a fir tree.

"The ice hasn't melted." He reached underneath a gray towel, gave Fritz, Rafferty and me each a chilled ten-ounce Coke, took one himself, held it to his cheek, pushed it up his temple.

"Mmmm, nice, perfect."

We had worked alongside him in the hot May sun since one o'clock, two hours without a break. I was so parched and dehydrated, I sucked my soda out of its green bottle in four icy swallows. The caramel foam oozed from the opening. The second bottle was slower, wetter. I paused, and carbonated bubbles came through my nostrils. We each had our own six-pack. Stevens had brought them back from Smithtown with him after driving the other Lower School kids in for the Saturday matinee.

Peep, first chick of our growing brood, toddled by. His yellow baby down was all gone now, the red and black feathers of his Rhode Island Red lineage taking over his four-week-old body; but his head was still naked, with tiny dot eyes, opaque, moving, his embryonic wattles emerging colorless underneath his beak.

"How did he get out of the pen, Woolf? Head him off."

Fritz and Rafferty cut him off in the rear. He ran into my feet. I had to pick him up or he would dart into the woods. No one else was near him. I grabbed his toothpick body with both hands, and the more he squawked, the tighter I squeezed his fragile breast. I was afraid I might crush him or provoke his rapid sharp beak. I held my breath, closed my eyes and rushed him toward the wire pen, dropping him into it.

"Atta boy, Woolf," Stevens shouted.

Phew, they hadn't noticed my panic.

I first saw Peep in his incubator at the Corner Store, where we usually stopped for cupcakes and soda on our Sunday hike with Stevens. He was an adorable yellow puffball like a Walt Disney animal until Stevens passed him around for approval and he was placed in my hands, shivering. He pecked my fingers, then released a green ooze in my palm, and I dropped him into Rafferty's lap. Eventually I adjusted, learned to mask my fear of touching him and the forty other chickens who comprised our flock. I more or less had to in order to do the chores: feeding and watering, maintaining the wire fences, completing the coop, running electricity out to it. These chores preoccupied me.

Stevens recorded the details of our common enterprise in an account ledger he kept in his room. We examined the entries every Friday night, when we made small contributions from our allowances. Our parents also helped out; even my father contributed, though he had never seen or planned to see our chicken coop. It was Stevens, however, who floated the operation with his own savings, ingenuity and sweat. We participated in certain decisions like whether to add ducks to the flock, but he was in charge of the big picture.

The following Saturday Rafferty and Fritz were screwing a hook and eye latch into the new panel door we'd cut in the coop so the chickens could go inside by themselves when the front door was bolted and we weren't around to shoo them inside. Stevens and I were above them laying tar paper on the new roof.

"What about these seams?" I asked Stevens as the last roll of paper was unfurled on the plywood roof. We had tapped metal tacks into aluminum push guards to hold the parallel rolls down. The push guards straddled the adjoining seams like silver nipples.

"See what I mean?" I ran my index finger along the unsecured tar paper seams. For the twelve inches between each aluminum circle they were free to pucker in the sun.

"We pour hot tar in that space. It hardens the seam."

"Where's the tar?"

"At Gould's. When we pick up the feed, we'll get some. Remind me, Mitchell."

I nodded, anticipating yet another process, a new skill. I stood up and looked out over the field of second-growth pine. A thick grove of maples and oaks divided us from the softball field. I wondered how my father would respond to the site. Would he approve of the quality of our postwar building materials and our craftsmanship? I spotted Rosenthal's wiry head moving up the dirt road toward the coop. He always showed up to kibbitz for a while on Saturday afternoon. He and Stevens were friends, though very different. Rosenthal had difficulty striking nails with a hammer. He was hopeless with tools, but terrific when muscle was needed to carry a hundred-pound feed sack or pull a tree stump out by the roots. He also understood electricity and was able to translate the diagram that came with our new fuse box.

"What's up, Rosie? Got something for us?" Stevens said in greeting.

"Some fuses, twenty-five amps so the new heater won't overload the box when it's plugged in." He went inside the coop and screwed the new fuses into the porcelain sockets, then walked back out, squinting at the sun, and heaved the old ten-amp fuses into the trash pile.

"Thanks, Rosie." Stevens was still on the roof.

"The station wagon's yours until six. Ma Kennedy left the keys in the usual place," Rosenthal announced to the blur on the roof.

"Hey, you guys, let's go get the feed!" Stevens was thrilled. "Rosie, help us out, will you?"

We scrambled off our ladders, ran down the pine field path and dashed, out of breath, across the softball field to the Pontiac station wagon. We did need supplies. Stevens and Rosenthal were in the front seat, the tailgate was down to receive the feed sacks. Fritz, Rafferty and I let our feet dangle from it as Stevens drove over the back roads to the gray silos of Gould's Feed and Supply.

Inside the cool storeroom Stevens ordered 400 pounds of Purina chicken feed. Fritz and Rafferty grabbed either end of a 100-pound sack. Rosenthal hoisted a sack over his shoulder. They began loading the back of the Pontiac.

"Don't forget the roofing tar," I reminded Stevens while the feed bill was tallied.

"Throw in some roofing tar also."

"Is that it now?" the salesman grumbled.

"That's it. What's it come to?"

"Twenty seventy-five."

Stevens wrote out a check.

Rafferty rushed back inside the store. "Hurry up, hurry up, you guys, it's raining!"

"Did you latch the panel door open after you screwed the new hook in?"

"I think so." Rafferty wasn't certain.

"I hope so." Stevens sounded worried.

The rain was so heavy on the ride back, the windshield wipers could not keep the windows clear. Rain flooded over the rubber blades.

"Jesus, I hope they had enough sense to go inside," Stevens mumbled.

We all knew the risks if they hadn't. No one said a word; even Rosenthal was somber. Stevens gunned the station wagon down the softball field. When he turned right up the pine field road, the rain stopped as suddenly as it had started. The hot sun burst through the clouds steaming the windshield dry. The hill we had to climb was awash with gushing rainwater. Stevens was afraid of losing traction if the road muddied, so he turned off the engine and yanked the emergency break out.

"Let's walk the rest!"

We all ran up the field to the coop, taking shortcuts through the dripping pine trees. We converged on the coop, a single consciousness, one set of disbelieving eyes. There, huddled before the panel door, which Rafferty *had* hooked open, were forty drenched chickens, their feathers plastered against their bodies. They were naked, drowning.

"Why the hell didn't they hop inside?" Rafferty asked.

"No one lead them," I guessed.

"Too dumb," Stevens replied, disgusted. "That's why their heads are so small—no fucking brains inside!"

Stevens began lifting the wet chicks in through the open door.

"This way, see. This is the way to stay dry," he mumbled to their limp heads, dejected, close to tears, which frightened us as much as the possibility of losing all the birds. Rosenthal helped by handing them in through the front door.

"Jesus Christ, what do we do now?" Stevens was undone.

"Are they dying?" I asked.

"Not yet."

We could see their bodies heaving on the cement floor of the coop. Rosenthal put his arm around Stevens. "We'll heat them back to life." He plugged in the new brood heater.

"That's not enough heat for an omelet." Stevens was still despondent.

While we unloaded the station wagon Rosenthal ran back to Mayall Hall, where he was in charge of the juniors and seniors. He gathered up all the electric heaters he could get his hands on and lugged them back to the coop, where he and Stevens arranged them in a semicircle around the waterlogged chicks.

"Nothing else to do," Rosenthal said. "Give it some time, maybe they'll dry out."

We sulked back to the dorm, convinced they would die and our venture would come to an end. In the morning, right after Sunday breakfast, we all ran directly to the coop, even Stevens and Rosenthal. Fritz, the quickest, opened the front door. A chorus of peeps filled the coop. The chicks were pecking at their grain trough, dipping into their water tin, scurrying about, feathers dry, as if nothing had happened the day before. It was a miracle—not one death, though a heater did blow a fuse. We shouted, hugged one another, swung around in a circle.

"They're too dumb to die!" Stevens shouted above our joyous huddle.

"And we're lucky they're so stupid," Rosenthal cried.

"Lucky, lucky, *lucky!*"

We were delirious with our rescue.

The whole campus was curious now, wanting to know more about the pine field, what we did there, especially Natalie and Carmen, the two sixth-grade girls. They had never observed such camaraderie between boys and teachers until we built the chicken coop. Our intimacy that Sunday morning, the collective urgency with which the five of us burst from the cellar dining room and ran toward the chicken coop was unusual.

Carmen and Natalie followed us up the steep path an hour later, after they had finished making their beds and cleaning the room they shared on the first floor of the South Dorm. I was back up on the roof, helping Stevens pour the tar we had bought at Gould's Feed. I pressed the seams of the paper as close together as I could while Stevens sealed the space between them with the warm tar. I turned away from the oily fumes to breathe in some clean air and saw Carmen's black shiny hair and Natalie's silly curls coming toward us.

"We have some visitors," I announced.

"Who?" Fritz asked.

"Mitchell's girl friend, La Señorita," Rafferty sassed.

He could see them too from his advanced position in the duck yard, where he was doing wire work.

"Come on, you guys, I didn't invite her out here," I pleaded.

"Why not? Too many chickens to spoil the necking pecking, I mean, pecking necking," Fritz came back.

I hopped off the roof, ready to go at Fritz, but Rosenthal came between us.

"Break it up." He held us apart. "Just two girls coming to look at the chickens. Act human." He let go of us.

Stevens welcomed them and displayed our flock, explaining the feeding ritual and building program. As Fritz, Rafferty and I relaxed with the two girls we competed for center stage, recreating the near mass drowning of our chicks.

Carmen was shy—perhaps because of her slight Spanish accent or the confusion she created in our midst with her womanly body. Though she was only a sixth grader, her breasts were developed, firm. Her face was serious, almost melancholy, with thick eyebrows, deep brown eyes. Natalie was the same height as Carmen, but she was flat-chested, had a little potbelly, a wide happy smile. She was still a kid like most of us in the Lower School. Natalie and Carmen both had older brothers in the Upper School, which was probably the reason they were at Lake Ronkonkoma School for its first coed year.

All the Upper and Lower School girls lived in the South Dorm, right across the way from us. The South Dorm freshmen and sophomore boys had been resettled in Mayall Hall. We had been casual observers of these changes until one evening when we were drawn to our second-floor bank of windows. Outside, a handful of Upper School girls and boys were petting just beneath our rooms. They were necking, with long breathless kisses, the girls straddleback against thick pine trunks for support, quiet, mature Spanish boy-men standing between their thighs, holding, caressing, swallowing, moving gently so they could come back the next night and the next and the next until there were no clothes or trees. Two couples wandered out of the lilac bushes, disheveled at ten P.M., curfew time. Some of these details were murky until Rafferty and Mayer turned their Eveready flash beams against the trees and bushes. We were innocent voyeurs; none of us knew exactly what we were missing except for Rafferty, who connected the barely visible acts with his own daydreams. He stared into the darkness, eyes enlarged, penis throbbing inside his flannel pajamas.

Every evening before dinner, all of us knew exactly what we were missing, what we could *see* but not *touch*. We ached to touch Rhoda Lane, clad in a lace brassiere, combing out her thick brown hair in front of her South Dorm windows. We could have sold seats, that was something we understood right off.

"Watch out, Austria, don't let her see your head. You want to ruin it for the rest of us?"

"Where did she go, Rafferty?" Austria pleaded.

"In her closet. She'll be back, always takes fifteen minutes to comb her hair."

"You lucky bastards!"

"Drop by anytime, Austria. Just keep your fucking head down, okay?"

Austria went back to his room.

"Jesus, it's blue tonight, Woolf." Rafferty socked my arm when Rhoda returned from her closet wearing a new brassiere. "I've never seen a blue one before! Look at it!"

I did. It was gorgeous. If only we could have them for a moment, look at them, take them out of their blue satin covers, touch them naked, that would be ecstacy beyond hugging and kissing in the darkness against rough bark.

I almost had my chance, or thought I would, one spring afternoon playing guns in the pine forest between the dorms and the softball field. Carmen was at my side, crouching under the bottom branches of a large fir tree. As everyone else scattered deeper into the

forest to find cover I dropped down just behind her on the soft
needles, my mobility hindered by her presence, which Mrs. Ryson
had forced on me. Where the hell could I hide with her tagging along?
I knew she liked me. The previous week she had pointed me out as
the boy she wanted to go to the senior prom with. "Him!" she had
whispered to Mrs. Ryson that Sunday before lunch when we were
lined up, ready to march into dinner. Some of us heard and turned
toward her. She was scarlet with shame. I was teased for several days
but had learned how to take it or at least not display my embarrassment. Now that I was trapped with her, what was I supposed to say?
"I'd love to take you to the prom—let's be friends"?

She'd tell Natalie and Mrs. Ryson, and everyone would make fun
of me. I was angered by that prospect and my own confusion, yet
there she was in a low-cut spring blouse, my head behind her bare
shoulders, her bosoms prominent. I could see the lacework of her bra
beneath the eyelet floral border of her blouse. Her deep breasts pulsed
with each heartbeat, lifting her cleavage into my eyes. I pushed both
hands inside her blouse.

"If you like me so much, why don't you let me hold them?" I
half-shouted.

Carmen tried to wrestle free of my grip. I cupped her breasts
more tightly, surprised at their heft. Confused by the elaborate construction of her wired bra, I tried again, this time approaching them
from underneath.

"Please, Mitchell, you're hurting me."

"If you really like me, let me feel. . . ." I wiggled my index finger
toward her nipple.

"I do. *You* don't like *me*. Stop!"

"You want me to take . . ."

She broke free, ran away crying. I followed her, frightened by her
sobbing. She stopped ten yards ahead, heaving against a cedar tree.

"I'm sorry, Carmen, I didn't mean to hurt you."

"Go away, Mitchell, leave me alone."

"Did I hurt you?"

"Yes, yes, you hurt me." And she started crying again, staring straight into my face, tears staining her blouse. I wanted to hold her in my arms, comfort her.

"Go away, please leave me!" She turned her head to the tree, her face against the smooth, silky trunk, her body dry-heaving.

"Did I break anything?" I was scared.

"What?" She turned away from the tree.

"Did I break anything?"

Carmen was dazed now, staring at my mouth.

"Like a bone?"

She rushed at me, hitting my head with her tight fists, laughing. "There aren't any bones in them, *estúpido*."

I didn't know how to defend myself without holding her against me to stop her fists. I smelled the oil in her hair, felt her tears on my arm. I didn't want to hurt her again, just to protect myself from her fists, calm her. I held on. She wouldn't stop laughing, crying in my arms.

"Bones?" she repeated into my flannel shirt pocket. *"Huesos?"*

"I'm sorry, Carmen." We both paused.

She broke away, running, then stopped to straighten out her blouse. On her way back to the South Dorm she tucked it into her dungarees.

I was overcome with shame and desire. Would she tell anyone? Expose my aggression, or worse, my stupidity about female anatomy? I thought about her often when we played guns at night in the pine field under the stars, wishing she were with me. I wouldn't hurt her again, make her cry, but just have her with me, a comrade in arms, maybe kiss her once or twice on the lips after attacking the enemy. She would observe my skill and bravery, moving around the slender pines with my three-battery flashlight off, ready for the kill.

Seeing Carmen now in the daylight of the pine field was not the same as my nighttime fantasy. I was no longer a gallant officer in the Resistance, but rather Mitchell Woolf with Rafferty, Fritz, Stevens and the goddamned chickens underfoot. Besides, Carmen didn't look so pretty in the hot sun with a duck in her hands. Fortunately I hadn't asked her to the prom.

"Quack survived the downpour easily," Stevens told Carmen as she dropped the duck back inside his pen. "He swam it out in his private mud puddle."

Carmen laughed. Damnit, she looked pretty again!

"Quittin' time!" Rosenthal sang out, mimicking the field hands in *Gone With the Wind.*

"Who says it's quittin' time?" Stevens drawled, playing out his part of the routine.

Rosenthal rose to the bait: "I does."

"*I* says when it's quittin' time around here," Stevens asserted. "I's the foreman. Quittin' time," he concluded, deadpan.

"Lunch, lunch!" Fritz, Rafferty and I shouted, dropping our tools.

Sunday lunch was the best meal of the week.

"Let's move it up to the dorm, you guys," Stevens ordered. "When's the last bath you took, Fritz, Rafferty? It's Sunday lunch. Move it!"

They did. Fritz and Rafferty dashed down the path, leaving me alone with the girls and four empty water buckets. Stevens and Rosenthal went off together toward Mayall Hall. There were showers there, and Stevens always took one before Sunday lunch.

Carmen and Natalie slouched ahead of me. I could tell they wanted me to catch up with them and Rafferty and Fritz to hurry back to the dorm, leaving us alone. I stacked the four cast-iron buckets, two to a pile, and carried one set in each hand. Even when empty they were cumbersome and heavy. We didn't have our own well up at the chicken coop, though we had almost everything else. So every day one of us had to lug two buckets of tap water out to the chickens and bring the empty pails back for the next day's water supply. Sunday was my turn. I wanted to avoid Carmen, not speak with her. My water boy responsibility was excellent camouflage until I was ten yards behind her and Natalie on the wooded path separating the fields. The dappled light set off sparkles in Carmen's black hair. I was caught by the arc of her back. Desire flooded into me, and I rushed ahead of them, trying to be nonchalant like Gary Cooper.

"Need any help, farmer?" Carmen surprised me.

"Nope." I didn't even turn my head.

"Come on, let us help." And they rushed up to my side.

"I'm fine, honest, I can handle them."

"Please!" Carmen grabbed one set of pails. I let her take them. She was strong. No more fighting, I resolved.

Natalie tried for the other set. I wouldn't release the wire handles, so she ran ahead, annoyed at her exclusion. Carmen and I walked in silence for thirty yards, swinging our pails.

This is it, I figured. *Now or never . . .* "Carmen." I could hear my own voice very loud. "Could . . . can . . . could I take you to the prom?"

She smiled up at my face. "Sure, Mitchell, I'd like that. I'd like to go with you."

I reached for her pails, and she let me hold them. Moving up a bluff toward the campus driveway, we paused in front of the cedar tree.

"Did you tell anyone?"

"What?" she asked.

"About . . ." I couldn't say *what,* so I pointed my head at the cedar.

She tossed her hair from side to side. "No!"

The blood tingled in my cheeks. I held my breath, walking beside her, unable to hug her because of my pails.

"See you," I said, half-promise, half-question, when we reached the dormitory sidewalk.

"At the prom." She smiled and swept into her dorm.

I dropped the four cast-iron buckets in the basement of the North Dorm under the water spigot and went upstairs for my Sunday bath.

There had never been a prom at Lake Ronkonkoma, only informal dances at camp. All the girls, Mrs. Ryson, and a handful of Upper School boys improvised what they thought a graduation prom should be. With hard work and whimsy they transformed the largest basketball court in Suffolk County into a fairyland. The walls, every inch of wainscotting, were draped with alternating rolls of white and blue crepe paper. White and Columbia blue were the school colors, a tribute to Mr. Kennedy's alma mater. One backboard was sheathed in white, the other in blue. The iron hoop of each basket was braided with both colors. Six-inch streamers dangled from every light fixture, muting their incandescent bulbs. From the largest one at mid-court white and blue streamers were festooned out to the backboards and walls, creating a canopy above the dance floor.

Ferdinand and I walked past the stuffy Ping-Pong rooms off the gymnasium entryway and into the white and blue bower. Flecks of silver gleamed on the polished dance floor. We were awed by the magic and our good fortune in being a part of it. No one else on our floor—not Rafferty, Daniels or Mayer—was going. They didn't have dates. Ferdinand had asked Natalie to the prom in a last-minute fit of gallantry. Carmen was my date. We waited for them at the ten-second line, dressed in our best Sunday clothes.

Three Upper School couples came in, the girls wearing long evening gowns. Someone turned on an enormous black phonograph. Harmonicas flooded the gymnasium with "Peg o' My Heart." Carmen and Natalie arrived in the middle of the record, part of a group Mr. and Mrs. Ryson had driven from the South Dorm.

"Thank you for the corsage, Mitchell," Carmen said as I helped her off with her evening jacket. We moved through the reprise holding each other.

"Da da da, I love you, Peg o' my heart," I sang softly. I knew the words from the Buddy Young recording. Carmen was bare-shouldered in a low-cut red gown, hair swept off her neck. The Harmonicats' beat was perfect for the foxtrot, a dance I had learned at camp on rainy afternoons. Though I was comfortable with its steps—breakaway walks, dips—it was difficult to relax with Carmen's body in a tight strapless gown. What to do with her in front of me, cheek to cheek, after I had performed so boorishly behind her in the woods?

Through the next record she moved snugly with me wherever my damp palms lead her, even though she was ten inches shorter. Frankie Laine cooed lyrics I had never quite listened to before: "To spend one night with you/ in our old rendezvous And reminisce with you,/ THAT'S MY DESIRE . . ." Conversation was beyond us.

Suddenly Donald Rich, a senior, tapped me on the left shoulder. "May I cut in?" He looked at Carmen. "And have the rest of this dance and the next?" He smiled. He was senior-class valedictorian.

"Yes," Carmen said. She was flattered. Rich swept her away.

"We'll sip a little glass of wine,/ I'll gaze into your eyes divine./ I'll feel the touch of your lips pressing on mine," Frankie Laine sang.

I noticed other couples were also switching partners. Mrs. Ryson seemed to be encouraging them. I asked Rich's stranded girl friend if I could dance with her.

"Of course, Mitchell."

She was a senior also, a shade taller than me, mature, exquisitely proportioned. I recalled her summertime one-piece bathing suit at Raynor's Beach. Now I was holding her entire body in my arms. Her breasts crushed against my white shirt, her nipples moving along my pockets when we dipped. She wasn't ashamed, why should I be? No one else was. I felt her stomach underneath, smooth against my pants, burning into me. We moved against each other.

"Where are you going to high school, Mitchell?" she asked. "Here?"

"Probably." I smiled, thinking of next year's prom.

"Have you thought about a different school?"

"Yeah." I remembered Stuyvesant. "But I'm not sure I'd do well."

"You'd do well anywhere." She shook my right shoulder gently. "Come on, Mitchell." She smiled at me with her spectacular white teeth. Her gray eyes glistened affection. I tried to hide the blush covering my face by pulling her closer to me.

After forty minutes of switching partners I was back with Carmen for what someone in authority announced was the last dance before intermission and refreshments.

"There was a boy,/ A very strange, enchanted boy,/ They say he wandered very far, very far/ Over land and sea," Nat King Cole mused. There was scattered applause, as if the trio were actually in the gymnasium. I held Carmen tenderly after dancing with Rich's girl. She sensed the difference and smiled. My penis started to expand, stiffen, push its head directly into the middle of her belly. I couldn't stop its thrust until it got so taut, it snapped up at a ninety degree angle against her lovely center. What had she felt through her silk gown and my gabardine pants? Would she bolt out of the white and blue gym? King Cole continued his voyage: "And then one day,/ One summer day,/ He passed my way,/ And as we spoke of many things,/ Fools and kings . . ."

We moved together slowly.

"You're a good dancer for a chicken farmer," Carmen said, looking into my eyes.

I couldn't stop laughing. Neither could she as I hugged her closer to contain our mirth.

Fritz, Rafferty and I gathered at the chicken coop dressed in flannel shirts on a Friday night in August after lights-out, five weeks into camp. Stevens revved Ma Kennedy's station wagon up the steep path to the clearing just outside the barren chicken pens. Rosenthal pulled up in Chef Swanson's ancient Ford. Stevens whirled the station wagon around until it was parked facing the Ford, thirty yards away. They let their engines idle when they left their cars so their crisscrossing headlights wouldn't drain the cars' batteries. Four white beams filtered over an area the size of a volleyball court. In the middle of it, away from the scrub underbrush, Stevens clamped a hundred and fifty watt floodlight on to the top rung of our eight-foot stepladder. He focused it directly at a waist-high oak stump. A black heavy-duty extension chord ran back to the fuse box in what was now our hen house.

We all knew why we were there nibbling pine needles, scuffing the ground with our moccasins in the circle of artificial light. When our flock of Rhode Island Reds and White Rocks had reached seventy-five and spread over three yards and into two coops, we were alarmed. Stevens would be unable to handle them all by himself between camp and school. Besides, Fritz would not be back this fall, and Rosenthal had taken a teaching job at a new junior high school in Hempstead. So Stevens and Rosenthal negotiated a deal with Chef Swanson, who already purchased our eggs: for all broilers four to six weeks old, dressed for the oven, COD, the second Sunday in August, fifteen cents a pound.

Not one of us had ever killed a chicken before, or even seen one killed. In the kosher butcher shops I had visited with Grandma Lufkin, the birds were naked, stone dead, like rubber playthings, their throats already punctured when the butcher finally sliced their tiny heads off. Now we were confronted with live, nervous red-, black- and white-feathered chickens clawing the ground with their scaled talons, shitting, flying, fighting behind wire-fenced yards we had built for them. To calm them down, we scattered corn in beside them. Their heads, coxcombed, beady-eyed, pecked at our offering like sewing machine needles out of control. How were we going to kill fifty of them?

Rosenthal lifted two immense aluminum kitchen pots from the trunk of Chef Swanson's car. He carried one of them toward the well, our latest capital improvement.

"Give me a hand, Woolf, Fritz. These monsters are heavy!" He pumped three gallons of water into the first one. Fritz and I each grabbed a handle and lifted it to make room for the next pot.

"Where to, Rosenthal?" I asked as he pumped fresh water into the second one.

"Over to the tree stump."

Why? I wondered but was too scared to ask. We were mute, willing to perform our tasks yet afraid to ask why. Maybe we'd drown them in the buckets. Hold each bird under.

"Where are the cleavers?" Stevens asked Rosenthal after both buckets were placed near the stump. "Did you forget?"

"No." Rosenthal went to the trunk of the Ford, still purring in neutral, and carried back a package wrapped in tattered dish towels.

"Compliments of the chef," he said, handing the bundle to Stevens, who unwrapped it quickly, revealing two steel cleavers. They were Chef Swanson's, polished for the occasion. Stevens grabbed one, tested the blade with his thumb.

"Jesus, that's sharp. Rafferty, Fritz, bring me two chickens."

Phew, he didn't ask me. He knew after all the months of my helping out I was still afraid to hold the fucking birds.

"Which ones?" they asked.

"The ones in the second pen, medium-size, four-to-six week brood, you guys know. Come on, we don't have all night. Woolf, stick with Rosenthal at the buckets. He'll show you what to do."

So drowning was still a possibility.

Rafferty came back with a medium-sized Red.

"Okay, hold him on the stump, Rafferty. His body, that's it. Sideways. Hold him still."

The chicken squawked, then stopped as Rafferty stroked its wings. Stevens placed his left hand over the bird's entire head, stretched out its neck, lifted the steel cleaver high over his own right ear and suddenly drove it down through the chicken's tense neck into the stump. Red blood spurted out. Stevens flinched, released his left hand, dropping the silent head on the stump.

"Jesus Christ, he's still moving!" Rafferty screamed. "Hit him again, he's not dead."

"Let him go, Rafferty, let him go. He's dead."

Rafferty released the body, and the chicken ran around us in a circle with its head cut off, finally thrashing into a patch of underbrush, blood gushing out of its neck as it sat down to die. Its recurring spasms, though it was officially dead, made the chicken seem human, pathetic, almost intelligent for one brief moment.

"Woolf, help Rosenthal with the dead chicken," Stevens ordered. I stopped breathing. Rosenthal sensed my panic.

"Wait here, Mitchell." He retrieved the dead bird and dumped it into the bucket of water.

Now we drown him. What's the point? "Why?" I asked Rosenthal.

"To pull his feathers off."

"Why now?"

"He's still warm, it's easier, see." Rosenthal pulled down on the bird's body and then released fistfuls of wet feathers on the ground. After five minutes of pulling and tugging he dropped the naked bird into a wooden crate. There were still some quills poking out of its yellow body, which I pointed out to Rosenthal.

"That's the best we can do. That's our deal. Swanson does the rest."

"Next one!" Rosenthal shouted, moving toward the underbrush. "Come on, Mitchell, watch me closely. You're going to start doing this too, or we'll be here all night. Pay attention, don't be a schmuck." His use of that word shocked me into responsibility, as if my father were there. No one had ever uttered it before at Lake Ronkonkoma. There were now three headless spastic chickens to choose from, each with its own choreographed dance.

Rosenthal and I came back to the pot. He carried the bird.

"Mitchell, let's go, pull off the feathers. Help out."

I placed my hand in the cold water, felt the dread feathers, pulled a fistful, petrified.

"Come on, Mitchell, *do* it! Don't be afraid," Rosenthal whispered and cuffed my hair with his dripping hand. "Do it, he's dead. Come on."

I plunged my hands in again, up to my forearms, and caught a leg.

"Pull down on it, Mitchell."

I did.

"Keep going, that's it. Hang down hard."

The bird was dead, though warm, buoyed up in the pot, floating. The more feathers I tore off, the less timid I was. I got my own bird next time, began yanking at the delicate wing feathers, then the body, the legs. Now there were five dead birds. Rafferty, Fritz and Stevens were way ahead of us. It was easier to kill than undress them. When the slaughter was almost completed with forty-five quiet chickens piled in three wooden crates, Rosenthal took a break, moved back from his pot, stood erect, cleaning his spattered glasses. He adjusted the wire temples around his ears and focused anew on my diligent activity.

"Hey, Woolf, you're a good chicken flicker, you know! One night, you're damned good, Woolf!"

I couldn't have been too good. The following Sunday when our chickens were served to the entire camp at lunch, I noticed tiny white needles on the baked skin of my portion. The quills were all gone, Chef Swanson had dealt with the obvious protrusions, but he had missed these tiny hairs, sticky, human, still growing, it seemed. I pushed my dish away, unable to eat. None of the campers noticed anything awry. We had decided not to tell anyone.

I was in front of the ball, felt it connect with the hard wood core of my bat as I drilled it, waist high inside the foul line over third base, where it bounced once before slicing out of bounds into the pine brush.

"Fair ball. Fair ball." Rosenthal leapt into the air, his body arched like a hairy parenthesis, to avoid being hit. He was the infield umpire in the last father-son softball game of the camp season. With runners on first and second, two outs, he was stationed behind third for a possible infield force-out.

"Play ball! Play ball!" he continued, staring at the imaginary left-field foul line which the softball had crossed on its trajectory into the pine scrub. He jumped behind the third base bag and pushed his arms over it toward the infield, shaking his fingers, indicating the ball had landed in bounds on its initial bounce and was thus playable regardless of where it came to rest. I rounded second, two runs scored, and the peg from left field allowed me to stretch for third standing up. Mr. Kennedy, who was pitching for the parents' side, rushed the bag after he cut off the left fielder's throw.

"Foul ball, Rosenthal. Give us a break! The ball went into the woods."

"After it bounced fair." Rosenthal pushed his arms over the bag again, replaying his decision, certifying the ball's flight path. "Tough call, tough call," he admitted, shaking his head from side to side, refusing to back down. Mr. Kennedy walked back to the mound, bald red head steaming with perspiration. He played to win every Sunday.

"Batter up! Play ball!" Rosenthal yelled to the home plate umpire. "Keep it moving!"

I had worked on my new batting stance all summer so I could hit line drive shots instead of my usual long fly balls to center field, which were okay against the Lower School opponents but were easily caught by the summertime grownups we played against every Sunday. I had learned to pull the ball, but my father would never see it; he missed the entire game as usual. Couldn't make the early 8:34

train out of Penn Station to see or play in the Sunday game. Even Fritz's father, the police captain, made it out for one Sunday game.

As we made our way back to wash up for Sunday lunch, carrying our gloves, bats and balls, victorious by one run, I saw a light gray Oldsmobile coming around the campus road, heading toward Mayall Hall. When our group hit the hard-top road, two little kids, fourth graders during the school year, came running at me.

"Your parents are here, Woolf!"

"Where?"

"Parked at Mayall Hall."

"Parked," I repeated, incredulous.

"Come on, Woolf, we're not kidding."

They were breathless sentinels. Whenever anyone's parents showed up during school the word was passed immediately, a search party sent out. This tradition was due to a mixture of surprise that anyone's parents actually made the effort to come out to Lake Ronkonkoma and fear that they might leave if their child wasn't produced within minutes.

Perhaps they got a ride with someone, maybe they were driven. By whom? I wondered as I raced around the curve to the Mayall Hall driveway, where I saw my father slide from behind the steering wheel of an Oldsmobile '88. Bea was already out of her seat, pacing the driveway, smoking.

"Dad!" I rushed up to him before his cordovan loafers hit the gravel. You drove *yourself?*"

He stood up smiling at me, realigning the pleats of his tan slacks.

"Why not? It's my car."

I ran into his arms, tingling with joy. Bea joined us.

"Isn't it something, Mitchell?"

"It's beautiful!" I ducked my head inside, examined the dashboard, popped back out into the sunlight. "When did you get it?"

"Last Monday."

"Monday! And you drive it already?"

"He took lessons, Mitchell."

"When? Where?" I wanted the whole story.

"Before the car arrived, for six weeks," Bea started, "at the Automobile Club."

"They have a great school near Columbus Circle," my father continued.

They were like two kids.

"Ten lessons and I can do everything. Of course it's Hydromatic. I even have a license." He reached into his back pocket.

"What's Hydromatic?" I asked.

"No clutch pedal for shifting gears. See, Mitchell!" he sat in the driver's seat again. "I just push this indicator over the steering column, see?"

"Yeah?"

"Move it with this handle and the car's in drive or reverse. Get in, we'll take you out for Sunday lunch."

"I need permission."

"Don't worry," Rafferty, who had watched the entire event mouth open in disbelief, said. "I'll tell Rosenthal. Have a good time, slugger."

"Thanks, Jimmy." I knew he could take care of it. They were easier about sudden interruptions at camp. "Tell Rosenthal I'm sorry for the short notice. . . ." Rafferty was gone up the stoop. It would be all right, more Sunday lunch for everyone else.

My father turned the key. The engine started up smoothly. We moved forward around Mayall Hall, down the campus road, heading toward the big highway, Route 25. The engine sounded clean, clock-like when my father accelerated. I was sitting next to him, inhaling the upholstery and dashboard plastic. Bea was in the back seat.

"Where would you like us to take you, Mitchell?"

"Anywhere. I don't care." I wasn't even interested in food for once.

Ten days later when camp let out on Thursday, Bea and my father reappeared in the gray Olds to take me home, just like the parents of some of the other kids who only attended camp. It was a last-minute surprise. I was prepared to take the Long Island Rail Road to

Penn Station, but the evening before at dinner Mr. Ryson had told me about the change.

"Woolf, your parents are coming up to get you tomorrow, drive you home."

They drove me along Northern State Parkway in lush green silence, over carefully engineered curves and dips, hills that stretched into the horizon. The center strip was inlaid with expensive rolls of turf that were beginning to take root, settle down, look like real grass. Mature oaks and maples stood twenty yards back on either side of the roadway, their leaves August tired. My two suitcases were in the car trunk. I relaxed in the front seat next to my father, dizzy.

Chapter
Six

◆◆◆

"PHILLY, LET'S SHOW Mitchell the house!"

"Which one?"

"Rockville Centre."

I woke up, the highway still rising in front of me, green on either side for miles ahead.

"The Dutch colonial?" he asked.

"That's it! Prewar."

"How do I get there? We're on Northern State."

"It's south." Bea knew the Island, had an Aunt Greta who had settled in Hempstead instead of Brooklyn, married into a big successful family, the Freeds. "We cross over to the Southern State somewhere, take that to Hempstead and . . . We'll ask, Phil, let's ask at the gas station."

"Think they know?" My father pulled off the roadway into a Texaco station constructed in the same style as the parkway. It was landscaped right into the road. He parked to the side, away from the Red Star pumps, brushed off his pants and walked into the fieldstone station to get directions. He returned in two minutes, smiling.

"It's twenty minutes at most. We can make the switch to Southern State five miles down. The mechanic lives in West Hempstead, takes the route every day. Bea, should we call Mr. Russo, make sure it's okay to drop by?"

"Good idea." She hopped out of the back seat and ran to the coin telephone in front of the ladies' room, leaking tobacco and small change in her trail.

My father twisted the ignition key, edged the gray Olds into the service area.

"Fill 'er up, chief!" He got out, and so did I. "And the windshield if you have a chance. Bugs all over!"

Bea was talking to someone on the other end of the line, pleading, cooing, laughing.

"Wonderful, Mr. Russo, we'll be there in twenty minutes. . . . Right . . . right . . . on to Hempstead Avenue from Southern State." She wrote the details on a scrap of paper. She raced over to the gasoline pump. "It's fine with them. They just found a dream ranch house themselves, so they're eager for us to stop by." She squeezed Philly's arm to make sure he was listening.

"Ouch!" He was paying the attendant for the gasoline, impressed with the gleaming windshield.

"That's a dollar seventy-five, mister."

"Here's a two."

The attendant clicked a quarter out of the silver change machine attached to his belt.

"Keep the change." My father's offer startled the man.

"Thanks, mister, thanks a lot!"

Philly drove off like the Lone Ranger, unaware of his altruism. No one is Nassau County tipped gasoline attendants. Philly was acting as if he were back in the Park Central, where everyone had to be tipped, particularly when their service excelled.

Southern State seemed much like Northern.

"Left here, Philly." Bea was reading from her scrap of paper in the back seat.

"Hempstead Avenue, Bea?"

"That's it, takes us right into Rockville Centre."

"How do we find the house on . . . what's the street?"

"Stay tuned until DeMott." Bea smiled, exuberant, almost silly. "It's two miles down."

"Then what?"

"I'll tell you if you're good."

From DeMott Avenue, Bea guided us onto Harvard Avenue, a glorious wide boulevard with comfortable prewar homes of wood and brick. Locusts and maples stood on either side, thick branches arched over the endless road, a canopy in the sky. It was awesome.

"No Minskoff trees here!" my father said.

Bea guffawed. "Character, Philly . . . character!" Her cigarette ashes floated harmlessly to the rubber floor mat. "Here, Philly, here it is. Everett, turn right . . . fourth house in!"

My father drove slowly up to a white clapboard house so we could take in all its details. It was smaller than most of the houses on Harvard Avenue but the same size as those on Everett. A black shingle roof hung low over the front of the house and extended down to the first story. The house was much wider than the Tudor gable we had inspected in Forest Hills. Mr. Russo appeared on the front brick stoop to greet us the moment we opened the car doors. A heavyset friendly man, he shook hands, touched my father's shoulder, squeezed Bea's wrists.

"Welcome, welcome, come on in! So, how are the Woolfs?"

"Fine, fine." Bea took over. "This is our son, Mitchell, Mr. Russo."

"A pleasure, Mitch, a pleasure." His hand was warm but not sweaty.

"We wanted to show him around and have a fresh look ourselves."

"Whatever you wish . . . anything. I love showing this house."

So why is he selling it? I wondered.

"My wife only wants one floor now. What can I tell you?" he said as though in answer to my thought.

I could see the staircase from the entryway, set in the middle of the house. It looked steep. In order to reach it, I had to cross the entire living room.

"Isn't it something, Mitchell?" Bea exclaimed.

"The stairs?"

"No, the living room!"

I stopped, looked right, then left. It was all one room running across the entire front of the house, thirty-two by fourteen.

"It's huge," I marveled.

"Used to be two rooms," Mr. Russo added. "Wall ran down the middle of it. We took it out."

A red brick fireplace dominated the left wall.

"It's real," my father said as I moved toward it.

Upstairs the bedrooms were large, airy, nothing extraordinary. Downstairs the dining room, just off the stairs, was also large, boxlike. The kitchen was charming: yellow and white Formica cabinets, a dishwasher, a windowed alcove with a knotty pine table and four armchairs around it.

"It *is* an eat-in kitchen! I was right, Phil!"

"We only use the dining room for company," Mr. Russo assured Bea.

The second toilet was at the head of a short staircase leading down to the fenced-in backyard. The four of us stood on the patio, gazing at the trees and plants.

"So, Phil, let me show you the garage."

My father trailed after him on the slate path.

"Mitch, come on, take a look at the mower, place for your bike." Russo beckoned to me.

The garage was a separate white house with a regular slanted roof. There were tools and tricycles, and oil stains splotched the cement floor. Mr. Russo's Mercury station wagon just fit inside.

"Phil, what do you think?" Mr. Russo was leaning against the Mercury tailgate with *Sunrise Appliances* in the center. My father surveyed the house from the garage doorway.

"Nice house."

"You gonna make an offer, or what?"

They were both still.

"What are the numbers again?" my father asked, staring at the rear of the house.

"Sixteen thousand nine hundred fifty dollars. Didn't the broker tell you?"

"I wasn't sure of all the O's. Just one zero?" My father looked straight at him.

"That's firm. Make me an offer. Go ahead."

"Sixteen thousand."

"You gotta be kidding, Phil! Sixteen thousand, that's robbery!" Russo leapt off the Mercury tailgate.

My father ignored his outrage. "That's it." He raised his palms up under Russo's black eyes, as if they were empty pockets. "All I can handle. Nothing else there."

"I said offer, Phil. Sixteen thousand dollars! Is that good faith? That's an insult!"

My father smirked to relieve the tension but held his ground, staring at Russo's blue-and-yellow-striped polo shirt. After thirty seconds Russo turned around, his rage dissolved. He was smiling.

"Listen, Phil, I've got a fantastic VA mortgage on this place. One and a half percent. You can take it over, reduce your nut."

"I don't qualify."

"Why not? My lawyer can work out the whole switch in ten minutes."

"I'm not a veteran."

"Oh?" Russo paused, grinning, his position suddenly strengthened by my father's lack of military service. "Anything wrong? You're all right, aren't you?"

"Yeah, I'm fine. What is this, a physical for Christsakes?" My father was steamed; he paced out into the driveway, kicked at some grass in the center strip, turned back to Russo. "Sixteen thousand!"

"Make a real offer."

"Okay. Sixteen three," my father conceded.

"Three hundred bucks? That's movement? Make it sixteen five!"

"Three fifty!"

"Five hundred!"

"Three fifty!"

"It's a deal!" Russo clapped my father around the back of the neck. "Deal, deal!" He was ready to dance with Philly.

My father stuck out his hand. Russo clutched it heartily. They walked along the driveway to the front of the house. When I joined them on the front lawn, Bea was there, listening to an edited replay of their deal. She was ecstatic.

"And the schools are the best. People move here just to be in the district." Russo was unstoppable now. "Mitch, what grade are you in?"

"Ninth, this year."

"South Side is the best high school in Nassau County. You'll go there, huh?"

"I don't know yet." I was surprised by his presumption. I'd never followed that one through, just accepted living in a house and going back to Lake Ronkonkoma as two distinct conditions. My answer stunned Russo.

"Mitchell goes to a prep school out in Suffolk County, the Lake Ronkonkoma School," Bea answered for me.

"Oh, I've heard of that, the one with the basketball team." Russo realized it was none of his business where I went to school. Bea, however, knew everything might hinge on which school I chose.

"How big is South Side?" she asked.

"Eight hundred students, I think." Russo's children were in grade school.

"It's small, Mitchell." Her capped teeth caught the sun.

When we finally pulled away from the curb in the gray Olds, I noticed the entrance of the house had its own roof over it. It was the same odd shape as the main roof except turned around, so the gambreled eaves were facing the street and the black shingled roof faced the side of the neighbor's house. It gave the entryway of the squat Dutch house an unexpected flamboyance, like my father had in the morning when he finished knotting his silk tie.

"Why does his wife want a one-story house?" I asked.

"Convenience, I guess," Bea answered from the front seat.

We had switched places for the last lap of our trip back to the city.

"Isn't it like an apartment, though? No stairs."

"Some people hate stairs."

"Why?"

"Hard to climb the steps."

She was getting funnier sometimes.

"It's taste. Everyone wants something different. The Russos were lucky, they found what they wanted," Philly explained.

"And so did we," Bea couldn't resist adding. "Didn't we?"

No one responded until we were on Sunrise Highway.

"I suppose. Who knows anymore." Philly stopped for a long light.

Bea surprised me by asking, "Who knows? Do you, Mitchell?"

When we finally got back to 2209, I unpacked my things and thought about the house. It was the nicest place they had showed me, spacious and well built. We could certainly use more room. The linens in my first valise were easy enough to slip in with the household's, but my socks, underwear, shirts and pants, in the second bag, were more difficult to store with each trip home. Bea's wardrobe was bountiful, her dresser and closet so full, some articles were stored in my father's bureau. Her winter garment bag now occupied a corner of his closet because the foyer one was brimming with electrical cooking gear hidden away between meals so the maid couldn't turn us in to Walsh, the house detective.

My father squeezed out some space for me in his bottom dresser drawer. It might be nice to have my own bureau and closet and bed in a room of my own. 2209 was definitely overcrowded. Everyone needed more space. A move was imminent. I got into my pajamas and slid between the sheets.

"Sixteen thousand three hundred fifty dollars! What does that come to a month, Bea?" My father was reviewing the details in the living room, more comfortable with the financial implications after four months of house hunting with Bea.

"I've got the breakdown in my bag, taxes and everything. Here it is, about a hundred twenty if we put twenty-five percent down."

"That's just like here."

"Phil, it's thirty dollars less per month. And look at the difference in space."

"I know."

"And if Mitchell doesn't go back to Lake Ronkonkoma . . ."
She was about to play her last card.

"Shh, shh, he's still up."

"If he goes to South Side High School . . ." she whispered.

"We'll be way ahead," he admitted.

"How much ahead?"

"That school now costs me twelve hundred dollars a year. But remember, he has to want it, Bea."

"How can he want it if he doesn't live there first?"

"I know, it's tricky, chicken and egg stuff."

"When do you call Russo?"

"Tomorrow, nine-thirty. Let's sleep on it."

He has to want it. . . . I rolled on my pillow. The unknown *it.*
What I had at Lake Ronkonkoma was familiar but evaporating, suddenly going elsewhere; Rosenthal to a new teaching job, Fritz to Bayshore, where his father had retired from the force, opened a bowling alley, Austria to prep school, Mayer to live with his mother during the week and his father on weekends. On our floor only Jimmy Rafferty would be back. He and Frank were lifers. There was no place else for them to go. Of course Stevens would return, but he would remain in charge of the Lower School. I would have to live in Mayall Hall with the Upper School.

So what did I want in its place? A revival of the old Lake Ronkonkoma, same friends and teachers . . . that would be impossible. Mr. Ryson was in charge now. He had bought the school from Mr. Kennedy during the summer. He had already made his policy clear: He would hire whomever he could get for the least money. In most instances this meant the feeble remnants of the boarding school circuit, like Mr. Schorer, an ancient nearsighted science teacher, or full-chested Mrs. Weimar, our Austro-Hungarian French and Spanish teacher. Many of the brightest girls were not returning because of the mediocre academic program. Even I was alarmed by my difficulty with the Stuyvesant test. So many of my friends were going to new and probably better high schools, why not try what they were doing?

Images of Lake Ronkonkoma flooded my senses in the morning. I was staring out the living room window while my father and Bea

slept late in the bedroom. The park was empty, and leaves were floating off the thick roadway trees. I remembered my last Sunday trip to
the chicken coop. There were fifteen birds left: Peep, a majestic cock
now, some fat hens, the ducks, and five broilers. The second pen and
coop were abandoned, so I only had one bucket of water to carry up
on Sunday morning. The place was desolate. No one liked going up
there anymore. Stevens would be all alone with the remnant of our
flock in four days, and he would probably sell off the equipment and
the birds. After I had watered the chickens and ducks, I started back
down the path with the empty bucket in my right hand. Carmen appeared, walking from the other direction, up the path toward the
coop. She remembered Sunday was my water day.

She stopped me. "Can I see them? Say good-bye to the ducks?"

"They're just about all that's left." I continued walking to the
softball field.

"Please, Mitchell."

We went back up. She held each duck, stroking its white feathers.
Then we returned down the path. The field grass was high, like ripe
winter wheat, with nervous grasshoppers everywhere inside the dry
stalks.

"I'm not coming back next year, Mitchell. My brother has to go
to a better high school."

"Where?"

"Forest Hills."

"Oh, I'm sorry for him."

"Why?"

"It's immense, twenty-five hundred kids."

"How do you know, farm boy?"

I told her about the Mahan House. She wasn't listening.

"We'll still be friends, right?" She took my free hand in hers. I
squeezed her palm tight, and she returned the pressure. We held on
to each other until we reached the opening before the softball field
where we knew the other campers might see us. I should have acted
before then, dropped the empty water bucket, taken her in my arms.
I wanted to kiss her lips.

"So, Mitchell, what'll it be for breakfast? Couple of eggs, bacon strips? What's your pleasure?" Bea broke into my revery, swept it aside. "Lost your voice? You'll need it for Cantor Gluck this afternoon. It's the home stretch. Can you believe it? Everything's happening at once. Phil, tea, corn muffins?"

"Tea and muffins." My father snapped into the living room, fully dressed except for his jacket, his tie knotted.

Bea was still in her housecoat and nightgown.

"Have you thought it over?" Bea sat down at the long table with a cup of black coffee.

My father was stirring his tea. "I slept on it." He smiled.

We knew that was his prescription for all important decisions.

"It's a good house, feels right. The town feels right."

"So?" she panted.

"The price—I'd like it under sixteen thousand."

"But, Phil, he came down from almost seventeen thousand. We have him in a bind."

"So what? Whose side are you on?"

Bea dropped her right hand under the table and stroked Philly's tense inner thigh. "On yours, honey," she whispered, her lips white. "Call him! Please, Phil!" She held on to his kneecap. "He may come down. Try. He needs an offer!"

"Isn't it too early? Nine-thirty on a Friday?"

"You said nine-thirty you'd call."

"I need some more tea, *hot*." He was temporizing.

Bea ran into the kitchenette to start up the kettle. "Fresh bag, Phil?"

"Sure."

"Coming right up!"

"Take your time." My father looked at me. "Mitchell, do you like the house?"

"It's very nice. I like the roof a lot."

"You'd have your own room when you came home."

"What if I stay home, like a real family?"

"What do you mean?"

"Don't go back to Lake Ronkonkoma."

"Why not?" He wasn't sure it would work out either.

"It's not the same anymore. The teachers stink. Everyone's left. Maybe South Side's a better high school."

Bea came back with hot tea, excited by what she'd overheard.

"They get into all the colleges from South Side." This was Russo's line—she had repeated it verbatim. "Want to go out there some time soon? Look over the school?"

My father got up, went into the bedroom to call Russo. Bea hovered at the door. In eight minutes it was done. Bea was all over his body when he returned to the dining table to announce our deal.

"Fifteen thousand nine hundred fifty dollars if we close one month from today, September twenty-fourth. After that the price goes back up to sixteen thousand three hundred fifty."

"Can you get a mortgage in one month?"

"I think so. Garrity at the Corn Exchange will help."

"When can we move in . . . start work?" Bea wanted every scrap of information.

"Right after we close."

"I want to paint, have the floors sanded, redo the bathrooms, it will be the end of October, beginning of . . ."

"Hey, not so fast!"

"Well, there's a lot to do, Phil."

"That house is in pretty good shape. Don't throw around the money."

"Well, I want to make it nice."

"It *is* nice! Russo took good care of it."

"The floors, though, Phil, the floors are terrible. He had them carpeted. They haven't been done in twenty years!"

"Stop it! We've got to take it easy . . . a little bit at a time."

"I want it all done before we move in."

"Well, painting, that makes sense, but the bathrooms are fine. I like the old tiles. I'm not a money tree."

"The floors, Phil, what about the floors?"

"We'll recarpet the living room."

"Really?"

"Wall to wall, give it warmth."

"Oh, wonderful, Phil, wonderful." She almost lifted him out of his shoes.

"Wait a second, what about Mitchell? Where will he go to school while you're doing all of this?" my father asked her.

"He can stay at Lake Ronkonkoma for one more semester." Bea looked at me for support.

"More money." Philly groaned.

"But I want to start at the beginning, come in when everyone else does in September," I said.

"How can you do it, Mitchell, if we're not living in the house?"

"There must be a way out to Rockville Centre."

"Every day?"

"Yes, whenever there's school."

"The Long Island Rail Road goes to Rockville Centre on the hour. It's a thirty-five to forty minute ride."

"I'll take it then," I said.

"You'd do that for us?" Bea rushed into my arms, her housecoat undone from all the thrashing about with my father. She kissed my lips. I turned my head away from the cigarette odor. Her breasts were exposed. I didn't want to see them. Carmen's weren't like that, flaccid and droopy.

I got up at six-forty-five to make the 7:30 train from Penn Station. I was too excited and rushed for more than a glass of cold tomato juice before leaving 2209 because I wasn't sure how long the IRT would take to 34th Street. It was unexpectedly fast, full of early-bird workers. The 7:30 train to Rockville Centre on the Babylon line was nearly empty, going against the commuter crowd, stopping at Woodside, Forest Hills, Kew Gardens, Jamaica, Valley Stream, lickety-split. I was a pioneer like my grandfather, Nathan, staking out a new location before Leah and the three boys joined him.

I arrived at Rockville Centre at 8:05 on the button. Famished, I headed across the street from the elevated concrete station to a coffee shop. Men in suits were gulping coffee, glancing at lead stories in their folded newspapers. A handful of them would dart out the screen door whenever a train to the city pulled in. I sat down on a red counter stool.

"What'll it be, kid?"

"A buttered roll and coffee."

The roll he slid over to me was crisp with a hint of egg, but no poppy seeds. Salt butter oozed out from between the sliced edges when I dunked it into my coffee. I wanted another one, two or three maybe, but I walked up to the cashier instead, forcing myself to be on time.

"How do I get to the high school?" I asked the cashier.

"Which one?"

"There's more than one?"

"Yeah, St. Agnes and South Side."

"South Side."

"I figured. Walk down North Park four blocks, hang a right, you can't miss it."

I had not gone out to the high school with Bea in August after my father spoke with Mr. Russo on the telephone. All the kids and teachers would have been on vacation, so there was no point. What could I learn? We had, however, driven past it in the gray Olds one Saturday on our way to meet a painter at the new house, so I knew what it looked like. A memorial to the townspeople killed in the Great War, the red brick high school was fifteen years older than Forest Hills High. The scale was much smaller, though it had a similar Greek Revival facade, multipaned windows and a cupola on top supported by peeling wooden columns. No trumpet salvos as I walked in a set of yellow doors to register and get my classroom assignments.

The whole system, everything was so different from the Lake Ronkonkoma School. There were four freshmen homerooms of twenty-five to thirty boys and girls, who mingled and marched through the halls together for eight periods of departmentalized classes. Most of them knew each other from the neighborhood grammar schools, churches, and scouting groups they had passed through together. The classroom work was serious but uninspired, taught by humorless middle-aged women who followed rigid course curriculums pegged to the year-end Regents examinations.

Sports were an obsession. The football team had been practicing for most of August, getting in shape for a seven-game season that began the week school opened. Seven of the largest freshmen were already on the varsity. Petrocelli and Krauss, actually on the starting eleven.

Petrocelli was the only kid in my homeroom who ate lunch in the cafeteria. Everyone else scattered out of the building to cars, luncheonettes or home. I usually ate alone, a couple of ice cream sandwiches if I was low on money, or one of the government-subsidized lunches, which were awful, worse than Lake Ronkonkoma food, except for the scoop of mashed potatoes with hot giblet gravy. Petrocelli had a short friend, Vito, from one of the other freshmen homerooms, who ate with him. Vito had algebra and history before lunch, Petrocelli after. Vito would give his friend all the correct homework answers and test questions while they ate. He was like a fight manager, except he didn't shave.

After school let out at three-ten, I took the Long Island Rail Road back to the city, got home at four-thirty and did my homework. There was a lot of it.

One morning on the trip out to South Side, I noticed Miss Rice, our English teacher, got on the train at Kew Gardens. I wasn't certain it was her at first because I'd only been in her class for two weeks. It looked like the same gaunt woman who was taking us through *The Rise of Silas Lapham* and red penciling my grammar and spelling errors. So I decided to greet her on my walk toward the front car after the Valley Stream stop.

"Hello, Miss Rice." I was standing above her seat, looking down at her head. "I guess we take the same train every day."

She looked up, but not at me, kind of through me, as if I weren't really there.

"Isn't it a coincidence?" I tried to hide my embarrassment.

She twisted her head away from my voice toward the train window. I noticed the center of her scalp was bald; her frizzy brown hair was arranged around it like a beehive to conceal the spot. I got off the train and went to the coffee shop for my morning hard roll and coffee. I didn't see her again until English class, when I checked her hairdo. It was the same woman I had seen on the train. How odd she wouldn't acknowledge me outside the classroom. Most of the students were like that, distant, unapproachable. They didn't tease me because I was new, they just ignored me, like Miss Rice on the train.

How could I make friends if we didn't eat together, play ball or talk after lights-out? Maybe it would all change once we actually moved into the Dutch colonial house on Everett Street or when I tried out for the basketball team in November. In the meantime I was an observer during school and a loyal fan at the varsity football games played on Saturday afternoon at North Memorial Stadium, off DeMott Avenue. I had no way of getting to the away games, but I took the Saturday morning train out for each home contest. The third one against our arch rival, Oceanside, took place on the last Saturday in October, the day the Mayflower moving men were bringing all our furniture and clothing from 2209 to the new house.

Bea suggested I sleep over at the house on Friday evening so I could let the movers in at ten-thirty, when they were supposed to arrive.

"They're terrible, Mitchell, you never know when they'll show up!"

"I'll spend Friday night at the house." I wanted to help. "There's a big game Saturday at twelve-forty-five."

"Mitchell, you must stay until the moving men come, or they'll screw everything up."

"I'll wait for them."

"They're unreliable."

"What will I sleep on?"

"Your mattress came yesterday from Sloane, but the schmucks forgot the headboard and slats. You can sleep on the mattress for one night. They promised Saturday delivery. It'll be something out there!"

Friday night alone in the new house was an adventure. I was camping out, making do. I set out for the empty house with a grinder, some chips, and an orange soda, unaware vinegar and oil were seeping out of the grocery bag until I reached my destination and shoved the mottled package into the icebox. I washed the grease off my hands and walked outside on the patio to examine the back yard.

At dusk I laid my sandwich out on the knotty pine breakfast table and ate it. I noticed the painters had left their portable radio on the window ledge over the stainless steel sink. I turned on the evening news, hoping to catch a weather report, walked into the living room with the spattered radio and sat crosslegged on the floor. Eager for a weather report, I turned the dial all the way right, suddenly hitting WQXR. The final moments of the Friday night service from Temple Emmanuel were being broadcast. The Rabbi's English accent made me miss Cantor Gluck's guttural baritone. He had been pleased with my Torah recitation, at the bar mitzvah service. "Good boychick," he had whispered when I left the onyx altar. The party at the Bolivar had been a treat. The Kagels all came. Uncle Alfie and Aunt Gracie brought Grandma Woolf. I gave a speech about fountain pens, making fun of Sam Levenson's routine. Bea was distracted. Her heart wasn't in the occasion. The house in Rockville Centre was all she could really talk about, Mitchell's new high school—all these symbols of real family life, mere weeks away, made my bar mitzvah suddenly irrelevant for her.

I switched off the radio, looked into the living room fireplace and knew it would work. I stretched out on the hearth and imagined the flames licking over the side tiles.

When I woke, it was pitch dark. I climbed upstairs to my bedroom, savoring each newly carpeted step. The mattress and box spring were centered on the floor. Some pieces of maple furniture had arrived, the dresser and secretary desk. I opened the desk's flap and put my school books inside and then undressed. Bea had already brought out a blanket and pillow. The sheets would be on the moving van.

I slept until seven-fifteen, when the morning sun rose through my east window. There was no food in the house, so I went down to the station coffee shop for a breakfast; two eggs over easy, sausage, English muffin and three cups of hot, fresh coffee. On my way back to Everett Street I felt expansive, hopeful. Maybe the three of us could make the Dutch colonial a real home. I was ready to begin when I got back to the house at nine-thirty-five and sat on the front stoop under the low roof.

When the movers didn't show by ten-fifty-five, I feared the worst: They had come while I was eating breakfast and left because no one was home. But was that possible with two rooms and a kitchenette to pack and load in midtown? Still no van at eleven-ten. The game was at twelve-forty-five, sharp. What the hell was I going to do? Nothing at eleven-thirty. Jesus Christ, they had come: I screwed up!

At eleven-forty a big yellow and green van turned into Everett. I ran to the middle of the street, hailing it. The harassed driver pulled in front of the house and hopped out of the cab.

"Woolf? P. Woolf?" he asked.

"This is the place," I assured him immediately.

"You got a phone inside, kid?"

"Not hooked up yet."

"Well, I don't unload this fucking truck until I get a helper! Not alone I don't work for any fucking body! Bastard got sick on me outside the hotel, vomiting, drunken asshole. I gotta call in for a temp. They got a phone next door, kid?"

"I guess." I was ashamed. What would the MacNeils think about the Mayflower man's language? Their children went to St. Agnes. Mr. MacNeil worked in Manhattan for Con Ed. Before I could advise restraint, the driver was at their door pushing the bell. He returned to the van even more agitated.

"The office can't get a man out here till twelve-thirty, one. That means two at the earliest. Fucking bastards want me to start unloading now!" He slapped the cab door with his open hand. "I'm supposed to bust my nuts until he gets here!" He sat down on the cab running board and dug both hands into his brown curls as if he were trying to rip his own brains out.

"I can give you a hand, at least until a quarter of one," I offered.

"You?" He paused, took in my five-feet-seven, 150-pound frame.

"I'm good at lifting and moving stuff."

"If you want to help out, kid, you're on!" He got up, unlocked the back door of the truck, rolled it up. Bea's vanity table and my father's bureau were on the ledge of the truck wrapped in green packing quilts.

"Do what I say kid, and we'll be all right."

The vanity table was a snap, but my father's bureau was cumbersome, a monster. We rested it every four steps before reaching the second-floor landing. The front doorbell rang.

"That's my guy," the mover gasped. He ran downstairs to greet him.

"Sloane's!"

"Shit. Hey, kid, you'd better come down. It's more stuff. I'll push the bureau into the bedroom myself."

The Sloane's delivery men were punctilious, dressed in matching brown uniforms with their names sewn on their left breast pockets.

"Where to?" The driver, Fred, held the maple headboard against his chest like a shield.

"The bedroom at the top of the stairs, turn right."

"Okay."

"Please assemble it."

"Certainly, we always assemble beds."

Drew, his helper, followed him in with two long sideboards. I closed the front door and watched them go up the stairwell. When Drew reached the landing, he swept the boards over the bannister rail so he could angle them into my bedroom from the narrow hallway. He maneuvered the front inside carefully but caught the Mayflower moving man in the face with the back end. The moving man had been charging down the dim hallway and didn't see the boards. He was stunned.

"Son of a bitch, you trying to kill me?" He grabbed the boards from behind and yanked them. They fell on the oak bannister, gashed the varnish off the railing. Drew came out of the bedroom empty-handed to retrieve the sideboards.

"What the hell?" He saw the Mayflower man, the boards resting at his feet against the bannister, and realized what had happened.

"Hey, I'm sorry, pal, I didn't realize anyone was working up here."

"Where the fuck should I deliver bedroom furniture? To the basement?"

"I didn't know where you were. Sorry, pal."

"Lemme know when you jokers are through so I don't get killed working in the same house with youse." He stormed down the stairs and out to his truck. I followed, wanting to see what he was going to do. He climbed into his cab.

"Hey, kid, there a grocery store around here?"

"Down Willow Street, near the train station."

He started his engine up.

"Where you going?" I yelled. "You can't leave now with all our stuff!"

"I need a brew, kid. This place is crazy. A goddamned madhouse." He drove off with the back gate of the truck still rolled up, our belongings exposed, jumping in the crisp fall air.

Ten minutes passed. One of the Sloane's men called to me from my bedroom.

"Son, could you come up here a second? We want to show you something before we leave." The bed was all assembled. "See the mark on the sideboard runner?" Drew pointed to the left one. "That's from falling on the bannister." He walked out to the stair landing, pointed at the railing. "That gash we also made."

Fred came out of the bedroom with a yellow invoice in his clipboard. He was scribbling on it with a ball point.

"I'm describing the damage, we'll make good on it, our liability covers it. Just have your father send the repair bill to Sloane's adjustment department."

"Sure." I nodded. They were decent, reasonable guys.

"And please, your John Hancock on the dotted line."

"My *what?*"

"Your signature!"

"Oh."

"It means you received the bed frame and accept the damage settlement."

It seemed fair. They had delivered the bed, so I signed.

"Thank you, Mitchell," he said, reading my name off the receipt, and handed me a blue carbon copy. They went out the front door and drove off. I watched them from the stoop. It was twelve-twenty.

When was the crazed Mayflower man coming back? Where the

hell were my parents? Everyone was letting me down. I was missing the warm-ups; I had to see the kickoff. At twelve-thirty-five I cut loose, walked away from the front stoop to Harvard Avenue. Lone ninth- and tenth- grade boys straggled along it toward DeMott. I rushed past them. Juniors and seniors, boys and girls together in old cars zipped by. A few parents even joined the procession. Mothers with wicker picnic hampers, fathers carrying plaid blankets. When our throng was outside the admission gate milling against one another, excited, eying the nearly filled bleachers, my moving day responsibilities evaporated.

It was a closely fought contest, which we won, 7–0, in a last-minute touchdown pass to the end zone from Stuart, the senior quarterback, to Petrocelli, the freshman tailback. Screaming erupted in the stands, pandemonium settling into back slapping and solitary hoots as we filled the neighboring streets, victorious.

I returned to Everett Street at four-fifteen. The moving van wasn't there, but three enormous packing boxes were in our driveway, so the Mayflower van must have come back. I walked in the front door. The living room was stuffed with 2209 furniture, none of it properly arranged. Garment bags were draped over the couch. I squeezed past to reach the kitchen, where Bea was ensconced in dishes.

"Where the hell have you been?" She whirled around from the sink, bubbles on her freckled arms.

"At the football game. We beat—"

"Football game? How could you leave before the moving man got . . . You promised us."

"I was here when he came at eleven-forty, helped him carry your vanity and Dad's bureau upstairs."

"I saw the scuff marks on the hall floor, thank you."

"His helper got sick."

"We know all about that episode and his own little trip to the grocery store. He came back pissy-eyed. You should have waited for us, Mitchell."

"I did! Until twelve-thirty. What took *you* so long?"

"Don't be fresh!" Bea snapped, sweat beaded on her forehead

and scarlet cheeks. "They wouldn't refund our security deposit when we settled accounts at the Park Central, said we owed them for towels and sheets. Bastards!"

She wiped her face dry with a dish towel, but the red was indelible, and perspiration reappeared on her face, curling down her cheeks with no relation to her physical activity.

"You all right?" I was startled. This was something new.

"It's a hot flash."

"Oh. Can I help out, Bea?"

"If you want, Mitchell. Please try to be a good boy. Get the china barrels in the driveway. I have to wash all the plates before I put them in the cupboard."

I lugged the three brown boxes up the back stairs into the kitchen, wondering why Bea called them barrels. They weren't wooden or round.

"What else is there?" I asked her back, eager for more chores, lifting, moving, pushing. It was like working on the chicken coop.

"Take your father's garment bag up to the bedroom, mine too. He went out to buy new hangers for the clothes. The old ones belonged to the hotel."

I returned in a few minutes. "That was easy. What else?"

"The boxes labeled 'Books' . . ."

"Yeah?"

"Put them in the guest room upstairs. We'll make a little library there. And take your own stuff up to your room."

Within minutes I came tumbling back into the kitchen laughing. "What else?"

"The night lamps, they're marked, put them in our bedroom."

They were packed in wide three-foot-high cartons, bulky but light. One fell on their double bed and bounced back up into my arms. I clutched it, shook it gently—nothing broken. I placed it on the floor in front of Bea's night table. I heard my father's voice downstairs in the kitchen, saw the gray Oldsmobile in the driveway. I was so afraid I had broken the lamp I didn't hear him drive in.

"I have to do everything around here, Phil! So much work!"

"Did Mitchell come back?"

"Yes."

"Where is he?"

"Upstairs."

"What's he doing?"

"See for yourself. Who knows *what* he does!"

That wasn't fair, telling him that. I *was* working and had before with the Mayflower man. I wanted to, but I also wanted to get credit for it, especially with my father.

"Bea, you're drenched. Slow down, babe. Did you take your medicine this afternoon?"

"How can I take anything around here? It's a madhouse. I have to do everything myself!"

"Just sit a minute, sit. I'll talk to Mitchell."

My father came upstairs.

"How's it going?" He walked into the bedroom, dumped the new wooden hangers on the bed.

"Fine." I showed him the garment bags, the lamps I'd brought up.

"How's your room? The maple furniture?"

"Come on. The men from Sloane's came and set up the bed this morning," I lead him down the hallway into my bedroom.

"Nice bed. Wait a minute . . . the mark on the sideboard . . . what the hell?"

He didn't miss a thing. "The guy from Sloane's hit the moving man in the face with it lifting it over the bannister. It fell on the rail."

"Did they knock any sense into the crazy bastard?"

"He left the house."

"So that's why no one was here. Thank God his replacement was sane and sober." He walked out to the bannister rail. "That's some gash there." He stared at it.

"They'll make good on it."

"Who?"

"Sloane."

"How do we get it out? Hah, we'll have to revarnish it!" He paced away from it, then crept back up. "Jesus!"

I took the carbon invoice out of my pocket. "See, they agreed to pay for it."

He took the piece of paper, examined the settlement.

Bea came upstairs with clean towels for the bathroom. Philly's scrutiny of the bannister drew Bea's attention.

"The Sloane's guy . . ." He pointed to the gash.

"My God!" Bea threw her arms up, letting the bath towels drop to the floor. "How could they do that? Where were you, Mitchell? I told you to watch them every minute, every second!"

I showed her the invoice.

"This?" she read it. "A scrap of paper! See, Phil, he's impossible. It's ruined, everything ruined!" She was heaving in my father's arms.

I crept into my room, stared out the window over the garage, confused, ready to cry myself.

That's how it was for days, weeks. Bea was enraged, flaming, never satisfied with my efforts.

"Once we're set up, then everything will calm down," my father assured me on a Saturday afternoon three weeks later. We were outside in the driveway, removing the wooden screens from the dining room windows and replacing them with matching storm windows. Mr. Russo had pointed to them on our basement tour saying, "Complete set of storms, great heat savers!" We had acknowledged their importance without knowing exactly what to do with them, but we were able to learn a lot from our neighbors' activities and our own common sense.

After a sudden chill in the evening air the second weekend in November, we knew the screens should come down. The mosquitoes, bugs and spiders had left. And I knew from watching Mr. MacNeil next door that the storm windows were held in place by the same clamp screws and hooks that held the screens. It was four o'clock in the afternoon when my father and I began taking all the first floor screens down. We rested them gingerly against the house. I was comfortable in my old chicken coop clothes. My father didn't own regular work clothes like Stevens. Instead he improvised with a cashmere sport shirt, old pinstripe suit pants and a herringbone topcoat. A soiled Dobbs hat covered his head.

"So where are the storm windows, Mitchell? Let's get them."

I went to the basement, turned on the light switch next to the furnace and examined four stacks of windows. All of them had adhesive labels indicating their proper location. I brushed the gray cobwebs off the first pile and lifted a dining room storm window, balancing it against my thighs as I maneuvered it up the cellar stairway and out the door.

"Need a hand?" My father poked his head into the cellar.

"No, I've got this one." I marched outside with it to the driveway. My father scurried alongside.

"Set it right there, Mitchell, next to the screens."

I put it down gently. My hands were creased red from the weight.

"Let me help now." My father noticed the marks.

"Sure."

It was easier carrying the second dining room storm upstairs with his help. We set it next to its mate beside the house.

"Jesus, that's filthy." My father sighed as he brushed a streak of black soot from his herringbone sleeve. "We can't put these up with all this *schmutz!*" He passed his fingers over the window glass, rubbed his thumb against the powdered dust they gathered.

"What do we do?" I asked.

"Wash them."

"With what?"

"Isn't there a hose? Water."

I ran to the garage, pulled a green tangled hose off the wall. I had hooked it up to the basement spigot at the front of the house before, so I had no difficulty repeating the procedure for my father. He was impressed.

"Here." I placed the brass nozzle in his strong, small hand.

"What now?"

"Unscrew it. Aim at the dirt. I'll turn on the water." I ran to the spigot, opened it, turned back to the driveway. A fine rainbow spray hissed over the storm window. I took the nozzle.

"Fine tune it. See, like this." I adjusted the spray to a steady stream.

"Good, Mitchell. Hit it all over." My father was excited, eager to examine the doused window when I cut off the rushing water.

"It's still dirty, streaked with film from the spray." He shook his head, kicked the water bubbles off his cordovan loafers.

"What now?" I was discouraged.

"Sponge it. Sponge and water, a little soap to cut the dirt."

"You sure?"

"That's what the window washer uses on Bookland every day."

"Every day?"

"That's right. He sponges off the dirt before wiping it clean with his squeegee in the morning. Every morning before the store opens. We need a sponge." My father walked to the back door.

"Where are you going?"

"To borrow a kitchen sponge from Bea. Hold on." He came back with a Maxwell House coffee can filled with warm soapy water and a pink round sponge in his hand.

"Let's go, Mitchell, this'll do it." He sponged the entire window with soapy water. "Okay, let it rip."

I opened the nozzle full blast, sprayed the corners, up and down the entire pane.

"That should do it. Let me inspect." He put his face up to the glass, examined it like his sapphire pinkie ring after a shower. I noticed the sun was beginning to set on the other side of the house. A wintery draught passed through the trees.

"Huh! It's still not clean!" He pulled out his white pocket handkerchief and ran it over the surface of the window, drying off the last traces of water. He scrutinized the window again, then spit on the handkerchief and rubbed one corner until it shone. "Mitchell, what's wrong? It's *still* dirty."

I examined the corner. "It's the other side. The other side is still dirty!"

"Holy mackerel . . . the other side!" He turned the window around, sponged it. I ran the water over it, cleaning off the suds.

"Well, we did it. Now it's clean. Next!" He waved his hat at the other dining room storm. "Hit it, maestro!" He winked at me.

I doused it, he sponged it and turned it around.

"Again, hit, maestro!" I did, and he sponged the other side. I sprayed off the suds.

"Clean!" he exclaimed. "We could be a team, do the whole block!"

"Whole town!" I shouted.

"More windows, maestro." My father fluttered his speckled hat at the cellar door.

"After you." I followed him down the stairs, giggling, eager for our next batch, the living room set. We washed them in half the time spent on the initial storms. However, my father noticed they were not drying clear but were streaked.

"We need a squeegee to get those last spots, or they'll spoil all our work."

"Does Bea have one?"

"No, it's a real window washer's item."

"She has old towels under the sink."

"They're no good. Leave lint all over the windows."

"Oh."

"Let's do this right . . . right?"

"Right!" I echoed.

"Grey's Hardware must have a squeegee. Bea, need anything in town?" my father yelled into the kitchen door.

"Why?" She emerged drying her hands on a floral apron.

"We're going to Grey's Hardware Store to buy a squeegee."

"Get a real sponge and pail while you're there. . . . And we could use mustard if you want to stop."

"What's the main course?" he asked.

"Virginia ham."

"Maybe something tart," he said, conjuring up the aftertaste of candied brown sauce.

"Whatever strikes your fancy, Phil. You pick." She looked at the dark overcast sky, clutched her arms shivering. "Isn't it very cold out here? Frosty."

"We'll be right back, Bea."

"Dinner's at seven-fifteen."

She went back upstairs into the kitchen.

We tore off in the Oldsmobile to Grey's Hardware Store and were back in the driveway by six-twenty-five, ready to use our new equipment, the rubber-edged squeegee, a fat, airy sponge, and a short stepladder for hooking up the storm windows when they were finally dry. The squeegee was magical. My father was using it on the last living room storm.

"Here, Mitchell." He handed it to me. "Bring over the stepladder. Let's hook it up. Ready?"

He climbed up to the second rung while I held the bottom half of the window.

"What this?" he exclaimed. "It's hard." He set the storm down on the ladder, pulled out his handkerchief again, rubbed it on a bump in the glass. "The water's hard, won't come off! Jesus Christ, it's ice! Mitchell, turn the hot on, we'll melt it off!"

I went back to the spigot expecting there would be a hot tap alongside the cold.

"There's no hot outside."

"How come?"

"It's not a bathroom."

"But we have cold."

"There's no pipe for hot."

"Get some anyway."

I ran inside to the little bathroom, poured hot water into the new pail. My father tried to melt the iced pane with the water. It only iced faster.

"Wait a minute, wait a minute! Stop the music! Hold everything! Something tells me this ain't gonna woik!" he announced, fedora tilted over his forehead.

"INK A DINK A DOO/ A dink a dee/ a dink a doo . . ." He hop-stepped away from the ladder, the pail of water steaming in his left hand. The streetlight caught the bridge of his large nose at an angle, magnifying it into a schnoz just like Durante's.

"INK A DINK A DOO/ A dink a dee/ a dink a doo . . ." He

continued prancing around the side of the house, down the driveway. He waved his hat back at me over his little head.

I laughed so hard, I had to cross my legs to stop from pissing in my already wet pants. I leaned against the white clapboards for support.

"INK A DINK A DOO/ A dink a dee/ a dink a doo." My father exited into the basement door, which muffled his voice and allowed me to regain control of my body. I picked up the discarded sponge and squeegee and headed toward the basement. The dining room screens remained lined up against the side of the house where we had put them when we began. As a result of all our spraying and sponging they had been doused repeatedly. Ice slivers glistened white inside the delicate black mesh of each screen. I carried them against my hip down to the basement, hoping they wouldn't thaw until my father and I returned for them next spring.

I was ravenous by the time I changed into dry clothes and returned to the kitchen alcove for dinner. The ham was set on the table next to my father's place, ready for carving. Bea pulled some hot biscuits out of the oven.

"Get the butter, Mitchell. How many times do I have to tell you? Always put the butter and the pepper on the table."

My father walked in, hair slicked back wet like mine. Still in his pinstripe pants.

"I have it, Mitchell, here's the pepper." He brought it to the table with him.

We both sat down.

"Like that oven, huh, Bea?"

"Mmmm," she purred. "I'm getting the hang of it."

My father and I smiled back, speechless with hunger.

There was no oven at the Park Central. Even in Bea's makeshift appliance world there was no surrogate oven like there had been an electric broiler, so using it became her new passion. Roasts, cakes, pies! The broiler was only used for steaks and chops, not chicken. In fact Bea never made broiled chicken again like she had at the Park Central. That taste was gone forever, and so were pressure-cooker vegetables. But new tastes were bountiful. So were the portions.

"Could I have another piece of ham?"

"It's your third helping." My father was startled, still on his first, though almost done.

"I love it!"

"Don't get sick!"

"It's good meat, Philly, well cooked," Bea said, defending her ham.

My father sliced through the brown fatty crust scored in squares with cloves stuck in the center of each box. He cut another top slice and then carved underneath the bone where there was less fat. The color and texture of this section was pale pink, essence of ham, it seemed. He dropped the three pieces on my empty plate. I was ready.

"Wait, have a touch of sauce." He ladled a spoon of brown glaze on my plate.

"Pineapple, Phil. Give him a slice, he's a growing boy."

He put half a slice of charred pineapple on top of the ham. I attacked, mixed all the ingredients together in my rush to possess the new flavors, so unlike any I'd ever tasted: sweet, smoky, soft meat, sugar-cured fat, spicy clove fiber, tart pineapple, all mingled together.

Bea and my father shared another piece. I poked my fork into the serving platter while they ate, gathering up the remnants of their slice, out of control. I couldn't get enough. I was ready to ask for more when Bea swept the serving platter from the kitchen table.

"So you liked my ham, Mitchell?"

"Yes, very much."

"Philly, some pie?"

"Really?" He always left room for dessert, paced himself toward it.

"It's apple with nuts and raisins."

He nodded his head with glee.

It was her own version of mince pie. She had begun experimenting with it at the Park Central, doctoring apple puddings with raisins and walnuts. Now she could mix her own dough and meld these ingredients into the crust. The filling steamed when she sliced into it with her sterling silver pie cutter. Opaque bubbles oozed from the hot apples and raisins, settled on Philly's dish, cooled into granulated spheres. He savored his first mouthful judiciously.

"Mitchell, a piece?"

"Not big." I was uncomfortable with the sour apple-raisin center. She cut two pieces, a small one for me and one for herself.

"Bea, this needs . . ." Philly's eyes were luminous. "What's missing?" he said to himself. "A top, I think."

Bea stiffened.

"Cream, that's it! A little cream."

She leapt to the icebox.

"Heavy?" She looked inside.

"Heavy," Philly assented.

"Shit, it's rancid. Nothing keeps anymore."

"Light. Do you have light?"

"Better." Bea swung around from the freezer compartment. "Schrafft's French vanilla!"

"Oh, boy!" Philly squealed. "Just a dab, Bea, just a spot on top of the crust . . . to melt in. . . . That's it . . . that's fine, babe."

She dropped two spoonfuls on his crust. They settled over the warm pie.

"Nice, nice."

She gave me and herself a scoop, put the container back in the freezer section and sat down.

"Perfect, Bea . . . perfect!" Philly orchestrated each forkful: apple, nut, raisin cluster, edge of crust, dip of cream. "Mmm, mmmm." From a different angle he rearranged the textures.

I stared at my piece of pie, put off by the hot fruit that delighted my father yet fascinated by the black dots floating inside the vanilla ice cream. My scoop curled behind the rim of the pie where the crust was thick and dark like a cookie. I drove my fork into this edge. It was delicious, like an ice cream butter cookie. The combination overpowered the sour fruit taste of the filling. Soon my ice cream was gone, but the rimless half of the pie remained uneaten. Bea sensed my difficulty.

"A little more ice cream to help with the pie?"

"Yes, yes!" I went on eating until my plate was clean.

"Woolf, go in at center now with the skins." I took my blue South Side T-shirt off and ran into mid-court. It was my second

249

chance in the scrimmage game. I had been on the shirt team first as a forward. The two teams were almost equal in ability, but Coach Wilson kept switching individual players around so he could find the best combination of guards to bring the ball up court and forwards to shoot and muscle under the boards.

Twenty-five of us had tried out for the junior varsity team. Fifteen freshmen and ten sophomores, five of them repeats from last year's team, annoyed they hadn't moved up to the varsity. We warmed up for twenty minutes, running lay-up drills, shooting baskets. Having played with the Upper School at Lake Ronkonkoma for the last two years, I had poise on the court; a quick jump shot to either side, a stylish one-hander from the top of the key, a tentative right-handed hook and an overhand lay-up. I displayed all these moves and shots before the scrimmage. Coach Wilson noticed me. So I started with the shirts at left forward, guarding Petrocelli, who was relieved from football practice so he could try out. There was only one more football game.

Schaffer, our six-foot-three center, slapped the opening tip-off to Krauss, who quickly tossed it toward me, cutting to our open basket. I dribbled twice, preparing for a routine lay-up off my right foot, but Petrocelli took the ball clean out of my right hand as I leapt up toward the backboard.

"Block! Foul! Block! Foul!"

Coach Wilson gave me a free throw, which I missed.

Back and forth, up and down the court we went. I was exhausted, dripping wet, my teeth ached. I went up for rebounds at either end of the court, but other fingers got them. My arms wouldn't move when I tried to lift them on defense. My body wouldn't respond to my will. It was spent after five minutes of all-out competition, whereas Petrocelli, Krauss and Schaffer got stronger and more accurate in their shooting. They stayed in; I came out after five minutes of playing time. I watched the shirt and skin teams rush pell-mell up and down the court. Somehow individual ability came through their wildness. Krauss, a large blond oak, all-county tackle, was deadly with a two-handed set shot from either corner. Schaffer, a clumsy black-haired rod, had an accurate jump shot, even though he often walked before he released it. Petrocelli was fierce.

After I'd spent fifteen minutes cooling off on the bench, Coach Wilson remembered me, stared at my thighs as he said, "Woolf, go in at center now with the skins." I had my second chance as a skin against Schaffer. Adrenaline filled my head and arms. I leapt so high for the center tap, I caught the middle seam of the ball as Schaffer, four inches taller, was pushing the other side of it toward Krauss. To my surprise we negated each other's tap, and the basketball fell between us.

"Rejump, you two, come on!" Coach Wilson blew his whistle, held the ball inert between us.

Schaffer was furious.

"Play ball!" Wilson threw the ball up again, and I never touched it. Schaffer slammed it to the other end of the court, where his little guard made an easy lay-up.

I tried to get back into the game but fell apart even more quickly guarding Schaffer. I couldn't play under the key anymore on offense I was so intimidated and battered by Schaffer and Krauss. I came out to greet our guards when they brought the ball over the ten-second line. One of them tossed it to me, which drew Schaffer away from the basket to guard me.

"Woolf, Woolf!" Petrocelli growled from the left forecourt. He was still playing for the skins, hungry for the ball, insatiable. I leaned around Schaffer with the ball. Petrocelli was guarded by two shirt players. He faked a give and go, darted around them, and I hit him with a bounce pass, which he caught running fifteen feet from the basket. Massive Krauss was in front of him. Petrocelli swiveled around him, elbowing Krauss's midsection, then flew toward the backboard, lifting the ball into the iron hoop underhanded, letting it roll off his fingertips.

"That's enough, Petrocelli, take a breather." Coach Wilson blew him out of the game. "Nice move," he added softly as Petrocelli trotted to the bench.

My accurate bounce pass and the flash of approval Petrocelli sent me after his score revitalized me. When the shirt guards dribbled the ball back to their basket, I hung over Schaffer, hands in front of his face. I anticipated the next pass into him, slapped it free, charged for the loose ball, grabbed it near the ten-second line and dribbled free toward our basket at the other end of the court. In the clear I drove for a lay-up. The two shirt guards gained on me screaming, "Clutch, Woolf, clutch!" breaking my concentration. One of them touched my shoulder. I lost control of the ball, and my legs wobbled when I reached for it, tapping it into the foul lane, pushing it out of bounds. I fell after it on the wrestling mat, sank to the floor exhausted.

"Shirt ball!" Coach Wilson blew his silver whistle. "Woolf, use the bench for a seat." His crack drew catcalls. My cheeks turned scarlet. I slumped toward the bench heaving wet.

The only empty spot was next to Petrocelli. He moved aside, indicating I was welcome. I sat down, my body flooded with perspiration draining into my shorts, staining the elastic top deep blue. Rivulets of sweat collected in the folds of my stomach. Petrocelli put his large dark hand on my knee. "Nice pass, Woolf." He stared at the game, his thick eyebrows menacing over his black eyes. He withdrew his hand. The back of it, like his arms, chest, stomach, every part of his tight body, was covered with hair. He had stubble on his face, a five o'clock shadow like my father. A few of the sophomores shaved, but most of the freshmen were still kids like me, with peach fuzz. My stomach used to be taut like Petrocelli's, without flat tires above my midriff. Bea's cuisine had transformed my body, slowed me down. Soon I wouldn't be able to break away from the kitchen alcove let alone score a lay-up. I remembered a snapshot of my father and me standing together at Raynor's Beach after my mother had sent me silver dollars for my birthday. I was a straight brown reed then.

The scrimmage was over. Everyone sat down on the benches.

"Okay, good workout, good effort. I appreciate all of you trying out. Unfortunately only twelve of you can make it. If your name isn't called, don't be discouraged. The following boys stick around." He read off their names. "I need your schedules. The rest of you . . ." He looked us over, up and down the bench, in case he had missed anyone. I tried to catch his eye but couldn't make contact. "The rest of you can get dressed." I put my shirt on, fighting back tears, pulled it over my face, got up.

"Don't leave any stuff under the bench!"

Petrocelli caught my eye as I was looking for my towel.

"See you in the lunchroom, Woolf." His grizzled man's face cracked into a smile.

"Thanks," I said and walked out of the gym.

I was so hurt and depressed when I got home, I wouldn't acknowledge Bea's greeting or accept her offer of a snack but went straight up to my room instead, speechless. I stared out the window at the top of the garage, mute with defeat, grieving, waiting for my father to drive in.

It was a long wait. He had changed his commuting routine, or rather it had been changed for him. Initially he used the Long Island Rail Road like most of the men who worked in the city. The thirty-five minute ride into Penn Station was one of the attractions of Rockville Centre. Trains left promptly every fifteen minutes between eight and nine-fifteen A.M. and returned in the evening between five-fifteen and six-thirty at similar intervals.

Philly drove himself to the station and parked the gray Olds in a commuter lot along with at least fifty other cars. He had difficulty interpreting the timetable, then meeting the trains on time. He was always five minutes late. He often came home after the six-thirty train at night because business at Bookland was so unpredictable. In the morning, he tried to make the nine-fifteen, which got him into Bookland at ten-twenty, his usual time when we lived at the Park Central. If he missed this one, he had to wait a half-hour. Harry and the salesmen were also left waiting, though he could call ahead if he wanted. Similarly, with Bea at night, if he missed an express home, he could call and pinpoint the later train he would be on. The timeable was thus a discipline, a deterrent to Philly's excessive dawdling. He even enjoyed the train at first when it wasn't crowded. But as the days went on he grew to resent the lack of control he had over his travel time. When he arrived and left Bookland should be his choice, not the railroad's. He couldn't forget the old days when he could chose between three bus lines, three subways, one trolley, and a taxicab to go a mere thirteen blocks.

Thus when the gray Oldsmobile was stolen one afternoon from the commuter lot in Rockville Centre right in front of the County Court House, Philly didn't interpret it as a disaster but rather as a sign, a portent.

"It was telling me something: Don't take the train to work anymore, commute by car!"

The stately green Chrysler Imperial he was able to purchase with the insurance money and a generous year-end discount made this decision a joyous relief. No more Long Island train schedule. He was his own boss on the open road just like he was in Bookland.

For Bea it was murder. Not in the mornings, but in the evenings, when she could no longer predict Philly's grand entrance. Her dinners were elaborate: appetizer, soup, main dish, two hot vegetables, salad, dessert. Timing was critical. Philly still called before leaving the store, but there was no way of holding him accountable, so many things could delay his trip home. Bea was wild with tension waiting for the new sound of the Chrysler in the driveway, not knowing whether to start the vegetables, turn down the oven, reheat the soup. The waiting was horrible.

I was still riveted to my bedroom window at seven-thirty when I heard the basso hum of the fluid drive engine as my father inched the Imperial into our driveway. He accelerated gently over a hump and glided into the clapboard garage. The massive car, a luxury land cruiser with bright headlights in front and smaller red ones sloped on the rear fins, could not quite fit inside the garage. The brake lights stuck outside in the night, their hue intensified as my father cut the engine off. He emerged from the garage with his briefcase and evening paper, paused beside the curved trunk, patted it as if it were an animal and walked briskly up the rear steps into the kitchen.

"I'm home, babe."

"What took you so long?"

"59th Street was murder . . . getting on the bridge . . ."

"You said you were leaving at six. You promised me, Phil. What is it?" She twirled around to the stove clock. "Ninety minutes since you called!"

"It was crazy until Van Wyck, jammed, Friday night, weekenders."

"How am I supposed to make dinner? Tell me!"

"I'll break away earlier on Friday."

"Look at the meat." She pointed at the top of the stove where a shriveled leg of lamb lay stuck in its own juices. "The soup is gone." A thick yellow film covered what had once been cream of mushroom soup. "I can't do it anymore, hot and timed for the minute you walk through the door. How can I do it? I want the meal to be perfect. It's important to *me*." Bea started trembling. Her potholder and dish towel fell to the floor as she raised both hands to her face. Philly caressed her shoulders, tried to pull her palms away from her wet eyes.

"Help me. Help me," she moaned. "Please help me!"

He held her heaving body against his outdoor smells. When she calmed, he pried her hands away from her face, one at a time. He kissed each eyelid.

"Phil." She smiled reluctantly. "No, no more, I'm really mad at you!"

"Let me wash up." He released her. "Two seconds, honest."

"I bet." She remained skeptical of his timing. "Get Mitchell to wash his hands." She dabbed her eyes with a tissue.

"Where is he?"

"Upstairs in his room . . . wouldn't come out."

"Why not?"

"Who knows what he's doing in there? Speak to him."

"Hey, champ." My father tapped on the door within seconds. "Can I come in?" He lowered his voice.

I turned away from the window toward the door, still mute, and put my hand on the porcelain knob.

"Champ, can I—" My father tumbled in as I turned the doorknob.

"I'm not a champ anymore, not even a contender. I was cut."

"Cut?"

"I didn't make the JV basketball team. Kaput, cut!" I sliced my hand through the air.

"I'm really sorry, Mitchell." He squeezed my shoulder. "Next year you'll make it."

"What do I do until then? Fart around in the bleachers?"

"Practice," he suggested.

"With whom? Where? I don't see how unless I'm on a team."

"You'll find out. Ask some of the other kids who didn't make the team."

"They're little schmucks. What do they know about anything?"

"It's not the end of the world."

"Hey, you two, dinner's on the table," Bea yelled from the foot of the stairs.

We scampered into the upstairs bathroom, and my father ran the hot and a touch of cold from the tap. He soaped his hands, then handed the bar to me.

"Come on, she's really steamed."

We shared the soap at the sink basin the way we used to when I was a little boy at the Park Central. It shot out of my hands into the air when my father asked for it back.

"Thank you, Alphonse!"

"Be my guest."

"No, be mine!" He shot the soap back through the air into my slippery fingers. We dried off using different ends of the same pink bath towel and tumbled down the carpeted stairs. We tiptoed into the kitchen, beaming, shiny faced.

"At last!" Bea said in greeting us. She ladled hot Campbell's tomato soup into our bowls. The mushroom soup was no more. The lamb was charred on the outside, pink near the bone. The garlic slivers masked the burned taste. It was edible, though not what we were used to. No one uttered a word. I even had seconds. The brussel sprouts were beyond me, nasty little cabbages. I pushed them to the rim of my plate under lamb gristle. Bea noticed.

"No sprouts, Mitchell? They'll make you strong."

"Hah, not strong enough!"

"What do you mean? Your father loves them and look—"

"Mitchell didn't make the basketball team, Bea," my father explained.

"So that's what's eating him. I'm sorry." She reached across the table.

"Sure you are."

"You should tell me what's bothering you, Mitchell. I can understand. I've been disappointed."

"Not like this."

"Well, close."

"I bet."

"Fresh!" Bea swept away from the table to the oven for a hot rhubarb pie. "Why can't he respect me, Philly?"

"He's upset, Bea. It's a big disappointment."

"Still, he shouldn't talk to me like that." She put the hot pie on the table, got clean dessert plates from the cupboard.

"I'm sorry," I said to my empty plate, saving my father the pain of asking me to apologize and hating Bea more.

"Well, that's better." She began cutting into the lattice crust. "Wasn't it Pee Wee Reese? Myron said he never made his high school baseball team."

"I think so." My father was amused at Bea's memory. She usually had no interest in sports.

"How come?" I asked. After all, he was the Dodger shortstop.

"Too small, I think. That's right, Myron said he was too small in high school . . . a peewee." Surprised at her bon mot, she cracked up. So did my father. I reddened, looked down at my fleshy stomach, the tight cordovan belt slicing into my midriff.

"That's not my problem." They continued laughing. At me, I assumed.

Finally, stifling her mouth with a dish towel, Bea tapped my forearm. "Rhubarb pie? Hot, a little cream on top?" They started giggling again.

"No, thanks."

They couldn't hear me their squealing was so infectious. Bea repeated her offer: "Rhubarb pie? Hot, a little cream on top?"

"*No, thanks!* Didn't you hear me?" I got up from the table.

"Sorree," Bea minced. "Where you going, mister? Dinner's not over."

"It is for me." I didn't want to hear them slobber through the bittersweet pie.

"Let him go, Bea. It's okay."

I moved away from the table alcove, darted toward the front stairs. At least I could break away from the kitchen table before the rhubarb pie was served. It was a start. Perhaps next year I'd be able to dribble full court and score a lay-up without losing control of the ball.

"Oh, Mitchell," Bea yelled out, her silliness gone. "If you use the bathroom for anything, try not to stain the bath mat." Her barb stopped me cold at the foot of the stairs. "Whatever that stuff is, it stains."

"It's snot," I yelled back through the kitchen doorway, furious at her innuendo.

"Snot?" She didn't believe me.

"Yeah, from my hayfever. Asshole," I added under my breath as I dashed upstairs and slammed the door to my room so hard the whole house shook. "Fucking asshole!" I screamed at the four walls.

The Chrysler Imperial was excessive; my father, self-contained. I couldn't understand why he chose it to replace the more compact Oldsmobile until I drove to work with him the following Saturday to help out with the pre-Christmas rush. He pulled the car out of the garage so I could get in without crushing myself against the lawn mower and rakes stored on the passenger side.

"Okay, Mitchell, the car is ready." He opened my door with a flourish. It closed like a vault. He scrambled around to the other side of the car, took off his overcoat and placed it carefully on the back seat. Then he centered a thick foam cushion over the driver's seat and got in. He could actually see six inches above the steering wheel with his new accessory.

"See the steering wheel, Mitchell?" He held it firmly in his pigskin gloves.

"Nice color." It was marble green.

"It's more than decoration! See?" He slammed the top of it full force with his palm. It bent inward.

"Don't break it," I cautioned him.

"That's the point. It bends, see?" He slammed into it again with his palm. "Suppose a car hits me head on, the steering wheel is pushed into my chest, right? But this one bends in half against me." And he pulled both sides up toward him as proof.

I shook my head at his doomsday scenario.

"See above the dashboard?" He touched a long padded strip covered with green leather. "That'll catch your head in case there's a sudden stop. Lean forward."

I did. The leather touched my forehead. Why the morbid preoccupation? I wondered as my father released the steel hand brake and we purred out of the driveway. Perhaps because the gray Olds had been stolen outside the County Court House he felt vulnerable, as if anything could happen to his car now, parked or with him at the wheel.

On Sunrise Highway he opened up on the accelerator, and we cruised along between the well-spaced stoplights at forty-five, fifty MPH. It felt like we were doing fifteen or twenty in local traffic. At a jammed intersection in Valley Stream where a large yellow overhead traffic light cautioned us to slow down, I noticed my father used both feet instead of one to bring the Imperial to a full stop.

"How come both feet? Too heavy for one to stop it?"

"No, no." He laughed. "See?" He pointed to the floor pedals. "One's the brake, the other, the clutch."

"Oh." I was surprised.

"It's not a Hydromatic like the Olds."

"You mean it's old-fashioned, like Uncle Myron's Ford?"

"Not exactly. I have a choice. It can handle like a three-speed shift. Or I can shift just once instead of three times to reach forty-five."

"How come?"

"There's fluid in the transmission that eases into second and third for me as I step on the gas."

"Is it better than Hydromatic?"

"I have more control over the engine, especially on hills, for starts and sudden stops. Watch." The overhead light turned green. My father depressed the clutch pedal. As he released it from the floor he stepped gently on the thin rubber accelerator with his right foot. We took off, gained speed, twenty, thirty, forty-five, and he didn't have to use the clutch or shift again after he was in gear. It was very smooth. No sudden clicks forward, like with the Olds when it "automatically" shifted gears. I was enthralled by the new fluid rhythm and watched my father deftly manipulate the pedals at each stop to achieve it. I noticed the break pedal was thicker than the one on the Oldsmobile. The clutch was of a similar thickness.

"Aren't the pedals bigger on this car, Dad?"

"Yep. The garage put blocks on them for me. I like the seat pushed back so far. I could barely reach them before. This way I can ride in comfort and see everything."

And still be five feet tall, I thought to myself, remembering the wooden blocks the bike man screwed on my tricycle pedals so I could reach them when I was four years old.

Off we sped onto the new Van Wyck Expressway, up hills with as much speed as down. The Imperial took the steepest incline without any decelerating effect on its powerful eight-cylinder engine. We cruised toward Bookland in upholstered living-room comfort, a wide armrest between us.

"How about some music, Mitchell?"

"Good idea. Martin Block, *Make Believe Ballroom.*"

My father pushed a chrome selection button right to WNEW.

"Number fifteen this week and moving up fast by the . . ." Block was well into his Saturday countdown of the top twenty-five songs of the week. The radio tone was rich, better than our cabinet Emerson with the green tuning eye. Block's patter was unadorned, comforting.

"Your Uncle Alfie started him off in Newark fifteen years ago, gave him his first few sponsors. I always liked him."

"So do I."

We talked about the songs but mostly over the music about Harry, the store, the basketball season at South Side, traffic. Bea and the house on Everett Street were not mentioned. Suddenly we were on Queens Boulevard in the three-lane center strip.

"I think Forest Hills High School is over there somewhere." My father swept his arm to the right.

"Too big," I replied.

"Too big," my father agreed, moving the Imperial quickly past local traffic, inexorably toward the East River, which we crossed over the cantilevered Queensboro Bridge, sparkling midtown visible through the rapid-fire openings in its erector set frame. Off the bridge at 59th in a racetrack rush. Left on 2nd, right at 57th, crawling slowly crosstown to the Gem Garage on 54th, just off 7th.

We climbed out of the Chrysler. My father retrieved his coat and briefcase from the back seat. An attendent, Ray, built like Jackie Robinson and with his grace and speed, took the car, revved it toward the elevator, stopped short, swung it expertly around into a first floor parking berth.

"Six-thirty, chief!" my father said when Ray returned to the front of the busy garage for another humming car.

"You got it, Mr. W."

With me in tow my father walked briskly to the bus stop, the same one we used in our Park Central days. He was vibrant for the new day. I was exhausted, ready for a second breakfast, a cup of coffee, a cruller, a little something to pick me up. A number 6 bus waddled in, farting, bumping up to the curb, still empty, only four blocks from its starting point on 59th Street. We were at the store in five minutes, but the entire trip, portal to portal, took an hour and ten. Why my father chose to commute in his car instead of on the faster Long Island Rail Road was something I thought about more at the busy store making change, wrapping books.

The answer became self-evident when we picked the Imperial up, returning on the now more crowded number 6 bus back up 7th Avenue to 54th Street at six-twenty-five. My father bought the *World-Telegram* and two Garcia y Vega panatelas, dark leaf, at the corner United Cigar Store.

Ray pulled the Imperial up a little bit off the main exit way so my father could take his time getting in without blocking the other cars.

He arranged his overcoat, briefcase and evening paper carefully in the back seat. I walked around to the passenger side, noticed the Fluid Drive logo welded to the lower fender beside my door. I realized the green Chrysler was large, but discreetly so; proportionate like my father's clothes, deemphasizing size, unlike the other luxury cars parked on the first floor of the Gem Garage.

My father rolled his window up, muffling the traffic noises. As we crawled back toward the Queensboro Bridge he was tight-lipped, preoccupied. December Saturdays at Bookland were always wild and full of interruptions. The driving seemed to relax him. He gradually unwound, though conversation was barely possible on Queens Boulevard. When we got to the Van Wyck Expressway, he unlocked his side window and nudged it open, breaking the rubber seal.

"You want to push that in for me, Mitchell?" He pointed to the dashboard cigarette lighter on my side of the radio. "Tell me when it pops out." He unwrapped the cellophane of his fresh cigar with his right hand and a twist of his teeth. The lighter snapped back out. I reached for it. My father intercepted my fingers.

"No, I'll get it. They're tricky." He pulled out the lighter. Its coils were dull gray, yet when my father held the cylinder to his cigar, the tip of it caught on fire. The coils were bright orange, like a miniature broiler, when he took the lighter away from his smoking cigar.

"You never know how hot the damned thing is until you light up!" He put it back in its dashboard hole, breathed in deeply on the panatela. "Nice, nice." He drew the leaf past his nose. Smoke circled out his side window. He was pleased, reflective.

"Dad, that *was* snot on the bath mat."

"What?" He didn't understand. Perhaps this wasn't the right moment. I was yelling at my side window rather than talking to him.

"Oh, God," I started again, "that was snot on the bath mat."

"I figured as much."

"I do it in my sleep, though."

He put his cigar in the ashtry underneath the radio.

"You know?" I prompted.

He was blank.

"Well, I do it in my sleep. Isn't that disgusting?"

"What?"

"I jerk off while I'm asleep. The stuff's all over me when I wake up. Can't stop. Once every two or three nights." I was looking at him now.

He smiled, hit the steering wheel so hard with his palm it snapped in. "That's wonderful, Mitchell!"

"Don't make fun. It's weird. I mean awake is bad enough, but while I'm asleep . . . ?"

"It's okay. You're not sick, for Christsakes!"

We were on Sunrise Highway at the Bayshore stoplight. He faced me. "There's nothing wrong with it. You're growing into a man. Grandpa Nathan would be proud!"

"Proud? He did it too?"

"You bet! Him, me, you, Milton Berle, Jimmy Durante, Al Jolson, everyone!"

"So I'm not sick? It's all right? Whew! I was so scared, ashamed . . . couldn't look at the girls walking in the hallways between classes anymore."

The light was green, we were off again.

"What about the clothes they wear?" my father asked. "Tight sexy sweaters?"

I nodded. "Shows everything, I mean, everything you can imagine."

"Well, at night you dream about that and explode. It's not your fault. How could it be anyone's fault?"

Suddenly we were in Rockville Centre. My father reached for his cigar. The aroma refilled the car as we pulled up our driveway into the garage. We got out on our own sides and met at the overhead door that couldn't be closed anymore.

"Wonderful!" My father was still smiling, eyes twinkling at me in the dark. "You know, Mitchell, your grandfather was a great fucker. He loved the ladies, and his father and his father before him." He slapped my shoulder. "You're part of that, all the way back." He laughed, tears in his eyes, shaking my hands in his.

"So when are you two lovebirds coming inside?" Bea called from the kitchen door. Light fell on the driveway as she opened it wider to see where we were and what we were doing. My father couldn't stop holding my hand, shaking it. I held his tight.

"What the hell are you two doing out there? The pot roast will dry out."

"We're coming, we're coming," my father answered back, deflecting her anger as we walked up the pathway into the Formica kitchen.

"What took you guys so long?" Bea saw us standing side by side, grinning at each other. She flinched and went back to the oven with her potholders.

The growing strain between Bea and me had intensified. Our informal alliance had fallen apart once its objectives were achieved and we were all living together like a real family. The old antagonisms, the rivalry for my father's affections took its place with a vengeance. Bea was jealous yet unable to compete with the new intimacy my father and I shared. She knew how to woo him when he walked through the door after work, even though the uncertainty of his arrival screwed up her timing. But pleasing him away from the kitchen table was a problem. Bea yearned for a social life in Rockville Centre. Philly wasn't interested. Partly he was exhausted from commuting five, sometimes six days a week. Deep down, however, he was always reluctant to have "company" over or go visiting on Sunday, unlike many of our neighbors on Everett Street.

Indeed, Jim Henson, a lawyer four houses down from us, even invited clients to large cocktail parties.

"Ridiculous!" my father said one Saturday evening, driving past their Tudor stucco house, an elaborate cocktail party spilling strangers on the lawn.

"Imagine doing all of that to impress. What kind of a lawyer can he be if he needs parties for his business?"

"A popular one," Bea answered.

"For how long, though? It's all phony baloney."

"That's how some people get clients. Bruce takes prospective ones to Broadway musicals. They remember the good time when they need an accountant for something."

"So what am I supposed to do, invite all the customers and

salesmen over on the weekend? Have publishers drop by so I can get special discounts? I gotta relax, Bea."

"So who's coming over, Phil? I'm making a nice stuffed chicken for lunch, and we'll take it easy all day tomorrow."

"Good, Bea." He was relieved. "Maybe we'll take a ride, see the sights."

"Whatever you say, hon."

There wasn't much to pull Philly out of the Dutch colonial house, no restaurants on Sunrise Highway worth the trouble. One movie theater showing last year's double features, a golf and a tennis club that were completely beyond him, a Georgian Reform temple Bea was occasionally able to get my father to if he came home early enough on Friday night.

So I was surprised the last Friday evening in February when I jumped off my Columbia three speed and bolted through the kitchen door to find out we were having company for Saturday dinner.

"Who?"

"The Freeds, remember? My Hempstead cousins."

"So I'll meet your tiny Aunt Greta?"

"She's not coming."

"Too small for the car?"

"No, no, she's visiting her youngest daughter on Staten Island. Her son, Jake, is coming and Beth, his wife, and Marge, their teenager." Bea rolled her eyes at me.

"What can I do to help?"

"Clean up your room and rake the front lawn. I asked this morning, remember?"

"It's too dark now."

"Come on, wise guy, your room has lights. Please?"

"We have a Rotary Club game tonight. Yale's coming by with his mother to pick me up."

"Mitchell, you promised! You promised me!"

"I forgot."

A horn blared in the driveway.

"It's your father. You left your damned bike in the way again. Move it."

"Okay, okay, I'm coming," I yelled out the window. "Can't make one mistake around here." I trailed down the back stairs.

"You make too many, kiddo!" Bea followed after me.

My father had his brights on. They filtered through the frame and spokes of my three speed, casting a shadow on the garage. I moved the bike aside, off the cement. Its shadow dissolved. My father waved as he drove the Chrysler past me into the garage. He wasn't mad. I walked my bike in after him, placed it against the wall on the passenger side of the car.

"How's it going, champ?"

"Fine. We're in the Rotary Club play-off tonight."

"Hey, good luck."

We walked toward the kitchen door.

"Bea's mad, I forgot to rake the leaves."

"Do it tomorrow."

"We have company then."

"Ooooooh, no, I forgot! The Freeds!" My father reached for his stomach, touched it gently. "They won't be here till the afternoon, will they?"

"Guess not."

"I hope not!" He smirked.

We entered the kitchen.

"He did it again, Philly."

"What?"

"*What?* His bike! I told him a million times! He doesn't listen to me . . . *ever!*"

"It's all right, he moved the bike."

"You take his side every time! Why?"

"I only said it was no big deal."

"He's always right, I'm always wrong!" She was red, dripping.

Philly sucked his chest up, turned away from her. "I'm going to wash up, Bea."

I trailed him into the dining room, up the stairs. Bea came after us and stood at the bottom of the stairwell braying: "What am I? His slave? I have to clean his room? I have to rake the lawn?"

"He'll do it tomorrow," my father answered.

"I want him to do it *now*." She was pounding the bannister rail with her palm.

"Son of a bitch!" my father yelled at the top of the stairs. "There it goes again. Jesus!" He put his briefcase down, massaged the underpart of his belly with both hands.

"Fucking cramps . . . uuuugh . . . there it goes! Oh, shit!" He winced.

Bea withdrew to the kitchen. I carried my father's coat and briefcase into the master bedroom. He stayed in the bathroom a long, long time, flushing the toilet, finally drawing a hot tub. Half an hour past. I sat in my room, numb, unable to clean up for Saturday. Bea returned to the foot of the stairs.

"When do you guys want dinner? Everything's ready now."

I wasn't hungry. I poked my head out the door to check on my father.

"See what he's up to," Bea urged sotto voce.

"Dad?" I tapped on the bathroom door.

"Come in, come in." He was staring up, afloat in the steaming water.

"You all right?"

His face was sweating.

"Bea says dinner's ready."

"Ooooh," he groaned. "I'm not."

"What should I tell her?"

"I can't eat anything."

"You'll be all right?"

"The water helps ease the muscle tension. Maybe later. Something light."

"I'll tell her."

"Have a good game." He splashed his hands in the water.

I tumbled down the stairs in my tight Keds. "Dad will be awhile."

Bea knew what that meant.

"When's your ride coming?"

"Ten minutes."

"I'll fix you a nice pot roast sandwich."

"No, no, that's all right, I'll eat after the game."

"You can't play on an empty stomach, you'll die." She pulled me into the kitchen, cut into the warm pot roast, placed the tender slabs of meat on a piece of rye bread, ladled minced onion and tomato gravy on the meat, placed another piece of rye on top and sliced. The bread soaked the grease out of the meat like a blotter. Only the caraway seeds retained their original color. I bit into the stain.

Yale's mother blew her station wagon horn. I flew out of the alcove, spilling some Pepsi on the floor. Bea was drawn to it like a yellow jacket.

"See ya." I was out the front door.

Yale, our tiny playmaker, was beside his mother, a kind brunette who dressed in moccasins, khaki skirts, and white shirt blouses.

"Up front, with us." She motioned me away from the rear door. "Sit with us, Mitchell." There was no more tension.

I slid in next to them.

"We need the back for the rest of the team." She gathered up six more boys and got us to the Rotary gym with fifteen minutes to spare for lay-up and foul practice.

The following Tuesday after school the front doorbell rang. I saw a village taxi shoot off empty into the downpour. The chimes sounded two, three more times before I opened the door. Bea stood there drenched, four shopping bags at her muddy shoes. I reached for two immediately.

"Mat . . . mat . . ." she gasped, out of breath. I didn't hear her words because of the rain and my own haste to reach the kitchen before the sodden bags split open. When I returned for the rest of them, Bea was livid.

"Where's the doormat? Can't you do anything for me?"

"I didn't hear you."

"You never listen. Look for it. My shoes are filthy."

It wasn't near the door or in the vestibule.

"There it is!" I yelled. A corner wedge of the mat jammed the hall closet open. I placed it over the sill for Bea to walk on.

"Who put it in there?"

"I don't know."

"Think, for Christsakes, think!"

"Why don't you? . . . Why don't you go fuck yourself?" I burst at her wet, angry face and went upstairs. But I could still hear Bea as she staggered into the living room with her two wet shopping bags, hyperventilating. The full ire of her response exploded through the late afternoon on into the night.

"You'll pay for this! You'll pay for this, you son of a bitch! Just wait till your father comes home." Blabbering, shrieking . . . up and down the hallway.

"To a mother he says, 'Go fuck yourself!' " she brayed the moment he opened the door. "Imagine . . . 'Go fuck yourself' to a mother! Do something, Philly! Philly, go in there, make him . . . Philly, I want you to go . . ."

In the morning Bea was still flaming by the kitchen sink.

"Are you ready to apologize now?"

"Maybe after breakfast."

"After breakfast, you little bastard?" She was on top of me in her dressing gown, swatting at my face, arms, anything she could hit. I squirmed away from her body, ran into the dining room. Around the mahogany table she chased me with a serrated bread knife.

"After breakfast, you bastard! I'll make you . . . I'll get you!" Faster, faster she ran, eyes engorged, reaching for my undershirt, touching it.

"Put the knife down, Bea!" My father was suddenly in the room, patches of toilet paper red and white on his chin.

"Make him apologize!"

I was under the table now.

"Put the knife down!" he repeated louder.

"Never! I'll kill . . . I'll kill . . ." She looked around the room for me. I remained in my hiding place.

"I'll kill . . . *MYSELF!* That's what you want, isn't it? Both of you?" She held the blade over her wrists. "Isn't it?"

Philly grabbed her knife hand from behind. "Let go, Bea. Drop it!"

The stainless steel blade stuck on its point in the oak floor.

"Don't ever raise a knife to him! Hear me?"

269

Bea was screaming, crying, terrified. Philly clutched her body to contain the writhing.

Nuts! Everyone was crazy, running around like chickens without any heads.

The following day I was back on the Long Island Rail Road, headed east toward Lake Ronkonkoma for the remainder of high school.

Chapter
Seven

"WOOLF'S COMING BACK." Zachery started the rumor.

"Woolf?" everyone asked.

"Yeah." Zachery was definite.

"When?" they all insisted.

"Tonight, sooner, lunch maybe."

Lunch. Jesus, what happened? Rafferty must have thought, though he didn't ask. Never asked, not later, when he told me how everybody had reacted to the news, or even when Mr. Ryson ushered me into his light corner room in Mayall Hall at one o'clock.

"You guys know each other?" Ryson chuckled at the unexpected irony of his question.

"Jimmy!"

"Woolf!"

"Holy mackerel!"

We slapped each other around.

"Nice room."

"Two windows." He pointed. One overlooked the tennis courts, the other a lilac bush.

"Bring your stuff inside."

I went back to the hall where I'd dropped my strap-around leather valise and laundry box. I carried them to the foot of the naked lower mattress. Ryson left us alone, went up to his apartment on the second floor.

"You missed lunch."

"Is that good or bad?" I asked.

"Grilled cheese, carrot strips, milk."

"I'll live without that meal."

"The canteen is better now. We'll get you stuff later."

"Don't worry about it."

Suddenly Ryson came back into the room breathing hard, brushing a stray wisp of hair out of his blue eyes, pressing it up to his hairline.

"Woolf, did you bring your basketball sneakers?"

"You bet."

"Get 'em out."

"What for?"

"Away game. East Islip. Bus leaves at two."

"But I don't have a uniform."

"You'll get one on the bus."

"I don't know the plays."

"Coach Berger will fill you in."

"Who?"

"Berger. New coach from Brooklyn, a regular guy. I'm coming along, I'll introduce you on the bus. We need you, Woolf. Everyone's getting sick. The second string is fading on us, but the starting five are healthy . . . damned good. They got us a 15-3 record. Rafferty, fill him in, okay?" Ryson huffed.

"Well, I'd love to help out, but I'm not in great shape."

"Come on, you were good last year, good enough for the JV. Now you're even bigger." Ryson touched both my shoulders with his calloused hands. He was six feet four, weighed 230 pounds and had played left tackle at Spartansburg Normal College before the war.

"He's also hungry—no lunch," Rafferty sassed.

"I'll get you a sandwich for the bus."

"Cold cheese," Rafferty whispered, cracking us both up.

"In fifteen minutes, Woolf, be ready."

"I'll get my stuff on."

While I pulled my jock strap, sweat socks, and Keds out of my valise Rafferty filled me in on the first team and the miraculous season Lake Ronkonkoma was having in basketball. So good, neither he or Zachery could make the team. The starting five came from Madison High School in the city. They had been imported as a unit by Berger. There was a high school coach's strike going on in New York City, which meant no basketball during their senior year, no exposure or athletic scholarships from the top college teams. Berger had seized on their misfortune and used it to bring the five Brooklyn hotshots out to the middle of Long Island. They got free room, board and tuition—full scholarships. The Lake Ronkonkoma School got a winning basketball season, the first since Mr. Kennedy's son and the World War II veterans had graced our long wooden court in 1946. All the prep schools we played recruited ballplayers: Stony Brook, Seton Hall, Carterette. Stringers, they were called when they suddenly appeared for games, not classes. But no school had ever recruited an entire team from New York City.

They were a formidable unit, in tune with one another's moves from years of school yard pickup games and high school contests they had watched or played in together. It was a different style of basketball they brought to the large, noisy East Islip gymnasium.

Glickman, the blond playmaker, brought the ball up court with Lewin, a deadly one-handed shooter from the twenty to thirty foot range. If Glickman didn't start a play, he worked one-on-one against his man. He could dribble or shoot with either hand, and he used this dexterity to change the flow of his body from the right side to the left as he switched hands, thus protecting the ball and faking out his man as he drove around him for an easy lay-up. Usually Glickman and Lewin ran plays off the center, Rosen, or the two forwards, Glazer and Franick. The plays had never been seen before on Long Island. Instead of hitting the inside big men around the key and running a conventional give-and-go or letting one of the big men hook off the pivot himself, Glickman and Lewin, who were only five eight and five nine, passed to each other cross-court, then cut under the basket to the opposite side, running an S pattern, pushing Rosen, Franick and Glazer in turn out to the guard positions, where they also passed off to the man opposite them and cut back under the basket. The result was a five-man weave in which everyone played each position. The object of all the motion was to shake someone loose for an open shot. East Islip never knew who was going to get the ball, who to concentrate on, who would shake free, where the pass would come from. It was too fluid an offense for them to contain. They were also confused by the starting five's jabbering, affectionate hum as they ran their weave.

"Here, baby Glaze, hit me!"

"Got you, Rosie!"

"See you, Lew!"

"Glick, pick, light the wick."

Suddenly Glickman winged the ball to Rosen all alone under the basket. He rammed the ball two-handed into the wire hoop. Our small bench cheered. The overhead score board flashed *Visitors 42, Home 36, 3.00 minutes, 4th quarter.* I couldn't believe the miracle. We had never controlled an East Islip game before. I was delirious; the world had been turned on its head. When our lead grew to 10, Berger, an emotional coach who spoke in the same monosyllabic bursts as the starting five, motioned three of us off the bench to his side.

"Okay. Muller for Franick, Ryan for Rosen, Woolf for Glazer. Next whistle, all of you go in."

I stared at Berger.

"It's okay, Woolf, you can do it, baby." He slapped my ass with his hand. The whistle blew; we were in the game for the final two minutes. Glickman and Lewin moved us around on offense. We tried to freeze the ball. I got two rebounds and blocked a desperation lay-up. My teeth didn't hurt. After the final buzzer Berger clapped me on both shoulders. "Woolf, we can use your muscle. Good effort!"

Mr. Ryson caught Berger's eye as I walked toward the shower room. "I told you Woolf was okay."

"Yeah, he'll help next week against LaSalle."

In the bus and at the Smithtown Diner, where we stopped for hamburgers, the starting five remained apart from the rest of us. They weren't hostile or deliberately exclusive, just uninterested in our company. Their clothes were different: suede shoes, pale blue and orange slacks, silk shirts. They went home every weekend there wasn't a Saturday game and returned on Monday, our Brooklyn mercenaries.

When the bus dropped us off at Mayall Hall it was ten-thirty, after lights-out. Rafferty was still awake when I got in.

"It's okay, Woolf, turn on the light," he sang out from the top bunk.

"Oh." I was relieved, not wanting to unpack and make my bed for the first time in the dark. I snapped on the overhead light. My bed was made, my suitcase was unpacked and standing next to my closet.

"Jimmy, who made . . . ?"

"I did. Figured you'd be late."

"Where did you put my clothes, my pajamas?" I asked.

"In the bureau over there, the green one."

Rafferty had laid out all my clothes: socks top drawer, underwear second, shirts third.

"How did you know where to put everything?"

"I know."

My bed was made with two sheets and a blanket folded into tight hospital corners, a technique Rafferty never used on his own bed.

"Thanks, Jimmy," I said, turning out the light, crawling into bed.

"So who won the game, Woolf? For Christsakes, tell me!"

"Us. 54–42." I told him every basket, every play.

"They're amazing, aren't they, Woolf? The starting five."

"Yeah." I stared up at the tarnished coil springs supporting his mattress. It was quiet, the lights were out all over the building.

"What's it like here . . . high school?" I asked.

"Different."

"How?"

"Teachers."

"Any good?"

"Some."

"Who?"

"Gold. English. Makes us read novels, recites poetry."

"Is he queer?"

"Na, he plays touch football with us; dirty, cheats sometimes."

"Anyone else?"

"Yeah, Dwight. Science and math, black Irish, Harvard graduate. Just out."

"Sounds better. Does he play touch also?"

"Yeah, but he doesn't cheat like Gold. He's a scrappy bastard."

"How are the girls?"

"La Seniorita's gone."

"I know about Carmen, wise guy!"

"A lot of girls didn't come back. Only eight in the Upper School."

"How are they?"

"Some are terrific. There's this one, Carla, thin toothpick legs, nice ass, but like most of them, she's taken. It's like they're married to the older guys. Can't touch Carla."

"Maybe later in the year when baseball starts. Don't give up the ship," I shouted into the nighttime silence.

Rafferty came back with John Paul Jones's retort: "I have not yet begun to fight."

"What's real high school like?" He poked his head down after two minutes of silence.

I told him about South Side, bald Miss Rice, Petrocelli, the cafeteria lunches. He wasn't too interested. Neither was I.

"How were the girls there, Mitchell?"

"Okay, I guess."

"Did you go out with anyone?"

"No."

"What did you do on the weekends?"

I described the Dutch colonial house, moving in, the chores, my three speed Columbia, Bea, the fights. Suddenly I was telling about the serrated bread knife stuck in the oak floor.

"Jesus, Woolf, it's good you got out of there in one piece."

"I guess so."

In the morning we sauntered down the cement path, side by side, weaving in step. It was great to be back in the chill basement dining room, where we had cornflakes, cinnamon toast and coffee for breakfast. There were changes, for sure. Daniels was gone, like Mayer, Austria and Castille. Few of the Lower School kids had stayed on for high school. But Stevens was still seated at the head of the fifth- and six-grader's table, bringing them along, his current favorites. He shot me a big smile, blushed almost.

Mr. and Mrs. Ryson occupied Mr. Kennedy's old headmaster's table. Their daughter, Clara, now ten, sat with a group of Lower School girls. Mrs. Borg, Dorothy Ryson's widowed mother, took Clara's place at the headmaster's table. A graceful, refined woman, she also seemed to have replaced Ma Kennedy in managing the kitchen and dining hall. It was rumored that she had put up the cash for Ryson's purchase of Lake Ronkonkoma.

Coach Berger sat with Glickman, Rosen and Franick, the only members of the starting five who ate breakfast. The Chief was gone.

"That's Gold, see him?" Rafferty whispered. "By the door. Carla's at his right."

"Nice," I assured him. "Nice ass."

He kicked me under the table.

Gold was bald and wore glasses, but he wasn't middle-aged like Harry from the bookstore. He was robust, animated, hairy somehow, except for his head. He probably did cheat in touch football. It was comforting, safe, back in the heart of old Long Island, sipping coffee next to Rafferty, our chairs resting against the Huck Finn wallpaper.

The new faculty certainly appeared more alert and approachable than Miss Rice and her colleagues at South Side High School. Gold exemplified this academic improvement. He was a recent MA from Columbia, a poet who actually cared about literature. When his GI benefits ran out, Ryson was able to hire him cheap because the job market was flooded.

Gold was repelled by the sterile hand-carved desks facing him in the third-floor English room, so he convinced Ryson to let him use the gymnasium Ping-Pong table instead. We sat around it. Gold vowed to preserve its white plastic net and return the table to the gym for the camp season. He kept the net up as a precaution so it wouldn't disappear into a musty closet. We adjusted to its bisecting white presence, aware of Gold's promise.

He was forced to use the same anthology, grammar book and Shakespeare volumes all past English teachers had, though he only made haphazard assignments in them to reinforce his own amorphous lesson plans. He seemed to know the anthology verse selections by heart. He rarely used the grammar book or assigned compositions. When we wrote papers, Gold ignored them or just put a letter grade on them three weeks later with a few words: "Excellent," "Good try," "Bullshit," "Read the poem." He never red-penciled spelling errors or ungrammatical sentences. What concerned him and us seated around our makeshift seminar table were his thoughts and impromptu recitations.

" 'Soft you; a word or two before you go.' " He was conversational yet stern during the second classroom discussion of *Othello*.

" 'I have done the state some service, and they know't./ No more of that." Gold got up from the green table, moved toward the side blackboard. " 'I pray you, in your letters,/ When you shall these unlucky deeds relate,/ Speak of me' "—he wiggled his tobacco-stained fingers—" 'as I am; nothing extenuate,/ Nor set down aught in malice.' " He knew the lines by heart, the stopping places, the rhythm. " 'Then must you speak/ Of one that lov'd not wisely, but too well.' " His voice was tremulous, a rich baritone. " 'Of one not easily jealous, but, being wrought,/ Perplex'd in the extreme. . . .' "

We could follow that, Othello had killed Desdemona already.

" '. . . of one whose hand/ (like the base Indian) threw a pearl away/ Richer than all his tribe; of one whose subdued eyes,/ Albeit unused to the melting mood,/ Drop tears as fast as the Arabian trees/ Their medicinal gum.' "

We could never articulate those words, or hear "medicinal gum," without remembering Gold's voice.

He paused as if the speech were done. " 'Set you down this,' " he continued quietly, surprising us as if it were another assignment, though he placed his book on the table. " 'And say besides that in Aleppo once,/ Where a malignant and a turban'd Turk/ Beat a Venetian and traduc'd the state' "—he spoke louder now, his vocal chords throbbing, popping from his neck—" 'I took by th' throat the circumcised dog/ And smote him, thus.' " Gold plunged both fists into his tweed jacket, fell back against the blackboard. Our hearts stopped. We were stunned by his intensity, his identification with the dying Moor.

" 'I kissed thee ere I killed thee. No way but this,/ Killing myself, to die upon a kiss.' " He lurched from the blackboard toward the Ping-Pong table, tumbled against his chair. The bell went off, and we gathered our notebooks, pencils and blue Ginn and Company *Othellos*, never touching the white plastic net.

"Don't forget, next week *Crime and Punishment* comes in," he boomed after us. "I want a dollar twenty-five from each one of you. Class dismissed."

Inspired, dazed, we moved down the hallway to Mr. Dwight's biology lab.

Mrs. Borg also changed things around when she moved into the Swansons' old house after Chef Swanson passed away and Mrs. Swanson retired. She promptly gutted the canteen from what was now her home and rebuilt it in the larger first floor of Windward Hall, where the Chief used to conduct our Friday night boxing matches. She installed a secondhand soda fountain, served ice cream sundaes, the usual candy and fresh cupcakes. Rafferty was right, there was much more in it, but Mrs. Borg had problems operating the canteen, keeping it clean and open twice a day for Lower and Upper School groups. She relied on student help.

Study, Work and Play was more than a shout in the middle of our school song; it actually gave Lake Ronkonkoma its daily structure. Work fit between morning study and afternoon play. Only those who waited on table were excused from the one-hour afternoon work period. On Saturdays there was a longer all-morning work session for everyone, even the little kids. Trees were felled, underbrush burned out, ball fields regraded. Mrs. Borg was dependent on this labor pool for her canteen help, a source she usually found disappointing.

On my first Saturday morning back Mr. Ryson sent me and Rafferty over to the canteen for work period. The grounds were too muddy for group landscaping efforts. We mopped the floors, took the garbage out to the school incinerator, set it on fire and returned to the canteen for our coats. Mrs. Borg was behind the counter.

"What'll it be boys?" she asked.

"Oh, that's okay, Mrs. Borg, you don't have to give us any—"

"Please. On the house. Vanilla, chocolate, strawberry . . . have a scoop."

Rafferty gave in: "Well, strawberry."

I followed suit. Ice cream in the morning was unusual anywhere. "Chocolate," I said.

"Good." She flipped open the silver lids and dug out a scoop of strawberry, released it into a paper-lined metal sundae holder. Did the same with my scoop of chocolate. Rafferty and I sat on red stools in front of the chromium fountain spigots, which were arced like swans' necks, the perpendicular knobs their heads, the black nozzles their beaks. Mrs. Borg rested her damp hands on the black knobs. She was a pretty woman, white-yellow hair, sparkling light blue eyes like her daughter's.

"Water?" she asked.

"Sure, we'll take anything we can get." Rafferty spoke for both of us.

She yanked the black handle down, and water flowed out of the nozzle into a paper cup set inside a convex metal holder.

"Here you go, boys." She pushed the holders from the aluminum drain onto the red Formica counter top. Her wrists were translucent, strung tight with blue veins.

"What's in the other spigot?" Rafferty asked.

She had filled both cups from the right one.

"Soda water, but I don't use it much."

"Why not?" I asked.

"I'm not sure."

"Of what?" I persisted.

"How to make an ice cream soda. What I use."

"*I* know."

"You do, Mitchell?" She was surprised. "Show me!"

I spun off my stool, ran behind the counter, recalling exactly what I'd seen the fountain men do at Schrafft's and the Park Central Drug Store.

"Okay." I grabbed a large holder, shoved a fresh cup inside. "Does the chocolate work?" I pointed to the double-jointed syrup dispenser.

"Yes," Mrs. Borg said, "Just filled."

"Three squirts down. Milk, I need milk!"

She got a container from the icebox.

"Good." I poured one ounce. "Now you push the spritzer handle backward." I did and a stiletto line of seltzer hit the bottom point of the cup, bubbling the syrup and milk together. "Then forward with the seltzer knob." A full flow of bubbling water filled the cup three-quarters full. "Now you put in the ice cream. What'll it be? Black and white? Strawberry? Your choice." I looked at Mrs. Borg.

"Vanilla."

I dropped in a scoop. "Do you have a thin spoon?"

"Only a fat serving spoon from the dining room," she replied.

I took it and stirred the best I could. "There you go!" I placed the soda on the counter.

Mrs. Borg sat down. I gave her a straw and a napkin. After two sips she smiled. "How much?"

"You're the boss."

"Well, twenty-five cents . . . twenty, make it twenty cents."

She put a dollar on the counter. "The cashbox is on the back table, see? Next to the refrigerator." It was a gray safe box which opened to penny, nickel, dime and quarter compartments. Just like a cash register. The bills fit under the change tray.

"Do you know how to make change, Mitchell?"

I laughed. "Can I make change?" I told her all about Bookland and the cash register.

She nodded her head in wonderment, wiped the soda cream from the corners of her mouth. "Could you help me this Sunday afternoon? We're so busy. Parents visit, allowances are given out, I can't handle it all."

"Sure, I'll help out."

"Thank you, Mitchell." She brushed the top of my hand with hers, squeezed my chilled knuckles. Mrs. Borg pronounced my name with a slight foreign accent, like Hans Brinker's grandmother might have, except her clothes were those of a Garden City matron.

Sunday was a banner day. We took in eighty dollars. I made at least forty ice cream sodas: black and white, strawberry, all chocolate. We ran out of chocolate and vanilla syrup at five o'clock. Rafferty brought fresh cupcakes and coffee from the kitchen to placate the hungry mob of departing parents.

I wrote about the canteen and the basketball team in my first letter home, addressed to my father and sent to Bookland, not Everett Street. He had called from the store at seven P.M. my first evening back at Lake Ronkonkoma to make sure I'd arrived in one piece. Since I was with the basketball team at East Islip, Mrs. Ryson told him I had arrived safely.

"He was pleased, Woolf," she had told me at breakfast.

I assumed Bea was still riled up or my father's call would have come from Rockville Centre. So I sent my first letter of good news to my father at the bookstore, trying to avoid any more confrontations, even pen and ink ones. Reading his answer ten days later confirmed the Bookland choice had been wise.

Dear Mitchell,

I'm glad things are working out so well for you on the basketball court and in your new corner room. Say hello to Rafferty for me. The canteen sounds terrific, must be in the blood, business sense. Things are tense at home with Bea still on the warpath. We better take it slow with weekends home and vacations until I give the high sign.

Love,

Dad

P.S. Harry fired me again; late coming into work and back from lunch two days in a row. He did it after returning from the post office. We sent you a package. It's your Pettit Brothers and Clayton basketball jacket, brand new. You sure they're undertakers? Sounds like Durante's old nightclub act, Jackson, Clayton and Durante.

P.P.S. Yale and his mother brought it over Sunday. They didn't know you had gone away. You should have said good-bye, let them know.

P.P.P.S. Harry says hello.

The jacket arrived a week later, parcel post, special handling, expertly sheathed in corrugated paper, the package taped and labeled. Rafferty brought it into the room from a late mail call I had missed.

"What is it, Woolf? Food?"

"I don't think so. It's a jacket."

"Well, open it for Christsakes, let's see!"

The jacket was purple and white satin, exactly the colors and ornamentation the team had selected when we were fitted in the Village Sport Shop four weeks before my sudden return to Lake Ronkonkoma. We had canvassed all the local merchants for a team sponsor so we could get uniforms and jackets. No one was interested, even though our team record was promising. Three of us wandered down the side streets off Sunrise Highway until we found Pettit Brothers and Clayton Funeral Home. They were interested, even flattered we'd considered them an appropriate sponsor.

I lifted the jacket out of the box.

"It's beautiful, Woolf!" Rafferty was smitten. "Put it on!"

Excellent fit, we agreed.

The front and back panels were purple, almost violet, the sleeves, white. So was the pocket trim.

"Is there really a business called Pettit Brothers and Clayton?" Rafferty stared at their white scripted name on my back.

"Yeah, they're undertakers."

He clutched his gut laughing. "You're kidding, Woolf!" He touched the purple satin on my shoulders. I caught his eyes, radiant behind me in the bureau mirror.

"Jimmy." I turned around. "You try it on, see if it fits."

"Naw, it's yours, Woolf, got your name on the front."

It did say *Mitch* in white over the left breast. I took off the jacket.

"Just try it on." I helped Rafferty get his arms into the gray sleeve lining, then pulled the back over his torso, smoothed out the purple shoulders. He snapped the white buttons together.

"What do you think?" I asked.

"It's gorgeous, a fucking knockout jacket. . . . And the Pettit Brothers on the back . . ." He started laughing again.

"Keep it."

"But it's your team."

"Not anymore. I'm on the Lake Ronkonkoma team now, eighth man."

'But your name is on it."

"Your kidding . . . 'Mitch'? " I shook my head, disgusted. Even Bea called me Mitchell. "Come on, Jimmy, I want you to have it."

"Really?" he began to soften. "You can always borrow it, Woolf."

"It's yours for keeps." I convinced him, and Jimmy wore it to breakfast, lunch, class, even dinner over his dress jacket. Everyone accepted it as Rafferty's jacket—my suburban nickname was ignored.

My father finally came up to see me in late May, two weeks before the semester ended. He parked the green Chrysler on the south side of Mayall Hall, just off the tar road. We could see it from our corner window. Rafferty and I dashed outside.

"Dad!" I hugged his cashmere arms and chest. He pressed the back of my neck with his strong hands. We were on the driver's side of the car, the door still open.

"You're still growing, huh? When are you going to stop?" He looked up at my big Lufkin head, smiling. "Rafferty, how are you?" He grabbed Jimmy's hand, shook it. "Jesus, you're as big as Mitchell. What is this, a conspiracy?"

We all laughed at his mock paranoia.

"So this is the new car?" Jimmy stared inside at the marble-green steering wheel, the leather-padded dash.

"Get in, I'll take you guys for a spin before lunch. Come on."

We both hopped in the front seat. There was plenty of room. My father chauffered us around the circular campus drive out to Route 25 for a ride to Center Moriches. On the way back we turned off the highway at the Corner Store, where Stevens had introduced us to Peep three years before.

It was exhilarating being in the car again. I showed Rafferty all its safety features, then turned on the radio. We edged back on campus, taking a road that cut across the center of the grounds. My father spotted Mr. Ryson on the canteen steps looking toward the dining hall. Mrs. Borg was beside him.

"I've got to speak to Ryson a minute. Mind if I intercept him?"

"Go ahead," I said.

"It's twelve-fifteen," Rafferty said, pointing at the car clock. "I've only got fifteen minutes to set my tables and eat."

My father stopped the Imperial midway between the dining hall and the canteen. We all got out.

"See you later, Mr. Woolf. Thanks." Rafferty tucked in his shirttails and ran for the kitchen door.

My father hailed Ryson, who started over to shake hands with him.

"Mitchell, why don't you change into something nicer for lunch while I talk with Ryson."

"Where are we eating?" I whispered.

"Friede's."

"Wow!" That was special. Stevens had taken Austria, Castille, Fritz and me there for a steak dinner the evening we graduated from the eighth grade.

I ran up the path to Mayall Hall as my father and Mr. Ryson moved toward the canteen and walked inside with Mrs. Borg.

After our steak sandwich lunch in the main dining room of Friede's, we moved outside for a talk.

"See over there?" My father pointed to three elegant wicker chairs facing a weeping willow tree. We walked down the porch stairs onto soft grass and across a miniature bridge to reach them. A clear brook raced beneath us toward the original Smithtown milling house. I had never been outside Friede's on their grounds. Few customers took advantage of them. We were truly alone. We angled our white armchairs tête-à-tête, stared past the brook at the porched-in diners finishing their desserts. Quietly we savored our good fortune. My father pierced his cigar with a peppermint flavored toothpick, lit up, drew in the aroma, let out the rich, comforting smoke. I studied his tired face, noticed his temples had turned silver against his fine black hair.

"Like Churchill at . . . remember where they were sitting in those pictures? Yalta?" I asked.

"I think Yalta," my father responded. "Or Teheran. Who are you, Mitchell, FDR with a cape and silver cane?"

"Not quite yet." I smiled. "So, how's everything at home?" It was time to ask, decide where I could go when school ended. We had talked around it, about everything else during lunch, on the ride out: school, the store, Harry, the canteen, Rafferty.

"It was awful, for days, weeks on end." My father drew on his cigar, almost inhaling the hot smoke, hoping to anesthetize his cramps. "Then it changed."

"What happened?"

"I told her to calm down, cut out the crap, or it was over. I couldn't take the tension anymore. My stomach knotted as soon as I walked in the door."

"What do you mean, 'over'?" I examined his eyes.

"Everything, the marriage."

"You'd get . . . ?"

"Divorced? That's right."

"What did she say?"

"Cried for a while, then got scared like a cornered animal, watching every move I made, listening, no words, just the glowering for days. The silent treatment was worse than the yelling. Her eyes bloodshot. I lived in the bathtub, my fingertips got waterlogged. Just the two of us. You were gone. Out of the house for a month, no longer an issue for combat, but she wouldn't let go of her anger over your exit. So I left too."

"You're kidding?" I was flabbergasted.

"I took off for Atlantic City in the Chrysler for a long weekend.

The car was a joy on the Garden State, made it in seven hours. I stayed at the Traymore. The ocean cleared my head. The sun was out every day on the Boardwalk. No more stomach pains. Best thing I could have done. Got my bearings. Driving back across Jersey, I tried to put myself in her shoes. Finally wondered how she felt about *me*, not just you and all the family shit."

I smiled, feeling a sense of relief.

"We finally talked when I got home. All night. In the kitchen, the bedroom. Bea unraveled her fears. I didn't like *her*, she wasn't enough alone without you in the house.

" 'He's gone now, forget that episode,' " I said. "But she held on to it, weeping again. 'Do you love me, Bea?,' I asked her. 'Just me . . . me, Philly?'

"She was stunned by a question I had never asked before, never had to.

" 'Phil, you know . . .'—she caught her breath. 'You're . . . everything to me!'

" 'Then act it—stop killing me with all your *mishegoss*, or—'

" 'I need you, Phil . . . honey, please let me change.' "

"How is it going now?" I didn't need the rest of that evening.

"Better, calmer most of the time, but she still flies off the handle at little stuff. Then it's awful again. The menopause doesn't help."

"Menopaw?"

"Her hot flashes . . ."

"You mean, the sweating, the red—"

"She's upset when it hits, makes everything harder."

"Why?"

"Her body's changing, chemistry throws her out of whack. She can't have babies anymore."

"Did she want kids?"

"Once, maybe, during her first marriage."

"She was married before you?"

"Yeah, when she was only eighteen. The guy was a monster. Beat her up at night. They got divorced in ten months. Must have been dreadful."

I imagined Bea at eighteen, all her curls and energy. "Did she have that menopause when you married her?"

"Well, she was missing periods then, though her doctor wasn't certain why. She was only thirty-eight, too young for menopause. After a year he diagnosed it as premature menopause. Then she wanted to adopt you, legally make you her son."

"We were closer then." I remembered how we had been allies at the hotel.

"Still, I wasn't sure; it didn't feel right somehow, after Hannah. Too soon to let anyone replace her legally. Have rights over you. Besides, I didn't want any more lawyers. I think I was right about that."

I agreed with my eyes, glad she would always be a stepmother.

"But I made a mistake with Hannah's family. Your cousins, Grandma Lufkin."

"I don't follow." I shook my head, confused.

"I wanted to punish them, not allow them to see you."

"Why?" I was upset, never having realized such a policy existed, though suspecting something was awry after Bea took me up to see Grandma Lufkin, always thinking it had been her doing.

"They hurt me, Mitchell, when your mother died. You too, though it wasn't personal, just money in your case. There was a life insurance policy your mother had and some war bonds both of us had put away in her name for your college. They wouldn't let them pass to you after she died because you were a minor and I would have control of the money until you were eighteen."

"How could they do that?"

"They got control of her will, didn't trust me."

"You're kidding!"

"Because of what happened between Hannah and me." Philly couldn't stop, he didn't want to. It all came out: the store, Hannah's fatigue, the new man, the train ride to Reno, her blood clot, the return home, their tentative reconciliation, her final illness.

" 'Cheap bastard, you'll marry again, Philly. You'll give your next wife everything! A mink . . . spoil her. Your third wife, she'll get two coats!' "

He was telling me a story, getting it off his chest, yet he was detached somehow, almost separated from it as he told it to me.

"I remember standing with you on the edge of Lake Ronkonkoma in front of Raynor's Beach Pavilion that summer she was in Reno, and asking, 'Did she send you silver dollars too?' "

"No, no," he answered, looking away into the brook.

"That's what you said then." I put my hand over his on the wicker armrest.

"She was exhausted," he continued, explaining the story. "Knew she was going to die, didn't mean what she said. They poisoned her thoughts." Philly stopped, not wanting to implicate Grandma Lufkin. "She was earthy, Mitchell, had a wonderful raucous laugh."

"You make me laugh too," I said after a pause drained us of memory.

The sun was behind the huge willow tree.

"What do we do about this summer, before and after camp? Is it safe for me to come—"

"*Home?*" My father was alarmed at the thought. "Things are still iffy, touch and go."

"I understand. Maybe I can stay on here awhile, help organize the canteen for camp."

"That's what Ryson and Mrs. Borg spoke to me about. They want you to run the canteen this summer for the entire camp. They'll pay you."

"I thought that might happen. Isn't Mrs. Borg special? Her face?"

"Yes." He nodded his head. "Nice lady."

The sun came around the side of the willow branches. We squinted into it.

"Mitchell, maybe if things work out with Bea, you could come home for a weekend before camp. We could see a doubleheader at the stadium."

"I'd get in the way. It's too delicate. You and Bea have to work stuff out alone. I'd screw it up."

"How about Labor Day, when the Yankees play the Athletics, Connie Mack. Remember him sitting in the dugout wearing a black gabardine suit?"

"Okay, Labor Day, it's a deal!"

We shook hands on it, standing, moving away from our chairs, back over the little bridge.

We never went to that Labor Day doubleheader. When the house was sold in August, Bea and Philly were too busy packing on Everett Street for their move back to the city, an easier place for them to work things out.

Thanksgiving, my father suggested over the telephone, was the best time for my first visit. "Four days to settle in, get used to the new apartment. Bea will make turkey with all the trimmings. Uncle Myron is coming over with his fiancée, Doris. How does that sound?"

"Wonderful!" I agreed.

"Come to the store, I'll bring you home. It's tricky getting to the Majestic from Penn Station."

"Four o'clock, Wednesday afternoon." I remembered the time-table.

"I'll be waiting."

Harry waved from the cash register as I swept open the glass door with my free hand.

"Stranger, look at you!"

I dropped my leather valise at the register wrapping counter. Harry measured the distance between our two heads, using his left hand for a ruler. He smiled at the growing differential, paused, then examined my face.

"Mitchell. You look exactly like her."

"Who?"

"Your mother. Honest, carbon copy: nose, eyes, full lips."

"Really?"

"She looked like you, the spit."

Voices erupted from my father's cubby office, reminding us that he was inside it.

"They're waiting for you now."

"*They?*"

"Yeah, Bea and your father."

"What's she doing here?"

"Helps out a few days a week, does the paper work, bills, payroll."

"Oh." I moved toward the back of the store, opened the office curtain.

"Dad, I'm—"

"Mitchell, you're early! Come in!"

There wasn't much room. We shook hands. Bea was seated at my father's tiny desk. She had been counting the afternoon deposit, entering the numbers in a black ledger. Now she stretched out her hand, willing to wipe the slate clean. I shook it firmly. She smiled.

"Just leaving, Mitchell, not much room for all of us in here, have to get dinner started anyway."

"I can squeeze over, there's enough room." I held my breath, pushing into the coats hung against the wall.

"Philly." She got up, reaching for her Persian lamb coat on a wooden hanger behind her.

"Bea, let me help you." They walked out to the Children's Section for more room. My father held up the black coat for her.

"Thanks, honey." She slid into the silk lining. He brushed some lint off the back of her coat.

"There you go, all set." He smiled at her.

"Remember to mail those checks, and don't forget the deposit," she reminded him.

"I won't forget that."

Bea was thinner; a new hairdo made her look like Claudette Colbert with a scowl.

"Need any oh-day?" he asked in pig latin.

"Maybe a ten, for the turkey."

"I just gave you one yesterday. What the hell happened to it?" His snappy reply had an edge to it.

"Your shirts, dry cleaning, everything is up, Phil. You know that."

"Come inside." He pulled at her sleeve. "I don't like flashing bills in the store."

"I know, hon." She followed him. "So, six o'clock sharp." she reemerged. "See you." Bea didn't look at me. "Night, Harry," she said at the register and was gone.

"Come in, come in, Mitchell, I'll just be a second," my father said.

He was back at his desk, like in the old times.

"I'm a big executive now. I can only sit down when the secretary leaves." We laughed at the incongruity of his office space. Things did seem better between them.

"When can I see the new apartment?"

"Forty-five minutes. I just have a few calls and the deposit drop on our way to the bus."

"What's it like?" I asked when we were finally outside between 7th Avenue and Broadway, in front of the *New York Times* building.

"Busy, busy, we're holding our own."

"I mean, things, you know. How is it working out?"

"Oh, much better. Couldn't you tell?"

I shook my head, not quite certain. We walked down 42nd Street toward 8th Avenue, past the New Amsterdam, the Apollo, the Laffmovie, all still there.

"Where are we headed?" I asked as we stepped onto a holiday-crowded number 10 bus.

"The Majestic. I told you, didn't I? In my letter?"

"Yeah, but where is it? This is 8th Avenue."

"72nd Street and Central Park West. The bus stops right at the door practically. 8th becomes Central Park West."

"Oh, uptown."

"Not too far, you'll see."

The Majestic was gigantic. Its twin art deco towers made it appear ten stories higher than the Park Central. A doorman saluted at the entrance.

"Left." My father motioned. "Last elevator."

We walked down a long carpeted hallway with floor to ceiling windows on the right side of it, opening on a gardened courtyard. Waiting for the elevator, my father ran his fingertips over the mahogany wall paneling behind him.

"I love this stuff, Mitchell." He caressed the reddish veneer with his open palm. "Don't you?"

I turned around. "Yeah, it's nice, but—"

"So classy."

A chrome elevator door whooshed open.

"How's Mr. Woolf tonight?"

"Fine, Clarence."

"And this must be your lad?"

"That's right. Mitchell will be staying with us for the holiday."

Clarence twisted his head around to take me in. "Big lad, isn't he?"

Clarence was wearing a black bow tie and stiff white shirt. His suit was like a tuxedo except it was dark blue with *Majestic* written across his pocket in red trim. He punched the number six button on his control panel. There was no manual lever controlling the up and down movement of the cab. Why was he running the elevator? I wondered. Anyone could push buttons. We got off on the sixth floor, stepped into a tiny hallway with only two other apartments on it. Bea opened the front door when Philly rang, and we entered a large parquet vestibule.

By the time dessert was served, I had unwound, taken in the kitchen and long, wide living room facing us off the dining alcove. The same green wall-to-wall carpeting that covered the Everett Street living room unified the living and dining areas of the new apartment.

"We were able to piece it together." My father noticed me scrutinizing its deep green pile.

"It's nice, they did a good job."

"We kept only the best new furniture and some old pieces of value we bought at country stores and auctions."

After the tea had steeped in its porcelain kettle, Bea poured Philly's hot cup. Her lips tightened.

"Tea, Mitchell?"

"No, thanks, keeps me up."

"You'll sleep like a log tonight," my father assured me.

"Where?" I asked, hoping there was a room for me off the hall-way that I had missed.

"There, Mitchell." Bea pointed to a new sofa facing the casement windows in the living room.

I got up and walked over to it.

"Isn't it too small?"

"It opens into a queen-sized bed." Bea rushed into the room and tossed the sofa pillows into my father's easy chair, folding out the metal bed frame with a two-inch mattress wrapped inside.

"I'll make it up in no time. Try it for size."

I lay down, dangling my shoes over the bottom of the frame. Certainly more width than my double-decker at Lake Ronkonkoma, but it wasn't as comfortable as the maple bed in my old room on Everett Street.

"Where's the maple bed?"

"We sold it to the people who bought the house."

"My dresser?"

"Ditto."

"Where do I unpack?"

"There's space in here." She opened two deep drawers at the base of an antique secretary.

"And hang my clothes?"

"Hall closet."

"Oh."

"Well, what did you expect? Your own room?" Bea said, raising her voice.

"I never . . . thought about—"

"Well, we don't have one for you anymore." Her control was gone. "That's over, those days."

My father walked into the living room. "Easy, Bea. He just asked."

"Why *Bea*? 'Easy, *Bea*'? It's always me, never him!" She was livid, screaming full force. "What does he expect, Phil? Always demands. What does he want from me?" She ran out of the living room and slammed herself into their white bedroom.

"Shit," my father said. "I was afraid of a blowup."

"I'll try not to upset her again, Dad."

"I don't know if this arrangement . . ." He waved his hand over the sofa bed. "Shit!" He made a fist and punched it into the loose pillows.

"I'll make the bed up," I offered.

The Telechron clock showed nine-fifteen.

"No linen." My father sighed.

"Where is it?"

"In the bedroom. The linen closet is in there." He pointed toward the slammed door.

"I'll sleep in my clothes."

"Naw, you'll screw up your slacks for tomorrow. Let's wait a few minutes. She'll calm down, then I'll go in there."

We sat quietly for a while, hoping the tension would seep away.

"Can I watch the parade from up here?" I said to break the silence. I walked to the metal living room windows, which opened on a steep courtyard lined with similar metal casements.

"Not much of a view," my father said. "But we got a deal on the place, two seventy-five a month. Facing the park, four rooms start at three twenty-five. It's crazy."

I agreed. We both noticed the clock, which said nine-thirty. Philly inched up to the bedroom door.

"Babe?" he whispered. "Open up. I have to get Mitchell's bedding." He closed the door gently after him.

"He gets away with murder!" filled the living room when my father reopened the door, his arms loaded with sheets, a blanket and pillow.

I made the bed up; folded the sheets and blanket into neat hospital corners, reversed the pillowcase inside out, pushed my fingers into the corners and fitted the case over the pillow, letting it fall back with the right side out. My father watched from the easy chair.

"She just sits there on the chaise, smoking those goddamned cigarettes. I have to get in the tub." He held the sides of his bloated stomach as he got up. "It's starting."

"I'm really sorry."

"Sleep, Mitchell, tomorrow will be better. Myron will be here with Doris."

"Can we see the parade in the street?" I asked.

"Sure, we'll take a little walk before they come over. Good night." Philly crept back into the bedroom.

I stared out at the courtyard, counted the other apartment lights, fascinated by their ugliness. I lowered the venetian slats. It wasn't going to work out, I could tell already. I heard the tub water running. Stop. Resume.

Somehow after thirty minutes I managed to fall asleep. Out until eight the next morning, when I woke up. I didn't know where I was, sitting upright in the sofa bed, staring around the dim living room. Intense morning light filtered through the venetian blinds. I pulled them up, pushed open the windows, surprised to see reflections of the rising sun. I looked for its face in the courtyard, but it was on the other side of the park, shining through a space between the north and south towers of the Majestic. Perfect day for a parade.

Bea and my father didn't make a waking sound for at least an hour, it seemed. Fortunately there were a toilet and sink next to the hall closet. I got some cold tomato juice from the icebox. Bea had returned to the kitchen while I was asleep to run the dishwasher. It was full of sparkling-clean dinnerware when I opened it for a clean glass. I paced the living room, sipping my juice, surprised at familiar objects rearranged, examining all their recent acquisitions, including "Philly and Bea" matchboxes and cocktail napkins.

The Queen Anne secretary held the family books on four shelves behind two glass doors. Mine were in the middle, the Heritage Club editions I had begun sending away for just before returning to Lake Ronkonkoma included. I was delighted to see *Crime and Punishment* among them. I had ordered but never received it. I pulled it out of its slipcase. The illustrations of Raskolnikov and the old pawnbroker were chilling. I began rereading the book. Gold had taken us through the first hundred and sixty pages before Thanksgiving in the Modern Library edition. I would take my boxed volume back to Lake Ronkonkoma. Show Gold the pictures.

The bedroom door finally opened at nine-thirty.

"I'll get the kettle started, Phil. You up, Mitchell?" Bea called from the kitchen.

"Yes."

"What are you doing?"

"Reading, just reading." I placed the open book on my lap.

"That's nice."

"Need a hand with breakfast?" I walked into the kitchen.

"No, just straighten the bed out. You can fold it, made up. Only the pillow has to be stored back in the linen closet. My God, they're coming at two-thirty! I've got so much to do," Bea gasped.

As I was putting the pillow in the linen closet my father came out of the bathroom.

"So how's the new sofa bed?"

"Okay. Can we still go to the parade? Remember?"

"Right after breakfast we'll run outside."

While my father finished his two-minute egg, pieces of buttered toast sprinkled inside the warm yolk, Bea composed a last-minute shopping list, hopping up from the table, darting to the icebox, stirring sauces on the stove, mixing the stuffing.

"Here, Philly. Please try to get these somewhere down on Broadway. There must be a store open. I really need the cream and butter."

"We'll do our best." He pecked at her cheek.

By the time we hit the sidewalk in front of the Majestic, it was eleven o'clock. A row of police cars passed the entrance, four abreast. Next came sanitation workers with their wheelbarrows and brooms, cleaning up isolated mounds of horse manure where the parade animals had relieved themselves. The men brushed at the brown piles until undigested oats were the sole remnants of their efforts.

"Did we miss the parade?" my father asked the distinguished doorman.

"Santa Claus passed maybe five, six minutes ago, Mr. Woolf. See?" He pointed south toward Columbus Circle.

We saw Santa's carriage four blocks down Central Park West. Mighty Mouse was seventy-five yards ahead of him, swaying aloft six stories high, his brilliant red cape and black head all we could see from behind.

"Let's catch up to them, Mitchell, come on!" We headed down the park side of the street as rapidly as the dispersing crowd would allow.

"How come it passed us so early?" I asked.

"It begins up here on 77th Street. They inflate the balloons beside the museum the night before. We'll catch it, Mitchell."

Side by side, my father and I pursued them. At 63rd Street we pulled a block ahead of Santa, winded. We waved and shouted joyously with the crowd when the plump red and white man rode past.

"Ho, ho, ho, to all a Merry Christmas and a Happy New Year!" was amplified over four loudspeakers with recorded music and bells. Santa moved his cherry lips to the holiday blessing. The same police cars drove by, four abreast, followed by the sanitation men.

"That building." I looked up high, across the street, where a yellow twin-tower apartment building stood. "It's like the Majestic. See the wide corner windows? Is it a sister or a cousin?"

"That's the Century." My father pointed to its green awning. "Same builder."

We crossed the street between the sanitation men and headed toward Broadway, where my father hoped a grocery store might be open.

"Holy mackerel!" he exclaimed at the corner. "There's the Hotel Empire."

It was a squat brown building with two red electric signs on top. One faced downtown, the other up toward 72nd Street.

"We used to stay there sometimes, Milton and I. They had special rates for show people."

"Can we look inside at the lobby?" I asked, recalling that one of our bachelor day amusements was exploring midtown hotels like the Taft, the Victoria, the Astor, even the Waldorf once.

My father checked his watch. "There's still some time."

We crossed Broadway and entered the lobby, walked into its carpeted three-story interior; desolate, not a soul.

"Elevators are still the same." We looked inside an open cab.

"How come you didn't sleep in Newark when you played Manhattan?"

"We did three shows on Saturday night, uptown somewhere. All these movie houses were vaudeville then. Couldn't get back to Newark that late and return for a matinee the next day. So we stayed here. I remember, each room had a private bath."

"How was the food?"

"You hungry already?"

"A candy bar would be nice."

"We'll be eating at three, save your appetite."

"Three!" I exclaimed.

"By the entrance there's a newsstand." My father smiled and threw up his hands.

"Oh, I missed it."

"Get the *Times* while you're at it. I'll ask at the front desk about grocery stores."

An old woman rose from behind the glass counter as I approached.

"Can I help, young man?"

"I'm just looking for a candy bar."

"We have them all." She passed her thick yellow fingers over the layered display case. "Milky Way, Mounds, Clark, Hershey, mints, gum."

I chose a Milky Way, gave her a dime. When I looked around for my father, he was talking to a man in a business suit standing in an office area beside the front desk mailbox. They both stared over at me. My father gestured with his left hand toward my head, as if he were measuring me off for the man.

"The *Times*, Mitchell," he reminded me.

I returned to the old woman, who was delighted to reduce her holiday pile of newspapers. I came back with the paper under my arm.

"Well, gotta run now." My father suddenly cut off their conversation. "Thanks for the tip, Mr. . . ."

"Salazar!"

"Let's go, Mitchell, the manager says there's a grocery open on 70th and Columbus till one. We'd better not miss it, or Bea will . . ."

I agreed.

Thanksgiving lunch was elaborate and plentiful. Though Bea's cooking only got better, I disliked most of the traditional dishes she had prepared, like sweet potatoes, brussel sprouts and mince meat pie. My plate was filled and refilled, however, with young turkey meat: chestnut stuffing beneath it, giblet gravy on top, fresh cranberry sauce on the side.

"Delicious," I cooed.

"Too bad you don't like the vegetables," Bea answered. "Try just a spoonful of sweet potatoes, a touch, one sprout, maybe."

"Please, I don't want any."

"Leave him, Bea," Uncle Myron said in my defense.

"But if he never tries, how will he know what it tastes like?"

"I bet he has tried it once."

"Twice," I concurred.

"I don't have a chance against you guys." She twisted her head away.

"Look at our plates." Myron gathered Bea's chin in his large, soft hand. "Look." He turned her head toward the table. Myron and Doris had taken generous second and third helpings of everything. My father had refilled his plate once. I had stuck with the turkey and its accoutrements.

"Well, I still wish he'd try different things."

After the mince pie, which I let cool, untouched on my plate, we carried our coffee and teacups into the living room.

Doris went to the bathroom, exhausted by the familiar in-law scrutiny. She was a large, good-natured woman, sandy haired, with gray eyes, a speech therapist in the city schools.

"Some schnapps, Myron?" My father offered him a selection of brandies from a brass tray which also held five pear-shaped liqueur glasses and a stack of "Philly and Bea" cocktail napkins.

"The cognac, please."

"Nice girl, Doris," my father said, handing Myron his glass. "Tall."

"I like her too . . . So how's Mitchell?" Myron wanted to change the subject.

We were sitting next to each other, sharing a leather tooled end table.

"Okay." I smiled. "I'm center on the basketball team now, two and two so far this season."

"I heard about it from Philly." Myron sipped the cognac. "Mmmm." Sipped again, breathed the aroma in. "Remember Thanksgiving at the Russian Tea Room?"

I nodded, saw the Wiener schnitzel, caviar, borscht, all the strange food on that long crowded table. "I'm reading Dostoevsky now at Lake Ronkonkoma."

"Really?"

"Crime and Punishment with Gold, our English teacher. Look." I reached for the Heritage Club edition on the open secretary flap and came around to Myron's chair with it.

"Exceptional illustrations!" He turned the pages.

"We use a different edition at school. This is my own."

"Says who?" Bea entered the living room, drying her hands on a soiled napkin.

"It's from my book club."

"I paid for it, *kiddo,* COD, after you left. Could have returned it."

"Or, sent it to me at Lake Ronkonkoma. Aren't there laws about forwarding mail?"

"Are you accusing *me?"*

"It's my book, goddamn it! I'm taking it back with me!"

"Like hell, you are!"

Myron placed it gingerly on the end table, as if it were a small bomb. I reached for it. Bea slapped her fist into the green cloth binding.

"Control yourselves!" Philly groaned.

"Bea!" Myron clutched her fist. "He's your son, what difference does it make who paid for it? A book . . ."

"Son? *Sonnnn?"* her voice inflected two octaves. "Is that how a *sonnnn"*—she hit the high notes again—"talks to a mother? 'Goddamn it!' 'Go fuck yourself!' she spit out through her cupped palms like a megaphone.

Philly dropped his head in his hands.

Myron turned white.

"Is that how you talk to a mother? 'Go fuck yourself!' he said to me!"

"When?" Myron asked. "I didn't hear 'Go—' "

"One afternoon I came home from shopping exhausted, dripping wet, arms loaded, rang the doorbell . . ."

Doris came out of the hall bathroom, her nose and cheeks freshly powdered, whiskers dusted silver. I ran past her into the bedroom, slammed the door. She walked into the living room.

"Is everything all right?" she asked her distraught hostess. "What happened?"

Philly's eyes were still closed. Myron, chalk white, could not speak.

I moved across the long white bedroom to the casements, stared out the windows into the overcast orange courtyard wondering how the three of us could share an apartment for two more nights. After forty minutes of screaming and sobbing in the living room, there was silence. The front door opened and shut. Then someone dialed the telephone. Finally my father poked his head inside the bedroom door.

"Psst, psst, Mitchell, want to take a walk? Get some air?"

"Where's Bea?"

"Myron took her for a spin in the Studebaker."

"Lucky!"

"Hurry up, let's get out of here! Bring your pajamas."

"What for?"

"Where the hell are they? Let's get going!"

"In here." I pulled them out of the bottom secretary drawer. "What's the rush, Dad?"

"I've got to get you out!" His cheeks were red.

"Why?"

"You can't stay here anymore."

"Why not?" My eyes started to fill.

"I can't take it, Mitchell. Let's go, please!" He gave me a Stern's shopping bag for my pajamas, opened the front door, buzzed the elevator.

Outside the street air was refreshing. We walked down 72nd

Street in silence, past Columbus, then Amsterdam, to Broadway and turned left.

"It won't work, Mitchell, we'll murder each other."

"It's that bad?"

"Worse." He could barely touch his stomach.

"I'm sorry."

"Well, it's not all your fault. Bea is excitable, *fermischt* sometimes."

"I thought you read the riot act, threatened divorce?"

"Yes, and she got the picture, calmed down. It's better now, much better until you showed up."

"So it *is* my fault?"

"Fault, schmalt, it's no good, Mitchell. I'm being ripped apart. I have to go on every day."

"With that madwoman?"

"She's a good person underneath."

So the balance of power had shifted since our luncheon at Friede's; they *had* worked things out.

"I'm sorry, Mitchell." My father grabbed my forearm just as the rooftop neon sign of the Hotel Empire came into focus.

Room 603 wasn't too bad—it had a full-sized bed, two pillows, a bureau, a cabinet radio, and a private bath.

"Not bad," my father agreed when he returned with my leather suitcase at eight P.M.

"You can stay till Sunday or go back tomorrow."

"No one's at Lake Ronkonkoma now," I said.

"It's up to you, Mitchell."

"Thanks!" I burst at his tight face. "Didn't you hear me? No one's on campus over Thanksgiving vacation. The Rysons and Mrs. Borg are visiting relatives in Garden City. Even the Spanish kids take off. The kitchen's shut tight."

"I didn't know that." Philly backed off.

"Well, now you do!" I walked to the window, hurt.

"Slow down, Mitchell. I had a tough day. Murder! And last night after my tub, Bea issued an ultimatum: 'You have to choose, mister, him or me!' "

"Some deal," I exclaimed.

"Half the store she's entitled to, maybe a third, that's Keppel-stein's opinion."

"And *me?*" I turned around to face him. "You just throw me out like a . . . lead me through the streets, pajamas in a shopping bag, to this place!" I opened both arms out full to encompass the entire twelve by eight room.

"What's wrong with this place?" He took in the wall-to-wall carpeting, the easy chair and floor lamp beside the window, the house phone without finger holes.

I followed his eyes. "It's not a home."

"Well, you can't stay at the Majestic."

"Ever?"

"After a day like this, Jesus, Mitchell, how?"

"But Thanksgiving is a holiday. It's special even for us. Remember the Russian Tea Room?"

"That was before you told Bea to go fuck herself every ten minutes."

"She was nicer then. Wanted us to live together like a real family. Needed me as a member of the trio."

"Real family!" Philly sighed. He took off his pearl-gray fedora, tossed it onto the glass top bureau. "Family, huh! Like Rockville Centre with the knife and hot tubs." He pushed both palms into his temples. "That was suicide, Mitchell. Like tonight if you had stayed."

I stared into his brown eyes. "Do I have a place anymore where we can be together? What's our deal going to be?"

Philly was stunned.

"I'm not a lifer you can dump at Lake Ronkonkoma!"

"You stayed there this summer, I thought a few more—"

"It was my *choice!* There were people there I liked. I had stuff to do at the canteen, in the gym. Gold was around, and I spent a few weeks at Rafferty's over Labor Day weekend, remember? While you and Bea moved."

Philly recalled the turbulance of that exodus.

"We have to work something out. You and me." I whispered the final pronouns.

"For the duration," my father stuck in, getting the point, surprised at my need yet trying to make light of my vehemence, to get me to laugh at the entire situation.

I wasn't amused.

"Like what?" He was hesitant. "Give me a for instance, Mitchell."

"How am I going to stay here until Sunday? Where do I eat? If I go downtown or up here to the Automat, Schrafft's or Hector's, doesn't it . . ."

"Cost money?" My father got the point.

I nodded my head.

"I'll take care of it, Mitchell. You're absolutely right. And when you're right, you're right." He pulled his money clip out. "Let's see." He peeled off three bills. "Five dollars a day seems fair, doesn't it? The room's taken care of."

"But I'm not."

"What more do you want?" he snapped.

"Not money, for Christsakes! I can take care of that soon enough, like running the canteen! I need—"

"Blood!" Philly challenged. "You want everything."

"Just care for me, Dad. Don't be cheap with that."

"You little punk!" He rushed at me. "I can still take you. Come on!" he shouted at my midsection, furious yet withholding his punches until I raised my hands in self-defense.

I caught his left and right jabs to my stomach, open fisted, slapping down his forearms. We circled in front of the bed.

"*Cheap?*" Philly roared, his face red. "Don't say that about me . . . *ever!*" He stung the tip of my chin with his fingers.

The tears stayed back inside. I got away from the bed. We slammed each other's arms, avoiding the face, relishing our physical animosity.

"We need a place, don't we?" I was out of breath.

"How about Stillman's Gym once every three weeks?"

"Ha ha." I dropped my hands.

"How about breakfast tomorrow, Mitchell? Ten o'clock?"

"That's late for me. . . . Jesus, don't you understand what I'm talking about?"

"I'll be prompt," he assured me, thinking I was concerned about his morning punctuality.

"Where? Your place?" I taunted.

"Too noisy, wiseass." Philly looked out the steel-framed window. "You know Bickford's at 60th and Broadway? Just north of Columbus Circle?"

"Not really, but I can find it, I guess."

"Great fries. Fifty-nine cents for the whole schmear, coffee included, ten sharp—"

"Bring the book," I interrupted.

"If I can find it." He looked back from the window.

"Ask Bea where it is."

"Not tonight, she'll start screaming again."

"Tomorrow morning ask her. I need it for school."

"I'll bring it for you."

"Promise?"

"Promise!" He nodded his head, got up, walked to the green metal door, weary. Things were changing so quickly. He turned around to face me, reached for the back of my head, the soft part where the hair starts. I grabbed his right hand, shook it. Our palms were dry.

After he left I stared out the window trying to orient myself. Broadway, Columbus, what happened to Amsterdam? Where did it go? The boundary lines kept shifting, I couldn't figure them out. I was unsure of everything. Where the hell would we end up, me and my father? What made him such a prick all of a sudden whenever Bea was involved?

"You'll marry again, Philly . . . give your next wife everything! A mink . . . you'll spoil her!"

Yet Bea still wore her Persian lamb coat with the tight black curls. He would never buy a mink for her either. Philly was trapped, caught. I couldn't be part of that vise. I wanted something else from him.

The phone rang at nine-thirty.

"Mitchell?"

"Rafferty! How did you find me?"

"Your old man gave me the number. What happened to you?"

I told him about Thanksgiving lunch, the book, our walk to the Empire.

"Well, at least you got your own room out of it. I still have to share with Francis."

"It's okay till Sunday when I go back. See you at the train."

"Listen, how about Friday night we go to the movies?" Rafferty had a plan.

"Sounds good," I agreed.

"On 42nd Street."

"Terrific! New Amsterdam, the Laffmovie. We can stay out all night."

"I'll meet you at Bookland, six o'clock."

"I don't know if I want to meet there."

"I understand. I'll call you tomorrow morning. Maybe I can think of a different place.

"Okay, what time?"

"Say ten o'clock?"

"I might be out then, having breakfast. I'm not sure yet."

"I'll leave a message if you're out."

"A message?"

"Yeah, with the operator at the switchboard."

"They take messages here?"

"Of course, Woolf! I thought you grew up in a hotel."

"Yeah, but I don't know much about telephone operators." We both roared.

"I'll call you, Mitchell, tomorrow morning."

"Or I'll call you, Jimmy. Good night." We both hung up.

In the morning I slid out of bed, brushed my teeth, turned on the radio while I dressed. Nine-twenty-five, the announcer said. I could hold out until ten if I wanted. My stomach was still in neutral.

I took the elevator down to the empty hotel lobby, walked over to the front desk, checked box 603 with my eyes. No messages yet, but there was an operator twirling around on a cushioned-back stool in front of the hotel switchboard, plugging in and disconnecting a series of long cloth-covered chords, writing little notes on a pad.

Mr. Salazar smiled at me. I nodded back, walked past the glass newstand and pushed the revolving door forward. The sun was warm on my cheeks as I turned right on Broadway and walked past the outside entrance of the hotel coffee shop. Its high awning blocked the sun. A menu was displayed on the glass entrance door—brunch: eggs, waffles, pancakes with bacon, ham or sausage links and baked apple, custard or tapioca pudding for dessert, all for a dollar twenty-five, no substitutions. I had enough money, but nothing was a la carte, and there was no counter, just separate tables with fresh cloths and linen napkins. I kept on walking down Broadway and passed the four-story Automobile Club where my father had signed up for his driving lessons.

In the distant traffic circle I could see Christopher Columbus aloft on his gray pedestal, the back of his cloak and Venetian skullcap all concrete, distinguishable by shape, not color. His head was angled staring down Broadway over Times Square to Bowling Green, Sandy Hook and the ocean beyond. Ever since my parents sent me off to the Lake Ronkonkoma School and my mother died I had been looking for a safe harbor. But the best times always occurred in transit—with Stevens and the iceboats, the chickens, dancing in the gym. Even as a family we were happiest away from home, up at the Cocoanut Grove, in the Russian Tea Room, or just my father and I together in the moving Chrysler. It was never a specific place that mattered but rather the way we held each other within it.

At the corner of 60th Street I crossed left over the trolley tracks, pausing in the center island for a red light. I could see my father inside Bickford's waiting for me on a counter stool, nursing a cup of tea, the green book next to his cup.

The light changed and I walked across the street to join him.